the Indian and Me

By Cathy Peebles
with the help of Linda Gosnell

Charleston, SC
www.PalmettoPublishing.com

The Indian and Me

Copyright © 2021 by Cathy Peebles

All rights reserved.

First Edition

Paperback ISBN: 978-1-64990-715-8
eBook ISBN: 978-1-64990-211-5

The Indian and Me

I want to state that three characters in this story actually lived and two of them I changed their names. First, Ben Walker was forced to marry into the Seneca world or be burned to death. As far as I know he did not have a family when he was captured, that part I made up, but I do know that when given the opportunity to leave after the Revolutionary War, when the Seneca were ordered to turn over all their captives numbering one hundred and one, Ben did not want to return to the world of the white man.

Tom Mulligan is the second one who was captured in his teens and later made a chief of the Seneca, because the Seneca loved and honored him so that when a British officer tried to buy him the Indians told the officer that no money was ever enough for Tom. He was raised a Christian and kept his faith the entire time he lived among the Indians. He felt God had put him there to save captives. He did set up a crude blacksmith shop and married a white captive but demanded a Christian wedding that he was granted. Later after the war he interpreted treaties brought to the Indians and set up trading between the white man and Indians. I changed his name, but his autobiography is one of the most interesting stories I have ever read in "Captured by Indians".

Daniel Morgan a man among men. George Washington knew he was exactly who he needed to win the war. He was not your highly educated military officer, but a scrapper who craved out a life for himself in the backwoods of America. I did not change his name and yes, he did all that I stated except he never knew Samuel Mckinny, the Rainsford sisters, or Ki, this I made up.

My admiration for George Washington has grown when I learned that not only did, he have to deal with the British but the entire Iroquois nation that was armed by the British. Most of the armies that Washington sent to battle the Indians did not turn out good. But the Patriots were able to burn out many of their settlements. Smallpox was another major thing he had to deal with, so he inoculated his entire army knowing that the coxpox was a less major sickness making one immune from smallpox.

My friend Linda Gosnell revised a lot of my writings. She is a master with the English language and I really am grateful for her help in taking my prose and turning it into something fun to read. She sews many period costumes for a local theater group and was able to put her imagination and research into what my characters wore. I never knew that Washington not being able to outfit all his army with uniforms, told the regulars to dress like Indians to scare the British, thus designing their clothing. This was the kind of research I was grateful that Linda did.

———

CHARACTERS IN BOOK

Jon DeRosssier *trapper*
Cholena *Ki's mother Seneca Indian*
Yuma *Seneca chief*
Kitchi - Ki *main character Seneca Indian*
John Townset *Julia's first husband*
Julia Townset *main character*
Megan Rainsford *Julia's sister main character*
Victora Rainsford *Julia's mother*
Jason Rainsford *Julia's father*
William Stuart *neighbor of Rainsford*
Joseph Grant *Ki's first teacher*
Lieutenant Stephens *British officer*
Adams *Farm in NY*
Sally *slave*
Ben *slave*
Yo da gent *Seneca Indian*
Tom Mulligan *white Indian captive*
Peta *white Indian captive*
Ben Walker *white Indian captive*
Kucma *John Townset's baby*
John Sullivan *worked with Daniel Morgan*
Daniel Morgan *rifleman for Patriots*
Jones *Farm NY*
Vicar Turner *minister*
Amy Walker *wife of Ben Walker*
Wiggins *lawyer for the Rainsford*
Mick Hall *British stalker*

Fanklin Townset John Townset's brother
John and Tom Sounder Patriots
Willie slave
Mia slave
Samuel, Molly, and Henry Mckinny indenture servants
Samuel is main character
Mr. Crowley British agent
Bobby Flanagan indenture servant
Moses Donavan doctor
Sarah Flynn old woman who lives near Julia
Running Wolf Seneca Indian
Raven Running Wolf's wife
Herman Mees German soldier
Fredrick Schmuer German soldier
Mr. McKay neighbor of Julia
Mr. Hall neighbor of Julia
Elsa Mees Robby's girlfriend
Koda and Bala wolves
Lucas Jones former owner of the Jones's Farm
Jack British guard
George British guard
Alexander Howard Megan's boyfriend
Darcy McGregor keeper of the horses in NYC
Caleb boat operator
Berkley Julia's neighbor
Little Bird clan mother of Seneca
Kane McLaughlin indentured servant
Mary McDouglas Kane's girlfriend
Joe slave

Seneca Indian Territory,

New York, 1755

J on emptied all the traps, pleased with the fruits of his labor. He had three beavers with huge pelts, two bulky rabbits, and best of all, three minks. Jon was worried about the dropping temperature. He needed to get back to the tiny cabin before nightfall. Getting caught in this weather and being forced to spend the night here in the open would not be good. He was tired and hungry and needed shelter. He was putting his catch on the horse when five Indians suddenly appeared as if by magic. One minute they were not there, and the next they stood before the trees, silent as falling leaves. He was taller and a lot heavier, but there were five of them. He knew they could fight to the end, but he would not last a minute. They made gestures for him to come while gathering all the pelts. They took the horse and led him through the forest. It was dark when they reached the Indian village, and everyone came out of the longhouses to see him. He felt closely watched and inspected, as if he were an insect, seen for the first time. They saw a white man a head taller than any of them, with eyes the color of the sky, straight, long nose, brown hair all over his face (and down his back.) When he stretched out his arms, hair peeked out of his clothes. He had big shoulders and long legs. The men looked him over in obvious jealousy and anger. Jon's anxiety rose. They marched him up to their apparent chief, who did not look happy. He pointed at Jon for a long time. Finally, Jon comprehended—*He wants my name!*

"Jon DeRossier, trapper."

"Trapper," repeated the chief.

"Yes," and Jon put a smile on his face. *Could not hurt,* he thought. The Indians displayed pelts on the ground in front of the chief, and he was looking closely at them. It occurred to Jon that this was their land, and they probably thought these were their animals. He had also heard what treatment strangers could receive from the Indians, and it was unholy. He swallowed and bent to the waist. Jon stretched his arm across the skins then up to the chief in a gesture of presentation.

The Indians made two lines and motioned him into their corridor. Many had unfriendly smiles on their faces. One Indian kicked him to make him move. When he reached the first two Indians, they began to hit him. The next pair had sticks, and they beat him. Two highly tattooed Indians kicked him in the legs, but he knew he had to keep going. One Indian took out a knife. Jon wrested it from his hand but quickly lost it to the kick of another attacking with a hatchet. Jon bent just in time to keep his head on. He retaliated with a kick in the chest, knocking his attacker to the ground. He was punched and kicked and beaten with sticks. One creative Indian kicked sand in his face while he bent over from a kick in the ribs. Jon kept going and took the hits without crying out. When he finally reached the end of the line, he bled from his face and felt bruised and dizzy, but he knew he had to stay on his feet or meet death. Suddenly an Indian rushed him with a hatchet. Jon tripped the Indian just in time to grasp the hatchet. By this time he was angry. If they were bent on killing him, he would fight back. Jon spun on the Indians and roared, "*If you want me, come and get it!*"

The din stopped suddenly. Having survived the gauntlet, Jon had earned their respect, if not their trust. The chief did not change expressions but nodded and gestured inside the longhouse. Jon went very cautiously inside. They all sat by the fire, where eyes closely watched him. A bowl of stew was put in his hand. Ravenously he smelled the bear meat. Jon ate all the food despite painful ribs and jaws. Some of the Indians brought in the skins and busied themselves, inspecting them. The chief, or sachem, was also looking closely at them. He gestured for his pipe, which passed around the group several times.

Jon had no trouble with the pipe. The Indians were beginning to talk to each other. The sachem appeared to debate something with one of the younger Indians. After about two minutes, the sachem put up his hand for silence. They quieted respectfully. Then the sachem gestured Jon in the direction of a woman. Finally, Jon realized he was to follow her. She led him to a raised compartment where massive animal skins made up a bed. He climbed into the bunk-like area, and to his surprise, Cholena, the woman, followed. She was large for a native, with straight black hair, a flat nose, and dark skin. She looked to be no more than fifteen. She did not smile or look happy but began to remove her clothes as if to say this was her lot in life. Jon could not help staring. He was curious to see her body, see if she was different from other women. Jon did not want to remove his clothes for fear of having to leave quickly without them. So when she tried to remove them, he stopped her. She cleaned his face cuts. He wanted her name, but how to ask? So like the sachem, and he pointed at her. At length, she said, "Cholena"

"Cholena," Jon repeated and lay down on the furs. He was exhausted but also nervous. He had not been with a woman for a long time, and it was obvious this one was only doing her duty. She lay down next to him and pulled skins over them. He could no longer keep his eyes from shutting. Fifteen minutes later he snored softly. Sometime in the night, he got hot and removed his shirt, thinking that if they hadn't attacked yet, then maybe he could relax. Cholena came awake and thought it was time to perform, so she reached for him. Her hand on his stomach made him gasp. She moved it lower. He came alive. After all, it had been a year since he had been with his wife. She was a tiny thing that did not like mating at all. This one looked made for it. He gave in and made what he thought to be sweet love to her twice in the night. She seemed to enjoy it after the second time, or so he thought.

In the morning, before sunrise, she got out of bed and dressed. Jon followed suit and let Cholena lead him out of the longhouse to his horse. His pelts were lost, but he was alive and free to go, thank heavens. He mounted, looked at Cholena, uttered a goodbye she could not understand, and left.

———

Later that day Jon was setting the traps again when a huge mother black bear came upon him. His focus was on fixing a broken trap next to a fast-running stream, so he did not hear her or her cubs. She charged, knocking him to his knees. Jon had time to pull his knife before she went in for his throat. One cub latched onto his arm. The other one bit his leg. He hardly felt them as he struggled to reach her throat. He longed for his gun, taken by the Indians. He got some decent knife cuts in before jaws sliced his neck in two. The Indians found the blood-soaked carcasses two days later, so they took the knife and dead bear back to the village. The cubs were long gone.

Five Months Later

"It is a good thing you are a captive," said Yuma, the chief, while staring at Cholena's growing stomach. Cholena could not help but wonder what was next for her. Her duties had increased, and her back was killing her. She kept her head up and did what was demanded. The sachem frowned.

"You are a strong woman." Cholena was Huron, captured in a conflict between the Seneca and Huron. She was fifteen and big for her age, the reason for her capture. She made a good slave for them. She hated it, but escape was not possible because they kept guards who watched out for enemies all the time. She was one of the whores of the Indian village now. But her first encounter had been with the white man who got her pregnant.

Four Months Later

Cholena cursed Jon in her native tongue as she was giving birth. She also prayed fruitlessly to her gods. Four doulas shook their heads. The women were not happy with this birth.

"The feet are first," said Keme. "It has been two days now, and the baby is not coming down." A day later Cholena's pulse got very weak. Keme knew Cholena was near death. She felt the stomach. The baby still moved but got weaker every minute. Stifling any possible screams with skins, Keme took her knife and cut the baby out. Cholena grew cold as her lifeblood spilled over the birthing place.

Keme was surprised to see the size of the male infant. He was blue and barely breathing, so she rubbed him, put him in warm water, then stroked him again. His color came back, and she was continuing to stroke and caress when he began to cry softly. Experienced from many births, she cleaned the airway out. When he had strength, she put him to her swollen breast. Keme herself had given birth seven days before to a stillborn girl. She still grieved the baby that she had so longed for, having hoped for a boy. Cholena's child began to suck weakly, and Keme's swollen breast shot milk into his mouth. He coughed and pulled away. Thirty minutes later Keme tried again after she had rubbed him more and wrapped him in tiny skins very securely. This time he took more of her breast, even more the next time. She went to Yuma, the chief, and her husband and presented the baby.

"This is not our child, but he is a big boy and looks to be healthy." Keme looked at the boy and wondered why she could not have borne him herself. The gods were cruel.

"Where is Cholena?"

"She was dying, so I cut the baby out."

Yuma only nodded and took the baby. Yuma was surprised at his size and weight. He had been very disappointed at their stillborn baby, but at least it had only been a girl.

"She gave us a son, so she will have noble burial." Yuma was looking sternly at Keme so that there would be no discussion on the subject, and Keme was wise enough not to utter a word of disapproval. Keme was happy to be holding a live baby in her hands. She knew she would have to watch him always to keep the blue skin from returning.

Seneca Indian Territory,

New York, 1767

"Yuma, why are my eyes the color of the sky?" Kitchi was looking at his father. "And why am I bigger than all the other boys?" Kitchi was a curious boy, always asking questions. Yuma was very proud.

"The gods wanted you to be special. That is why Keme named you Kitchi the brave. You are not like the others and never will be. You are big and strong, as the gods wanted you to be." Kitchi's chest swelled up, and he stood even taller. He was learning to be a chief, and he took his lessons seriously. Keme was also proud of the son, who had given her so much joy. The boy was a pleasure to have around. The other women were jealous of her big, strong boy. Of course, they kept their mouths shut as to whose he was. They never mentioned Jon or Cholena, or there would have been severe repercussions. Thus, Kitchi thrived in the Indian way of life.

Seneca Indian Territory,
New York, January 1774

K eme was worried; she stared at Yuma until he protested angrily. Now nineteen years old, Kitchi had never seen them so edgy. He thought he knew why. In the past years, the white man had come closer and closer to the village. Everyday white settlers stole more game and cropland; they fenced land, built homes, and planted crops of corn, potatoes, beans, and onions the Haudenosaunee had given them one hundred years ago. Two years ago red-coated soldiers had arrived, apparently in opposition to the settlers. Sometimes they would enforce their treaty with the Indians and clear out the settlers. But soon another white settler would move in.

A soldier in a red coat now stood in the village with an English-speaking Huron. Yuma knew some villages were making treaties to fight for the redcoats against the settlers. It was a warm day for January, so the travelers had no trouble getting to the village.

"Ask him who his parents are." The redcoat leader was staring at Kitchi with matching sky-blue eyes. The Huron translated the question. Kitchi stood taller and responded that Yuma, the village sachem, was his father and Keme, his mother. When the Huron replied, the redcoat rudely stared at him and snorted a half laugh while shaking his head. Lord Townset bowed before Yuma.

"Tell him we come in peace to ask a favor of him," he directed the Huron. "Tell him the settlers are forming an army to drive all Indians from their territory and turn it into farms. We, the English army, want to stop their army and keep them from taking more of your lands and game animals."

Yuma's eyes burned brighter, for this was very problematic for him. But he did not trust any white man. One may work the land as a farmer, and the other live as a warrior, but none were honorable. Any of them might kill you with their guns, envied by the Indians.

Lord Townset, knowing what Yuma wanted, quickly offered, "Tell him that we will give them guns and horses in return for aid."

Yuma sat forward with great interest. But, unwilling to commit, he stood up and talked to the Huron. "I must discuss this with my people and decide. Come back at the next full moon, and I will have an answer."

When Townset understood, he nodded his assent. But then he thought of an added assurance he could gain. "We will also need guides from your tribe to show us through the forest so that we may catch these armies that mean to take your lands."

Yuma nodded. "I will talk to my people. Come back."

Lord Townset looked sternly at Yuma, gauging his thoughts. "I will need the guide now. He will have to learn English, customs, the way we do battle, including how to handle a gun and who the commanders are. When I return with the supplies, if you do not agree to fight for us, then I will return the guide."

Yuma sat back, and Townset could see he was perplexed. Townset took a deep breath and said, "How about your son? We will take him to Boston and give him a fine place to sleep and all the food he wants. He will learn the ways of the white man and probably learn to read our language. Of course, this will take some time and effort, but if ever a white man was to bring a treaty to your village, you would have a son who could read it."

Yuma was even more thoughtful now because he had heard of the white man's treaties and how they turned out to be a source of trouble for the tribes. But if he could let his son be a spy in the camp of the white man and, yes, learn his ways, then maybe they would know how to defeat him. Yuma turned to the Huron and told him, "Take Kitchi."

London, 1775

Townset knew he had to act fast. He was lucky that the military had let him go back to England based on family matters. The damned trip back to England had taken one and a half months. He had to sail back to America in four. A year-and-a-half ago, his father had paid nearly the entirety of John's inheritance to secure him a commission as lieutenant colonel in the British army. But after he had been made lieutenant colonel, what did the British do but send him straight to New York in the colonies? His brother, Franklin, had sent a threatening letter warning that the family was almost destitute.

Well, tonight he would strike hard on Julia Rainsford and win her hand. He was bent on it. She was coming out tonight, a very rich, beautiful, somewhat elderly nineteen-year-old. He savored the prospect. This would make life so much simpler. Of course, they would have to pay their dues by living in America for two years, possibly, until they showed those idiotic "Patriots" just how powerful was the British Empire. Then home again, they would return—to fame and fortune and the life he intended to live. John would be the savior of the family when he wed that beautiful brat, who thought herself better than anyone. She was unmarried because no one was good enough. He licked his lips as he played in his head a scene of bedding Julia in a most insensitive way. Talk about killing two birds with one stone. He shouted at the servant to make sure his uniform was clean and his boots were polished.

Rainsford House

Julia readied herself for the coming-out ball. Her mother had had a unique dress of scarlet satin made for the occasion. Handmade off-white lace surrounded the daring neckline. After all, this was her debut, and she had to be on display. She wore a lace necklace with a ruby set in the center, from her mother, around her throat. Her slippers were scarlet, and her gloves were made of delicate lace.

Julia's little sister, Megan, was enviously watching her dress. "Mother outdid herself having that dress made for you. I only hope I can get one that fine when my time comes."

"Do you know how I feel?" Julia looked into the mirror. "I read how they put slaves on a pedestal for buyers to view, and the buyers circle the slave and check even the teeth to make sure their purchase is in good health." Julia was turning this way and that in the mirror.

"Are they naked?" Megan's eyes were huge.

"Usually. One must know what one is getting. Well, at least I am not naked. Is this me? I don't like to get this formal."

"What woman does not like dressing up? Is it not fun to flirt and be adored and dance, and have men wait on you? How is that bad?"

"And then what?" Julia looked into her sister's eyes,

"Then you pick one," Megan shouted.

"Really? I get to select, or does the family choose for me?" Julia gazed ironically at her beautiful sibling, who loved to flirt—especially with the handsome stable boy of seventeen. Julia picked up her fan and pointed at her sister. "I will be watching you, so you had better not make for the stables while no one is looking." Julia smiled at Megan and winked.

Megan looked at Julia, again with envy, seeing a beautiful woman with black-as-night hair, white skin, and dark blue eyes. Eyes ringed with black lashes that made them look like liquid gems. Julia was not tiny but not overly tall either, and like a decent English aristocrat, she stood erect. Megan was jealous of her sister's breasts. She felt her breasts and prayed that they would grow. Megan was imitating Julia's pouty smile when she spotted her mother coming down the hall in full battle mode.

"Megan! You get dressed now! If you give me any trouble tonight, I swear I will turn you over my knee and spank your bottom. I may need help from your father to do it, but I *will* do it!" Victoria Rainsford was red in the face. How could an apple have fallen so far from her conventional Welsh Anglican tree?

"People will soon be here! I had better not see you near the stables." Victoria took a deep breath and looked sadly at her daughter. "You try my patience, but I do love you, Megan. Please be a good girl tonight."

"Of course! I will be down in a trice."

Victoria watched her sable-haired daughter walk away. Her eyes could appear to be different shades of sherry, depending on mood. Unfortunately, she seemed to be developing fast and was already tall for seventeen. All the boys looked twice. Victoria turned her eyes heavenward and prayed that she could get both her daughters into good marriages before some disastrous event. Having two beautiful daughters was a blessing but also a curse. She had to keep the men and boys at bay for the cost of her frazzled nerves. Megan was not helping the situation. She would have run wildly all over the countryside if allowed.

On the other hand, Julia was a thinker who would repeatedly analyze every event so that one wanted to scream. Julia wanted to help people, and she saw the good in them. Julia refused a personal maid, which was so unconventional for the time, because she valued her privacy. She informed her mother that she was perfectly capable of dressing herself, and if Julia needed help, she would ask her sister. Victoria had to laugh at her worries. Thank God they were all healthy. She prayed this debut would be a success for Julia. At nineteen she needed to secure a husband.

———

Townset could not stop looking at Julia. He had asked her to dance thrice and fetched three glasses of punch for her, yet Lord Clinton appeared to be making more progress than he was. She leaned on Clinton's arm and laughed at some feeble joke. If John wanted his plan to work, he would have to come up with something fast. He had stepped outside to think and get fresh air when he spied Megan slipping into the barn. John followed at a slow pace to see what she was up to. When he caught up, Megan was showing off her dress to the stable boy.

"Do you think I look pretty?" Megan whirled around the stable.

"You have no idea how beautiful you are!" The stable boy's eyes followed her every move.

"Do you want to dance?" Megan motioned for him to join her. "Come, I will teach you." He immediately came forward, and Megan began to instruct him. They danced to soft music from the house.

Townset began devising his plan. He would have to plan well but act fast.

———

"Who is it?" Julia called to the butler.

"Lord Townset. Do you want me to tell him you will be right down?"

"Yes, and have some tea and cakes served." *If I get bored, I can fill my mouth with food instead of talking*, she thought, checking her hair and dress as she was heading to the door. Julia liked John Townset; she thought of him as a friend. She remembered the ball where Townset had talked nonstop about his military conquests. She found it dubious that in just a year and a half of service, he had performed so many amazing feats, all with hardly a scratch, broken limb, or even missing tooth. They had been neighbors for as long as Julia could remember, trading visits on holidays. Occasionally her father would do business with the elder Lord Townset. But lately John seemed to have romantic ideas. His uniform looked very fine with his tall stature. However, something made Julia distrust him. She had witnessed him berating servants for imagined faults. Once he became enraged and whipped his horse for not jumping correctly. She noticed he was quick-tempered—especially with people he felt were inferior to him. Julia always felt that God had been gracious to put her into the right family and provide for her generously. When she saw people who had to struggle in life, she would try and help them when she could. She felt this was the Christian thing to do.

"Lord Townset, how nice to see you again." Julia wore her white day dress and soft leather boots. After they had tea, he invited her to walk in the gardens.

"Julia, you have grown into a most beautiful woman. I have fallen in love with you. I have always been fond of you. But I thought about you constantly while in America. Please do not think me forward, for I have wanted you as my wife for a long time."

John was indeed very handsome in his uniform. He was tall and blond, with large blue eyes and a generous mouth. Any woman would think John exceptionally elegant. This time he did not just kiss her hand and release it; he took her arm and turned her to face him. But Julia thought of him as only a friend.

"John, please. You are my dear friend, but I do not feel the same for you. Surely you understand. I cannot help my feelings. You will find the right woman for you one day, and I have no doubt." Julia put on her winningest smile, searching for a quick exit from this situation. "Mayhap we should return to the house. Look! Mother is watching us!"

"Well, then, please tell me you will save me several dances next week at Stuart's ball?"

"Of course I will, John." Julia sighed with relief and untangled herself from his arm.

"That stable boy, the handsome one, will he be driving your coach over to the ball?" John tried to sound casual.

"Why, yes. Why do you ask?" Julia looked curiously at John.

"Only that I noticed he is adept with horses. We need a good stable boy, and I would like to talk to him to see if he has any brothers that need work." John put on his most sincere face.

"Would you like me to find out?"

"No, no. I need to interview him myself for skills that you would not comprehend. I can wait until the ball," John said, taking the matter out of Julia's hands. His plan might work after all.

———

Julia wore a midnight blue satin dress with freshwater pearls sown around the low-cut neckline, a pearl choker necklace, and lace gloves. She arrived with her parents and Megan. John Townset and his father met them.

John was on edge. Tonight would be his only chance to execute his plan and save his family financially. He would be their hero for keeping them from the debtor's prison. Julia had danced with John twice when he saw Megan leave the ballroom without her parents' notice. He followed quietly, watching her make her way to the stable. Quickly, John returned to the hall and found Julia dancing with another man. He stepped in.

"I am sorry, but I have an urgent message for Julia." The man was irritated, but John ignored him. He bent down and whispered in her ear.

"Julia, I just saw Megan go into the stables alone." John put on a very concerned face.

"Oh, no! John, please bring her back!" Julia pleaded with John.

"Julia, she won't obey me. She *will* listen to you. We can slip in and out before anyone sees us. Now come quickly." They took a step toward the door, but Julia objected. It would be better if they were not seen leaving together. There would be gossip. They watched the crowd. When it appeared no one was watching, John went first, then Julia. In the stable, they found Megan kissing the stable boy.

John roared, "Get your hands off her!"

"John! Not so loud. You will draw in everyone."

Seven grooms who had been playing cards in the back room scraped back their chairs to run over. Now was John's chance! He swept Julia forward while tripping her with his foot. She landed face-first in a mound of hay. He gently fell on top of her and inserted his hand up her skirts. As luck would have it, not only the seven grooms appeared, but also Lord William Stuart, looking for his man. Stuart's mouth fell open. He bellowed, "Just what do you think you are doing!"

John quickly jumped up and mimed, fastening his clothes with faux embarrassment. Julia gasped at John, shocked and betrayed. She slapped him smartly with a piercing look and turned to Stuart.

"This was not what it appears to be, Lord Stuart. I came out here to get my sister away from the stable boy, and John came with me, and we tripped, and he fell on top of me." Julia babbled.

"His hand was up to your skirt." With that, Lord Stuart immediately made for the house, calling to his servant, "Fetch Lord and Lady Rainsford immediately!"

Julia slapped John again—so hard she left a handprint on his face.

"What have you done?" she screamed.

Marriage

"**D**addy, he did it on purpose because he wants to marry me, but I do not love him and will not marry him." Julia was hysterical. "I only was out there to save Megan. John told me he had seen her sneaking into the stables. I asked him to retrieve her, but he insisted that I come. I had to get her away from the stable boy!"

"Would it be so bad marrying him, Julia? He *is* handsome. I don't know *who* will marry you now that you are compromised." Victoria sadly gazed at her daughter, thinking this was just the disaster she had been trying to avoid. She thought it would be Megan and not Julia who would end up in such a nightmare.

"Yes, it would. John is determined to take me to America, to New York. We would have to live in some rich farmer's house, confiscated by the army. We would evict the poor man from his own bedroom. We would eat at this man's table every night and use his horses whenever we wanted. Can you think of a more awkward situation?"

"Julia, it is the Crown's right to support their soldiers, you know that. Your stay will be relatively short. Soon you will be back here and living as a true lady does." Lord Rainsford was trying to be patient and not raise his voice. "I don't see another way out of this."

"Daddy, please don't do this," wailed Julia, but it was to a rock-solid wall of obduracy. In the eyes of the aristocracy, her reputation was sullied. There was not a man of a decent position that would consider her for marriage.

"I have made up a very thoughtful marriage contract. John will have to sign if he is to marry you. If he should die, all property will revert to your name only. Additionally, John provides you with a jointure, a large section of land in your name. He will be required to purchase it to see you through widowhood in the case he predeceases you. Julia, you realize that most women have no such assurance. There is a good chance that John will not sign the contract." Her father gazed meaningfully at her, and Julia was hopeful for the first time. John might *not* sign the contract. She had never heard of any woman requiring this. Her father *did* love her and wanted to take care of her. Julia stood up and threw her arms around his neck to kiss him.

———

John was livid when he learned of the contract. He smashed a glass of brandy on the fireplace in the great hall. His brother was very concerned that the whole thing would fall apart.

"You must sign it anyway. We are *desperate* for money. Do it for the family, and please take no unnecessary risks over there in America. Rainsford is a bastard! When he dies, let us hire a lawyer and contest the reversion of the inheritance somehow. I have never heard of such a contract before! That cursed Julia must be a cosseted brat.

Jointure is going to be a problem. We have no money to buy the property."

Franklin thought hard with his hand to his mouth, and then he looked up suddenly. "Perhaps you can forestall the purchase by creating a suspicion that Julia is expecting." Franklin looked at his brother and hopefully shrugged his shoulders. "What if Julia's parents thought she was pregnant? It could still work."

"I will go and see him tomorrow and discreetly tell him that haste may be necessary." John felt the marriage might go forward, but how would he survive talking to Julia's father?

———

When Rainsford heard that Julia could be with child, he seized John's throat right there in the sitting room. Chairs were overturned, tables were knocked out of the way, pictures fell off the wall as the two men crashed into them, china crashed to the floor, all hell broke loose. With great anguish, Victoria intervened in John's strangulation. "Jason, please! We need to face the truth of the situation. This is a disaster. Julia's reputation is ruined." She calmed Rainsford while pulling him away from John and made him see reality. Victoria appealed to her husband. They needed to effect a wedding soon to forestall gossip. It was for the best that Julia was going to America. People could not be counting on their fingers when the baby came.

But when John did recover and picked himself off the floor, while he was straightening his clothes and catching his breath, the Rainsfords handed him a pen and made him sign the contract. Worried that they would deduce that he did not have the money for the jointure, John declared, "I have no time to buy land before returning to America. Could it not wait until I return to England ?"

"Unacceptable! Do it before you may have her!" Rainford was livid.

Victoria put her hand on Rainsford's arm. "Please, she could be pregnant."

Thus, with only a disinclined handshake, Rainsford decided that John would buy the land after the couple returned to England. He did not secure release from the jointure. Her parents wanted to believe Julia's denials of sexual congress, but even if she was telling the truth, who else would ever want her after this? Julia felt their betrayal—no matter how things were supposed to take place in polite society.

Middle of the Atlantic Ocean

Julia watched yet another dead horse be thrown over-board. Before her eyes, sharks tore the carcass apart. She could not help vomiting for the third time over the side of the boat.

Unsympathetic, John laughed. "When are you going to get over the seasickness? You have been using this as an excuse for staying out of bed with me, but I will not accept it much longer."

"You planned to have me come with you. How could I have known that I would be seasick? I feel horrible all the time." Julia was trying to stay on her feet as the boat swayed from another enormous wave, and she caught hold of the side to steady herself.

"Julia, I have tried to be patient with you, you know I have, but my patience is running out."

"This was not my idea. I did not desire to do this, so do not blame me for this outcome!" With that, Julia threw up again.

"I have told you to keep your voice down so the other men will not hear you. I am the lieutenant colonel on this boat, and my men cannot hear you yelling like a fishwife at me."

"John, I am trying! Just now, I feel I am dying. Perhaps we can feel better about each other when I get off this damnable boat. Please give me time."

Boston, 1775

Kitchi woke up in a pool of vomit. He could not remember what had happened last night, but it was not good. Corporal Joseph Grant, assigned to orient Ki, stood over him with arms akimbo. Joseph could not pronounce Kitchi, nor could any other white men, so he was "Ki."

"If I did not think you would spew on me, I would kick your arse. Probably this is my best chance to get the better of you. We will not have your reading lesson today because we are moving out of Boston to New York. Damn you! Do you even remember what you did last night? You were drunk after only three tankards. You tried to kill a man because he asked you how an Indian could have blue eyes. You told him some story about the gods thinking you were special. When everyone laughed, you went for his throat. I thought we would not leave the tavern alive. I heard that you Indians could not hold your liquor. We need to report to Lieutenant Colonel Townset, so hurry up and get your things." Joseph was looking at Ki crossly.

Ki lived in a barn in Boston, while Joseph lived in a house with many other soldiers. The food was not bad, but he wondered why only he lived in the barn. If truth be told, Ki preferred it over sleeping inside a house. For the first time, he had privacy. He watched the soldiers take over households, put the people out of their sleeping rooms, and make them provide food for the soldiers. If that wasn't enough, they weren't even grateful. These people had beautiful horses. The soldiers were saddling them up to take them. They took only the best of the breed. Ki was homesick and hated being away from his tribe.

When he first came into Boston, he could not believe his eyes. The buildings were so tall and close together. He did not like the trash and human waste that filled the streets, emitting a filthy odor. He liked the wagons— until they fell apart and you had to fix them. That was the problem with a lot of the white man's things: they were pleasing until they broke and you had to figure out how to fix them. That was what Ki was learning, more than the language or how to read. He was learning how to shoot, take a gun apart, and clean it. Ki was also learning how to take care of the horses and saddles. He enjoyed that part a lot. He quickly took to riding, and he realized he loved horses and had a sense for them. He loved riding fast. He soon learned you could not do that in the middle of Boston when people went screaming out of his way one afternoon. A man threatened to shoot him if he did it again. "Fucking Indian" was on more than one man's lips. He was the outsider, and it seemed that they enjoyed making sure he knew it.

The soldiers did have a healthy respect for his ability with a knife. He was frequently asked to teach them how to use one and throw it. Realistically, they *had* to accord him respect because of his size and quickness. When Ki also took to shooting well, the soldiers realized he could be a deadly ally in the field. Even with their crude muskets, he could hit a target two hundred feet away.

Ki found the white man's ways strange, from the way they ate food at a table to the silly hair that they would put on their heads. The women's dresses were massive and cumbersome. They regularly had to pick them up so they would not drag them in the mud. Ki wondered why they did not just make them shorter. All the women were delicate and weak. They were fearful of everything and would faint or scream over the smallest things. He had come into a store with Joseph wearing his buckskins and knife, his hair long to his shoulders. A woman had all but fainted as if he were going to kill her right there.

It was a different world for him. The white man had a lot of possessions; dishes, furniture, lamps, and the like. Now they were moving to a new place. His father had put much faith in him and told him how honorable he was. His actions would drive the white man out of their land. They desperately needed the guns and horses that Townset brought to the tribe. Ki had a feeling the soldiers had stolen those horses. Taking colonist horses was a common occurrence, one he had witnessed. The soldiers said it was for the king of England, whom he never saw because he lived across the ocean.

"We going to New York." Ki was trying to stand up without his stomach turning from the brew he had had drunk the night before.

"A big battle is coming, and we need to meet up with Townset. You are going to hunt meat for the army on our way there. Also, you will scout ahead to see if any Patriots are lurking around." Grant was gathering up items in the barn. "Also, you will let us know if there are any hostile Indians on the way. Your job is to make sure we only meet friendly ones." Ki only nodded and began his preparations.

———

The journey took two weeks, with Ki hunting for the army as planned. In the second week, they came to a farm with cabbage and potatoes growing in the fields. The soldiers were ordered to harvest as many as they could for now and later. The farmer arose out of the barn and asked what was going on. He was told that the British army needed his harvest and would camp around his house that night.

The camp set up, and the soldiers having eaten, the daughter of the farmer came out to help with the cattle. Ki noticed Grant looking at her and sneaking off toward the barn. Ki followed and watched as Grant waited to get the daughter alone. When her father went off into the field to find missing cows, Grant ran into the barn and grabbed the daughter. The poor girl was fighting for her life and had scratched his face. Her eyes were terrified, with tears were running down her cheeks. He had her bent over a feeding box and was about to rape her when Ki came in quietly behind him, knife drawn. Rape was not a thing in Ki's world; that was losing control of oneself. Ki caught Grant in a chokehold and put his blade to his balls.

"Let her go," said Ki softly.

"You will regret this, you fucking savage!" Grant was sweating as Ki slowly released him. He ran back to camp, pulling up his pants.

"You hurt?" The girl looked traumatized and uncertain. Here was a massive Indian. He had just saved her. But she did not know if she was safe from him either. "I take you back your house."

Ki gently took her arm and led her to the house. When they got to the door, the poor girl turned and said, "Thank you so much! I don't know what I could have done had you not stopped him."

"Lock door; don't open until father comes." Ki almost pushed her inside. "Does father have gun?" Ki stood in the open doorway, and she nodded. "Tell him keep until we leave."

She nodded. "Thank you!"

———————

"That fucking Indian almost cut off my balls!" screamed Grant into the face of Lieutenant Stephens. They were standing in the lieutenant's tent the next morning. Grant had seized Ki and shoved him into the tent. But Ki had already informed the lieutenant of the incident, fearing the farmer and for his daughter's safety.

"We are trying to bring law and order into New York, not rape women, Grant. If I hear of you *ever* doing this again, I will have you hanging! Do you understand?" Stephens was just as maddened. His order from Townset had been exact—bring law and order into the land so that people will have faith again in the British government.

"Now get out of my tent, and do not let me hear from you again." With that, he turned to Ki. "Thank you for diverting a horrible mess, Ki. This could have been disastrous for us. And thank you for all the hunting and scouting you have done for the army."

Ki just nodded his head and left the tent. His opinion of the army was dropping every day. The hard-drinking and gambling were not what he had expected. He was beginning to wonder if the British had any respect for people who were not British. They seemed to have an attitude that they were above the colonists and natives who lived here. He felt this attitude himself every day.

Adams Farmhouse, outside of New York City 1776

J ulia's cases had arrived in the Adams farmhouse; they were put in the master bedroom, which Julia refused. She said the guest room would be perfectly acceptable for them. John, of course, was not happy at all with the situation. He wanted the master bedroom. Julia was trying not to be a bother to their hosts.

"John, we do not need to inconvenience these people. Please remember we are guests in their house."

"Britain is having trouble with colonists, Julia. We need to show them that we are in charge here until this attitude of revolt stops."

"Well, since we are living in their houses, eating their food, and riding their horses, we are dependent upon their goodwill. Please keep your voice down, so at least they don't have to endure us shouting at each other," Julia said while going through her cases of clothes. She was happy that she had brought comfortable clothing. She had several pocketed linen skirts and woolen jackets that could be mixed or matched in practical dark colors over her stays. Formal events would be few and far between.

"This house is so tiny that I feel we are living on top of each other. Look at the wardrobe! Your clothes will barely fit, and where will I put mine?" John looked irritated.

"I will keep mine in the cases, and you can put your clothes in the wardrobe."

"Thank you, Julia." And with that John put his hands on her shoulders and began to rub her back while kissing her neck. Julia was trying not to feel repulsion. John was her husband, but try as she might, she could not will herself to love him. You could hear everything in this house. When lovemaking occurred, she had to pretend that she felt something like passion and, at the same time, try to keep John from being too loud.

"John, I need something to do. I can't stay in this room all day pretending to sew or read." Julia pried his hands from her shoulders.

"Well, actually, I have a job I think you might like. We have an Indian guide who needs to learn English and to read. Would you like to school him on this?"

"Indian?" Julia looked perplexed.

"Yes. He is from the Seneca tribe. He will guide us through the forests and hunt meat for the army."

"Is he a savage?"

"No, not at all; I went to his tribe because the army desperately needs guides. I promised his father the chief that if he helped us, I would try to drive some of the settlers off their land, plus bring supplies to them—horses and pots to cook in."

"Where are you getting the horses? Most of ours died on the way over here."

"Well, you know it is part of the responsibility of the army to scavenge what it needs in these uncertain times."

Julia drew in a deep breath and closed her eyes. It was very awkward living in a place where the people were obliged to hand over anything the Crown might feel they needed. Most of these people were not rich, and they had worked hard for their possessions. Julia admired what they had carved out for themselves here with their bare hands. It took a lot of courage and fortitude to accomplish what they had done. Julia often wondered if she could have done it. Starting from scratch, chopping the wood to build a house while at the same time preparing fields for planting so you did not starve. They must have worked from sun up to nightfall, then fell in bed exhausted every day. She thought about how tedious and trivial her tasks were at home in England. The strenuous colonial life inspired her respect as she began to learn about the new world. These were proud people who held their heads up high and would bow to no one.

"The job sounds interesting. I will try it. Should I start tomorrow?"

"Yes. I will take you to the barn and introduce you to Ki." John was looking very pleased with himself.

"He lives in the barn? Why? All the other soldiers have taken up residence in houses around here; why not him?" Julia was beginning to wonder if they treated this Indian like a commoner or a stable boy.

"Don't get all righteous, Julia. He is used to living rough. They have longhouses where up to twenty families live. He wouldn't fit in living in a house like this. He was never taught to sit at a table and eat with silverware and napkins. Their lives are very primitive and simple compared to ours. But they can be ruthless when provoked. Don't worry; Ki is not bad. He stopped a rape when one of the soldiers wanted a farmer's daughter."

"One of the soldiers wanted to rape a farmer's daughter? For heaven's sake, John; I thought this whole mission was to bring law and order to the colonies. How could such a primitive have the boldness to flout a soldier?" Julia was amazed every day at the things she heard about this place.

"Don't worry about it now; come to bed." John pushed her down on the pillow.

"What did you say his name was?

"Ki."

———

"Ki, this is my wife, Julia. She will teach you our ways and reading. You will meet here every day in the parlor right after lunch." John had fetched Ki from the barn to the house. Julia was surprised to see an Indian with what appeared to be European features, especially the blue eyes. Julia had seen paintings of Indians, and this one did not look at all like the pictures she had seen. He had a straight nose, black hair to his shoulders, and a broad face with high cheekbones. His skin was darkly tanned but not to the hue of that of other Indians she had seen. His intense slanted blue eyes were watching her as if he had just seen something new and profound. She found him to be handsome and strange at the same time. His buck-skins outlined muscular thighs with two separate pants legs hung on a string around his waist, with a breechclout suspended front to back between on a cord. Tattooed on each arm were ovals with icicle-shaped triangles point-ing downward. On his neck were rectangles bisected by lines with small triangles pointing up on the top. Julia offered her hand to kiss in greeting but quickly withdrew it when she realized that he had no notion what to do with it. His sleeveless shirt was cut in a V in the front with laces of deerskin looped through holes. It opened now, displaying a hairless chest, and she could see his skin was perfectly smooth, as was his face: not a trace of a beard. His shoes were of buckskin, molded to his feet. You could not hear his footsteps coming at all.

Julia felt she needed to say something, instead of just staring at him, so with blushing cheeks, she said, "We will start by writing the letters and then go to the sounds of the letters." She smiled as if speaking to a child.

"I know letters, sounds; Grant teach me. We dis-agreed." his voice was deep and subdued. Julia was sur-prised to find he could speak English reasonably well.

"Oh, well, then we will start to read books. I will begin by reading to you and pointing to the words so that you can learn them. Then I will have you write some of the words. Later I may give you a spelling test."

"Spelling test?" Ki looked perplexed.

"Yes. After you learn the words, you write them down from memory on a piece of paper."

Ki nodded uncertainly. John stifled a laugh by putting his hand to his mouth. Ki felt uneasy and distrustful of John, as if he mocked him.

"I try. He want to learn read maps." Ki looked at Townset. How did such a man get so beautiful a wife? He turned his gaze on Julia, making her blush even more. The blush went all the way to her breasts, which Ki noticed with amazement. Indian women never did that. Her low square-cut neckline displayed pretty pink flushed globes instead of snow-white flesh. The gold cross around her neck accented her breasts.

Warily, she said, "I know, and we will learn that also." She felt it was rude for a man to stare so openly at a woman. Suddenly, she longed for her fichu, still hanging on a hook by the door.

"It is crucial that you instruct him how to read and draw maps if you accomplish nothing else. Ki, you may go back to whatever you were doing. Julia will see you inside the dining room every day at one o'clock. Hmm, you don't know how to tell time, do you? Let us say after the noon meal." John took Julia's arm and led her back upstairs, but not before she turned her head and saw Ki looking at her languidly. He held her gaze until John shook her arm and she had to give him her attention.

"These Indians are ignorant of our customs, so keep your distance while instructing him. There will be someone in the house all the time you are teaching him. If you feel threatened, or if he cannot learn how to behave indoors, let me know, and I will get another instructor."

"Let me try and make it work first." Julia stole one last glimpse only to see the tall, good-looking Indian still staring at her. This time without volition, she explored his body with her eyes; Ki seemed to know what she was doing as he nodded his head to her make her blush even more, bringing a hint of a smile across his face.

———

Joseph Adams did not have many slaves. He had only two—siblings, Sally and Ben. They lived in a cottage Joseph had built for them on the farm with one room and a fireplace. Eighteen-year-old Sally was light-skinned with long, black, curly hair. Fifteen-year-old Ben was stocky and not as tall. Sally was cleaning the lieutenant colonel's room when he came in.

"Sally, did you clean my uniform and polish my boots?" John looked at her with intensity.

"Yes, sir. They are right here in the wardrobe." She pulled the door open. John took hold of her arms and raked her with appraising eyes. Then he bent his head and kissed her. Sally squirmed and tried to throw an elbow, but her wrists were in a trap.

As he crushed her tightly against the wall, he hissed, "Don't you scream or say a thing, else I will accuse you of stealing my gold watch. I will have Mr. Adams sell you. I could even buy you and give you to my soldiers. Tonight, I will come to your cabin when everyone is asleep. You must leave your door open."

Her fear seemingly arousing him even more, Sally stopped resisting. She knew that she would have to stay quiet. Nothing would be worse than separating from her brother.

———————

When she told Ben what would happen, he was angry.

"We don't have to let him in," shouted Ben.

"He will say I stole his watch. Mr. Adams will have to sell me. He even said he would buy me himself and give me to his soldiers. We will be separated forever."

Ben looked miserably at Sally. "I guess I will leave when he comes; I will not be able to stomach listening."

Sally hugged her brother, trying to be brave. As a big sister, she felt responsible for him. The thought of leaving Ben was horrible, much less being the whore for all the soldiers. Because she was a slave, she could not hope to keep her virginity for long, anyway. Tears ran down her cheeks as she thought about these facts.

"That's a good idea. Then I will not have to worry about you."

———————

Julia was sound asleep when she aroused, feeling that something terrible was about to happen. She realized John was out of bed as she listened to him moving in the farm house and out the front door. Finally, Julia rose and peered out the window to see John entering the slave cabin. Compelled to see what he was up to, she donned her robe and slipped down the stairs. At the slave cabin door, she heard John talking to Sally as she pulled the door open.

"John, what are you doing?"

"Julia, go back to the house; this is not your concern." Julia noticed that John had Sally's arm and that Sally looked terrified. Sally silently looked for help from Julia. Julia had a feeling of evil. She sternly looked at John.

"John, please come back to the house." John pulled Julia into the slave cabin and slapped her hard, leaving a huge red mark across her cheek. He pointed a gun at Ben and ordered him out. "John, have you gone mad? Why do you have a gun?"

"I told you to go back to the house now!"

Julia could not believe what she was witnessing. She now knew John was amoral, for this was a new low. She held her face where he had slapped her while tears ran down her nightgown. But for the first time, Julia let her anger take control.

"John, come back to the house now! Stop being a sordid human being." With that, John pushed Julia out and slammed the door of the slave cabin in her face. In total shock, Julia saw Grant come to parade rest in front of the door with a musket in his hand. Grant was guarding John. Julia could not forget the look of desperation on Sally's face. Grant gave her a challenging look. Julia slowly turned to go back to the farmhouse. She saw Ki watching her from the barn door. When Julia got to the farmhouse, with tears running down her face, Ki came to her, "Do you want me to stop him?"

"No! You will be hurt! Grant will shoot you!" Julia looked into Ki's eyes. "Leave him alone," she said with despair, slowly turning to Ben. "Come into the farmhouse with me."

When they got to the house, Julia told Ben she would try and talk some sense into her husband, but Ben was still worried for his sister.

"Is he raping her?"

Julia hung her head and put her hands to her face. She did not know what to do. All she could think to do was repeat what she had said. "I will talk to him. Do not be shot over this. I will try and think of a solution. Please listen to me. Ben, please *stay out of his way.*"

Ben was angry and hurt, feeling completely helpless and useless. They both could hear the cries of Sally from the cabin.

———

"Your husband bad!" Ki was in the parlor for his lesson the next day. In Ki's world, it was inhumane for a man to act like this. All Julia could do was put on a brave face and nod her head. Julia could see the anger in Ki's eyes. Even though they were alone in the parlor, the rest of the household was busy doing chores but in earshot of every word. Julia felt Ki's judgment strong on her, so she felt in need of explaining.

"I don't know what to do. I don't know how to stop John. He has a lot of power here. He is the law." Julia was embarrassed and felt overwhelmed with dismay at the situation she found herself in. Now she was being confronted by this Indian she needed to teach. What was she supposed to do? Act as though nothing had happened?

Even this morning, Mr. Adams could not look her in the eye. Mrs. Adams's hands shook as she served the food, avoiding eye contact with Julia.

Before Julia knew it, tears ran down her face, then sobs began, making it worse. Everything Julia had endured was coming to a boiling point. At the wretched wedding, she didn't want the horrible wedding night. John had taken her roughly and made her bleed, then laughed about it. John told her she could expect more of this regularly. Julia felt like he was punishing her sexually for rejecting him.

Slowly, so as not to frighten her, Ki took her hand. He pulled her up and out of the chair in the dining room and out the door. Ki felt sorry for the beautiful woman who was hurt by the disrespect her husband was showing her. If she were his, he would never look at another woman—much less rape another. Ki had studied different women in the white man's world. Some of the rich ones were lovely yet very standoffish. Others that had been attractive once had worked themselves to death. The soldiers liked prostitutes. That cost money, something Ki had little of. Some of these ladies of the night communicated to him they would come to him for free, but Ki did not believe them. He heard they carried diseases, so he kept away.

"What are you doing?" Julia thought Ki somewhat forward, taking her arm and moving her along to God knows where. Ki did not look at her but led her along with determination while gently holding her hand. The intimacy made her blush. Ki turned once to look at her, and when he saw her flush, he smiled. Her embarrassed flush deepened as she realized her sense of magnetism to this man. But how could that be? He was a stranger from a primitive culture. For some reason, she felt she could trust him. This was something new to Julia, who had learned she could *not* trust John. Julia had not known other men in her short life; hearing stories of abuse and infidelity from her peers had discouraged her from wanting a suitor.

"You will like beautiful place." They moved into the woods and headed to the river. Julia looked back and saw the house, hoping that if she screamed, someone would come.

There was a clearing with wildflowers that inclined down to the river. Several deer were feeding there but quickly moved on. A massive flat rock jutted into the river above the water, making a perfect surface to walk out onto without getting wet. This peaceful place was where Ki had led her. They both sat down—and just perceived the serenity as she spread her dress out around her. The sun shone on the water so that one had to squint, and beautiful butterflies stopped at all the flowers. One landed on her arm, and she smiled. They were quiet, and it felt commonplace and easeful. Julia felt that if she spoke, she would break the calm that she so desperately needed. The sun was in her face, and it felt good.

"Thank you for this. It is beautiful here." Julia felt in control again. "We are both strangers in a strange land. You do not know British customs, and I know nothing about your people, this land, or American settlers. I feel I don't know anything anymore."

"Miss your home?" Ki was looking at Julia.

"Yes, very much. It is very different where I come from."

"This my home, now the white man here."

"Here? This was your home? But what happened?"

"The white settlers out our villages farther and farther." Ki pointed to the west while Julia looked in that direction.

"We fight them; they had guns, horses, disease. Villages destroyed; we move, trading with white man for iron. White men pay iron and horses for land. We move and move." Ki was quiet.

Julia did not know what to say. She was trying to comprehend what it would be like to be displaced farther and farther by the white man. "It sounds horrible for your people—to once have had all of this. It is so beautiful, and the crops grow so well. We don't grow these foods in Europe."

"The Haudenosaunee showed settlers how to grow corn, beans, and squash. But too many kept moving in."

"Now there is a war going on, and you are in the middle of it." Julia was looking into Ki's face. For a long minute, they both stared at each other until Julia looked away.

"We try stay out; husband came to my village, asked my father for guide. He said would give horses, supplies we help him. When British win war, we get lands back."

Julia had never heard any of this before. She wondered if they really would push settlers out of their farms to give the land back to the Indians. She could not see them doing that. The British had profited from the crops. Next, she tried to visualize John going to Ki's village to speak with his father. Julia could not see him doing that, either. She did not know John as well as she thought she had. What had she gotten herself into here?

"What your land like?" Ki asked.

"We live in huge houses," Julia smiled, feeling shy.

"Bigger than farmer's house?"

"Yes—much bigger and taller. We have castles made of stone and many servants to cook for us and wash our clothes and drive us in our carriages." Julia was beginning to relax again, and Ki found her fascinating. Her cheeks were red when she got excited, making her eyes very blue. Her lips were small and delicate. "I have a sister whom I miss, and parents. What about you? Do you have a sister or brother?

"No. Father village sachem; mother runs village with women."

Julia could not believe her ears. "Are you saying the women have a say in what happens to your village?" Her eyes were wide open, and Ki wanted to laugh.

"Yes, clans follow mothers' lines."

Now Julia was amazed. "You have clans?"

"Yes. Wolf clan, bear clan, beaver clan. Child born into mother's clan; if he takes woman, he goes her clan to live. Clan lives longhouse, different these houses. There many clans in village; fifteen more families live in longhouse." Julia shook her head, thinking what a different world he lived in from hers.

"Julia! Julia! Where are you?" John's voice called for her. Julia's face darkened, and Ki could see fear.

"I must go!" She gathered up her dress quickly. Ki helped her up by offering his hand, noticing her low-cut neckline and suddenly wanting to touch the lovely white bosom.

"You stay here. Don't let John see us out here together, or he will get angry." She started to flee but turned around. "Come to your lesson tomorrow." Julia had a microscopic flirty smile on her face when she looked at Ki, making his heart jump. Julia knew she had no right to look as if she was leading him on, but for some reason, she did not care; all she knew was that she had been happy for a short while with Ki.

Relationships

"Today, we shall learn to eat politely, so I have set the table as we do in England. We will learn how to grasp a fork, spoon, or knife, and why more than one of each is needed." Julia used her most cheerful voice while holding up the utensils. Ki regarded the silverware as he would a new snake he had never seen before.

"Unfold your napkin, and place it in your lap. Unwind your feet from the chair legs, please. We will begin with the soup." Julia was still ladling soup into his bowl when he picked it up with both hands and started drinking from the vessel. Julia lifted it out of his grasp and replaced it on the table. This action caused her to blush, which brought a smile to Ki's face.

"No. You must use proper silver to eat from the dish. But even before you can begin, you must sit up perfectly straight" Julia demonstrated this with her back straight as an arrow. "Then we pick up the spoon like this. Dip the leading edge into the soup, and follow through smoothly. Hold your elbow slightly away from your body, and bring it to your mouth." Ki wanted to take this seriously for Julia's sake, but a snigger almost escaped. He brought spoon to mouth, and he carefully slurped up every drop with smacking lips.

"No, no, no!" Julia stifled a giggle. "You must not make a noise! Just try to get it into your mouth without making a sound." Finding this funny also, Julia realized how ridiculous all this was. But if she failed to teach him their customs, and he ever ate with white men at a table, he would be mocked. Why his humiliation should unsettle her, she could not say, but it did.

"Now put your bowl aside, and I will serve the meat and vegetables." Julia was enjoying herself. She piled food on his plate. Julia showed him how to pick up the fork and hold it, reminding him to keep his back straight and elbows out slightly. His efforts pleased her until she showed him how to use the knife. He kept holding it in his fist, so Julia got up and tried to place it into his hand correctly. As their hands met, she nearly gasped at the spark she felt. She quickly demonstrated the act of cutting the meat and sat back down quickly. Her low-cut dress had allowed his breathing to hit her breasts, causing them to blush and sweat at the same time. He smiled at her, knowing what had just happened. Julia tried to ignore it and act as if nothing had happened.

"Thanking Providence for this food, let us eat." Julia slowly began. Ki hurriedly began to shovel food in his mouth. "No, you have to eat unhurriedly."

"I starving." Ki's look of dissent told her wolfing down food was the normal mode in his culture.

"I know. But you must behave as though you are not hungry. Eat slowly."

Ki looked at her in bewilderment. "Why?" He found this dishonesty incomprehensible. Ki was looking at Julia with such confusion and wonder that Julia could not contain her laughter. She shook her head and held her hand to her mouth so food wouldn't fly out. "I don't know why! Our customs seem ridiculous now that I think of it. Even aristocrats get very hungry. Oh, for heaven's sake! Since you are starved, then I give you leave to gobble it. I think you will enjoy the dessert."

"Dessert?"

"Yes, it is a blueberry pie."

"You made?"

"No." This made Julia feel embarrassed, for she did not know how to cook.

"Mrs. Adams made it."

"You make this food?" Ki asked curiously.

"No. Mrs. Adams made it." Julia's gaze fell to the napkin in her lap. She suspected that all the women of his clan were taught from a young age how to cook and this must seem utterly strange to him.

"You know to make food?" Ki's curiosity rose. He had never known a woman who could not cook. Most women of the tribe even dressed out the animals brought in by hunters. To cover the awkward minute, Julia quickly cut the pie and handed Ki a piece. He grabbed the big fork. Julia put her hand on his without thinking. Once again, she felt the intimacy and quickly withdrew it.

"Don't eat it with the large fork. That is only for the main course. This *small* fork is for dessert."

"Why?" now Ki looked utterly astonished. Julia could not help but laugh. It felt so good to laugh and have an enjoyable time, for she had been unhappy for so long. All Julia could do was shrug and dig into her pie. Ki had eaten the white man's desserts before, even though he was not used to eating a lot of sweet food, but this was good. The Indians used berries to sweeten foods having no access to sugar, only honey.

"Do you like it" Julia looked hopefully at Ki?

"Yes. A lot to wash." Ki was moving his hand over the entire table, and once more laughter bubbled out of her as Julia shook her head.

"I know! I never realized how unnecessary these customs are until now." Good God! It felt good to really laugh and be herself and not play games of intrigue and mystery, always trying to guess the hidden meaning behind someone's words.

"Well, this concludes our lesson today. I really should help Mrs. Adams with all these additional dirty dishes." Julia began to laugh again. She stopped to smile at Ki. "See you tomorrow?"

The lessons after that went very well. Ki was a fast learner who seemed keen on education. He certainly enjoyed being around Julia and could not wait to be with her; it was the highlight of his day. She was so beautiful, so kind; he could go on and on. How could her husband even think of hitting her? He knew her husband was down at Sally's cabin at least two times a week, and sometimes he could see Julia looking out the window when John went to Sally's home.

Townset was a strange man. He would start the day reasonably, then turn ridiculous for no reason. Ki thrived on the strenuous drills he gave the soldiers and enjoyed learning the whites' military ways, even though they made little sense. He preferred the Indian way, to make your body blend into the environment and ambush the enemy. When he tried to explain this to Townset, he was looked at as if he were crazy. Ki could tell that Townset had never fought like this. Well, the "Patriots" were learning the strategy and successfully using it. Ki heard the soldiers' whispers about how one minute their friend was talking to them and the next there was a bullet through his head because they never saw it coming until it was too late.

Ki had to prepare for a journey to Long Island, the army's next destination. With the help of Julia, he drew a map with tribal areas marked. All the military equipment was loaded on ox carts, with food, clothing, and bedding gathered and sorted for the trip. They took what few medical supplies they could collect from farmhouses, along with horses, mules, cattle, and goats. Ki felt sorry for the farmers who had been plowing their fields when the army commandeered the horses out from under them. They even grabbed a few chickens on the way out.

Julia waved goodbye to her husband without a tear. Ki noticed that when John tried to kiss her, she quickly turned her head aside. He felt jealous. The soldiers staying in nearby farmhouses had all gathered, dressed smartly in uniform with muskets shouldered. Most were on foot, all ready for some action. Ki scouted ahead for danger, doubling back to make sure they were on the right path. Once, he narrowly escaped a militia of Patriots crossing a river and had to hide in a tree for hours as they stopped to water the horses and eat a bite of lunch. By the time the British army got there, they had disappeared. He did his usual hunting deer chores, occasionally bagging a tur-key; the British were unaccustomed to eating this meat. In lean times they ate rabbit and squirrel.

Adams Farmhouse, 1776

Sally was cleaning the Townset bedroom when Julia first noticed the girl's swelling abdomen; the situation hit Julia like a slap. She put a hand over her mouth, dropping suddenly onto the bed, wagging her head in denial, crying. Julia realized that they were both pregnant. She did not want to be pregnant, but she had to try to love this child, innocent of the father's sins.

"What is wrong, Ms. Townset?"

"I am so sorry for my husband's ill use of you. You do not deserve this at all. He is a pig!" Sally could only hang her head, gently rubbing her stomach. Neither could speak for a while. Then Julia looked at Sally and said, "I will have to think of some means to help you. I don't control enough money to buy you. I must find some other way." Julia grabbed Sally's hand. "Please trust me; I can't reverse his misdeeds, but I will help you."

Sally began to cry, and Julia put her arms around her. "Are you getting enough food? Are you warm enough in your cabin? While John is gone, you can sleep with me here in the room."

"Yes, I am all right. I have my brother, Ben, to look out for me."

Julia was amazed at the strength of the young girl. She not only had to put up with John but also take care of her little brother. Suddenly Julia realized Ben had probably been present at her violations. Julia could not speak for a moment with embarrassment. "Is Ben there when—" Julia could not finish.

"No. He leaves and waits outside because Grant will not let him in." Julia put her hands to her face in total despair. Then fury filled her, and she knew she truly hated John.

Long Island 1776

Ki heard deafening cannon fire from the hundred British ships lined up along Long Island. In all of his short life, he would remember this scene of destruction by the British. Ki avoided the fires as best he could, but the heat was overwhelming. The Patriots fought hard, but it was apparent Washington's troops were spread too thin. Desperately they fought for their lives.

"Retreat! Retreat!" screamed the Patriot commanders. Ki lost count of the dead bodies. He saw small children screaming for their mothers; one stood crying over his mother's dead body. British soldiers searched, finishing off as many men as possible with their bayonets. The slaughter and destruction awed Ki, who was new to explosives. General Howe's fifteen thousand troops laid waste to the city. Ki headed for the ships to join the general. His feet struck a British officer's corpse wearing many gold rings. Gold meant little to Ki, but he knew it was valuable to the white man, so he took the jewelry and hid it in his pouch.

"We need to capture Washington." Townset gave orders that this was the main objective.

When they finally reached the shore, Ki alerted Townset. "We need to watch the rivers, so Washington cannot escape."

To Ki's surprise, Townset shook his head. "No, we need to deal with all these prisoners and get them onto the ships using these rowboats." Ki looked at the wounded men in chains. Townset continued. "Take them down to the hull of the ship and shackle them when you get them on the big boat."

"Too many. Take days. You want Washington?" Ki couldn't believe what he had heard. But Townset said, "We have thousands of captured men, so get busy and secure them now!"

There were so many prisoners; it was almost impossible to count them. At least three thousand captured Patriots would see the end of their lives on the old warships. As Ki took prisoners down, the stench of the hull nearly knocked him over. What he saw was nightmarish: Rats gnawed on chained corpses. Feces and urine overpowered his nose. The prisoners he led were unable to walk, so Ki carried them to their shackles. The ones who hung back were bayoneted and thrown over the side of the ship. Ki realized this was a better death than being starved and left to the rats. Ki felt the bile rise into his mouth. He swallowed it as best he could. He told himself that if this was the white man's world, he had to bear it. But deep in his soul, he felt disgusted over the whole scene.

When he left the ship to find Townset, a woman with three small children hanging on her arm stopped him.

"Please help me; my house has burned, and there is no shelter or food."

He gave her the gold rings. Scavengers were already at work, looking for anything of value left on the bodies.

"Take children; hide! Go, *go!*" Ki yelled at the woman. "Someone robs you!" She ran for her life, with the children trying to keep up as best they could. One child, about two, fell on his face, and his older brother came back, picked him up, grasped him around his knees, and carried him to his running mother. Ki could taste the fire, and it burned his eyes with the smell of death everywhere.

Blowback

"**G**od fucking damn you! You let him escape! You had orders to guard the rivers, but *no, you disobeyed your orders!*" General Howe was beside himself. He had had Washington where he wanted him, and now he had gotten away. Washington had retreated off Long Island in the dense fog of night with the remaining Patriots.

"I can't believe it." Howe sat down, tired as a result of the events; he could not stand any longer.

"I had three thousand prisoners I had to deal with!" Townset couldn't believe he was being held responsible for this.

"We could have ended it here!" Howe could not even lift his head. Townset only shook his head. What should he have done? Let thousands of prisoners go free so he could find Washington? This was going to look incompetent to the Crown. God only knew what the report would read.

"General Howe, we now control the city and the harbor. We have dealt a terrible blow to the Patriots. Washington is on the run. We will find him. I am sure of it."

Howe controlled his disgust. Regrettably, he needed this fool. "Go back to the interior, and try to bring law and order back under our command. Root out any minutemen or militia you find. Discover their hiding places and their plans. It is dangerous territory, so don't stay too far from the city." He spoke slowly, with emphasis. "This is very important. Do you understand?"

All Townset could do was nod and leave. The army headed back into the countryside, fighting minor battles with the Patriots. Before Ki left New York City, he saw many prisoners being led back to the ships, where certain death awaited them.

Adams Farmhouse, 1776

"You know that idiot Washington and their moronic Congress declared themselves to be independent of Britain?" John was pacing up and down the bedroom.

Julia nodded her head, trying to pay attention. "We received word the battle of Long Island went well. Washington evaded capture, but it is only a matter of time before you catch him." Julia was trying to be encouraging. Since John's return, he had been more out of sorts than ever. The smallest thing would set him off. When he noticed Sally's belly, he screamed at her to get out of the house. Julia wanted to keep peace in the place, but the Adamses grew more and more concerned every minute, and one could cut the tension with a knife. Julia worried that John might physically hurt Sally, so she talked to the Adams about keeping Sally out of the house while John was there. She was ashamed that John had raped Sally and, worse, had felt it had been his right to do so. John, fortunately, had taken offices in the small church half a mile away. She did not see him for most of the day.

"I want you to keep your eyes open. If you see anything that I need to know, tell me. I have heard there are spies everywhere." John spoke with authority, and Julia did not doubt what he was saying was true. The few people she mingled with had become secretive and wary. The tension was not just in the Adams house, but everywhere. When Julia would go into the small store, everyone would stop talking and watch her intensely. She was an outsider in this strange land.

Ki bathed in the river and washed his skins as best he could. He had resumed his residence in the barn. Ki wanted to see Julia again and take up their lessons. When he got to the house, she greeted him at the door, smiling. For a long minute, they just stood and took each other in to see if something had changed. He almost embarrassed himself when he noted the small bulge in her dress with distress; she was with child. He had greatly missed her and was hoping that maybe she had missed him also. He needed to be around her happiness and beauty because he had seen so much slaughter that nightmares kept him up all night long. The ships with those doomed men in them kept playing in his head; he could see their faces. Ki knew even now they were dying of neglect and starvation. Yes, he needed to see her face again, and he so wanted to touch her and feel her.

When he had come back from the river after bathing, he had heard John talking to Grant in the barn. Ki could move in such a way that no one would ever see or hear him, and he made his way to the doorway.

"You could go for a ride in the countryside and push her off her horse." Grant was talking almost silently, but Ki could hear everything.

"Do you actually think that would work? What if she doesn't die? Then what should I do? Get off my horse and strangle her?"

"Well, that is one thing, but you can get pretty bruised up falling off a horse, so if you beat her to death, no one will question you when you say that she fell off the horse."

"I don't know if I can do that!" John was shaking his head.

"Let me follow you secretly, and I can do it. You can leave and not look if it bothers you so much." Grant thought rape would be fun also.

"Let me think about it more and then give you an answer." John was about to leave when Grant put his hand out to stop him,

"What if we make it look like the Indian did it?" Grant was smiling, and John's face lit up.

"That would be perfect! Let's work more on this and come up with something! But remember, we will need a body to bring back to England, or no one will believe us."

John and Grant left without seeing Ki. Ki thought hard on the subject of telling Julia. Would she believe him? He was the outsider who had no authority in her life; he was in her world and not his. Did John seriously want to go through with it? Would Julia believe him or get mad at him and not want to see him again, telling him to go away and then running to John and telling him everything. Julia was a white woman; why would she believe an Indian? No, he had to keep quiet about it, but he would also keep watch. So they were going to make it look like he had done it!

"I have a surprise for you. I found *Romeo and Juliet* on the bookshelf in the parlor. Someone must have brought it from England, and I am going to read it to you." With that, she led him into the parlor. When her governess had read Shakespeare, the sisters had played the parts of Juliet and Romeo, so Julia knew all the characters' lines. Slowly her voice began to calm his soul. She explained details of the story he did not understand, and he became more and more taken with the tale. When she got to the end, where Juliet stabs herself, Julia got up and started to act out the parts. Ki watched in fascination as Juliet dramatically stabbed herself upon seeing Romeo dead. Julia wilted to the ground. Ki sat there for what seemed like a long time, but she did not move. He got up and began calling,

"Julia, Julia!" He was kneeling beside her when he noticed her sides were shaking from laughter.

She sprang up, giggling, two inches from his face. Suddenly they ceased laughing, and her face became very tender. He held his breath as she slowly brought her mouth to his. Her kiss was warm—and very soft. She drew away, blushing.

"I'm sorry. I should not have done that." The kiss had been freshwater to a man dying of thirst. Ki retook her mouth in a much deeper kiss. Julia had missed him, and every thought was of him and his safety while he was gone. She had dreams of them making love. The kiss turned very sexual as Ki pulled her into his lap, and his hands went for her breasts, reality struck Julia. Someone could find them, and all hell would break loose. Julia shook her head.

"No, no! This is not right—I am married, and John will kill you if he finds out."

It was Ki's turn to shake his head. "How you love John when he dishonors you?"

Julia lowered her head in despair. "There is nothing I can do about it. I must endure it."

"No. Come away with me." Julia could not believe her ears.

"I cannot; I am married, and our laws are on his side. The English law is not very favorable to women who run away from their husbands. No. I am sorry if I have misled you." Julia got up and smoothed out her dress. "Besides, where would we go?"

"My village. I *make* the women accept you." Ki was very serious.

Julia was astonished. She was ignorant of Indian life. Going by what little she knew, it would be very different from how she was living now. They were known as savages.

"It is very kind of you to want to take me there, but my life is here"—she wanted to add "unfortunately." She smiled at Ki. "Besides, I don't think I would do well there." Tears had formed in her eyes; it was making her so depressed that they could not be together.

"I teach you. You learn quickly." Ki was thinking about how wonderful it would be to have her there with him. He would love to be her teacher. But then he thought of her clothes. They would get in the way of everyday living.

"You need different clothes," he said, smiling, and gently whisked the tears from her eyes. "The women not dress like you. They move much more. They jump on horse."

"Really! There are days I hate these dresses. But I cannot imagine wearing anything else. No, Ki. I am sorry for kissing you. I don't see any other way. We will not talk about this again. I have to stay here." With that, Julia stood up and walked Ki to the door. Ki thought hard about telling Julia what he had heard John and Grant talking about in the barn, but he still felt she would not believe him. She was already making excuses for John.

"I will see you again tomorrow, won't I?" Julia said with a flushed face and a dismissive tone.

"No!" Ki's eyes burned into hers; anger overtook him. He felt she was not even going to try and work things out with him. She was telling him that they had no future together.

Julia could not believe her ears. What had she done! Not seeing Ki again would be the end of her sanity. Being with Ki was the best part of every day, she realized. She had never really seen him angry at her before; the last thing she wanted to do was to hurt him.

"I am so sorry for what I did! I want you to come back. Please? Tomorrow I will have another surprise for you." Julia was talking fast, eyes wide and tearful, pleading with him. Making him want her even more and feel very frustrated.

"What?" Ki was looking suspiciously at Julia.

"It is a surprise! I can't tell you, or it would be spoiled."
Ki finally agreed to come back the next day. Julia breathed
a sigh of relief.

Julia's plight captivated Ki. In the Seneca world, a
woman's family could expel an abusive husband from the
fireside. If a couple did not get along, he could live with
his birth clan. Having no line here, he could understand
why she did not just leave. But why had she left her own
family? The white man's world often made no sense.

———

When Ki showed up, Julia was wearing her riding outfit
of navy blue worsted with a waist-length fitted jacket. The
jacket had wide, collar-like lapels showing a frothy lace-
trimmed white linen neckcloth and full skirt with extra
length, allowing modest sidesaddle riding.

"Let's go for a ride." They walked to the barn, and Ki
put the saddles on the horses while Julia sat watching him,
admiring his body and the ease with which he moved.

"Where we going?" Ki queried.

"I told you; it is a surprise."

Ki noticed her pink complexion even more than
usual in juxtaposition with the very deep blue wool, colors he rarely saw in nature. Her beauty fascinated him.
But he could not help feeling rejected from yesterday. He
did not know why he should continue to be around her
if she did not want to leave with him. He desired to take
her away more and more, primarily since he had heard
what Grant and John had said in the barn. He thought
again about telling her what they were planning, but he

still was unsure if Julia would believe him. They rode into town and stopped at the tailor's shop. Ki looked curiously at Julia.

"Today is another lesson on the use of money and clothes. Do you think you could sometimes wear different clothes?"

"I have to see; I move around in them. They not feel like red coats?"

"No, this is not a uniform. This will be a suit of clothes to wear too—maybe it should be clothes you could work in." Julia was thinking, *He does not go to church, so all he needs is work clothes.*

They went into the tailor's shop, and Ki watched as the tailor measured him for pants and two shirts. If he found it strange, so did the tailor, who had never measured an Indian before. The tailor said he had just made some pants that might fit Ki, so Ki went into the backroom to change. When he came out wearing only the pants, Julia was shocked at how handsome he looked; she openly admired his body.

Ki wondered if he could get used to these clothes, but he was willing to try. The shirts were a little strange, with the huge sleeves. He looked at Julia to see if she liked them. She was looking at him intensely. Suddenly she smiled and said, "We will take these." Julia showed Ki how to buy the clothes with money she had saved from what John had given her when he had left to fight on Long Island.

"Do you think you can wear them? You don't have to wear them all the time, but I thought since you are living

among white people now, maybe you should look like us."
They were riding back to the farmhouse.

"Do you want me look like white men?"

"No—not if you don't want to. You are you, and I think
it is wonderful. But you are in our world now. I remember
you telling me that if I went to your village, I would have
to change my clothes."

"You right. I live in world of white man, and I saw
many things I like, but many things I not like. I saw in
New York City I not like."

"Do you want to go back to your village?" Julia looked
sadly at Ki.

"Yes, miss my people, our ways. I go back, but I promised father I help the white man with his war." Ki wanted
to say, "And I don't want to go back without you."

—————

John was very discouraged because the Crown was dis-
pleased with Washington's escape down the East River.
Howe had demoted him. In a fit of rage, he had cleared
his desk with one swipe. Grant entered at that time.

"I saw your wife with the Indian. She took him to the
tailor in town and bought him clothes with your money."
Grant looked severe, but really, he wanted to laugh. He
thought this would put fuel on the fire of John's anger.
Grant still fumed at his humiliation by Ki. He was getting his revenge. They were at the church John used for a
headquarters for his troops.

"I will deal with this in my way," John said through
his teeth.

CATHY PEEBLES

Nothing had gone right since he had returned, and it had been a huge mistake bringing Julia here, so maybe it was time to put their plan into place? He should have left her in England, he realized. When he got back to England, he could do what he wanted. Many men of his resources had mistresses. He and Julia were not happy together, and just the other day, Mr. Adams had tried to talk to him about being more considerate of her. He was incredulous that a mere farmer could advise him about marriage. Julia had caused some loud arguments that John knew the whole house could hear. She had had the gall to bring up Sally and question what he was going to do about the baby! Hell if he knew! It was not his problem. God damned woman! He should have chosen better. If only he hadn't needed her money so urgently.

The suggestion of Grant was looking better and better. She was spending more and more time with this heathen Indian. This was not England, where eyes were everywhere plus, everyone here had seen her spending time with Ki. He would have to act the heartbroken widower for a while, but it would be worth it. The thought of being rid of her and her constant judgmental ways was an increasingly welcomed feeling. He would have to put a plan in motion and be very careful about how he implemented it. He would have all her money and none of the tiresome duties of a husband, no longer having to answer for everything. It was worth losing the child; he had never wanted children anyway, especially from Julia. Everyone in England would believe the story of Julia trying to help the heathen Indian and then the violent creature turning on her. He could see their faces as he told the story of how he had found Julia utterly destroyed by Ki; he also would have to remember to put the scalping part into the story of how she died.

The Last Straw

"Yes, I bought Ki those clothes. Just remember where that money came from, John! I know you brought no money to the marriage. Money was your total motivation for marrying me. I will spend *my* money the way I see fit."

Completely red in the face, John trembled with fury. He grabbed Julia's arm and raised his hand to her face. "You will do as I say, or I will force you!"

"No, you will not. I am weary of catering to you, of your fits and rages and your whoring around. I know Sally is not the only one you see. You have the gall to sleep with her in front of her brother! You are a whore dog!"

With that, John slapped Julia hard across the face, knocking her to the floor. In a black rage, he kicked her in the ribs. She screamed. She covered her abdomen to protect her unborn baby. He picked her up by the hair and drove a blow into her stomach. Mr. and Mrs. Adams could not take the abuse any longer and began banging on the door.

"Lord Townset, stop! You are hurting your wife! Do you want to harm the baby? Please stop and think about what you are doing!" Mr. Adams stood like a constable, with his wife red-faced right behind him. John knew he had gone too far as he was supposed to keep law and order in the county, not create a peace disturbance. He dashed open the door, pushing past the Adamses, and quickly fled the house to the stables.

———

Ki had risen before dawn to go hunting for the household. He had been asleep in the hay, mired in a nightmare about New York City, seeing again those horrible ships where the prisoners died a cruel death. He heard them screaming. Ki had sat up and realized that it was Julia screaming. He quickly grabbed his knife and headed for the house as he almost collided with John.

"You leave my wife alone. Don't even think about coming to the house again or seeing her anywhere. Do you understand? I am sending her back on the next ship to England." John's pride had gotten the best of him, so he clutched Ki's shirt to scream into his face, with his spit flying. John was hoping everyone could witness what was happening so it would look as if John had warned Ki to stay away from Julia. Before John knew what was happening, Ki's strong forearm drew John's throat to his knife. He had never seen Ki in action, and suddenly, John feared for his life, feeling a force stronger than him.

"Not touch her again!" Small blood cuts appeared on John's neck. Ki longed to let the blade sink into the coward's throat and be done with him, but odds were against Ki in the white man's world. Ki slowly let John go, holding eye contact and whispering, "I hear your plan!"
John's pride got in the way again. Who did this dumb

Indian think he was? "She is mine!" John mounted in too much haste to even use a saddle. He galloped out of the stable, heading for town. Twenty minutes later, at the tavern, John was drinking heavily with Grant.

———

Ki threw a stone at Julia's window. When she opened it, he could tell she had been crying.

"Bring things; come down." His face was intense, and Julia knew this was the moment at which she had to make a decision.

"You not come down, I leave tonight, never see you again. He kill you; I not watch. Come with me! We go my village you, safe from him." Julia's eyes were huge. She took a deep breath, then nodded. Without hesitation, she gathered a few clothes and blankets. Julia realized that John could kill her here in America and no one would investigate it. The British officials were busy with the war, and even then, John could make it look like an accident if he wanted to. John would have all her money, and she would no longer bother him, make him feel guilty about seeing other women. He could even marry another rich woman and live even better than he was living now. Julia realized that she feared for her life and that of her unborn child. If he hurt her, what would he do to the child? She felt a sharp pain in her abdomen, making her bend over in pain; panting hard, Julia thought about staying, but the aching stopped. She continued to gather what belongings she thought would serve her best in the new world she was about to enter.

As she was leaving the house, Mr. Adams came to her and said, "Will you be taking the horses?" Julia knew that these were his only horses, so she took off her wedding ring and gave it to him. He looked worried but then said, "You must go! He is getting more and more violent. I do not want to predict what will happen. I will pray for you; I hope that Indian treats you well. He appears to be a good man, and I hope he protects you." His eyes were serious as he looked into Julia's face.

She just nodded. When she was leaving, she saw Sally.

"I cannot remain here. If you can leave, do so."

With that, they left.

———

They traveled all night long and into the next day, stopping long enough for Ki to try and cover their tracks and water the horses. Julia was so tired she could have fallen off the horse, but higher than her weariness was her hunger. Her ribs and abdomen pained her, and she carried a bruise where John had slapped her. Ki saw that it was hard for her to ride the horse. The weather favored them by not raining. Ki sought a cave he had found as a boy, and when they reached it, daylight still lit the back of the space, so they drew the horses inside with them and Ki lit a fire.

"Why did you say you would leave and not come back if I didn't come with you?" Julia was feeling shy and uncertain.

"I not let your husband beat you. I killed him and the army after me. Julia, you mine. I hear John plans kill you make look I did it." Julia looked down because of the shame she felt in regard to John. The bastard! There were no words to describe what she felt. She then limped over to Ki and kissed him with everything she had in her. He knew if he ever got the chance, he would kill John for doing this to Julia. The kiss became deep, but Ki pushed her away gently.

"I need hunt, we need sleep; long way to my village."

The rabbit Ki had caught was roasting on the fire when Julia felt an overwhelming pain in her abdomen. It erupted violently, Julia screamed in excruciating pain, and Ki saw she was losing her baby.

"Julia, take off clothes. The baby dying." Ki shucked her skirts before the flood of blood started, and Julia delivered the dead fetus in excruciating pain, with Ki trying to help as best he could. Ki carried water from the river to bathe her as he held her tightly while washing her off. Finally, she slept while he buried the fetus in the cave. The next morning when he woke her and dressed her, she was delirious from fever. He managed to mount her onto his horse. They started home, leading her horse.

After five hours' ride, Ki came to the burnt-out village that had been his home. He couldn't believe it.

"What is wrong?" Julia spoke weakly from Ki's arms.

"They burned village."

"Who would do that?"

"Patriots; we support British."

"Was anyone killed, do you think?"

"No bodies."

"Do you want to look around?"

"No, I know where tribe went. You need help. I come back.

———

John had gotten so drunk that night he could not even climb the stairs to his bedroom. He gave way on the front porch and woke up with a massive headache. When he finally could rise to his bedroom, Julia was gone. He quickly found Mrs. Adams.

"Where is my wife?"

"She left with the Indian."

John gaped incredulously. "How long ago?"

"Yesterday, after you left for the tavern."

John turned, ran for his horse, and rode to the small church where he saw his men drilling. He called to Grant. "Assemble the men; we are heading out. We need provisions for several days."

"Why? Is Washington on the move?" Grant looked excited to be going somewhere.

"No, that goddamned Indian stole my wife. I want her back. Keep your lips sealed about this." Grant could not believe his luck. He would finally seek revenge for that damned Indian's insolence. Grant wanted to tell John that now he could file for Julia's desertion and still have all her money, but he longed to see Ki punished. The punishment would be over the top for an Indian running away with an officer's wife. He even had a depraved thought about what John would do to Julia when he got her back.

"The farmer and his wife know Julia ran away with Ki, along with Sally and Ben. We could never get away with the story of Ki killing her without a body. We have to get her back! I am afraid of what that stupid farmer will say to the community and authorities about our relationship. This could look bad for me, so I have to take a body back to England, and it has to be Julia."

As they gathered provisions, a rider entered the churchyard with Howe's message, which canceled John's plans. Washington was on the move again, and John was to stop him at any cost. Instead of going to look for his wife he had to look for Washington. They were two horses short at Adams's barn—probably the ones Julia and Ki had taken. John sought two horses from the closest horse farm and there saw Mr. Adams buying two replacement horses. When Adams had left, John inquired how he had paid for the horses, knowing that Adams had little money.

"Adams had no coin for two horses, so I am wondering how he paid for them?"

"He just handed me this valuable gold ring, and I said, 'Yes, that will get you two horses all right.'"

John's eyes burned with outrage to see Julia's ring in the owner's hand. He cursed as he got on his horse.

———

In a small tavern near White Plains, New York, Grant drank with his fellow soldiers, playing cards and losing badly. He already owed ten silver coins. His opponent grew suspicious that he couldn't pay.

"You don't have the goddamned money, do you?" Another soldier grabbed Grant by the collar and hauled him up out of his chair.

"No, but I have some interesting information." Grant was hoping he would not get a beating if he could distract him from the silver coins.

"To the devil with your blasted information! I want my money. Now God damn you, hand it over, or I will make a joke of your face." The rest of the soldiers laughed at that and began to cheer the soldier to act.

"Oh, I think you will want to hear this one. It is worth knowing." Grant was sweating heavily now. "I *don't* have the money, but if you beat the hell out of me, then you won't hear what I have to tell."

"You sheep fucker!" The soldier punched Grant in the face. "What is so goddamned interesting?" He had not let go of Grant's collar.

"Have you heard that Townset's wife is missing?" Grant tried to make his secret sound like the fountain of youth.

"No! What of it?" The soldier was getting impatient.

"Have you heard of the Indian guide named Ki?"

"No! God damn you! Get on with it!" The soldier aimed his fist at Grant's face again.

"Townset's wife ran off with that Indian. They went back to his village. We were supposed to retrieve her, but Washington began to move again, so we had to look for Washington instead of getting his wife back."

The tavern had grown very quiet. The soldier thought about it for a moment. "Is there a reward for her return?"

"I am sure there will be. You can be the first to find Julia and get the reward!" The soldier knocked Grant out cold.

No one knew a Patriot spy was sitting in the corner listening to this news. The spy ran back to the camp hidden in the woods and reported to Daniel Morgan.

"I just learned that the Seneca guide Ki, who works for Townset, ran off with his wife." The man was laughing. Morgan could scarcely believe his ears. Morgan had just taken charge of a large group of Patriot soldiers in New York known as Morgan's Riflemen. If the story was true, he could gain an undue advantage by capturing this woman for her ransom.

"Let all our men know that they should be on the lookout for her. Capture her at all costs." Morgan was thinking about how badly the Patriots needed the money. It would humiliate the British if the Patriots were to catch her and hold her for ramson.

The Village

Ki found the new village assembled in a somewhat hasty way. Julia was in worse condition and had a high fever, so he searched the stony faces for Keme. The villagers were unhappy to see Ki come in with a white woman. At last, Keme stepped forward.

"Mother, this woman needs your help. She has lost a baby and is very sick." Keme marshaled her clan women to carry Julia into the medicine hut.

"Who is this, Kitchi?" Keme was taking Julia's clothes off to inspect her.

"Her name is Julia. Her baby died because her husband kicked her. She is a good woman whom I do not want to die. She is to have our protection."

Yuma stood in the doorway. "I want to speak to you!" Ki turned to him. He could see that his father was unhappy. "Who is this? Why is she here? I sent you to guide the British, and now you bring one of their women here!"

"Her husband was trying to kill her. He kicked her so hard she lost her baby. She is very sick."

"What has this got to do with you?"

Ki looked down at his feet and then into the eyes of his father. "She deserves a better man than her husband, so I took her. I know he will look for her, but I think he is busy now with Washington."

"You trade our village for her safety! How could you do this to us? You saw what the Patriots did to our village. They sent an army out to destroy us, and we were able to escape but had to abandon our fields and fruit trees. Now the British will come for us also. I hate all whites even more than before. I should never have let you guide them. They cannot be forgiven for what they did to our village. You will keep guard! You will make sure that we know when they come!"

Shamefaced, Ki nodded his agreement. "I know I brought danger to our village, but I will protect us. Yuma, her husband was going to kill her and make it look like I did it. I heard the plans they were making when they did not know I was there."

His father looked at him in frustration, and then concerned washed over him for his son's safety. Yuma knew that his son needed to come back from the untrustworthy white man. "What is her name?"

"Julia"

When Keme finally returned to her longhouse after breaking Julia's fever, Yuma was there, angry about the whole situation. "Is the white woman to live?"

"Yes, but she will need constant care for a while."

"Kitchi has brought harm to this village. We will regret the day he brought her into our life."

"Your son has returned to us. Enjoy this time."

"No good can come of this."

"His face shows me he will only be happy with her. I would have preferred a Haudenosaunee woman for him,

but I will protect her from harm. I do this for my son."
Her concentrated gaze told him he had lost this battle.

A New Life

Julia bathed in warm water; she felt gentle hands exploring her body while the fever still gripped her. She was wrapped in a blanket and put by the fire, then given a bitter drink. She screamed when taken to the river and dunked in cold water. Then she was wrapped in warm blankets and placed close to the fire to steam the infection away. The women did this every day until the fever stopped. To Julia's marvel, she began to feel better. Ki came to see her, looking worried.

"You better?"

Julia tried to sit up with Ki's help. "Yes. Whatever your mother did seems to be helping. What did you do with the baby?"

Ki held her in his arms. "I buried baby in cave; girl."

Tears began to flow down Julia's face. Ki took her face into his hands,

"Not your fault; Townset did this. Dishonorable man. We not talk of him again.

"But his soldiers will come looking with guns!"

"We keep the village in guard. The guards notice they approach. They do not know country; hard for them to find us.

"Maybe I should go back. I can only bring trouble to your people. He will do his worst to kill you."

"*No.* You stay here with me. I protect you. I keep you as mine." Julia put her hand on his face with relief and tenderness. Their desire was growing. Ki slowly pushed her away,

"You get well. Later we live man and wife in clan's longhouse. When you stronger, you work and help with the women's chores. I help you, teaching you as you teach me. You happy here, different, you love it as I do."

She felt safe with Ki, whom she trusted and was beginning to love. Was there any other option? Ki wanted her for his wife, and she was married to another man. Living as Ki's wife was so against everything that she knew to be true. She felt that she was going against God's will. But what else was she to do? John had killed their baby, and if he loved her, he would never have done that. John was supposed to protect and love her. John never loved her; he only wanted her money.

"It take time for people trust you. I teach you language first. Julia, life very different from old life; people work to grow and harvest food, or we starve. You carry water every day, help with food gathering, storing. Keme and me talked clothes. I help you make new clothes."

Julia's eyes widened. She realized her options were limited. She could return to an abusive, despicable fortune hunter to retain her lifestyle or learn a hard new way with a man she knew she could love. Julia, filled with the optimism of a twenty-year-old, knew she could meet the challenge. She wanted to make these people like her and would work hard to do it. In the confidence of youth, she welcomed the new world with its strange and intense ways so different from the one in which she had learned to live. Her parents and sister would be horrified to know what she was doing. She was giving up a life of privilege— no more servants, money, and wealth. She was reinventing herself.

What choice did she have? John had killed their baby. Tears came to her eyes just thinking about it. She hated John and never wanted to see him again. Here she would live as the wife of Ki, all the time knowing that she was legally married to John. She smiled at the idea of being Ki's wife. But Julia would not give up her religion, the people would have to understand that, and at the same time, she would strive not to burden anyone. Julia had often watched the servants in her house and thought about what it would feel like to be them, working all the time. Now she would learn firsthand how they felt.

Julia regained more strength day by day. Keme came in with her food, and Julia placed her hand on her shoulder. "Thank you; you have been kind to me."

Keme smiled, rubbing Julia's hands, "You better?"

"Much better, thanks to you," Julia said in her broken Algonquin. This woman was old and wise. Julia could see she was trying to be friendly. She was beginning to trust her. They mainly signed their conversations. Keme had been very patient with Julia, showing her how to take care of herself in this first natural world. This woman, who always spoke in a soft voice, had a power and strength that commanded authority. Her eyes were kind but intense, seeing into one's soul.

Julia was trying to comb out the tangles in her hair when Ki came into the longhouse.

"Let's go for a ride." They rode in silence for a while, just enjoying time together.

Julia gazed around at the beauty of the place, marveling how uninhabited it seemed.

"Do any other tribes live nearby?"

Ki shook his head. "No. Far away; we talk to them." Ki was leading the horse to a high bluff.

"Are they friendly?" Julia had to turn to look at Ki; she was riding in front of him on his horse.

"We treat them with respect. Our guards know when strangers coming. We don't get along the Huron."

They passed before a lovely waterfall. The air was warm and balmy.

"This place is so beautiful and peaceful." Ki picked Julia up and turned her around so they were facing each other. Their bodies rubbed together with the rhythm of the horse as they began kissing, and it soon became erotic. He raised her legs, wrapping them around him, then stopped the horse and lifted her so his manhood entered her smoothly. The exquisite stimulation was a revelation to Julia, causing her to climax for the first time in her life. She could see in his darkening eyes that he enjoyed her response as much as she did. They explored every inch of each other's bodies with hands and mouth. Julia thought that as long as she lived, she would never forget these moments.

They moved on to the waterfall and got down from the horse. Ki laid down a blanket behind the waterfall in a dry area, and they made love once more. He had brought food, and they ate quietly, smiling at each other the whole time. As soon as they finished eating and sleepiness came, they made love again. This was the most romantic thing Julia had ever encountered in her life. It was rustic but beautiful and peaceful and full of love and the wonder of exploring each other's bodies.

"You never before."

"No. It is so delicious; I love it. I thought sexual congress was something a woman had to endure, and I hated it with John. With you, it is something wonderful." Julia enjoyed stretching out naked in front of Ki in a flirtatious way and laughed when she saw its effect on him. Julia realized that she could sexually do anything she wanted with Ki and that there would be no judgment, which gave her great joy and anticipation of their future together.

———

The next day villagers busied themselves with many tasks. They got up at dawn and ate what looked like thick corn mush with bear meat. It was not that enticing to Julia, but she was hungry, so she ate it. Ki started the language lesson. They went all over the village, naming everything, including the women, children, and men. Julia's head was aching by the time they went back to their compartment in the longhouse. The women harvested crops and gathered seasonal fruit, with the men building new longhouses or hunting, always keeping a lookout for trouble. The men also cleared land for planting and practiced daily with their weapons, especially bow and arrow.

The village was organized and clean; it followed a river; sixty Indians lived there with everyone busy doing something, so Julia knew she had to pitch in. She rolled up her sleeves and got to work, getting the water, and that meant assembling the clay pots. Julia thought maybe she could carry two at a time, but it was too hard when they were filled because the liquid was continuously spilling out. It was some distance to the river, and Julia was breathing hard by the time she got it to the longhouse. She deduced this was the work of women because no men in sight were carrying water.

Ki showed her the collection baskets, and she decided that her next task would be to help with the corn harvesting. The next day Keme took her to the cornfields and showed her how to use a large knife to cut the corn. By the time they stopped to eat a stew of corn, beans, and squash, it tasted better than the best cuisine Julia had ever eaten. When she got back to the longhouse at dusk, Ki had killed a deer. He was cleaning it and drying the skin. He noticed her hands had blisters, so he rubbed in bear grease.

"You need this, in winter, when hands get cold dry." All Julia could do was nod and drop down on the bear-skins, desperately wanting sleep. "No. Stay awake, eat, keep strength up. Tomorrow another busy day, much food harvested for winter." Ki was pulling Julia up. "winter comes, we need all of it. Come. Eat now. I have something to show you."

Julia rose and followed Ki to where the women had made a giant pot of stew with corn, beans, squash, and venison. While they were eating, Ki resumed the language lesson. Julia tried to attend to it, but as soon as her belly was full, she got sleepy again. Ki took her by the hand and led her down by the river to a secluded spot. He took off her outer clothes.

"You need bath in river, will help feel better." As soon as she was in her shift, they started kissing and caressing each other. Julia felt her strength return in full while they made love. Then they entered the cold river to wash off. The sun was setting, making the water surface golden. Ki embraced her to share his warmth.

"What do you do in the winter? Please tell me you don't jump in when there are ice and snow?" Julia was trying to stop shivering and keep her teeth from chattering.

"Yes, makes you strong, able to take cold. You want warm water. You carry it to longhouse, warm it." Ki said in warning.

"I know this makes me sound spoiled, but I will miss the servants doing it for me. I never thought about what hard work they did getting my bath ready."

"Julia, no servants. You are strong woman. You can do it." Ki was laughing but serious.

"Keep telling me that. I am going to need to hear it." Julia looked a little doubtful. They headed back to the longhouse, Ki pulling her behind a tree for a kiss. Julia's mood had improved. She had become more resolved to acclimate to the new world that she had fallen headfirst into.

Julia tried picking beans, but as she was working so close to the ground, her back ached terribly. Keme then showed her how to mash the corn in an iron pot with a big paddle, so she made dinner that night with the corn she had ground and venison. Ki was proud of her because it actually tasted good, and everyone who ate it agreed. Creating food that was edible astonished Julia, who had never cooked before. She enjoyed picking blueberries, strawberries, and raspberries and watching the women prepare them for drying. They gathered all kinds of nuts for drying. The longhouses were filling up with baskets of food and vegetables hanging from the ceiling to dry. Collecting wood was another task of the women, so every day Julia went deep into the forest looking for wood with the other women.

Dreams and Visions

Every night Julia would get on her knees and pray. She asked God to forgive her for running away from her husband, the husband whom she could not love, the husband who killed their child, the husband who was not faithful and, most importantly, wanted to kill her. Julia felt guilty for having not lived up to the Christian religion's standards and white society's rules. Nonetheless, she was not sorry she had left John and knew she would never be ashamed of her love of Ki, which made her happy. The Indian village was not really where she meant to live her life, but it was far better than living with John. In the Indian town, she received adequate treatment, while her mind was kept active in learning their skills. There was so much to learn about herbs, crops, game, and women's roles in the village's governing. She had to remind herself not to walk ahead of Ki; she always had to walk behind him.

"Why you pray on your knees?" Ki was lying on their bed, watching Julia pray.

"I do it out of respect for my God." Julia had tried to explain Christianity to Ki. He continually asked questions about what she believed.

"Why you pray every night?"

"So God can protect and guide me. He watches me and leads me. He forgives me when I sin."

"You sinned? You good woman."

"I left my husband, which a wife should not do, so I ask for his forgiveness."

Ki sat up and faced Julia, looking curiously into her face. "Your God wants stay with man who beats you, lies with other women?"

"Maybe God let that happen so that I could run away with you and find real love. Maybe that was his plan? God wants us to be happy, and I am happy with you." Julia put her arms around Ki and kissed him deeply.

"Do you sin with me? God punish you?" Ki was willingly being pushed down on the bed by Julia.

"This is why I ask for his forgiveness every night. I am not sorry for what I have done and never will be. But I do not want to provoke his anger. He is a powerful God, and if you become evil-minded, you will go to hell."

"Hell?" Ki was lying on his back with his arms around Julia.

"A horrible place where bad people go. When you die, you want to go to heaven and be with God. There is only happiness there."

"I go to heaven with you?"

"Yes, but only if you have faith in Jesus Christ, who is God's only son." Julia smiled down at Ki. She knew this was a lot for him to take in.

"I can't do that? Your gods different. I want go with you, we die." Ki moved on top of Julia, and once again, she marveled at the incredible climax she had with him. If this was sinning, then she could not help herself; she would love every minute of it. When they had finished, Julia still wanted to talk.

"What about your gods? Tell me about them."

"Hiawatha bring Great Peace. He, Master of Life. He made Haudenosaunee, Mohawks, Oneidas, Onondagas, Cayugas, and Senecas. Whites no respect for us; we have no writing. But we live under law—a creed made in council. I live by our belief; I free to live as I choose. Our clan matron picks male from family who make our sachem for council. She sees problems with building, food gathering, ceremonies; we make right in village council. All the nations speak of war or trade, decide in tribal council in Onondaga territory. Each nation send sachems, all the sachems must agree. Is this 'representation' Patriots fight for? We have it here."

Julia was sitting up in amazement. "What if someone doesn't obey? Who punishes them?"

"They shunned, losing help, protection. Shunned not only shameful but dangerous. My mother leads fireside, all her descendants from our ohwachira. Son marries; he goes longhouse of bride's clan. He welcome back home, they don't get along."

"This is unbelievable! Women in our society never have power. Men would never ask our opinions on anything. White men consider us inferior, although England can have women rulers. One was especially good at it, but she inherited it through her father's line. She would never have been there otherwise. So Haudenosaunee women are considered equals with men?"

"Yes, one is killed, worth ten wampum beads more." Ki was astonished when Julia grabbed him and kissed him with great enthusiasm. Even with Ki telling her that she was equal, she knew that there were jobs only the women did and responsibilities only the men had and that would be the same in every culture and time.

Boots

Julia stood next to their shelf with arms outstretched, being measured for her new winter clothes by Keme and some other village women. The deerskin was very soft and warm. They were making a long dress with pants while Keme decorated the yoke with beads.

"This feels wonderful! How can hide get so pliable?" Julia credited Keme with hours of patient stretching, chewing, and lubricating. She nodded her thanks. Julia progressed slowly with the language. Keme had been very kind in teaching her Seneca ways, and Julia was grateful. When they were alone, Ki said, "I have surprise." He had her sit down, and he brought out the boots he had made from deerskin lined with rabbit fur. They went halfway up her calf.

"These feel so good." Julia could not believe how beautiful they were. "My feet will never get cold in these." Ki laced them up. Julia could not contain her love for Ki. "You are always so good to me, but I have nothing for you. Ki, I love you." Julia could not keep the tears out of her eyes.

"Love?" Ki wanted her to explain her love for him so he could entrench it in his heart.

"Well, I don't know your word for it. It is when you cannot be apart from another human without being miserable. In other words, you always think of them and want to be with them. Remember when I read you *Romeo and Juliet*? That was love."

"I want you all time." Ki put his arms around Julia, and they sank to the bearskins and took off their clothes, kissing each part of the other's body. Having at first been shy about making love in the longhouse, Julia lost her reserve as she learned to ignore other couples. Against their customs, Ki had put up skins on their bunk's three inner sides for Julia's privacy. She realized that the Indians felt no shame over nakedness the way people of the Book did, and neither were they ashamed of sex, which was taboo in the white man's world.

———

Out of kindness toward Julia, Ki was building a house for them. The house, made of logs, had crevices of mud and sticks. The roof was sheets of bark overlapping each other. There was a square opening for a window with a layer of bark to close it at night. The door hung on loose wooden hinges, and it was there only to stop the wind and creatures from coming in. Stealing was a crime; no one would even think about doing it, so there was no need for locks. The floor was the bare ground; it had a fireplace in the middle, and smoke was supposed to go out the square opening in the roof, but it filled the room a lot of the time. The whole structure was about ten by twelve feet.

There were crude benches along the wall for seats and to hold a pestle for pounding corn. Pegs in the front wall supported a rifle and tomahawk. Crotched sticks at each side of the fireplace reinforced a cross pole from which kettles and roasting meat hung. Flat stones were used in baking and put in the ashes of the fire. Julia had a copper kettle that she cooked their meals in. She felt pride in cooking for them; she became a natural and even enjoyed doing it. To her surprise, she liked to pound corn and loved the homemade bread she would make of it, putting it on the baking stones. They had thick skins for a bed at night when it was cold. The bed was on the ground, and Julia got used to a rigid support. At the end of the day of challenging work, Ki and Julia would eat their dinner in their unfinished house and point out things they needed to change or marvel at the hard work they had accomplished. One night when it was quiet and they were lying next to each other in bed, Julia shyly brought up the subject of Ki's looks.

"Ki, I have to ask why your physical characteristics are so different from those of the other men. Where did you get white facial features and blue eyes?" Julia held her breath, fearing this was an uncomfortable subject for him.

Ki seemed embarrassed. "Do not know. I got in fight in Boston with man who laugh about having blue eyes. I ask Keme. Father told me, gods favored me; I believe him. Now I want know why I different."

Two days later, Keme came into their room in the longhouse and sat down. She spoke in Seneca. "Kitchi, you ask me why you don't look like a true Indian. Well, your blood father was white. He was a French fur trader who had come into our lands trapping. We caught him with many pelts. Out of fear or respect, he presented them as gifts to Yuma."

"What was his name?" Ki looked wide-eyed at his mother.

"His name was Jon DeRossier. He was a very bulky, hairy man with blue eyes. Your father didn't want to kill him after he came out of the gauntlet on his feet. Yuma even gave him your Huron mother, Cholena, for the night as a gift. We took her captive because she was a big, strong teenager. I wanted to tell you this, but your father said no. I was unable to give him a son. We had just lost a baby girl, so I was able to nurse you."

"Cholena was my real mother?"

"Yes. Cholena made a good captive—strong and hardworking. But when her time came, you got stuck backward. I was there." Keme hung her head and then looked up at Ki and took his hands. "She died trying to push you out. I knew you were alive, so I cut you a door."

"But look, you are now the strong, beautiful son whom your father and I had longed to have. We love you. You will always be our son."

"Why did you not tell me? I wanted the truth." Ki was shocked by what he had heard.

"You are special to us and always will be." With that, Keme left.

Ki told Julia everything, and when he got to the part of cutting out the baby, Julia couldn't help but put her hand over her mouth in shock. Ki did not see a problem with doing this, but Julia was horrified. Ki realized that there were some things in his culture that Julia would always look upon as wrong.

There was a lot of commotion one day in the village, and Julia asked Ki what was happening. He replied that visitors were coming. The woman coming in was a relative of Keme, who was, as Ki tried to explain, his cousin. Her name was Yo da gent. Julia watched in wonder as the woman rode in with two warriors that Julia had never seen before. To her horror, she saw a white child of not more than three sitting in front of one of the warriors. The female child had blond hair with blue eyes and was looking very frightened. The woman was one of the most beautiful Indian women Julia had ever seen. Ki informed Julia that she had just lost her husband in a battle with the Patriots and was very upset and had come to Keme for comfort. Keme was trying to find another husband for her, but she had rejected all prospects put before her. Julia still was in wonder that the Indian women had more say in their futures than white women.

"Ki, who is the child! It is a white child?" Julia couldn't take her eyes off the child being handed to Yo da gent by one of the warriors. Julia could tell the child wanted to cry but was afraid so that her little chin trembled. The child's eyes looked around wildly, trying to take in her surroundings.

"Yo da gent's husband killed by Patriot, had a little girl; child is now Yo da gent. When white men kill one of ours, we take one of theirs. The warriors killed Patriot and took child."

Julia was recovering from this when another unusual thing happened. A white young man came riding in dressed in Indian clothes. He would not have been that different from the Indians except his hair was blond; his mannerisms were Indian, and he spoke the language well when he greeted the host of Indians waiting to welcome the newcomers. He was smiling until he saw Julia, then his eyes seemed to widen in surprise. This young man was very handsome and seemed to be completely comfortable in this alien world.

"Who is that?" Julia couldn't take her eyes off of him.

"Tom Mulligan, taken in battle, replace dead warrior. He is great warrior. Hair strange in our world."

"What do you mean?"

"He strong; take down strongest, fastest warriors."

"So this man is captured then challenged to see if he will make a great warrior?" Julia felt this to be unfair to Tom.

"Yes, our way."

"What about that poor little white girl? Is she going to be challenged also?"

"No, become Indian, one day marry warrior, have children from him."

Julia was trying to process this strange world. It was the first time she was seeing white people who had been taken captive. Julia couldn't help but think about how worried the family of the little girl must be. Then she realized this child must have witnessed her family being killed in front of her, making her afraid to cry for fear of losing her own life. It was all Julia could do not to run to the child and comfort her.

Ki noticed that Julia was uncomfortable with all of this. "White man not take our children, kills them, receives bounty for scalps."

This Julia knew to be true. She had heard stories of the rewards offered for the scalps of Indians, and the fact that it didn't matter that they were children or women to Patriot soldiers.

Tom walked up to Ki and greeted him in the Indian way and then began to talk in English. He indicated that he wanted to speak in private. So Ki and Julia moved to a more private place where they could not be overheard.

"You have hidden her well, Ki. That is what the white woman now calls you, so I have heard, and I will call you that also." Tom had a smile on his face as he looked at Julia, but he became serious again. "The British are looking for Julia and have offered a reward. I suspect it is from her husband, Townset. The British are not happy that you have taken one of their own, especially the wife of an officer."

"Many know Julia here? You tell?" Ki looked worried.

"No, I did not. I would not betray you; I know it is not the Indian way. But be careful; they are looking for her, and you know what happens when money is offered. Indians will want to buy the drink, and anything could happen."

"Thank you; I need know anything changes."

Tom was now looking at Julia and smiling. "Your husband wants you back and has offered a reward, but Washington is keeping him very busy, so you are in luck and can hide here for some time." Julia wanted to talk further with Tom, but Ki took her arm and led her off. Julia was looking over her shoulder at Tom and the child when Ki turned her around and spoke sternly in her ear.

"You not talk to white people here. You plan escape; do not do it." Julia looked at Ki, confused.

"Where would I run away to? Tom looks like he has accepted Indian life. I must admit it is confusing for me right now because I would think he would want to be with his people. And that poor child back there! Her family must be crazy with worry!" Ki took Julia's arm sternly and looked deep into her eyes.

"Our way, you accept it."

Julia had never seen Ki so forceful with her, and she felt this was important to him. She slowly nodded her head in acceptance. "Ki, I will try; I am trying! I am grateful for all you have done for me, but you have got to understand this is so different from our ways! I am learning to walk behind you." Julia said this with a timid smile that made Ki laugh.

Julia noticed that Tom and Yo da gent lived in the longhouse with Keme. Tom would even call Keme mother. Ki told her that he was captured at the age of fourteen and has adapted well to Indian life. Julia noticed that he seemed to enjoy living among them. Tom easily laughed and relished being challenged to manly feats like foot racing, hunting, and fishing. He was even teaching Ki how to wrestle, for this was an action unfamiliar to the Indians. Tom was a natural athlete who showed a prowess that the Indians loved. During one wrestling lesson, a prominent warrior came up to Tom and challenged him to a match. Tom accepted the challenge and received several blows from the challenger before Tom reached for his throat, restricting his breathing, causing the Indian to fall to his knees and almost lose consciousness. Tom was able to do this with one hand. It was then that Tom put his hands under the Indian's hips, raising him and throwing him to the ground. The Indian reared up, shouting, "I will kill you." He ran for his tomahawk to kill Tom. Tom stood still and did not move, with a smirk on his face, as if he knew what was going to happen.

Ki stepped forward, talking in Seneca. "You lost; now you will continue to dishonor yourself by killing your challenger. You need to accept that you have lost." Everyone held their breath, while Tom appeared not to be concerned. The Indian slowly dropped the tomahawk and offered the sign of peace to Tom, which he accepted with his good humor.

The next day, as Julia was picking blueberries to dry for the winter, Tom came along, and she called out to him.

"Why don't you try and escape? You did not come here willingly, and you seem skilled enough to know how to leave without the Indians finding you." As Julia spoke, she saw Tom's easygoing personality come out.

"I did leave, and I left for a day; they tried to come after me. I saw them from my hiding place, but then I thought of all the white prisoners I have helped. I have saved lives. I act as translator for the Seneca when they want to know if a prisoner has ever killed an Indian. If you have killed an Indian, you are tortured to death, so I lie for the prisoner most of the time. You have not had the pleasure of seeing a person put to the fire. They roast them, and a large man can take two days to die." Julia recoiled from that and put her hand to her mouth. "You did not think of that when you willingly came here, did you?"

"Do the British know about this?"

"Yes, and they will even bring in Patriots for them to kill, especially if they know those Patriots killed Indians.

Now the British will do a prisoner exchange, or the family will offer money for their release, which the Indians will take. I have helped get Patriots exchanged for British soldiers that were captured; I know both languages well and act as their interpreter. Julia, I am a Christian and have not lost my faith. I don't let the tribe know it, but I feel that I am doing God's work. I know that I am walking a fine line between their world and mine, but God protects me."

Julia had tears in her eyes as she took his hand. "You truly are a child of God, and you are doing God's work. But what about that poor little girl? Surely her family must be worried about her. She does not look happy at all. Did she witness her family being killed in front of her?"

"Yes she probably did. But she will be treated as a child of the Indian nation and will not be molested in any way. Yo da gent needs a companion with her now that she is a widow, or else the unmarried warriors will be after her for her attention."

"Is that why she has the child?" Julia could not believe what she was hearing.

"It was not the original reason for taking the child— to replace her husband. You know that the Indians believe that if you take one of theirs, they will take one of yours to replace the person. That is their belief. But now that Yo da gent is a window, she needs a companion to keep the single warriors from giving her unwanted attention. She will treat the child with loving respect, as if it were her own. Yo da gent is my sister because of the family that adopted me. She is very picky about who she wants for a husband in the future."

"It is nice to know that some women have the pleasure of picking their husbands. I never got that choice, and now I find myself hiding here with the help of Ki."

"You know the British have offered a reward for your return and are very angry at Ki for hiding you here."

"Do they know where I am hiding?"

"They do not, but it is just a matter of time before they find out and come looking for you. But the British do not want to anger the Indians who have willingly taken up arms for them. How are you faring in this alien world? You talk like a woman of means."

"I am happy to be away from my husband. He is a horrible person; I was miserable living with him. Ki told me John, my husband, had planned to kill me and make it look like Ki did it. Like you, I adapted to my circumstances and have even taken it on as a challenge to endure here. There are a lot of things to admire about Indian life. Women hold power here, and I think that is wonderful. The chiefs are elected to their positions, and women have a say in that. Aren't these some of the same principles that the Patriots are fighting for?"

"It was what I was fighting for before the Indians took me. The British told the Indians that they would drive the settlers back out of their land if they come to their side. I don't blame the Indians for wanting their land back."

Both Julia and Tom noticed that they were being watched, so they silently decided to stop talking, but not before Julia quickly took Tom's hand and said, "You are doing God's work, and you are courageous." She quickly went back to picking blueberries.

———

One night, after Ki had killed a deer and was trying to teach Julia how to clean it, Tom couldn't help but laugh at Julia's queasiness over gutting the animal. Tom knew this was not a task that she would have ever dreamt of doing in her privileged life. When they had completed the job, Julia invited Tom to dinner. While they sat on the ground in their house, Julia couldn't help bringing up Tom's former life.

"How were you captured?"

"I was captured when I joined the Patriots to fight the Indians. My father told me not to go with the Rebel militia, but I did not listen. We had gotten tired of the Indians raiding our homes and formed a militia to fight them." Julia looked over to Ki to see if this bothered him, but it did not seem to, so she continued.

"Do you think that maybe your family wants to see you and know what has happened? They would have peace of mind knowing that you are safe and not dead."

"One day, I will see them again and explain everything to them."

"Do you mean when you are in heaven?"

"No. When this war is over, and the Patriots have won, I will talk to them again." Both Julia and Ki were shocked at what he had said.

"We lose! Why?" Ki had stopped eating.

"Ki, I feel that I can talk true to you. You have lived with the British and know what it is like out there." Tom was pointing to the east. "The Rebel militia had many councils, just like the war councils that are held by the

Iroquois Nation. The Rebels, or Patriots, talked long and hard about starting a war with the British, and we talked about strategies we could use to win."

"Do you truly think that the Patriots can win against the strongest military in the world?" Julia couldn't believe what she was hearing.

"Julia, when I was with the Rebel militia, we discussed that the colonies have a thousand-mile coast that the British cannot blockade. We figured that we could muster a force of one hundred thousand or so citizen-soldiers, one that would be four times the size of the British army in America. The British would have to be sending supplies regularly across the thirteen colonies. The thirteen colonies are six times the size of England, and their army would be spread out over a vast area. Have you seen what the Patriots do to the British when we get them deep in the woods? We fight like the Indian's taught us to fight, and we have snipers."

"Snipers?" Ki was tensely listening to all of this with a feeling of dread. What if he was right? What would happen to the Indian nations?

"They are men who hide in trees and shoot the British, who never see them." Julia was stunned.

"You loyal to us!" Ki was suddenly mad and felt that Tom was a traitor to the Indians and British, never having accepted them as he had led them to believe.

"When the time comes, when the Patriots win, I will be here to make sure the white man does not take advantage of the Seneca. I will protect them as best I can. I can speak both languages and know your ways very well. I will not let the white man dishonor these wonderful people whom I have come to love. I will be loyal to them. Ki, I believe this is what is coming, and you need to prepare yourself for it."

Tom's good nature had disappeared as he slowly got up to leave. It was overwhelming to think of a future where the British would not control everything. What would happen?

That night Julia and Ki held each other, thinking in many different directions. Julia wondered what kind of government would replace the British realm and where that would leave her. Ki wondered if this could be his people's downfall, for he knew the Patriots did not like the Indians, especially his tribe.

———

Over the weeks that followed, Julia got to know Yo da gent and grew to like her. She named the child Peta, meaning golden eagle, for her blond hair. At first, Julia was shy about showing affection to the child, thinking that the Indians would see it as Julia sympathizing with her over the capture. But slowly everyone accepted the situation. One night, as they all gathered to eat, Peta quietly spoke to Julia.

"Will I ever see my people again?" The child looked so helpless and lost that Julia picked her up and held her.

"No, I think not; this is your new home. These are your people now" With that, Peta's eyes filled with tears.

"I miss them and want to go home!"

Julia looked around as she held the child and secretly came to a resolution. "I will not let anyone hurt you, and

I will protect you. But you must accept that these are your people now, and Yo da gent is your mother. She treats you well?" Peta nodded. "Then forget about your other life; this is your new life." Julia hugged Peta again, this time with a greater degree of warmth, to let the little girl know that she would protect her. When Yo da gent observed them, Julia smiled at her, letting her know that she was not conspiring with the child to escape. Yo da gent knew some English and could talk with Julia.

"You love Kitchi?" Yo da gent smiled at Julia.

"Yes."

"I see he love you much. He happy, but Yuma mad."

"I know that Yuma does not want me here, and I don't blame him. I have brought trouble to the tribe by coming here."

"The British, friends, want you back? You another husband?"

"You are right. That husband was a cruel man who beat me."

Yo da gent made a troubled face. "Kitchi not do that; not our way. I call Ki now, what you call him?" Yo da gent smiled at Julia.

"The British gave him the name because they could not pronounce his real name."

"The British give us new names, new names where we live. If they not say warrior's name, they give him title of colonel, colonel James."

"That is called the last name, like my last name is Townset."

"My husband Colonel James Hunt."

"I have observed that." Julia had heard the Indians using the English words for rivers, and even some of the Indian villages had an English name. They always used the English term for the many forts that the British had built.

"Yuma me married again; I don't want. I love my husband; he gone. No replace him." Yo da gent looked sad, remembering her husband.

"It is a miserable life if you marry someone you don't love. I was beginning to hate my life. Then Ki came into it." Julia felt herself smiling as she spoke of Ki, and the realization that she did love him hit her hard. How much easier it would have been if she could have married a man of means, someone in her position in society. But how often did that happen in her old world? She never really thought to ask her mother if she was in love with her father when they married. She was instructed to accept whomever her parents wanted for her to marry, that eventually they would love each other. But did that happen? Julia was beginning to think not.

"Do you think you can love Peta?" Much of the communication took place in signing, but Julia and Yo da gent were beginning to converse well together.

"Yes, daughter I never had." Once again, Yo da gent was sad, so Julia just put her hand on her arm for comfort. Then she thought how fragile this world was. Ki could be killed, and what would happen to her? Would she be handed back to John by the Indians? Suddenly Julia looked for Ki and found him looking at her. When he saw the concern on her face, he motioned for her to come to him. They left and went to their small house.

"What, Julia?"

"Ki, what if something happens to you? What will then happen to me?" Julia grabbed Ki and held him tightly to her.

"I not die."

"You don't know that; look what happened to Yo da gent. She is miserable without her husband, and now your father wants her to marry again. Your people will hand me back to the English and then back to John."

"I speak to Keme, make you into tribe."

"Can she do that? Will she do that?"

"Clan mother, power to do that; I make her know to do it."

"Thank you, Ki; I love you!"

Once again, Julia marveled at the joy of making love to someone you genuinely love.

Julia felt she had found a friend in Yo da gent, and the two were beginning to converse more and more, sometimes in English and sometimes in Seneca. There still was signing between them when they could not come up with a word that neither of them understood. It was nice to have a female friend her age. Keme asked her if she had found a warrior that she wanted to marry weekly, and Yo da gent was holding out but knew it was only a matter of time before she had to decide on one of the warriors.

Julia was bringing water to their new home when she heard the incoming warriors' war shouts. Running Wolf and several warriors had gone on the warpath with British soldiers and were returning. Julia saw two white men in ropes being led into the middle of the village. Even though they had been beaten badly, she could tell one was a large and very handsome man. The other looked to have on a severely torn uniform. Both were young and seemed to be in their early thirties. Julia was surprised to see everyone grabbing sticks, knives, and tomahawks, going to the village center, and forming two lines where the men were being forced to go through. The two were fighting back, trying to protect themselves as best they could, but the blows were coming in fast. Julia watched in horror as the men were stabbed and nicked; even the children took part in the abuse, hitting them with sticks. She wanted to help them somehow but did not know what to do, and instinct told her that it would not be considered a good thing if she did. Finally, the poor men made it to the end and were still standing when they bound one of them up again and threw him in a hut.

Ki looked up and saw the shocked expression on Julia's face, knowing she had seen him taking part in the beating, and then he saw her turning away with disgust. He stopped and ran to her, but she put up her hand to indicate "Don't touch" when she heard him coming up to her. Ki grabbed her hand and pulled it down in anger.

"That was horrible; those poor men!" Julia was sick to her stomach after what she had just watched.

"Julia! Men are enemies to us. They and more take all our lands. We do this when we get them."

"What will happen now? "

"We hold for ransom, see anyone offers money; British want for prisoner exchange. One with uniform offered back to Patriots."

"What happens if that doesn't work?"

"We burn them."

"I can't watch this; they are human beings!" Julia walked back to their house with a heavy heart. Had she made a mistake coming here? Then she remembered seeing a man drawn and quartered in England on a trip to London. Her mother had told her not to look, but she hadn't been able to turn away, and the whole thing had made her throw up—when they took out his guts after hanging him until he was blue, then cut off his head. Was the white man so different? Julia wondered how often these beatings and burnings occurred here She watched as the man in the uniform was led to a fort for a prisoner exchange.

That night Julia and Ki didn't talk to each other because they knew it would lead to an argument. Julia couldn't sleep over what she had seen, but Ki was soundly sleeping, turned away from Julia, who was turned away from him when she decided to get up quietly. She saw Yo da gent walking by their small window, walking very silently, almost unnoticeable. Julia decided to follow, throwing on a shawl, watching as Yo da gent went to the hut where the man was imprisoned. Yo da gent turned to see if anyone was watching; as she was about to duck into the hut, she noticed Julia following her. She put her hand to her lips to indicate silence.

"Food, water, medicine." Yo da gent spoke very quietly. Julia nodded in agreement, and both women went into the hut. The man lay on his back with his hands and feet tied. Yo da gent brought a knife and cut him loose. His eyes were wide open in terror.

"Will you let me go free? Please, I beg you!"

"No, not escape; help you, not leave. Seneca hunt you down, kill you, far away from white settlements." Yo da gent was whispering.

"My God, are you a white woman? Did they capture you also?" He was looking at Julia.

"I was not captured. Now let us help you. Yo da gent held a water jug to his mouth, and he drank with abandon. Then she handed him a bowl of corn, squash, and venison. He ate the entire thing in less than two minutes. Yo da gent was putting medicine on his feet, legs, arms, and head, wrapping them so the deep cuts wouldn't get infected from dirt.

"What is she doing?"

"She is helping you with food and medicine; what is your name?

"Ben Walker"

"My name is Julia, and this is Yo da gent. I repeat, do not try and escape; they will hunt you down and kill you. We are far away, and you will get lost in the forest. We will try and help you. They are holding you for ransom. Does your family have money?"

"No, my wife Amy and I have children, but we are just poor farmers. I was fighting with the Rebel militia, and that is when I was captured."

"They may use you for a prisoner exchange." As Julia spoke, the man put his large hands to his head in grief. Julia studied him; he had dark brown hair and was indeed handsome, with broad shoulders and big blue eyes blackened from fighting. Ben appeared to have his teeth still intact, which was a good thing. He looked to be about six-foot-three.

"I have to go, and I will try and help you as best I can." Julia got up to go and noticed that Yo da gent did not get up to leave but continued to clean his wounds and care for him with a gentleness that made Julia wonder what she was doing.

Becoming Seneca

J ulia woke up to all the women standing around her door. "Ki, what is going on?" Peta was there also.

"You want Seneca; we make you Seneca today. Come with me." Ki began leading her out of the house to the river, where she and Peta had to take their clothes off and get in the cold river. Both of them were given the sign not to worry. Julia was embarrassed, but both she and Peta immediately were dunked underwater. The women began to scrub both Julia and Peta with sand, then leaves. When they dried them off, Keme gave Julia a long leather dress decorated with beads and quills. Peta also had a long robe of leather and boots to match.

"You now Seneca." Ki held Julia, smiling. "Peta also Seneca. Seneca give new names; you keep your old name."

"Thank you for doing this; so now, if something were to happen to you, I could stay here and not be turned over to John?"

"Yes. You, Seneca."

Yo Da Gent

E very night Yo da gent went to see Ben in his hut with food and water. He had not tried to escape, so the tribe had not tied him up but left him in the hut. Ben realized that when the Indians took them, they did not follow a direct route back to the camp but took a roundabout path to confuse the prisoners. If he did escape, he would not know what direction to go in. It had been weeks now, and no one had heard of a ransom or prisoner exchange.

"Yo da gent, what is going to happen to Ben?"

"Burn him; I not let that happen." The beautiful Indian woman looked stern, as if she had a plan.

"What are you planning?" Julia was whispering as they pounded corn together in big bowls.

"Marry him." Yo da gent looked defiant as she spoke. "I talk to Keme, tell, I want him. He gunsmith." At first, Julia didn't understand, then she realized Yo do gent's meaning. The Seneca did not have these skills, and their guns were always breaking or jamming. They would have to take them to the British forts to repair them. But if they had a person in the tribe who could fix them, it would make it a lot easier. "He tell me he married, children; I want my husband. If he not, he burn."

"Let me talk to him and tell him he has other options. It is a sin in our world to marry when you are already married to another person. That is why I have not married Ki. I am legally married to John Townset. I know you don't understand all I am speaking, but understand, it will be hard for him to do this when he already has a wife and children." Julia could see that Yo da gent understood but was determined to do this.

Ki was not happy when he heard about the situation.

"Yo da gent marry him!"

"Yes, he already has a wife and children, but he will need to forget about them. Think about it, Ki. Ben knows the art of gunsmithing, which can be very helpful when your guns break because he can fix them!"

"You do this because a white man, you want save him?"

"Yes, but also, I think he could make Yo da gent happy and help your tribe at the same time."

"I go with you to him." Julia and Ki entered the hut, and Ben looked surprised to see Ki, thinking something fearful was about to happen.

"Ben, Yo da gent wants to marry you, and if you agree, then your life will be spared." Julia was looking persuasively at Ben.

"I am married to Amy and have five children, what about them? It is a sin for me to marry two women in our religion." Ben was looking very worried.

"I know, but to stay alive, you will have to forget about Amy and your children and marry Yo da gent."

"I don't know if I can do that!"

At that point Ki spoke up. "Warriors bet how long take you to die when burn you. You large man, take two days." Ki's words brought terror to the face of Ben.

"I guess I have no choice then. I was farming when the Patriots came to me and asked me to help them. All I want is to be free of a king; is that so bad?" Julia felt sorry for this poor man who had had the bad luck of being captured by the Seneca.

"Your people take more lands, British promise drive back to sea; why we fight with them."

"I am British, so why are you trying to kill me, besides? Do you believe that the British will stop all the white people from farming your lands? They are making a fortune off of us. They make money off our crops and then tax us for it. I heard that the Seneca elect all their leaders, so why can't we have the same thing? You don't live under a king that you hate, but I do, so why is it so wrong to want to be able to live as you do?"

"You take our land, the land we hunt; we move villages for your farms!" Julia was afraid that the two would get into an argument and that Ben would lose his life.

"Ben, you have no choice but to wed Yo da gent—otherwise you will be killed." Ben hung his head, and Julia could see that this was tearing him apart. Slowly he nodded his head.

"Yo da gent has been very kind to me, and I am grateful for her. She is saving my life."

That night a council was held to discuss the marriage, and Tom Mulligan showed up to advise on the matter. Tom explained that the tribe could use a gunsmith to fix their broken guns. Ki could see on the warriors' faces that this was something they would welcome, a skill the Seneca did not have. Their weapons had become their very survival. Ben knew how to make bullets and how to outfit the coveted long rifle of the Patriots. Ben could offer them skills that the British could not give them. Keme, the wolf clan's head mother, then stood up and told the warriors that she would honor the marriage.

That is when Running Wolf angrily said, "He does not have a gift to present."

Ben did not have a valuable prize to offer Keme for the hand of Yo da gent. This was a custom of the Seneca when a man wanted to marry. The council agreed to think upon the issue and decide later what would happen to Ben. Julia was waiting for Ki to come back from the council meeting, praying that they would agree to the marriage.

"They want Ben marry Yo da gent. We use skills with guns. Running Wolf said he need gift of value to Keme. He not have one, a problem." Julia knew of the custom. What would happen now? She could not stand to see Ben burned to death. A gift of value was all Julia could think about since the poor man had nothing. That is when she put her hand on her chest to think and felt the solid gold cross that her parents had given her for her fifteenth birthday. Could Julia part with the cross that was the only thread left of her old life? She had boldly told Ki that she would not give up her religion when she first came to the Seneca. Now, could she give up the one thing that symbolized that belief? A voice echoed loudly in her head. "This will save his life." Without another thought, Julia took the necklace off. The chain was solid gold also. These would do for a gift. Ki could not believe it when Julia handed him the cross and chain.

"Julia?" Ki looked at her, knowing this was of value, seeing tears running down her face.

"If Ben has to burn because I would not give up my cross, then I could never live with myself. Giving the gold cross is what my God would expect me to do." After saying this out loud, Julia felt even more determined. Ki took the chain and cross from Julia, knowing that they would be more than sufficient.

———

Two days later the tribe gathered to witness Ben's wedding and a very happy Yo da gent. Ben went through the ritual of becoming a Seneca. He was stripped of the white man's clothes, scrubbed in the river with sand, and given Seneca clothes that Yo da gent had made for him. The two of them began building a small rustic one-room house in the same fashion as Julia and Ki, and Ben welcomed Peta as his child. Tom started to set up a crude blacksmith shop with Ben. They amazed the Indians with what they could do with old iron pots that had burned out or iron hooks that had broken. The Indians watched in wonder as they melted down the old iron into bullets, buttons, gardening tools, and even jewelry pieces much desired in the Indian world.

———

William Conner was the second prisoner taken by Running Wolf and delivered to the British fort for a prisoner exchange. He was flogged a hundred times for being a Patriot and then handed over to Samuel McKinny in exchange for a British officer taken by the Patriots. The minute they were away from the fort and watchful of not being followed, William told Samuel what he witnessed in the Indian village.

"I saw a white woman in the village living freely there. She was with one of the warriors and appeared to be English. Do you think she has run away from her family or was taken prisoner? She appeared to be highborn, and most strangely, she did not look distressed about being there."

"Don't know, but that is odd. We need to get you to the settlement without these spies following us and knowing where we are; how is your back doing? Did you put salt on it so it will not become infected?"

"It hurts like the devil, but I will live. Thank you for getting me; the poor fellow that they kept there had to marry some Indian woman, or else they were going to kill him."

"Hope she was at least good-looking?"

"Yeah, she was right nice for an Indian." Suddenly Samuel stopped and looked at William. "This could be that British woman who ran away with the Indian guide! He was a Seneca! We need to tell Daniel Morgan immediately."

Julia woke up feeling unwell. She thought maybe the harvest feasting had gone on so late into the night that she had become overly tired. Ki and other warriors had danced around the fire. At first, she feared the pagan ceremony would offend God, but eventually the rhythm soothed her. She got up to start her morning chores and went outside, where she saw Keme leaving for the fields. Julia caught up with her to learn more about the language. A woman started cleaning a deer, with the entrails spilling out; that is when Julia's stomach rebelled. Why should this make her vomit? She had seen it many times. Her irritation in herself continued when Keme laughed and patted Julia's stomach with the other women mimicking Keme. That night Julia discussed this with Ki in their room.

"All morning, I felt sick. I threw up at the sight of a deer cleaned and dressed, which I see all the time. All the women started laughing at me and put their hands on my stomach."

"You have a baby." Ki looked seriously at Julia, who did not seem to be taking the news well.

"How do you know this?" No sooner had she uttered the statement than she recalled she had not menstruated but twice at the Indian village.

"A woman sick in morning, she have baby." Ki studied Julia to see her reaction. He could not believe she hadn't recognized this.

"How stupid of me not to realize I'm going to have a baby. I will be without my mother or sister here! No doctor. Last time I never got sick at all. Do you think something is wrong?" The reality was dawning on Julia as her anxiety rose.

"Keme help you. She bring many babies. You happy?" Julia was thinking of Keme cutting Ki out when his mother was probably still alive.

"I don't know." Ki, who was happy, held Julia. Then Julia thought of the pregnant Indian women she had seen working right up to the day they delivered. Some did not even go back to the longhouse but stayed in the field, delivering the baby on the ground. "I am not birthing our baby in the field while I work," Julia said very sternly, which triggered a laugh from Ki.

"What is so funny?"

"Julia, be all right; woman work carrying baby is good, makes strong."

"You mean carrying water from the river to the long-house will make my pain easier because I will be stronger?" Julia's ire grew. She knew she was being absurd, but her emotions had been out of control lately. When Ki put his hand on her shoulder, she turned away. This rejection was new to both of them. They had never been angry at each other; not knowing what to do, Ki sighed and left the longhouse. Julia was frightened—what if something happened? All she could think about was Keme cutting the baby out of Cholena. Who would be there to help her? What if she died? Her parents had no idea where she was. No one would even know she had left this world.

Would her child grow up as a non-Christian? Would he or she learn to hate the white man and kill him? Would she want her child beating a captive while going through the gauntlet? Julia got even angrier with herself for having not thought this through when she accompanied Ki. But again, what was she to do? "I could have gone back to England, but I still would have been married to John, whom I hate." Julia started talking out loud to herself. "All my life, I would have thought about Ki and wondered what he was doing. Every minute of every day, I would have thought about him." Julia knew she had to accept this life and everything that came with it.

Ki was sitting outside of the longhouse when Running Wolf walked up and told him of a weeklong deer hunt with fishing. He knew he was needed, but Ki hated to leave when they were not getting along. He knew Julia was agitated and out of her element in the natural world. She had not even realized it when she was pregnant. He thought she should be happy about it, but then he remembered that white women of privilege like Julia did not work when pregnant. He rose to find Julia, but she had gone to see Keme.

When Keme saw Julia, she was weeping and holding her stomach. Suddenly Keme pitied this delicate woman who had worked so hard to fit in. "Will you help me?" Julia said in appeal. Keme took Julia's hand. "If I die, will you cut out the baby?"

Keme looked seriously at Julia. "What you need me to do? What Ki want?

"I don't know what I want."

"Yes, I help you, herbs help pain, you gather with me? You have for time comes?"

Julia agreed with relief, and she noted that she should observe Keme birthing the babies in the village. She would also learn more about the herbs.

———

Julia was returning to her room when she realized she had not yet fetched water, so she picked up two pots and headed to the river. She was coming back when she tripped and spilled the water. Unreasonable anger filled her at the thought of doing this when she is heavy with child. Ki was observing Julia but not offering to help because this was a woman's job. When he saw her fall, he offered his hand, but Julia held up her hands in rejection and turned her head away, telling him silently not to touch her. The unreasonable anger took hold of her again, even though she knew it had not been his fault.

"No. Do not help me. Remember, you told me this would make me strong, so I must go back down and get more water." For reasons Julia did not know, she wanted to throw these rules in his face. Maybe this had something to do with the morning sickness and her breasts being tender. She made her way back down to the river.

"Julia, I go away to hunt, few days."

"How many days?

"Seven, longer; need meat for winter."

"Maybe it is best that we are away from each other for a few days." Julia felt her reaction was mean but could not rule them in. She was confused and needed to think about her future with a newborn baby. Would she have everything she needed? Would she have to make everything herself? Could she do that? Could she raise a baby as a Seneca?

With a heavy heart, Ki slowly turned around and left with his gear. He knew women became very sensitive at this time of pregnancy, and she had rebuffed every approach from him. He would have to discuss this with some of the men and see what they did when their women got so upset. Maybe that is why men went on hunting trips—not just to get meat. Hopefully, being away would make her miss him.

———

The next day Julia was washing clothes at the river. She glimpsed her reflection in the water with disbelief. Braids bound with white thongs hung on each side of her face, held back by a beaded headband. She did not recognize herself as she sat back to consider this. At that minute, a warrior arrived with news; Keme talked to him as Julia asked what was going on.

"What is it, Keme?

"At burned village, black people living there."

"Was it a woman and a man with a baby?"

"Yes." Keme looked at Julia curiously.

"I think I know them. They may have lived at the house where I met Ki. Keme, I need to go and see for myself. These are good people enslaved to the white man."

"I go with you. Many herbs grow there. We go now." Keme made her way to the longhouse as Julia went to saddle up the horses, and they left soon after gathering supplies.

London, 1777

Megan could not believe she was utterly left alone in the world. Victoria had contracted a cough that plagued her for a long time. It appeared to overtake her body until she was coughing blood. She got weaker and weaker until one day she just died. They went to their London house to escape the old one, where her mother had died, with all the memories. That was when Rainsford started drinking heavily, and Megan would overhear him in the garden late at night, crying. One morning he was found after she thought she had put him to bed, frozen with a bottle of gin in his hand. *Great God, I wish Julia were here to help me*, she thought with yearning. Her letters to her sister were answered at first, but then all replies stopped. Julia needed to learn that their parents had died.

"Madam, there is a man to see you." The maid looked worriedly at Megan.

"Show him into the parlor." Megan took a quick look at herself and went downstairs.

"Well, hello, Franklin Townset, what brings you to London?" Megan was suspicious of the fellow. Franklin was a handsome man like his brother, with blond hair and blue eyes. He always dressed in the best fashion for a man of his position, but that position was now in question. The family was living beyond their means. The boys did like to gamble, and it had cost the family dearly. Franklin had tried to get Rainsford involved in questionable investments during his decline, but her father had resisted his schemes.

"Megan, I am worried about you living here by yourself with no one to help you. Please consider moving to Townset House so we can look after you. Mother would love to have you there. To be truthful, we all would love it if you moved there."

I'll wager you would, Megan thought to herself. "Franklin, I am fine. This is my home. Please tell me, have you heard from John? I have had no post from Julia, and I am anxious." Franklin *had* received letters from John, and it sounded as if he and Julia were not getting along. The last few had been very vague about Julia.

"John is kept busy with the war. They are doing capitally. I don't know why Julia has not written to you. Does she know about your parents?" Franklin had written John immediately upon the death of Rainsford. He wanted his brother to be aware Megan was alone in London.

"I don't know. Has John told her?"

"I would think so. I know Julia would not want you to be alone right now." Franklin had risen and moved to where Megan was sitting on the couch.

"It is so odd not to hear from her."

"That is exactly why you need to move to Townset House, so we can help you, at least until you hear from Julia." Now Franklin touched her arm consolingly.

"No! I will stay here." Megan shrugged off Franklin's hand and moved to the fireplace.

"Megan, may I remind you that it is indecent for a young woman to live alone in this fashion." Now Franklin put on a very fatherly face. Megan wanted to slap it.

"Madam, the bookkeeper has arrived." The butler had been listening. He somewhat grabbed the little man at the door, and gratefully threw him into the room with Megan and Franklin.

"Splendid. I have been expecting Wiggins. Now, if you please, Franklin, I must see to business." Megan motioned Franklin toward the door, without introducing Wiggins, but he would not move.

"Please, Megan, I am very good with numbers and accounts. This is not a woman's task. I can help you, if you would let me. Our families are combined now, and your sister's share belongs to John."

"Franklin, my father apportioned his estate in his will, so I really will not be needing your help." With that, the butler handed Franklin his cane and hat.

"Very well; I will leave," he said coldly. "Good day to you all."

"Goodbye, Franklin, and please do not worry about me."

"You have not seen the last of me, Megan. As I pointed out, it is indecent for a young woman to live by herself." He left with a menacing expression.

"Did he upset you, Miss Megan?" The butler seemed worried about his young mistress.

"He would not *go*!" Megan sat down on the couch, worried.

"I am afraid this will only get worse, mistress, with you being so young and alone in London." Mr. Wiggins was talking in his anxious way. He was a tiny man with a nervous tic that made his head twitch every so often. "Every bachelor will be breaking the door down once it is identified that you are very wealthy and alone."

"Well, am I not fortunate! My new name is 'Moneybags.'" Megan wanted to cry despite her humorous words. She had never felt so alone in her life. She had thought she wanted independence to do what pleased her, and now that she had it, she knew not what to do with it.

"Mr. Wiggins, I am so glad that you have secured the family's finances for me and no one can touch them." Megan went over to the little man and took his hands. He felt proud.

"We still need Julia's signature on some things. Have *you* heard from her? Remember that half the estate is hers and John's."

"I have sent letters. Nothing has come back. I am so worried. I want to talk to Julia badly!" Megan was trying to keep the tears and frustration from showing.

"I will help you in every way I can. I did get a response from John; this is the reason why I am here. He wrote not a word about Julia. He is asking for his share of the estate. I will hold him off as long as I can. Each of their signatures is necessary to release the estate."

"I need my sister. I am beginning to worry about her safety. John will not mention her at all! Mr. Wiggins, what if something has happened to her?

Wiggins was a small man who had never married. He had been a sickly child of poor, bookish parents. Their humble diet had done nothing to improve his health. He had excelled at school numbers—a wonderful gift since he was unable to do heavy work. His grandfather was determined to see him well schooled to support the low-income family. Wiggins served an apprenticeship with a Scottish bank, where his law and finance aptitude earned him high esteem. A client of the bank, Lord Rainsford, had hired Wiggins to serve in the management of his assets. Wiggins's siblings had not been so thoughtful as to invite him home once his parents and grandparent were gone. His sisters and brothers felt he had become too fancy for them, and therefore he felt alone. He had become familiar with the little girls while consulting with Rainsford, and the girls had grown to love him.

As Wiggins walked in town, he sought for toys or candy he thought they might like. When they knew he was coming, they would wait outside, and at the sight of him, they would bounce in unladylike excitement to meet his carriage and see what he had bought them. Three days before Christmas, they determined that he would not spend the holidays alone. The tenderhearted imps invited him to join them for Christmas. He looked at Rainsford in embarrassment, but Rainsford could rarely resist his daughters. After that, the girls insisted that he spend every holiday with them. When Wiggins had heard about the incident in the stable, he had accepted Julia's account. He knew Townset was after their money, and now the girls were alone. He felt love and responsibility for them because Rainsford would desire that he look after the girls.

He had tried only once to talk to Rainsford about his drinking, without success, and he almost forfeited his job at that point. He never mentioned it again, even when Megan asked him to intervene. He was not surprised to find Rainsford dead that winter day. Rainsford had been falling down a dark hole ever since his wife's death. Wiggins worried about the girls now, and he felt dread for some eventuality he could not fully understand and explain. Rainsford had left a will; because Townset had never provided the jointure, the marriage was not even recognized in the estate. The estate was divided evenly between the girls as if both were unmarried. Wiggins knew Townset would appeal the will since it was widely accepted that when a woman married, her earnings, inheritance, and all worldly goods were given over to her husband. They would probably lose on the appeal, to Wiggins's dismay and disgust.

America

"Mr. Wiggins, please, have you never wanted to travel?" Megan wore her most winning face.

"No! Most especially not to the uncivilized colonies!" His twitch was worse, and he scarcely believed what he was hearing.

"I must have someone to accompany me to America to find my sister. Besides, is it not your obligation to inform my sister of her inheritance?" Megan wore a stern expression.

"Megan, it is dangerous. We could be killed!" The twitch accelerated.

Megan inhaled deeply. "You have been with my family forever. Now is not the time to back out on me." She looked angry and helpless at the same time. "All right, I will pay you twofold, but that is my final offer; I may have to replace you." Megan was holding her breath. She had no idea what she would do if he said no or what her alternate plan would be.

"All right, but I protest. This is most unusual." Wiggins wiped his forehead with his handkerchief. Megan put her arms around him and kissed him on the cheek.

"I will get the house in order and leave the butler here to see to things. Thank you very much."

"Megan, we could regret this greatly. The Americans have taken up arms against the Crown. George is hated and reviled. Besides, hostile Indians may kill us." But Wiggins knew he could never deny Megan anything, no more than his former employer could. So he took a deep breath; they were in for a hair-raising adventure.

Franklin Townset loitered at a tavern in the shipyard. He needed to recruit a man to tail Megan. His inquiries turned up Mick Hall's name. From all reports, this man would do anything for money, including murder. Not more than thirty-five, he was a stocky man whose face showed a hard life of heavy drinking.

"I need a man to tail Megan Rainsford and report back to me. Note her activities, movements, and associates." Franklin nursed a tankard of beer.

"I am your man, but I must have me money upfront." Mick wobbled a bit.

"You will get half now, half when you finish."

"How long will I be employed?" spittle sprayed from Mick's mouth.

"Until I tell you to stop!" Franklin hated dealing with this class of people.

"This upper crust don't stay put. They gets bored and moves about. What then?" Mick's eyebrows rose.

"I will give you the money to follow her. Attend me well! It is crucial that you stay on her and keep me informed."

Three days later Mick reported Megan had purchased two tickets to America.

"Curse it!" Franklin paced the parlor. "That bitch is planning to find her sister!"

"What's me orders today, guv?" Mick besmirched the couch with dirty clothes and the smell of old beer.

"You will have to follow her to America. I will pay for your expenses."

"You're mad! The colonies are rebelling. I could get impressed into the navy." Mick looked at Franklin with outrage.

"I will pay you double and write you a letter of employment. Would that make you feel more secure?" Sweat sprang up on Townset's upper lip.

"Weh-yul, that could work, I s'pose. Need some new clothes so as I can look respectable..."

"Yes. I will clothe you respectably, but you must also behave respectably. You must refrain from drunkenness and cursing like a heathen. Can you read and write?" Franklin's color rose.

"Enough to tell you what's 'apnin."

"Beside tailing Megan, I want you to find my brother and his wife. Julia, his wife, is the important one here; I need to know she is with John. He is a colonel in the British army, so he won't be hard to find. I will give you a letter to him. Megan is landing in New York, correct?"

"Yeh, and is your brother in New York?

"Yes. Megan will be looking for him. Tomorrow we will buy you new clothes, but first, you need to bathe.

On this assignment, you must wash regularly. Can you do this?

"For me fee—yes, I c'n do this, and act like a refine' gen'lmun if I mus'." With that, Mick loudly burped a vaporous cloud of stale beer, stood up proudly, and smiled evilly at Franklin's wrinkled nose.

Burned Seneca Village

U pon their arrival, Keme and Julia spied Sally and Ben, who were living in a tent. Sally held the baby in her arms while Julia stared helplessly at the baby boy, John's baby. He had chocolate skin and light brown curly hair.

"What is his name?"

"Kucma." Sally happily drew Julia close.

After their embrace, Julia turned to Keme. "This is Keme, Ki's mother. This is Sally and Ben, who worked at the house where I met Ki. May I hold the baby?" As Julia held Kucma, Sally described how they had run away. They had come upon the village and decided to stay there and try to make a go of it.

"Ben took a musket, and he's been hunting. Some fields were not burnt, so we have gotten food from them and planted also." Sally retrieved Kucma, and they all went into the tent to sit and decide what to do.

"Keme, would it be possible for Sally and Ben to live in the village? They are good people and work hard." Julia held her breath, hoping Keme would agree to this.

Suddenly the noise of riders coming in hard surrounded them. Ben was out of the tent with the rifle raised, but he quickly put up his hands when he saw how many there were. At least ten men rode in with guns drawn.

"Julia Townset? We have been on the hunt for you." John Sullivan was looking down at Julia.

"Who are you? You don't sound British." Julia was terrified.

"No, madam. We are Patriots. We heard you deserted your husband. We intend to sell you back to him for a large ransom. So, we are holding you." Men were already grasping Julia's arms and leading her to a horse when Ben tried to stop them. The men clubbed him in the face and stomach. Julia realized she had to gain control fast.

"No! Ben! You go back with Keme and Sally to the village." Julia then appealed to Sullivan. "Let them go; they are of no value to you." Sullivan agreed.

"I don't need them. You are the prize we've been looking for. Now get on that horse, quickly! We need to get out of here now!

Julia looked at Keme's desolate face. "Tell Ki that I will never stop loving him. He is not to come for me because they will kill him. I never could live with that. Your kindness will never be forgotten." Julia's words were strangled with emotion. For a brief minute, Keme clutched Julia's hand. Julia's happy life was over. Keme just caught her eye, nodding in agreement, and then they were gone.

New York City 1777

"I know you are uncomfortable, Wiggins, but I must find my sister!" Megan was tired of his complaints and warnings of doom. Wiggins had been violently ill the whole voyage, preventing any pleasure in the trip. Now they found New York half-burned to the ground and people living in tents. Their captain told her the name of the British commanding general so that they could inquire of *him* where the Townsets were.

"We will book a room at the Queen's Head, try to get some decent food, and settle in before we look for General Howe." They plodded toward the hotel in a cart drawn by a very tired-looking horse. The deplorable conditions of the city depressed them after their harrowing sail. In their misery they failed to notice a fellow passenger following them.

Mick had tried to make himself invisible to Megan and Wiggins in order to overhear their conversations. He knew they were looking for General Howe, and it would take careful dealings on his part to remain unnoticed once they reached the general's headquarters.

———

After some refreshing stability, Wiggins's queasiness abated. He left the hotel to find directions to General Howe, and when queried about their goal for meeting him, he hinted there was money in it for the British. He was given an appointment within days. The general looked tired and busy with the vast task of bringing the colonies under control. They had taken complete control of New York City; beyond that were wild Indians and Patriot country.

"General Howe, your critical duties must keep you very busy, so I will be brief. I must find Lieutenant Colonel John Townset, my brother-in-law, and my sister, Julia Townset." Howe was taken with the beauty standing before him. "I have traveled from England and have a great need to contact them." Howe showed Megan to a chair and ordered tea.

"Miss Rainsford, I hate to be the one to inform you of the unfortunate situation your sister is in right now. I don't know how to put this, so I will just come out with it. Your sister, Julia, deserted her husband and ran away with an Indian scout employed to guide our troops. The Rebels have captured her and are demanding a ransom of one hundred and twenty-five pounds for her return." He felt pity for this lovely young woman as shock and grief filled her eyes with tears.

Megan's hands fluttered unsteadily. "I don't know what to say! I could not imagine less likely behavior from Julia! Is she safe?" Megan marshaled her emotions and squared her shoulders. "I have the money to pay for her return."

"For the time being, she is safe. Her captors regard her as a prize."

"What has John Townset said about all this? He must be keen to retrieve her. Why has he not paid?

"By all appearances, he was heartsick over her departure, but he has not the money for her return. He begged relief from the British military, but we can hardly afford to give in to the Patriots, I'm sure you can understand." Howe used his most calming voice as he calculated how much she could be carrying with her right then.

"I will gladly pay for my sister's return." Megan lifted her chin defiantly. But she pictured her vivacious sister being violated by God knows whom. All she knew of Indians was that they were violent heathens.

"Will you order secret negotiations with her captors? I beg of you, General Howe. I will be forever grateful for your kindness. I will contribute to your cause."

"I can only try my best. The Rebels want to ransom Julia quickly. We can now tell them the money is available. But it is a dangerous situation."

Megan stood up and looked, pleading, into General Howe's face. "I know you will do your best. I will make it worth your effort."

Farmhouse near Yonkers, New York

The Joneses were a nice enough couple, Patriots who supported the rebellion. They were surprised when a young woman was brought to them for shelter under guard; they hesitantly offered their care service. They received the message directly from Daniel Morgan to watch her while she was held for ransom. She will bring in an excellent price from the British. What surprised them was how she dressed and that she willingly was living with the Seneca.

"Where on earth did you get those clothes? I know you are not an Indian, but my goodness, girl, you are dressed like one." Mrs. Jones could not believe her eyes.

"I have been living with the Seneca." Julia held up her chin.

"You are not Indian; you are British!" Mrs. Jones shook her head in confusion.

"My story is long. I suppose I should now wear what you consider normal clothes." But when Julia began to remove the boots that Ki had made, she could not let them go; tears filled her eyes and sobs burst out.

"I have to keep these. I can't let you have them." She held them to her breast, "Please do not destroy these clothes. I want to keep them."

"Do you want to go back?" Mrs. Jones was astonished.

"That is quite impossible now with guards surrounding the house. I am worth a large ransom to the Patriots." All Mrs. Jones could do was nod.

"Well, I will match your size and make you a dress."

"Thank you. But if you have material, could you teach me to sew it? It seems I will have a lot of time on my hands." Julia dabbed at the tears on her face. Without warning, Julia ran to the dresser and threw up in the washbowl.

"Are you sick, girl? Did you catch something?" Mrs. Jones was very concerned. Smallpox and other disease worried them continuously.

"No, I am going to have a baby."

"Oh my, oh my" was all Mrs. Jones could express. Had the girl been raped? What had those Indians done to her? Her hand flew to her throat. "Well, we will deal with this just as we do everything else." Head high, with a determined expression on her face, she asked, "Would you like to speak to the vicar, Turner? You still believe in the Almighty, don't you?"

"Yes, I would like that. I often prayed when I was there."

"Did you try to escape while you were there?" Mrs. Jones could not help asking.

"No, I went willingly, Mrs. Jones. I believed my husband would harm me fatally; he killed the baby I was carrying, his baby. Ki, the Indian guide I was teaching, took pity on me, and we ran away to his village."

"You had no family to go to?"

"I was brought here by my husband, who is a British officer; I am far from my home and family." Julia bowed her head with tears running down her face. Mrs. Jones couldn't help but hug the poor young woman. It had to be hard being so far from home and having a cruel husband. Mrs. Jones had never heard of an Indian doing a good deed.

"Ki was kind to me and protected me when I had no one. My parents made me marry that horrible man. I did not know what to do."

"You could have gone back home to your family."

"He was getting more and more violent; he was going down to the slave quarters and got Sally with child." Julia couldn't stop herself from talking because this was the first opportunity she had had to speak about what had happened to her with a person in her culture. Mrs. Jones reminded Julia of her mother in her very straightforward and unadorned manner. She appeared to be kind and caring based on the way she welcomed Julia into her house. They lived a simple life and loathed the aristocracy's habits, for they viewed the nobility as self-serving and two-faced. But Mrs. Jones could still not come to terms with Julia running away with an Indian, much less going to bed with one. She took a deep breath and stroked Julia's arms with hands that were work-worn, telling her everything was going to be better as she left the room.

When Julia glanced at the boots, she felt new tears coming. Why had they left the village? Now she would be forced to return to John and her horrible life. What would he do when he learned she was pregnant? He would know the baby couldn't be his and throw another hellish fit, probably striking her again. But without her, he would not get what he wanted—her money. Her father would withhold it, for John had not fulfilled the contract. But her situation! What would her parents think? Could they ever take her back? She had disgraced them and herself. Most likely, a convent would be her destination. But her one desire and ambition was to be a mother to her child, come hell or high water. *And I might as well prepare for hell,* she though.

She missed Ki and regretted the way they had parted. She had taken out her fears on him, especially when the morning sickness had started. That was utterly unfair of her. Did she think that they could go on making love forever without conceiving?

"Ki, I am so very sorry. Please forgive me. All you have tried to do is protect me." Only silence replied. "I will never see you again, but I love you so much. You taught me what true love is."

The next day Vicar Turner came to the house to talk to Julia to reaffirm her faith in God. Mrs. Jones repeated what she had learned from Julia, and he told her he wanted to speak to Julia alone. Mrs. Jones bought Julia to the small drawing room with a dress she had hastily put together over the course of the night so Julia could get out of those Indian clothes. Reverend Turner sat Julia down and took her hand.

"You have been through a terrible ordeal, my poor child. I am sorry to have to ask you this, but were you raped?" Julia could not believe what the man was saying to her. These people mistrusted Indians and even hated them, but there was no way she would deceive Ki and lie about what had happened. She loved Ki and felt he was an honorable man.

"I went willingly and would do it again. Ki is an honorable person, and I know you find this strange since he is an Indian. But you must believe me; he took me from a horrible situation. My husband beat me and killed the child I was carrying. John was planning on killing me for my money. He thought it would be easier in America than in England, and he would make it look like Ki did it. I was Ki's teacher for English and reading." Julia looked down into her hands and wondered if she should be telling him everything. "That was when Ki asked me to go to his village where I would be safe."

"But you told Mrs. Jones you are with child now? Did you have to act like his wife when you were married to another man?"

"No, I wanted him for my husband, but I told him I could not marry him since I was already married. I know you think I am horrible, but I fell in love with him. He was kind to me and protected me. I had no one else, especially since my family lives in England."

"You know Daniel Morgan is going to ransom you back to your husband?

"Yes, I know that, and I pray he will send me back to my family without harming me when he finds out I am with child."

Turner didn't know what to say to this poor woman who found herself in a horrible situation. The Patriots would be returning her to a man who could harm her. The upper classes were strange—they could get away with murder if they so chose. He could tell she was highborn by her manners and speech. He had thought he would never feel sorry for one of them, but here he was with this poor creature who had been abused by her husband and done the unthinkable, running away with an Indian! She was young and impressionable; that was why she had fallen in love with this savage. She was one of God's children, and he needed to bring her back into the fold.

"Pray for me, please, because I will need God's help." Julia was crying again, and with that, they prayed a very long prayer.

———

Three days later a woman came to the house to see Julia. She wore a shabby dress that had seen better days. The poor woman had walked miles to see Julia and was given food and tea while sitting in the small drawing room. The woman stood up quickly when Julia came into the room with a highly expectant expression. When Julia sat next to her, the woman looked imploringly into Julia's face.

"Mrs. Townset, my husband was with a group of men who were ordered to fight the Indians by directions of Washington. He did this for the safety of the community, but he was captured." At this point Mrs. Walker had to put her head down, and a tear rolled down her cheek. "I was told the Seneca took him. I heard that you were with them and lived in one of their villages. Mrs. Townset, did you see my husband? Did they kill him? Please. Did they torture him? His name is Ben Walker."

At this point, Mrs. Walker had her arm on Julia's arm, and tears were pouring down her face. Julia was so shocked that all she could do was stare at the woman. Julia could see herself telling Walker that he had to marry Yo da gent to survive. Now she had to face his wife, and what should she tell her? The truth? She knew never to lie, that no good would ever come of it. Well, what good would come of Julia telling Mrs. Walker the truth? Julia was so stunned that words wouldn't come out of her mouth, and she realized that she was making Mrs. Walker very uneasy.

"Mrs. Townset, you know something! Please tell me! I miss my husband every day, and if he is alive, I want to know. We have five children who need their daddy. Please, if you know anything..."

Julia's face had lost all color. She wanted to cry for Mrs. Walker and cry for everything that had happened since coming to America. Julia wanted to weep for the five children without a daddy and all the unfairness of the world, but she realized that it wouldn't help. So she drew up her shoulders and took a deep breath. "Mrs. Walker, your husband was killed honorably. I really did not see it happen, but I am sure he was courageous. He was never brought into the village where I lived, but another man was, a Mr. Connor, and your husband was not with him." Julia put her arm around the poor woman.

"Please call me Amy...I knew Mr. Connor and knew he was in a prisoner exchange. I was just hoping that maybe you knew what had happened to my husband. I wish I could bury him properly. The children ask for him every day."

A new wave of guilt swept over Julia, and she tried to stop the memories of Yo da gent attending to his wounds. But she could not tell this woman the truth because it would kill her, and what would she say to her children?

"I need to leave; thank you for talking to me. I just had to find out what happened. I was told that he had been captured, but now I know he was killed."

New tears came, and Julia had to look away to hide the shame she was feeling. Julia accompanied her to the door and saw the sad woman walk down the road.

When Ki heard of the capture, he could not believe it. He got ready to look for Julia; Ki made sure he had all his weapons, but he wanted a long rifle, the kind the Patriots had. He could kill from a distance with a gun like that.

"Where are you going?" Yuma had a worried look that was changing quickly into one of anger.

"To get her back!" Ki was trying to get on his horse, but his father stopped him.

"Are you crazy! If the Patriots don't kill you, then the British will! How will you find her?"

No sooner had Yuma spoken than he remembered that Ki was an expert at tracking people down because he had been his teacher. Yuma had a fear of never seeing his son again. He held on to his son's arm to try and stop him and looked into the man's eyes and felt the love Ki had for this woman. For many years Yuma had been everything to Ki. Ki worshipped him, but now Yuma realized he was second place in Ki's world. But isn't this how the world worked? His love of this woman was the only thing that mattered. Slowly Yuma let this wonderful son go, and he prayed that the spirits would guard him against all harm, especially the white man. Keme came to stand beside Yuma as they watched Ki ride away, and both felt a terrible omen in the fact that Keme couldn't stop her tears.

The Exchange

Daniel Morgan had picked the spot carefully, a field with surrounding trees where he could place snipers if something went wrong. He knew only that the British side had the money for the trade. If this worked out, they could afford many needed supplies. A young messenger instructed him to bring the Townset woman with no more than ten soldiers. The British could also bring in no more than ten soldiers and the money. Townset would retrieve his soiled wife and hand over her ransom.

Unknown to Morgan, Ki had been tracking them for a week. He knew where Julia was being held, but there were too many guards for him to rescue her. He surmised that they were holding her for ransom because he knew the Patriots were desperate for money, and this was the standard operating procedure of action during the war. Ki knew Townset had offered a reward for her return. He was trying to come up with a plan to retrieve her during the exchange somehow. He fleeced a long rifle from Morgan's soldiers as they slept off a drunken, much-needed rest after skirmishing with the British outside of New York City. Ki knew the storeroom was guarded, so he watched the men drink themselves into a stupor, and when Ki looked down from the storeroom roof, he spied only one unlucky guard. Ki fell on him with his hatchet, knocking him out. He found little ammunition and only a few long rifles. Ki had only practiced with the long gun once, when the British had confiscated one from a captured Patriot teen while Ki was with the British in Boston. Fascinated, Ki had induced the boy to teach him to use the odd gun in exchange for letting him escape in the night. They had planned the escape together. The teen had taught Ki how to wrap buckskin around the bullet and adequately sight the gun in, and it had taken some time for Ki to learn how to do this. The trigger was incredibly hard, but he knew how to "hold over" to compensate for wind with much practice. Ki had a powder horn that he poured down the gun's barrel, then rammed a wad down, then rimed the pan. Before Ki could plan the teen's escape, the British had executed the poor Patriot teen.

Now he took his booty out of earshot in the forest to test how far he could shoot. He had to go some miles away so as not to be heard. Excellent eyesight made him accurate at over two hundred and fifty feet. He returned to spy; he was tortured by the fear that Townset would again get his hands on Julia. Ki had slept and eaten little, and he had been backtracking the Rebels to this camp and patiently looking for an opportunity to rescue Julia. Now that Julia carried their child, Ki was desperate to prevent her from falling back into Townset's violent control. Ki had labored so long to help her recover from Townset's abuse, and he could not risk their child being destroyed by Townset.

Finally, he spied the Rebels leading Julia out of the house and followed at a safe distance. They stopped in a field, where several soldiers climbed into the trees with their rifles and hid, and Ki followed suit. The others went to the middle of the area with Julia, and it was not long before the British came, with Townset leading ten heavily armed redcoats. Ki had an excellent view of Julia from his tree and saw Grant ride forward to grab her; he was carrying a heavy bag of coin on his pommel. Ki aimed with his loaded rifle and fired, hitting Grant in the chest. All hell broke out.

Morgan snatched Julia back and returned British fire with deadly aim, shooting several of the redcoats. Morgan scanned the trees. "Hold fire, hold fire. That shot came from none of my men."

Feeling outnumber and outgunned, Townset called a retreat, with the bag of coins having been retrieved from Grant's horse. "This is not over," he snarled at Morgan. "This is not over." Townset spurred out of the field.

A New Sharpshooter Recruit

"**W**ho the hell fired?" Morgan looked around, trying to locate the traitor. Ki was spotted and shot at by several soldiers, and when he tried to run, they surrounded him. Exhausted and relieved at Julia's escape from danger, he felt he had at least one win. They circled him with pointed rifles. Morgan escorted Julia back to the farmhouse, a reasonable distance from the exchange place. Ki was bound and brought to the farmhouse yard. Julia knew Ki had come for her, but she couldn't get a look at him.

They unloaded and dragged Ki into the barn at the farmhouse, where they rained blows and kicks on him by turns.

Morgan quickly made his way to the barn, where a bloody Ki sagged, almost unconscious, against a barn wall.

"Stop." Morgan wanted to execute Ki on the spot because he quickly deduced he must be Julia's lover.

"Goddamned savage! You have cost us a fortune!" He slammed his boot into Ki's ribs.

"Morgan, first consider this; the Indian shot from a distance of over two hundred and fifty paces. Maybe we can put him to good use for all the money he has cost us," said Samuel McKinny.

Morgan thought about it for a moment. Then he said, "Bring the girl here. We will see how good he is." Julia was fetched from the house and handed a small plate no larger than seven inches across. Ki hauled up to stand 280 feet from Julia, and when given a rifle, he would not take hold of it. Ki saw Julia crying; he knew what the bastards wanted him to do. His child would die if he shot Julia. *He* would die. He shook his head in rejection.

"Oh, yes. You will shoot that plate out of her hand, or else you will never see her again. I might even have her for myself. So, if you don't want that to happen, then shoot the damned plate out of her hand. She then will go back to the house." Ki was sweating and knew he had no choice, so he aimed as best he could while praying to every spirit he could think of for help. He held his breath. Ki fired and dropped to his knees when he saw that he had missed the plate. Julia had cried out, but he hadn't hit her. He thanked the gods, but Morgan was yelling at him to do it again. This time sweat dripped from his forehead. He wiped it out of his eyes and aimed, staying on one knee for better support. He had to stop and wipe the sweat off his hands. Then he aimed for what seemed a long time; his heart thundered in his chest, and with his head pounding, he fired. He could hear Julia cry out when the plate exploded out of her hand.

Julia then fell to her knees, and Ki could see that she was crying because she had put her hands to her face; but thank the gods, there was no blood. The rest of the men hollered in wonderment at what they had just witnessed. He waited to see if she showed pain, but she did not, only a look of despair as she was seized and hurried back into the house. She strained to keep Ki in her field of vision as he saw her lips moving but could not make out what she was saying. Morgan walked over to Ki, who was slowly getting up.

"If you want to see Julia again, then you will kill as many Brits as I want you to kill. Understand me? You will take their scalps and bring them to me. Do you understand? Because if you don't, I will bed that pretty Brit myself. Then I will give her back to that stupid husband of hers after selling your child, or maybe I will kill it. Yes, I know she is pregnant with your child. She was throwing up the whole way back here. Do we have a deal?" Morgan's face was so close to Ki's that his spit was all over Ki's face. Ki slowly nodded his head in agreement as Morgan walked away, ordering, "Watch him closely."

Ki got one day to recuperate from his beating before leaving on a mission to the north. They stopped to camp, and Samuel McKinny came over to Ki with a long rifle leaning on his shoulder. Samuel was from the old country, as were most of the men. He had a strong Irish accent and a handsome face with a prominent square chin, deep-set blue eyes, and curly reddish-brown hair. For a man of his time, he had very straight white teeth. He was about six-foot-two. He wore a thigh-length fringed cloth hunting shirt following the pattern sent around by George Washington, a thigh-high pair of leggings, breechclout, and moccasins.

McKinny had worked his way over on a boat while his indentured parents served out their contracts. He took on odd jobs, trying to help his parents as best he could. They had lived in a small log cabin on the farm to which his parents were indentured. There had been some Indian attacks, so McKinny knew what it was to sleep with one eye open. When the revolution started, McKinny quickly signed up. His skills with the rifle became well known. Daniel Morgan recruited men with special rifle skills to target the British officers. Looked upon as cowardly behavior by the British, this strategy was, in reality, having a very devastating effect on them. To be selected for Morgan's Provisional Rifle Corps, you had to be able to shoot a seven-inch bull's-eye from two hundred and fifty feet away while climbing and hiding in a tree.

"You were about two hundred and sixty feet from that British soldier when you shot him. But shooting that plate out of her hand was unbelievable."

"Grant?"

"You knew that soldier before you shot him? So this was personal for you? Well, we need you to keep shooting British soldiers. Then you can take their scalps. Orders from Morgan, our commander. You are now under his command and will do as you are told. If you don't, then we will have to kill you."

"I understand." Ki met Samuel's eyes.

"Good. So let's get started practicing. Do you think that maybe you could shoot even farther? And if you are asking, 'What will happen after we beat the hell out of the

British?'—who knows? Hopefully, that pretty young girl back there will still be waiting for you."

"I go to battle, I need bow and knife. I shoot many arrows by time you reload guns. Where is Julia to be kept?"

"If I knew, I wouldn't tell you."

America, New York

Megan could not believe her ears. She had wanted to talk to John but had been informed that he was busy with his men and the war, making it impossible for him to take time to see her in New York. General Howe had just informed her that the transfer had been a disaster, and the money had disappeared. So everything had not worked out as planned. Megan felt despair and hopelessness, but she loved her sister and needed to help her in any way she could. Wiggins did not think the money had been lost but rather stolen by the British.

"We need to go home. There is nothing we can do, Megan."

"I need to find my sister, for the last time!" Megan did not care if people were listening in the tavern connected to the hotel where they stayed, but Mick Hall heard from a table a few feet away.

"Well, we dare not go into Rebel territory. That would be utterly reckless." Wiggins twitched and sweated uncomfortably.

"That is exactly where we are going to find her. I have learned of an inn where we can stay. Now, all we need is an escort to help us." Megan strained to be upbeat.

"Savage Indians could attack us!"

"A good escort will avoid dangerous areas. I want to try again to pay the ransom for my sister." Megan placed a hand over Wiggins's. "Let us retire to the rooms and talk privately."

Megan was uncomfortable with so many people around her. Mick Hall got up from the table when they left, going to the bartender. He passed a crown to him to make a map of the area, especially of the terrain to the west. The man became suspicious and wanted to know why, so Mick slipped him another crown. The man started to draw on a napkin a crude map of New York City and the surrounding area.

"Do you know of a tavern west of the city?" Mick asked.

"There is one, and it is a stronghold of the Rebels. Are you planning on going there? What business do you have there?"

Mick had to think fast. "I won a bet in London, and the loser sold me his land. I have come to claim it, so if you could maybe draw where I can find it on the map, I would be grateful. I think it is close to that tavern west of the city." Mick held his breath and used his best English, not wanting to let the man see that he was of a lower class. Mick was in luck when the bartender began drawing the route to the tavern on the napkin.

"You better watch yourself because you will be in Rebel country." The bartender gave him a warning look.

Now Mick had to convince Megan and that idiot Wiggins to hire him. He knew they were carrying a lot of money on them. He decided to rob them on the road, leave them for dead, then take the money and run. Somehow, he would have to avoid entanglement in the

conflict. It would be dangerous going into enemy territory. He had bought a gun from a displaced citizen of
New York desperate for food and shelter for his family.

———

Upstairs Megan laid out her plans for Wiggins. "I will
sew money into my dress somehow to make it silent when
I walk."

"Do you think that will work? Wiggins mopped his
brow.

"You hide some too—in your socks, maybe? Wherever
you think you can get away with it. I will hide my jewelry—
somewhere." Megan did not want to mention her corset.

"Do you think you can mount a horse with all that?

"I will manage somehow. Now please try to find us
an escort out of this city, someone who knows what he is
doing."

"How am I supposed to do that?" The sweat was dripping off his head like a river.

"Use your intelligence!" Megan threw up her hands.

While Megan tried on the cleverly sewn new clothes
hiding coin and jewelry, Wiggins stood outside the house
of the seamstress who had been kind enough to sew all
night and day for Megan. The seamstress badly needed
the money, and she promised not to tell anyone about the
money and jewelry in the dress. Wiggins noticed a man
from their ship coming up to him slowly.

"Do you recognize me? Mick Hall," he said, holding
out his hand. "I was on the ship with you from England,
where I concluded some business. Now I am headed back

to my farm west of here. I have been in this country for only twelve years and have done very well for myself. I have thirty slaves." Mick lied glibly to make a good impression.

"I do recognize you. Have you lodged at the Queen's Head also?" Wiggins wondered if he could trust this strange man.

"Yes. I do business here in New York buying staples and cloth for my wife and my many slaves." Mick could tell he had Wiggins's interest, so he used his best English and manners. The money he was about to attain from them excited him. He had no idea what he was talking about, but he did know large landowners used black slaves instead of indentured people. Mick so hoped that he was able to make his lie believable.

"J. Wiggins, esquire." Wiggins was holding out his hand to try to establish a friendly relationship. "We require an escort west to an inn where Patriots have been known to stay. Is there any chance we could pay you to take us along?"

"Sir, that could be quite dangerous. What business do you have there?" Jubilation elevated Mick's performance as he peered suspiciously at Wiggins.

"Mr. Hall, it is a delicate family situation that we must handle. I assure you it is not to spy on anyone, but in fact, to retrieve Mistress Rainsford's sister." Wiggins feared he had given too much away.

"Why do you propose to do that? Is she there against her will?

"Well, we need her to return willingly." He carefully avoided mentioning the money they had on them. "If that does not work, well, I don't know. We will just have to come up with some other idea."

Mick Hall threw back his head and laughed. "That is total bollocks. But if you want me to take you, I will, for a fee of twelve pounds." Mick changed his manner to a friendly one. Again Wiggins held out his hand in agreement.

"Is the mistress going to be a problem on the road?"

"No. She rides well. I think she can handle herself."

"What is your mistress's name?

"Megan Rainsford. We will look forward to traveling with you. When do we leave?

"In two days. Do you have mounts?"

"No. Would you be so kind as to show me where to buy horses? We shall need a lady's saddle."

"Of course. I think I can procure some good horses and a lady's saddle." Mick was delighted with the situation.

Two days later they left after giving Mick money for horses and supplies. Megan was not happy to be going with Mick, who, she felt she could not trust for some reason. She had seen him on the ship and thought he was watching her, and then when he was at the hotel, she felt it was not a coincidence; she sensed a creepiness about him. But what else could she do? They did not know anyone else in New York City, and it was not reasonable to let everyone know that they were headed into Rebel territory.

When the three came to the King's Bridge out of New York City, they were prevented from passing by British guards wanting to know their business. Mick stepped up and told the guards he had a farm and needed to return to it.

"Where is your pass, sir, and do you have papers showing that you own this place?" Mick began to sweat, for he had not anticipated this. Megan also had not thought about this, and it could be a situation that they would not be able to overcome. She could not go to the general because he would inquire about the reason for their departure and would not consent to give them a pass. Megan did not know what to do.

"Sir, we did not know about the passes, and we are with this man who needs to get back to his home."

"Everyone needs a pass, little lady, and what is a fine looking lady like you leaving New York for?"

Megan noticed that the guard had been looking at her breasts. She came in closer and whispered in his ear, "If you let us go, then I will come back tonight. What time do you get off your shift, sir?"

Now the guard was all but drooling. "I get off at seven. Will you be at the gate? They will not let you in without a pass."

"I will most certainly be here because we will need to get back in, but I will leave my friends so that I can be with you." Megan gave him the most sexual smile that she could produce and watched his eyes widened in anticipation.

"Let these people pass."

When they got away from the guards, Wiggins gave Megan the most disagreeable stare.

"I don't need your judgment right now!" This was turning out to be a lot harder than Megan had expected.

Mick noticed and pondered why Megan had had a hard time getting on the horse. Could it be that she had a lot of gold on her? He would stop every hour and a half, pleading necessary relief in the bushes or rest for the horses. In reality, he would consult the map to confirm they were heading in the right direction. Mick had wanted to laugh when Megan pulled that phony ploy over on that guard. He was finding out she wasn't so innocent after all.

"Do you think he knows where he is going? He has a worried look on his face most of the time." Megan was getting worried herself because she could not believe she was doing this. There were animals, savage Indians, and Patriots lurking everywhere. She felt she was right in the middle of the war. What if they got caught in a fight? Wiggins might have been right. She probably should not have risked this. But Megan would never forgive herself if she did not bring aid to her sister. And she felt she should not trouble Wiggins with her anxiety. His spasms would only get worse.

"Let us mount and act as if we know what we are doing." Wiggin's jerky head shone as he scanned their surroundings, talking in whispers to Megan. They had been hearing noises that scared him, and suddenly both heard horses coming up close. Mick came out of the bushes fast with his gun pointed. Five men surrounded them with guns as they reared their horses in.

"What is your business? Show your passes." The men wore buckskins and fur hats. Ranging in age from teens to greybeards, they looked determined, and all pointed rifles at them. Mick was taken aback and lowered his gun. His robbery plan had no contingency for Patriot capture and would catch him in his lie about having a farmhouse with thirty slaves. Megan nervously waited for Mick to speak. She realized he was not going to.

"Would you be spies?" One of the older ones looked menacingly at them.

"Come now, tell us what you are doing."

"I am looking for my sister. She was captured by Patriots and held for ransom. I did not know we needed passes." Megan had decided to tell the truth. At some point she would be forced to tell someone why she was there.

An older man looked earnestly into her face. "I heard about your sister. Everyone needs passes, or they are considered spies. What is your name?"

"My name is Megan Rainsford, and my sister is Julia Townset." Megan felt her legs shaking. "Gentlemen, I have to ask, are you Patriots fighting for the cause?" Megan knew she was pushing her luck. Wiggins blanched. Mick just stood there, saying nothing. Megan took a huge breath. "I would like to contribute to the cause by offering money for my sister's release." If she was very circumspect, she could act like all she had on her was her necklace and they would not find out about the rest of the jewelry and coin on her.

"Well, now, where would that money be?" The men were enjoying this. When Megan unhooked her bodice and pulled out a diamond and ruby necklace, the men lost their grins, now wide-eyed at the spectacle. Their mouths gaped open.

"Gentlemen, I heard that your commander in chief, Washington, needs this. I am here to bring it to him for the cause, but I would like my sister back. I know you will do the right thing for the cause and give this to

Washington." In the hope that these were honest men, she mainly played to their sense of duty. She knew she had them when confusion appeared on their faces. No longer focused on spies, their gazes turned inward and they tried to figure out what to do. One of the younger men spoke first.

"She is right. Washington needs this desperately, and we will put ourselves in good order with him if we bring this." He tried to whisper, but Megan heard every word. What Megan did not know was that the younger men wanted to join up with Morgan. The older man looked doubtfully at the younger man, thinking he probably wanted the necklace for himself. One could buy a farm with it. Megan had to think fast on her feet and pray that they would believe her and not rob them.

"Gentlemen, there is more in a hidden place in New York City. I can get it for the cause, but first I need my sister back." Megan was doing her best to disguise the weight she was carrying. Centuries of entitlement straightened her posture, but a trickle of terror made its way down her leg. "I believe in this cause and want to see this country free of British rule."

"Why? You appear to be British. Why should we believe you?" Now all eyes were on her.

"I was not treated very well in England. To add insult to injury, I gave Howe money for my sister's ransom and he stole the money and totally wrecked the scheme we had to get my sister back from the Patriots. Now I want to help the Patriots." Megan raised her chin.

"How *much* money did you give them?" The older man asked.

"One hundred and twenty-five pounds." This figure matched his knowledge of the exchange the men had heard about. There was a discussion of what to do. The youngsters were idealistic Patriots who wanted to help the cause, but the older man was an opportunist.

"We could improve the farm with this, and to hell with her sister," the older man said.

"You sound like a Loyalist! Pa, you were the one who got flogged by the British, and your brother was impressed by the British, and you never saw him again. What if Washington finds out about this and is informed that we never turned the necklace over? There could be dire trouble for us."

The young men overruled him, and they voted to contribute the necklace to the cause, to Megan's surprise. Megan said a prayer of thanks to God. This episode was the first time Megan had witnessed true loyalty to the roots of independence. She had been searching so hard for her sister that she had not considered the war's true motives and why it had to be fought. She *had* felt betrayed by Howe for losing or stealing her money, but she had lied about having thoughts of betraying her country. Now such thoughts whirled in her head, making her draw in a breath; giving a priceless necklace to the Patriots could be seen as treason on her part.

"Where were you headed to make these offers? Why don't these men talk? Why let a lady do all the talking?" Now suspicious looks fell on the men.

Finally, Mick spoke. "I have a small farm west of here. I am only guiding these people to the inn on the way to my farm." Hall looked very nervous.

"Your name is?"

"Mick Hall."

"I never heard of any Halls in this area. Anybody heard of a Hall farm?" Now the men were shaking their heads.

"I just bought it last year. I am new to the country. Came over from England because I, too, believe in the cause and have come to hate my fellow Englishmen." Hall could only hope they would believe this.

"This man is Mr. Wiggins, my man at large. As you know, a proper female does not go unchaperoned." Megan indicated Wiggins. She truly wanted to ask Hall some questions about this so-called farm he had led them to believe he owned.

The older man instructed his son, "Go find Daniel Morgan, and tell him we have the sister of the woman he wants to ransom. Take your brother, and don't get caught by the British. I will take these people to the inn and wait for you." The two younger men turned their horses and went in search of Morgan.

Megan looked at the older man. "What is your name, sir?"

"John Sounder. Now get back on your horse, and I will take you to the inn. It lies not far from here. You better be telling the truth, young lady, and not be a spy because there could be severe trouble for you. We make our laws here in the country that don't be true to British laws.

"You are kind, sir. I will repay you for your kindness." Megan was beginning to feel more optimistic. "Mick Hall, must you come along?"

Sounder examined Mick suspiciously, and one of the young Patriots chimed in. "Damn right, he comes. I disbelieve him, never heard of him in these parts, and until his story is cleared up, he is coming with us."

Ki's Rebel Service

Ki and Samuel had spotted a dragoon of British soldiers coming through the woods. They quickly signaled the others to hide and take aim. Ki and Samuel climbed into the trees as fast as they could. When the British were close, they did not detect they were in the trees, so all got shot, except for three of them. These three were able to close in on Ki and Samuel as they reloaded. Ki and Samuel descended from the trees so fast that Samuel fell to the ground after catching his foot on a branch. Balanced and agile, Ki drew his bow from a crouch. At lightning speed three deadly arrows hit their targets before the Brits could react. One went into the eye, the other two straight through the necks, of the soldiers. Samuel gasped in wonder then he saw Ki bent to his task of efficient butchery. Sick fascination glued Samuel's eyes to the scene, and he walked up to Ki.

"Thank you for saving my life; that was incredible." It turned his stomach to watch Ki do what they had asked him to do. "You will have to teach me to use the bow and arrow. You are very quick with weapons. Who taught you to scalp?"

"Father, whites put bounty on Haudensaunee scalps, women and children."

175

Ki never looked up from his gruesome task. Samuel knew of the bounty on Indian scalps. He had seen men claim money on scalps; some were young Indian children. In minutes Ki carried three bleeding scalps on his belt. "Morgan? Back, he took off shirt." Ki was pointing to his back.

"Morgan was captured by the British in the French war. They gave him the death penalty of four hundred and ninety-nine lashes. Against all the odds, he survived; no one knows how. I think he is in a lot of pain most days, which tells you about his moods, and now he hates the British. He also hates Indians, so stay clear of him as best you can. Washington ordered him to form this rifle company. One day Morgan announced he was looking for men who could shoot, so I tried out and qualified. We thought we could all shoot pretty well until you came along and beat us all."

Morgan's Response

Tom Sounder finally found Daniel Morgan in camp, drilling his men. Morgan turned to the puppy-like recruit with irritation. Everything aggravated his ill-used body. The war had not been going well, and he wondered if there was a snowball's chance in hell of winning it.

"Sir! I have good news for you. I am Tom Sounder. We found the sister of Julia Townset. She wants to ransom her sister." Daniel stood staring at this young man, wondering if he had come from heaven.

"She has money?"

"Not money. Megan Rainsford has a huge diamond and ruby necklace that must bring a lot of money for the cause."

"Where did you find her?"

"Making her way to the inn with two men. One, she said, was her man at large. The other claims to be a farmer who lives west and who led them from the city. But no one has ever heard of him."

"Did you see the necklace?"

"Yes!"

"Well, why did you not just take it, God damn it!" But when he saw confusion set in on the young man's face, he turned around and yelled for Samuel to come.

Then Morgan got in front of the young man. "This better be accurate, son, or I will have your head. Julia is from England, so her sister must be English too. She has traveled from England?"

"It appeared so. They are traveling with baggage. Megan Rainsford seems to want her sister back as soon as possible. General Howe stole the money she gave him to get her back. So now she is using her jewelry, I guess."

With that, Daniel laughed and started to feel some hope, a thing he had not felt in a long time. Samuel came up to him, and Daniel took him aside. "A situation has developed. Julia Townset's sister has turned up with a huge diamond necklace to ransom her sister. She is at the inn, and I want you to get that necklace. If it is real, return the sister and bring me the necklace. Bite each piece to make sure it is real, *and watch for a trap. Do not let the Indian know what is happening.*" Daniel knew that Ki had saved Samuel's life, so he stared hard at Samuel to ensure his obedience. "Do you understand me?" Samuel felt a second of guilt about deceiving his rescuer, but he was a soldier and knew how to obey orders, so he nodded his head.

Tom approached Daniel again. "I have three brothers who want to join up, sir; they are eighteen, seventeen, and sixteen." Tom looked hopeful.

"Do they have guns?" Daniel crossed his fingers.

"No, only pa and I have."

Daniel rolled his eyes and shook his head. This was why he needed money so badly. Hell, half the soldiers were almost barefooted.

"Go with Samuel back to the inn, and bring your brothers back. They will serve under Washington, not me, because this is a limited company for riflemen." Daniel turned to Samuel. "Take three extra guns for his brothers, and bring everyone back quickly.

Samuel was annoyed at having to do this. The kid kept up a steady stream of questions, wanting to know about the army and what it was like to kill someone. It was a constant strain watching out for the British. What Samuel would do if he encountered their soldiers was always foremost on his mind. Ki had asked where he was going, and Samuel had lied that he had personal business back home to attend to; he had even added that his father was dying.

When he got to the inn and walked up to the proprietor, he learned that all rooms were occupied. What was offered was a small former storeroom that could be cleaned out and furnished with a pallet. Samuel sighed and nodded assent. He started up the stairs, looking sorrowfully at the door of a room he wanted.

Out came a beautiful woman dressed in a fern brocade gown, the like never before seen on the frontier. Thick, rose gold waves held up her bonnet. Her full amber gaze, framed by expressive dark arched brows and a generous peach mouth, now formed into an O. The light gleamed off the folds of her silk gown, drawn up in the polonaise style. Her off foot hit the floor in a sudden stop. A wave of Muguet de Bois scent wafted over him. The guns suddenly decided to free themselves from the hole in the sack that Samuel carried on his back. They hit the floor with a loud clatter in front of Megan.

"Those look like regimental muskets. Sir?"

Samuel noted her British accent. The way she dressed told him she was not long in America. Upper-class British were incredibly annoying to him. These people who thought he was mud on their boots. He had no use for them at all. What the hell was she doing here?

"They are. You would not enjoy viewing the soldiers from whom I retrieved them." Samuel leaned in toward her face with scorn, making her eyes widened in fear; his breath smelled of smoked meat and whiskey. Abruptly, it was clear to Megan that this Patriot soldier had collected the guns from dead British soldiers. She turned red, offended, and a sense of being threatened emerged in her. She had never been overly patriotic; however, witnessing actual evidence of murdered British soldiers sobered her. She was near the epicenter of rebellion, and it was overwhelming. What the hell was she doing here? Samuel, on the other hand, felt very patriotic to the cause. He was proud of what he was doing. As if having been challenged to justify his presence, he needed to show her the Patriots were in charge of this region. Her eyes riveted on a flash of muscular brown thigh showing above his leggings. Why was he (un)clothed so? Megan quickly stepped aside from the guns and moved down the stairs rapidly without saying another word. The bottom floor of the inn was a tavern where men took their ideas with equal part spirits. Megan saw Mick there.

"What are you doing here still? I thought you would have left." Megan hid her distrust of his motives.

"I have business here," Mick replied in confidential tones, trying to cover his lies. He knew people would be wondering who he was and why he was there and his story of having a farm would not hold water long and he could be looked upon as a spy. Mick was beginning to realize these Patriots made their own rules. He had been trying to devise some plan to kidnap Julia and bring her back to England, but being amid all these Patriots was unnerving. If they found out he was the agent of a British officer, he would be shot instantly. He needed to locate Townset, but he dared not ask questions here.

"Are you lodging here? And why did you lie to us about that so-called farm you have?" Megan hoped he would leave.

"No. Just supping until my business is concluded. I see that Morgan's man is here to trade your sister." Mick avoided her other question.

"Was that the man with the sack of guns over his shoulder?" Megan quickly looked upstairs again; she couldn't believe that it was him. "I heard him say his name is Samuel. Tom brought him in."

Megan could not contain her joy at the thought of being reunited with Julia. "Then I guess I will see my sister soon!"

"That was some trick, keeping that necklace in your bosom." Mick's look was leering, and she backed up suddenly in disgust.

Samuel had come back down from his tiny room and ordered a beer when he noticed their interaction. Megan picked up her skirts and fled upstairs to her room. Samuel collected his beer and went over to Mick.

"Was *that* the Rainsford woman?" Samuel asked.

"It be, indeed. I be the man who brought her party from New York! Mick Hall, sir." Mick was holding out his hand, friendly as the day was long. Samuel took his hand in a firm shake.

"Samuel McKinny. Did *you* see the necklace that will be the ransom payment?" Samuel's close study noted that Mick appeared to be British, of a lower class judging by his speech and clothing.

"I did. It looked authentic. Hard to look on it, when she pulled it out from her corset, Megan did." He moistened his fat lips and looked at Samuel with a lusty stare.

"From where do you hale, man? You sound English." Mick's bonhomie wilted. He looked guilty for some reason.

"I bought a farm west of here with some slaves, and I have business to attend to before I leave." Mick tried to puff out his chest and look essential, but he was failing.

"Tom told me he has never heard of you or your farm with thirty slaves." Samuel looked closely at Mick now.

"I was trying to impress the lady and may have embellished the number of slaves I have." Sweat beaded on Mick's forehead. "I have only three."

"She has a man at large?" Samuel's suspicion of the man grew.

"Wiggins, a little squirrel of a man. He has this twitch that makes his head go up and down." Mick was chipper again.

"I haven't seen him." Samuel scanned the tavern.

"He never leaves his room except to eat. Must be afraid of his own shadow, he must. His room is next to his mistress'."

"I will see the necklace for myself." Samuel drank his tankard down and rose.

When Megan answered his knock, she had just washed her hair and was drying it with a towel. Megan threw a short cut jacket over her semitransparent shift, but it failed to cover a good deal of the vaunted bosom. She began fastening the many fiddly hooks, a flush rising on her neck.

"Yes. What do you want?" She looked embarrassed and a little lost because here stood that overforbidding man.

"I have come from Daniel Morgan," he said officially." My name is Samuel McKinny. I need to see the necklace you propose to trade for your sister to make sure it is real."

"Come in, and leave the door open. I will get my man at large." She edged past him in the doorway. In the next room, she knocked loudly. When Wiggins came, she all but grabbed him by the collar and hauled him into her room.

"Samuel McKinny, this is Mr. Wiggins. He helps me with all my accounts and transactions." Megan was trying to appear as if she knew what she was doing. She went to her bags, found the necklace, and handed it to Samuel. He had seen nothing like this in his short life. Megan noticed his eyes widen for a moment, but then he recovered his composure and started biting on the stones.

"I assure you they are real! I must know the condition of my sister before I give you this." Megan held her head high.

"She is in fine fettle. We found her at an Indian village that we burned. She had run off with an Indian guide named Ki."

The color drained from Megan's face. "Why should she leave her husband to run off with this Indian?"

"You will have to ask her that! She was all dressed up as an Indian when we found her."

Megan was dumbfounded. Her hand sought the bed-post to steady herself.

"Did she look relieved when you found her?" Wiggins finally spoke.

"No, she did not. This old Indian woman she was with clung to her hands. She told the old Indian to tell Ki she loved him and would probably never see him again. But on the day of the exchange, Ki showed up and killed one of the British soldiers. Everybody was fighting mad, and the exchange fell through."

"What happened to Ki?" Megan asked.

"There are very few men who can shoot as Ki can. We need them to defeat you self-righteous British. You think it is cowardly of us to shoot from trees and long distances to kill the commanders. But we don't give a good god-damn what you think! We will continue whether you like it or not." Samuel was getting red in the face, and his Irish accent was coming out. Megan felt he was full of hostility; the English considered the Irish to be lower-class people.

"Well, I mean to accompany you tomorrow. I want to see for myself how well Julia is doing." Megan looked reso-lutely at Samuel.

"That is not a good idea. Too dangerous." Samuel did not want to escort this woman with whom he felt awkward for some strange reason.

"I will do it, sir, whether you like it or not!'" She stopped and continued in a more conciliatory tone, realizing that being pushy probably wouldn't get her any place with this man. "I must see my sister, my last living relative. It has been years since we parted." Megan's sweet face softened. Shyly, she smiled, "Please?" Megan knew from the past what effect she could have on men when she acted the helpless and silly maid.

"Goddamn it! I warned you! So if something happens, it is your fault. There is a lot of danger out there. I won't even start with the many Indians roaming the area." His Irish brogue was evident. Samuel was cursing this job, but Megan stood there with such an imploring look. "Be ready to go first thing in the morning." With that, he stomped out to his little room, then turned around and went downstairs, where he drank three jugs of beer

"Is it safe going with him?" Wiggins was looking worriedly at Megan.

"I will take that risk. You stay here and guard our valuables. I don't like leaving them where someone can come in and just take them." Megan was still reeling from the shock of what her sister had done. Her parents would be so ashamed of them. They had given the girls what they hoped was a good upbringing, taught them to do the right thing and marry the right person. But *why* had Julia left John—for an Indian, for heaven's sake, a savage?

She then thought about her behavior. Her plan for tomorrow would have pushed her parents over the cliff. It was not safe riding sidesaddle in this untamed country, so she would have to omit some petticoats under her dress tomorrow. Maybe *one* would not impede her putting a leg over the pommel. In England, this would have been unthinkable. She would have to take care of mounting so that no one could peek up her dress. She shocked herself with these plans, but what if they ran into trouble and had to run for it? Riding sidesaddle was the superior risk, and one had to prepare for the dangerous environment.

The next day Samuel tried to avert his eyes when Megan mounted. She had requested a regular saddle, and he had given her a boost, shocked when her leg crossed over the pommel. He had rarely seen a woman of her high standards astride, leaving him speechless, so they rode in silence for a good while. The more he thought about it, the more he liked it. She had just pointed her toe and whipped that leg over the saddle, then settled her skirts down quickly and acted like it was nothing. He spurred forward at a fast pace to see if she could keep up and found she had no problem doing so, even when jumping over logs and splashing through creeks. It appeared she was enjoying herself, as if saying, "You want to play, then let's play." Her face flushed with excitement, relishing the challenge that he was giving her. They slowed down, and Megan moved to his side.

"This country is beautiful and untamed and huge. As a soldier, do you have to move constantly?" Megan was trying to be sociable.

"Yes, we are constantly on the move." Samuel did not know how much to tell her, in case she was a spy. For all he knew, she was headed back to Howe for debriefing.

"I am not a spy, in case you were wondering; all I am trying to do is get my sister back so we can return to England." It was as if she had read his mind.

"How can you be sure she will want to go back?" Samuel thought Ki might have more attraction to Julia than Megan understood.

"Why on earth would she want to stay here?"

"You know she chose to run off with the Indian. It looked like she wanted to be with him."

"Surely not, sir. I cannot fathom why she would do that. When she sees me, I will clear this all up. We will go back and live as before, probably with her husband."

Megan discounted the shocking behavior of Julia. She did not doubt that she could make the situation right and they would go on as before. They rode on in silence, with Megan contemplating the future. Then she started to notice plowed fields, indicating they were close to a farm. They came through a forest on the hill, and there stood the New England farm nestled in a rolling valley with giant trees on the sides of the hills. Pastures had been carved out of the valley and on some of the hills. Megan surveyed the white-painted farmhouse, two stories with a vast slanting roof and one enormous chimney in the middle. There were many windows. Megan also saw three small rough wood houses about thirty feet from the main house. She had seen many English farms in her life, but this one took her breath away. It had been hand carved out of the untamed, rugged land. She realized that these people did not have a land baron that they had to bow down to, for this was all theirs, and it was awesome.

"When we get there, you stay mounted, and I will get Julia." Samuel instructed Megan sternly. She nodded, excited to see Julia again.

Close to the house, a black man waited for them. Samuel held up his hand in greeting and told the man why they were there. He also showed the man the pass that all Patriots kept handy. The man held Samuel's horse while he approached the house and went in. Megan sat there, watching the black man, and speculated what his life was like. The man did not attempt to talk to Megan, and she turned her attention to the massive barn with a large *J* on the door. There were horses, cattle, chickens, goats, and pigs. The place looked well cared for and orderly. Megan noticed several black women in the garden, with three small children. Samuel came out with Julia, and she ran joyously to Megan.

"Julia," screamed Megan. Not giving a thought to her hasty dismount, she ran to her sister. Julia wore the modest clothes of a farm wife, unmatched jacket and skirt overstays and chemise covered by a pinafore and fichu, scavenged from Mrs. Jones's trunks and supplemented by her work.

"Megan, thank God you came for me. How could you possibly be here!" The sisters embraced for a long time until Samuel interrupted, for they needed to be on their way.

"You two ride together, and I will stay behind you. We need to hurry." Samuel helped Megan into the saddle, then lifted Julia, who also had to ride astride.

"Whatever made you leave John and run away with an Indian, for heaven's sake? Julia, I was so worried about you!" Julia looked distressed, and they both glanced at Samuel.

"Let's not talk about this right now, Megan; I will tell you everything later. Thank you for putting up the ransom and coming for me. I know it was a huge endeavor for you. I am so grateful. Tell me, how are mother and father doing?" Megan's eyes were downcast for such a long time that Julia became concerned. "Megan, they *are* all right?" Megan's head shook a no. "What happened? Megan?"

Slowly Megan took a deep breath. "Mother got sick and died, and father could not deal with it at all and started drinking even more, and one night..." Tears dripped from Megan's face, and she was having a hard time getting the words out. Samuel noticed tears tracking down Julia's face also.

"How did it happen, Megan? I am so sorry I was not there to help you."

Finally, the words poured out. "Julia, he got drunk and went out of the house at night when I was asleep and—it was freezing out so—he...Wiggins found him in the garden." Megan could not continue and began sobbing into her handkerchief while Julia just listened, in tears. Megan had a hard time controlling the horse and talking, but she was able to keep the horse on the trail. They were going much slower now than Samuel wanted to, compelling him to continually watching out for Indians and soldiers.

"Megan, I am so sorry I was not there. Did mother suffer long?"

"No. She went quickly. That is why father could not adjust to the situation. Mr. Wiggins has been a big help and has even come with me to act as my chaperone." Samuel was thinking that not even rich people could escape problems.

"I would not think that Mr. Wiggins would be the type of man to take on such a task." Julia could not help but feel amazed at the little man.

"Well, I had to encourage him. I even offered double payment." Megan quickly looked at Samuel to see how much of this he was taking in, making Samuel look away, as if not listening. "Julia, how could you run off with a savage, an Indian? For heaven's sake, are you crazy?" Megan berated Julia.

"Megan, Ki is a wonderful man, and I love him. He saved me from John, who is very abusive."

"But Julia, an Indian!" Megan was not mollified, and Samuel could hold his tongue no longer.

"That Indian saved my life!" He studied Megan's reaction. "Yes, Julia is right, Megan. He is a good man, and I believe he would save your sister from her abusive husband." Samuel was speaking boldly, and Julia tried to turn around and catch Samuel's eye.

"Is Ki all right? Where is he?"

"He is in camp with Daniel Morgan. He is doing all right."

"Thank God. I was so worried!" Julia closed her eyes. Megan was shocked at her sister and could not believe Samuel was standing up for this Indian.

"What is his name? Ki?"

"Yes! I will tell you everything when we are alone!" Julia had just run out of patience with her sister, who finally got the hint and shut up. "I would like to see Ki. Would that be possible?" Julia was looking at Samuel, hopefully.

"Not possible; Ki is busy working for Daniel Morgan." Samuel had a stern look on his face.

"When you next see Ki, tell him I am waiting for his return!"

Sisters

J ulia told Megan and Wiggins everything, and John's abuse shocked both of them.

"He impregnated a servant? And then kicked you?" Megan's eyes burned with resentment and anger. "He was planning on killing you? I wonder if that is why he wanted you over here with him. He could get away with it more efficiently over here than in England."

Julia nodded. "I hate him! He killed our baby. Ki had to bury her. Ki took me to his village, where the women helped me because I was failing. Without Ki, I would have died from my injuries and fever. He saved me. John would have killed me, and no one would have stopped him. He is out of control. Megan, I love Ki and owe him my life."

"Franklin came to me and tried to get me to move in with the Townset family after mother and father died. He kept belaboring the indecency of a young woman living alone. I needed to move in with his family so they could take care of everything, Franklin claimed. But he was trying to get his hands on the money. If the butler hadn't announced Mr. Wiggins when he did—let's say he was coming at me closer and closer." Megan had a terrible taste in her mouth as she recalled the situation. "Julia, I always believed you about John! I would never have made you marry him! I tried to tell your father this, but he wouldn't listen to me."

Wiggins was sitting next to Julia and holding her hand. Julia was so happy that she kissed him on the cheek while hugging him and felt a little more normal being around him. "It was a horrible day that we got involved with that family. They are running out of money and hunting for coinage like vultures. I hate John. I will never return to him. I guess Franklin did not know all that happened between John and me."

Megan shook her head no at Julia. "What will we do now, Julia? We have the money to choose what we want." Megan was wide-eyed, looking at both Julia and Wiggins.

"I want to wait for Ki because I am pregnant with his child. Other than that, I don't know what to do."

"Julia, you could never marry someone like that! In England you could not hold your head up. No one there would ever accept you again." Megan's eyes were huge as she tried to talk to her sister in reasonable terms.

Wiggins nodded his agreement. "Julia, think about your future!" His head was beginning to twitch.

"Then I suppose I shall not return to England." Julia held up her chin.

"But what if England prevails? Then what? You could be considered a traitor!" Wiggins was trying to control the twitching.

"Many men oppose England. If *they* win, this will be a new world." Julia stood her ground.

"But to give up England! Julia, I will have to think long and hard on that one." Megan was all but stamping her foot.

"For now, I need to rest." Julia sat upon the bed, and Megan helped her unfasten her dress and settle in bed after Wiggins had left and said he badly needed a drink. The two sisters were sharing a bed and a room.

"I will leave you to sleep for a while. I have paid for a week here at the inn. We can talk about what will happen after you have rested. Wiggins and I have a lot to talk about downstairs."

Julia tenderly grasped Megan's hand. "Not many people would have been as brave as you were, coming across the ocean, my true and loyal sister."

"I had to know you were alive and tell you everything. I could not bear not knowing your fate." Megan kissed her sister's cheek and went down to the tavern to meet Wiggins. Mick was watching from the side of the inn. He knew it was now or never as regarded catching Julia. He had devised a scheme to get into her room.

Wiggins informed Megan that they needed money. "I need to convert more of your jewelry to money. I learned that Washington prints money for the Patriots. So, if we stay here, we must obtain some. Now that Julia is back, what is your plan?" Wiggins's endurance had just about reached its limit. He dearly wanted to be in England.

"I don't have a plan, but I know that Julia does not want to leave here. John mistreated her; he struck and kicked her and planned for her demise." Mortified, Wiggins pressed his hands to his face. "This is why she ran off with the Indian, Ki. She says she loves him. They have a child coming. She waits for him to return from fighting on Washington's side. What are we going to do?"

"Good Lord, this is a nightmare. Megan, I don't know how safe we are staying here." Wiggins lowered his voice. "We are British, and they don't like us. Now that they have the necklace, we are of no further use to the Patriots. Those rough men who apprehended us don't seem to have conveyed your lie about money hidden in New York. Megan, we could be killed—for heaven's sake! It is a wonder we have not been already. It is just a matter of time before they realize we have money in our room." The tic was back, and his head was shaking nervously; it was embarrassing. Megan looked around the tavern to see if anyone was watching. It was then that she saw Mick stealing up the stairs to their rooms. Megan knew he was not lodging up there but rather had the only room downstairs. Something told her to follow him, but she waited to see if he was meeting someone for business or something sexual.

Mick entered the room quietly and pounced on Julia, gagging her to muffle any screams with the pillowcase. He planned on taking her out the window to his waiting horse. Mick would have to drop her from the window, and then he would jump also. He thought it was a good plan and hoped he wouldn't break anything jumping. Then they would have to keep low until they found the Brits somehow. Mick packed his waiting horse with supplies for the journey. He would rape Julia as many times as he wanted along the way. He thought of the rich reward waiting for him when he brought Julia into the waiting arms of her family.

Mick's knee held her face down while he tied her hands and feet behind her. Megan peered through the crack in the doorway, observing this with rising rage. Samuel's room was down the hallway with the looted guns. Megan doubted screaming would work amid the tavern's natural uproar. She ran to Samuel's room, searching for the muskets. By the time Megan found a pistol under loose floorboards, there was no time to check if it was loaded— not that Megan knew how. She ran back to their room as Mick was about to head for the window with Julia.

Megan held out the gun and shouted, "Stop! Villain! Put her down *now*!" Taken by surprise, Mick dropped Julia back on the bed. "Hands up, and come out of the room!" Megan stood around in the hallway in case he tried to grab the gun. "Head for the front door!" she yelled.

Mick cautiously raised his hands with a murderous look on his face. If he failed to gain control of the situation, his plans were doomed. It occurred to him that a knowledge of guns was rare in fine ladies. But Megan had surprised him before, and now she was in a towering rage. He complied.

Meanwhile Samuel sat at the bar with his third jug, regaling his audience with stories of Morgan's riflemen. He could not help but brag about their feats, telling how they used apples on their heads as target practice. The older men were skeptical when Samuel said that no one ever got shot. Suddenly Samuel spied that slimy Brit coming down the stairs with his hands up and Megan pointing one of *his* guns at Mick's back! The din died to a deathly quiet. The spectacle was riveting. Megan wore a furious expression, one that he had never seen on the face of a woman before. His beer was forgotten; he pulled his gun out and followed.

When they reached Mick's horse, Mick turned to challenge Megan. "You don't know how to use that gun, do you? Probably not loaded." He stepped toward her menacingly. Megan's hands began to tremble. She cocked the gun and realized too late she should have done that earlier. Closer and closer Mick approached. Suddenly from the door of the tavern came a deep voice.

"She may not shoot you, but I will! Get on that horse, and ride the hell out of here. Never come back, or I will kill you myself!" Mick peered into the mouth of Samuel's gun barrel and sized him up. He made his decision quickly, mounted, and rode out of sight. Samuel turned to Megan with a lot of questions, but she had headed back into the tavern, where she grabbed Samuel's beer and swallowed the whole thing in one gulp, then ran back out of the inn and threw up. Samuel tried not to laugh. "What the hell were you going to do with him? Have you ever shot a gun in your life? What the hell happened up there?"

"Not now! I have to go up and untie my sister." Megan was retching and spitting. "He has been following us. Mick thinks I have money. I think he may have even followed us from England. That bastard pretended to be someone he is not. He tried to take Julia. I had to stop him." Samuel had never known a woman like her before. She had shown unexpected bravery for a female aristocrat, not to mention she was also beautiful.

"May I have my gun back, please?"

Megan pulled herself together. "I hope you do not mind, but I needed it badly." She was wiping her mouth and did not at all appear to be the flirty high-born woman he had thought her to be. She was a woman who could get serious when she had to, and if he had known what Megan was feeling at that moment, he would have been surprised to find that it was new for her also. With a very sullen expression, Megan handed him back his gun and went upstairs.

Gold Cross

T ownset had to go to the British fort for supplies; he needed guns to be repaired and all the usual necessities. He also wanted to hear the latest gossip and news. He went into the supply room and found the sergeant looking at Julia's cross and necklace. His eyes almost came out of his head.

"Where did you get that?" Townset could not help but grab it.

"Sir, I will need that back! It was payment for many guns and three horses brought here by a Seneca Indian."

"What was his name?" John was screaming into the man's face, and he realized he was out of control, so he stepped back and tried to contain himself.

"I believe his name was Running Wolf; you won't want to turn your back on that one, sir; he looks like he would scalp your hair off without a moment's notice. Now I need that cross and necklace back!"

Slowly Townset handed it back. His throat filled with bile, and hatred overflowed in his heart. He desperately wanted revenge on that bitch. He knew he had to move with caution because of the Seneca siding with the British in this war. They were welcomed here at the British forts because they traded for many goods. He had known it would not be wise to ride into a Seneca village demanding his wife back; that would be suicidal. But that was just what he had wanted desperately to do. The Patriots had her now, and he was surprised that she had not been offered up again for ransom. What was going on?

—

Mick was trying to make his way back to New York City. But having lost his map, he was having trouble. Tired, hungry, and disgruntled, he slept out in the open for fear of more Patriots finding him. He was near giving up on reaching New York City when a British dragoon came upon him and demanded to know his business.

"Thank God you are here. I am on assignment for the brother of John Townset to return his wife to him. I got in trouble with the Patriots and nearly lost my life trying to capture her." Mick showed them the documents with which Franklin had supplied him. "I was assigned to follow the sister of Julia Townset from England. Her name is Megan Rainsford; Megan ransomed her sister from the Patriots."

Although it was common knowledge that Townset's wife had run away with an Indian, they had no idea who he was. The men started arguing over what to do. "I don't believe him. Maybe we should take him to Major General Clinton, under whom Townset serves; Clinton will know what to do with him." The speaker decided to take this decision. They tied his hands in front so he could stay astride his horse. It was a day's journey to Clinton's camp.

Mick was viewed suspiciously upon arrival. General Clinton heard his incredible tale of following Megan and Wiggins from England to America to find out about Julia and possibly capture her.

"Where is Townset? He needs to hear this." Clinton disbelieved Mick's account, but he knew Townset's wife had run away.

Townset was found drilling soldiers in a nearby field. He quickly mounted and rode to camp.

"Your bruver Franklin paid me to tail Megan and Wiggins to America and follo' them to Julia. I did this, pretendin' to be a planter returnin' from England. I even led them from New York to the Patriot's inn outside New York, claimin' I knew the way. I got the directions from a victualer in New York. Patriots seized us. They took us to the inn for the promise Megan would give over a huge diamond necklace to Washington's cause if he would order her sister released. The exchange was completed." Mick had reverted to his old speech.

"Megan is here! And she ransomed Julia with a diamond necklace!" John was dismayed to think of the fortune being frittered away on traitorous females. It was not unexpected that he'd had no notification from Franklin after being at the frontier for so long. (He was still ignorant of his in-laws' deaths.)

"Yes, the Patriots were keeping her at a farmhouse owned by the Joneses. A man named Samuel McKinny took Julia after accepting the necklace from Megan. I tried to sneak Julia out of the inn, but her sister held a gun on me. I was not afraid of her. I knew she did not know how to shoot the damned thing. Then that big Patriot showed up with his gun and forced me to leave." Mick clung to his pride while he talked in his refined speech.

"So, Julia and Megan are at this Patriot's inn, and the place is full of Rebels?" Townset's mind groped for a plan.

"I have heard of the place. It swarms with Rebels. Too risky." Clinton looked seriously at John.

"But I would like to get my wife back, sir!" If he could get both of them, and if their parents ever wanted to see them alive again, then he would be in an excellent position to get most of Rainsford's money in ransom, he rapidly reasoned. "Why did Megan come without her father? Why did Wiggins come?" John asked with rising hope.

"Well, from watching the house in England and tailing her, there ain't any parents."

"There aren't any parents?" John was beside himself. He could see the prize within his hands, if only he could get Julia back. Her sister added that much more to the potential gain. He could control both of them by marrying Megan off to one of his brothers. He would be set for life. If he could escape this confounded war and return to England, he would live like a king.

"That little man with them, Wiggins, would pee his pants if you looked at him wrong. What a joke he is, but he had to act as chaperone for Megan." Mick was laughing.

"I have heard of Wiggins. I met him once. Do you remember where the Jones farmhouse is?" A plan was forming in John's head.

Willie's Tale

J ohn Townset called his five-man party to a halt one-
quarter of a mile from the Jones's farmhouse. They
dismounted when they spotted smoke rising from the
chimney. They hid on top of the hill overlooking the
farm. They could see the slaves working the barn and
garden. The harvest looked to be complete. It was a beautiful place with a two-story house and fertile black soil.
The corral was full of animals: goats, chickens, and pigs.
There were around twenty cows that roamed in the pasture. Mature oak trees spread huge limbs over the natural
green grasses. For a minute John felt envious of America
and its abundant natural resources.

"Make sure your rifles are loaded, pistols too. We are
going in there as a force. Anyone who fails to comply will
be shot. Mick, you are *sure* Megan and Julia are not here?"
John turned to Mick.

"Seemed like they were staying at the inn. No plans
of going anywhere." He had secretly followed Samuel and
Megan some of the way to Julia's rescue before turning
back, finding it difficult to follow and wondering if he
would get lost on the way back. Now he was just thankful
he had not gotten lost on their way to the Jones farm.

"I would like to know how close the Patriots are. We must plan how to get Julia and Megan back here quickly. Once we take over, we will lie in wait for them and kill any Patriots they have with them. Mount up, and let us ride in fast with guns pointed and ready."

John sprang to a horse, the men following, and they rode down hard on the farm. Mr. Jones came running out with his rifle pointed. The redcoats immediately shot him. Mrs. Jones came screaming out of the house after him. She, too, was shot and killed. The servants were frozen in shock, unsure of what to do.

"I come in the name of the king. This house has been harboring Patriots, a capital offense. Stand in line with hands raised, or you will be shot." They fanned out, searching for anyone with a gun. When they were satisfied all stood in the yard, John declared his party would stay and lodge there. Four slaves hauled the bodies of the Joneses away for burial while the women wept. They returned slowly to their usual tasks of housekeeping and food preparation. John got off his horse and motioned his men to follow. He stationed one man in the front of the house and another in the back. As John took Mr. Jones's chair and ordered a whiskey, Mick approached him with a plan.

"More than likely, these slaves are all relatives. We send a black man to the inn to tell Julia she left something, and if the servant blabs at the inn, they never see their relative alive again. Get them to bring Megan too." Mick was smiling broadly.

John spoke to the woman slave crossing the room. "When the woman Julia was here, did she leave anything?"

John assumed a nonthreatening air. She ran up the stairs and quickly came back with a pair of Indian boots. John looked at them in disgust.

"Was she actually wearing this?"

The woman nodded. "When she come, she was dressed like an Injun." The woman was trembling so hard her teeth chattered.

John suppressed anger and shock. How could a high-born woman prefer this mode of dress? Gad, it was a mistake bringing her here! John strove for casualness.

"Do you have an older son here?" Now the woman took fright. "I will not hurt your son; I only want him to deliver a message for me. You have my word that nothing will happen to him if he does not reveal our presence to the Patriots. But if he alerts them, I will kill you both. Bring him to me so I can tell him the message."

Moments later a terrified fourteen-year-old stood in front of John, near tears. He had respected the Joneses. Their deaths saddened him.

"What is your name?" queried John.

"Willie"

"Willie, do you remember a woman named Julia Townset who was staying here?"

"Yassuh"

"Well, we need her to return with her sister, and I want you to help me with that." John spoke in a very calm, low voice so as not to scare the boy. "You need to go to the inn and tell her that she has left some things here."

"What ifn she aks why I din' bring 'em wid' me, suh?"

John considered the question. What would motivate a woman to take a dangerous journey to the scene of her incarceration? He never met one that didn't like fine clothes, except Julia. "What do you think would draw her back?"

"Well, ah ges' ifn Misus Jones need' huh for sompin,' like mehbe Mistuh Jones wus sick."

"Yes, that sounds pretty good, boy. Now for the important part." John took the boy by the shoulders and looked him in his face earnestly. "If you tell anyone that we are here, your mother will be killed, and I will sell you far away. Do you understand?"

"Yassuh." Tears spilled down Willie's face.

"Good. I am glad we understand each other. If you do a good job, you will remain here with your mother, and nothing bad will happen to you." John let go of the boy's shoulders and smiled broadly at him. "Now, get ready to leave." Willie nodded and headed for the kitchen.

What Have I Done?

"A cup of tea would suit so well. Blasted Patriots will not buy the British tea." Megan groused as she searched for Samuel in the tavern where they were eating breakfast. She wanted more practice with a gun before he returned to the Patriots. She also was needing to see him again for her pleasure. Julia was about to speak when a small black boy shyly came up to them.

"Missus Townset, yoah—yoah new dress be finished an' yo' boots-you lef' back at de house, an' ma'am want' a fit you in yoah dress so please come back an' she will make you dinnah—and bring yoah sister!" The boy was so cute, his knees shaking so hard that Megan put her hand on his shoulder to calm him.

"My boots! I left them." Julia realized the fact with dismay. "It is so kind of your mistress to do this, Willie, but I don't think I can go right now. It is not safe to travel, and I have a hard time on a horse right now. Tell her I will come to see her as soon as I can." Julia smiled at the boy as she pointed to her growing belly.

"Maybe Samuel and I can get the boots for you." Megan's gaze was warmhearted.

"I heard my name. Who is the boy here?" Samuel entered the tavern.

"Willie, suh. Mah mistrus wan' see Missus Julia again foah to give huh back huh boots an' fit huh dress." Willie still shook unhappily.

While Julia and Megan made room for Samuel at the table, he gazed curiously at the boy.

"Are you hungry? Do you want some of this food?" Julia was concerned about the boy. Willie looked at the food, and his mouth watered. He had not eaten since the killings.

"Samuel, could *we* get the boots and dress? You could teach me to shoot." Megan's eyes were on Samuel when Willie started to cry.

"*Missus Julia* has t' come quick! The missus needs huh *bad*!" Tears in his eyes, and without another word, Willie ran out of the tavern.

"That was strange." Samuel was watching the boy flee. "I think I will go and find out what is going on over there."

"I really would like to go. I need to learn to shoot. I have been thinking of buying a gun; if we remain here for any length of time, I need to know how to defend myself." Megan said.

"I don't feel good about this at all." Samuel shook his head.

"Please, it will be fun, and there might be a home-cooked meal in it."

"I cannot believe I left the boots. They mean a lot to me. Ki made them for me; I do not want a long ride on a horse right now." Julia studied Samuel.

Samuel took a deep breath and rolled his eyes. When both of them came at him, it was hard to resist. So once again, he said, "Agreed. We'll leave tomorrow, early."

———

Knowing instinctively her sister wanted to be left alone with Samuel, Julia decided to stay and help Wiggins look after their wealth. Now was not the time to be the big sister and lecture Megan on morality. Julia was still amazed that Megan had come all this way for her. Megan chose not to ride sidesaddle; she left her petticoats at the inn and wore an informal dress. After all, she would learn to shoot and was beginning to like not wearing formal clothing.

It was a beautiful autumn day. Birds sang overhead, and leaves fell, and Megan wondered what the winter would be like here in this wild country. Samuel was very quiet and looked around restlessly, as if someone were about to jump out of the bushes.

"Does it snow a lot here?" Megan tried to make conservation with him.

"Yes, it gets freezing and stormy. We will stop here and practice. But mind you, I don't have a lot of ammunition to spare from our campaign." He stopped and helped her dismount. With a businesslike attitude, he demonstrated loading the pistols and set up a target. He showed her how to hold the weapon. He also warned her there would be a kickback. She needed to stand with feet apart and hold the gun with both hands. She pointed it as instructed and fired. Her hand went up, and she took a step back, her ears ringing. She very much enjoyed the look on Samuel's face when he examined the target. She had not hit the bull's-eye but was quite close.

"I can't believe it! You almost hit the bull's-eye!" Samuel smiled broadly at her. "Now let's try it again."

This time Megan steadied herself better and fired again.

"Fancy that; you are a natural at this!" Samuel could not believe it. A lot of men couldn't shoot like this. "I am impressed!" Megan did a curtsy and blushed down to the bosom showing in her low-cut dress. Samuel suddenly wanted to pull her down and kiss her hard. He turned quickly to hide his sexual reaction. Damn, she was great at this. He cleared his voice in a calming manner and said, "We had better get going."

This time, when he helped her on the horse, he breathed in her scent and watched her dress as it gently moved around her legs. They traveled on in good humor and at a leisurely pace. Samuel was more talkative, telling her how he had learned to shoot and the game he would put on the table. He even started to talk about his boyhood in Ireland. After an hour the euphoria left, and the strange reaction of Willie took over his mind. After working with Daniel Morgan, he had developed a sixth sense for trouble. This foreboding had kept them alive on the trail many a time. The hair on the back of his neck was beginning to rise, and he took notice.

"What happened? You were so happy talking about your childhood, and now I cannot get a word out of you." Megan peered at him, head cocked.

"The hair is beginning to stand up on my neck. If there is one thing I have learned, it is to trust this warning. I should not have let you come. I must ask you to hide while I take stock of the farm before we go in." Samuel's transition from a calm, romantic mood to a solemn, thoughtful one alarmed Megan.

"If you think that best, I trust you." Megan watched Samuel with wide eyes.

"I will leave you this gun. Hide in these bushes, and if I have not returned in four hours, then ride back to the inn and bring help." Samuel's expression was so severe that Megan regretted coming. She accepted the pistol, dismounted, and towed her horse into the bushes with her. "I mean to come back for you." With that, he turned and left.

Samuel watched the house from a spot on top of the hill and heard a soft crunching of leaves coming from the left. He pointed his gun to the sound of it. Quietly Willie crept toward him, wearing a distressed look. Samuel could read anxiety in his body language. Willie put a finger to his lips. He whispered in Samuel's ear.

"There be five, one redcoat behin' de barn standin' guard an' two in de barn an' two in de house. De leaduh be called Townset. Dey kilt' de massuh an' missus."

Shocked, Samuel grasped Willie by the shoulders. "You did well. How did you know I was here?"

"I bin waitin' an' prayin', watchin' an' prayin' an' I thought I saw you, sos I come up to warn you."

"Follow behind me, and keep quiet. I will need your help. Can you do this?" Willie's eyes were huge, but he nodded yes. The guard behind the barn was resting on the ground as his head nodded, fighting off sleep. Samuel studied the situation. He attacked from behind, cutting the guard's throat and quietly hiding the body. "Now we have to draw another one out of the barn." Samuel was covered with blood.

"I know how. I tell em dat Townset wan' talk to em."

"So Townset is in the house? Let's hope he hasn't seen us already. Go in there and bring another one out, but be careful." Again Samuel grasped Willie's shoulders to lend him strength. Willie gulped and entered the barn. He saw the men playing cards in the middle of the barn amid quiet animal noise from chickens and pigs.

"Masuh Townset sen' me heuh to fetch one a' you." Willie was shaking again but kept it somewhat under control.

"Which one?" the soldiers did not look up.

"Di'n say."

"All right, I will go." One of the soldiers got up, threw down his cards, headed to the barn door, and closed it behind him. Samuel quickly grabbed the redcoat in a neck hold from behind and slit his throat. But the soldier inside heard the scuffling noise and came running with a shout of warning to the house. Townset came out firing and almost hit Samuel.

"Run! hide!" Samuel pushed Willie out of the way. Samuel ran back to his horse; Townset, Mick, and the other soldier were after him in a heartbeat, firing away. The redcoats got on their horses without saddling them. Samuel managed to shoot the horse out from under one redcoat with his pistol as they were coming upon him. He continued heading toward Megan, fearing she might take a stray shot. He was riding in a zigzag to keep from getting hit. He halted to aim his long rifle and was able to hit Mick squarely in the chest. But Townset's fire finally hit him in turn, and Samuel felt a burning in his arm. Now Townset's gun was emptied, so Samuel rushed forward to unhorse Townset with the butt of his rifle. Townset drew his broad sword from the sheath in readiness for Samuel as Megan Rainsford emerged, gun pointed at Townset's chest. Megan was close to Townset as he pulled up his startled mount and quickly recovered his attention to a trembling Megan. Townset was able to keep Samuel at bay with his sword since Samuel couldn't reload fast enough. Townset's face showed the contempt he felt for the Rainsfords as he came upon Megan.

"You have changed, Megan. I should have known you would seek out your sister. You are now an enemy of the Crown." His face was distorted. "I will warn the British of your defection." With that, he turned to go.

"Shoot!" Samuel yelled as he rode to Megan. "Shoot him now!" But he saw that Megan was terrified and confused and did not have the nerve to shoot him. He was finally able to grab the gun from Megan and fired, but John rode away unharmed.

"I could not. I could not kill." Megan was shaking and could not stand up; she kept falling to the ground. "I never thought I would have to kill my brother-in-law."

"If you are going to hold a gun on a man, then for God's sake, use it!" All patience had left Samuel as he shouted, causing Megan to cry harder.

Samuel rolled his eyes up and prayed to the Lord to help him, then sighed and put his arm around her.

"You are from a more polite world. Now you must adopt this one." Samuel's eyes locked with hers.

"What?" Megan was still shaking.

"If Townset follows through, if you become an enemy of the Crown, I don't think you can go back."

"Go back?"

"Go back to England. You are now their enemy, and the British will imprison you, deprive you of your possessions, kill you." Samuel's insistence was relentless.

"But...England is home. My belongings remain there, at my parent's house. They can't do that!" Tears spilled down her face.

Megan then spied blood dripping from Samuel's wound. "Your arm! My God, you have been hit!" Megan inspected his arm. "Thank God the bullet only grazed you." She tore off part of her dress, not caring that she had lifted it over her knees, showing a fair amount of her leg, and wrapped it around his arm. Samuel tried to hide his surprise as he slugged whiskey from his pocket flask and soaked the bullet hole before Megan wrapped it.

———

"Ma, Ma, we got to hide." Willie grabbed his mother; they ran to the woods and hid for two days. Townset retrieved the surviving redcoat, who had been knocked out when his horse was shot out from under him, and returned to his camp with a tale of being overcome by a horde of Patriots. Five male slaves went with Townset to serve in the army, knowing that they would be free after the war. The rest of the servants ran away when they realized that they had no master. Willie and Mia came out of the woods hungry; not knowing where else to go, they returned to the farm.

When the Joneses were not in church two Sundays in a row, Vicar Turner came to call. Willie and his mother greeted him and recounted what had happened. He called on the local magistrate to come out and evaluate the situation.

"Is there a living relative to be notified?" The magistrate was livid over what had happened. He could not dispute that the Jones were harboring Patriots, which was against the law. "I know they had a son who joined the Patriots, but I think he was killed in the Battle of New York, wasn't he? Does anyone know for sure? Anyone else?"

"None I knows of, suh. We don't hear from Master Lucas in many ah moons; I think he killed, like you say. Jones worried cause they don't hear from him." Willie's mama was looking sad and wiping tears. She knew that the Joneses had been good people. What was to become of her and her son now? Were they to be sold again?

"I will let the place sit for a while to see if someone comes forward with the proof they have a claim to ownership. For now, stay here and take care of the place. Harvest the crops as best you can. We will conduct proper burial and funerals for the Joneses." With that, he left them.

"Mama, wha's gonna becom' of us? The Joneses wus good to us, an' now they gone and we don' know who be comin' heuh. What if dey beats us?"

Mia looked at her son and sighed. She shook her head. "I know 'is bad now, not knowin' what be hap'nen to us, but we got to pray an' hope for de bes."

Enemies of the Crown

One week later a notice was posted: Megan Rainsford and Julia Townset were enemies of England's king. If seen, they were to be arrested and given over to the authorities of the king.

"What are we going to do?" Megan wept quietly as she sat in the tavern with Julia, Samuel, and Wiggins. They were stunned to have had this happen to them, but at least they were deep in Patriot country, where the British would have a hard time coming for them. Samuel remembered this feeling of being an exile from one's realm.

"I did not see this coming, believe me. And I had no idea when I set out that I would never see England again, much less be expelled as a common criminal!" Megan said through tears.

"Welcome to the world of the commoners! You can take the king and stick him up their Loyalist arses." Samuel said.

"Sorry, Samuel. I am not putting on airs; I just did not expect this." Megan looked at Samuel.

Samuel took a deep breath and let out a sigh. "Wiggins, do you think you can go back on your own and sell everything? And what about that money you told the men you had in New York?"

Samuel looked at Megan, but Wiggins answered. "I think that I will be arrested if I go back. The British know I work for Julia and Megan." Wiggins took a deep breath and looked sternly at Samuel. "Megan made up the money in New York." His head twitched.

"Well, we cannot go back with him; that is certain." Julia shook her head.

"I know of someone who could. It would take money… On second thought, sorry I said anything; I should not have spoken." For the first time, Julia and Megan witnessed Samuel turn bright red, suddenly uncomfortable.

He had turned to retreat when Megan caught his arm demanding, "What on earth is wrong with you? Who is it?"

"I should have stayed silent." Samuel tried to free his arm, but Megan gripped harder, trying to draw him back to the table, feeling the stares.

"Who, Samuel? We need help here." Megan was shocked at Samuel's shyness.

"My parents could go with Wiggins and deflect suspicion. But there is one hurdle. They are indentured servants. They have worked most of their term, but not all." Samuel still blushed, and Megan could see for the first time how he felt about being destitute.

"We can pay for their release. I would console myself that Wiggins had locals watching over him. Wiggins, we will dress you as an American so no one will recognize you." Megan was looking at her sister for confirmation of this.

Julia lowered her voice and assumed a tone of confidentiality. "Of course! Samuel, your idea could work!

Megan managed to bring a lot of the family's jewelry, which we can sell. Set this in motion straight away; can you? We must hasten to sell our assets in England. Megan is right, and I would feel calmed knowing Wiggins had friendly companions. Franklin spies for John, but if you act rapidly, John and Franklin might not find out before you sell everything." Julia was whispering to everyone at the table.

Wiggins looked very downcast. "*I* cannot devise another workable plan. But think, after returning your proceeds, I could never see England again. Besides, I have no pass to get into New York."

"You will always have us for a family; we will always take care of you! I guess you will have to leave through the Boston ports. The Patriots have run the British out of Boston. It might be tricky, but you can do it." Both Megan and Julia put their arms around Wiggins, and Samuel rolled his eyes up as he witnessed the surrender of Wiggins to two very imitating women, both of whom showed love for this little man.

"I don't know! This whole thing is so crazy!" Wiggins's head was twitching.

"My father is good with guns, and he will help protect you. They will take care of you," Samuel said, trying to reassure Wiggins.

We Will Always Love You

Wiggins was not happy about going back to England and selling the Rainsfords' estate; it would be difficult and dangerous. He knew the Townsets would demand their share of Julia's estate. He would have to make these arrangements in secrecy before the Townsets knew what was happening. To get back to England, they would have to take an American naval ship to France from Boston, then from there to England. Wiggins was ready to back out because it was much too dangerous. The British ruled the seas, and they could be sent to the bottom of the ocean in an American warship.

On the other hand, it was easy for Samuel to buy the release of his parents from their indentureship. His parents were more than happy to leave with Samuel from the backbreaking work they had to do every day. It took Samuel two weeks to retrieve them from the farm they were working on in Pennsylvania. Molly and Henry McKinny had all the markings of peasants from Ireland with their Irish brogue. It was apparent that Henry would be a good protector of Wiggins because of this size and street knowledge. Henry was around forty-five, and Molly was forty-one, but they looked a lot older because of their stations in life; they were decent, honest, religious, and hardworking.

Luck was with them, and they made an uneventful journey to France, where they rested for two days, then boarded a ship to England. France and England were not at war with each other at the time. Wiggins was unhappy about having to share a room with Henry McKinny aboard the first ship. Samuel's plan of having both parents go had to be modified because Samuel's mother was frail and barely able to walk, which ruled out an intercontinental voyage. When Samuel brought them to the inn, they looked overworked, making Wiggins afraid that Samuel had taken advantage of the ladies' predicament to free his parents.

———

During the first few days on the American warship, tension stiffened Wiggins's and Henry's attitude toward each other. Slowly Henry's good nature and positive outlook began to rub off on Wiggins. Henry tactfully never mentioned Wiggins's affliction; Henry would avert his gaze when the head would twitch. He offered his whiskey cache to Wiggins to calm his nerves. At first Wiggins barely indulged, but then his seasickness abated after a time, and he started taking a few drinks in the evening with Henry. He noticed that after two strong ones, the twitch died down. Thus the men slowly started a friendship that surprised both.

"What is the plan?" Henry was on his third drink.

"We will have to advertise the sale of the estate and try and sell it before the Townsets find out. Otherwise, we will be in court for God knows how long, fighting their claim on Julia's portion. They did not live up to the contract that John Townset signed because of the coverture. We have that on our side. The Townsets will contest under the old law that states that the woman's property at marriage becomes her husband's. Still, Jason Rainsford made Townset sign a coverture agreement that said he had to buy land in Julia's name. He did not do this because he did not have the money, even though he signed the document. Townset said when he came back from America, he would buy the land, so a handshake finalized it. We will have to pretend that we do not know of the handshake. The marriage could be null because of that, but they will demand half of the estate's selling price. This family is desperate for money and will stop at nothing to collect. We have to hope that the Townset family does not know about the enemy-of-the-Crown situation."

"I have a gun." Henry looked seriously at Wiggins.

"I am afraid the law falls on their side. The one thing we do have is the contract that John signed and did not fulfill."

"Where is the contract?"

"Hidden within the house with important papers and the rest of the jewelry."

"Is anyone guarding the house?"

"Yes. I left the butler and some servants there to look after the place. They were told not to let the Townsets come in under any conditions.

"Do you trust these people?"

"They have been with the family for years. They are trustworthy, in my opinion. I intend to pension them off when we sell. I am confident they know we will look after them and not just turn them out into the streets."

"That is what happened to us. I was a footman, and Molly was a maid on a large estate in Ireland. The master gambled it all away, and we were turned out. Samuel was only twelve, his little brother ten. James got sick. We couldn't afford a doctor, so he died in an alley. We were thrown into debtors' prison and sold as indentured servants. Samuel was placed in an orphanage, but he ran away. He found us and followed us to America by working on a ship. He is a good boy, and I love him very much."

A tear rolled down Henry's cheek. Wiggins looked away. He wanted to know what had happened to the body of James but was afraid to ask. "We must, immediately upon arrival, look for buyers for the house in London and the country estate. We will have to show the estate. Also, we must retrieve the jewelry and the contract that John Townset signed. We will need to be believable as professional representatives when dealing with all this. Do you think you can do this?"

"Sure, I can play the gentleman and put on airs. In truth, there *is* one thing."

"What is that?"

"I cannot read."

Becoming American

"Mama, I 'm goin' take these boots to Julia. She is at inn. I will tell her farm be for sale." Willie had a plan, and Mia knew just what he was up to.

"She loved boots. I saw her hold 'em a long time. I will jus' mention the farm be up for sale. If no one proves they owns it."

Mia smiled down at her son. She admired him for trying to take control of the situation. As yet no one had come forth with evidence of ownership. People wanted to claim it but were turned away by the magistrate. Because of the "enemy of the Crown" fliers, Mia surmised that the sisters could no longer return to their country. But that did not mean they wanted to live in America, much less buy a farm that was quickly falling to pieces. She and her son might have run like the other slaves, but they had nowhere to run to. Several had already been caught and sold again. The thought of being captured by the Indians in the woods terrified Mia. She had heard of the gauntlet. She knew she and her son would not overcome it.

"Put Sunday clothes on, son. We only hope they wantin' to take over the farm. Julia be sad the las' time she stay here. Maybe she doan' want to return. But do yoah bes'." She smiled and hugged her only son. She dearly loved Willie and worried about seeing him off on another errand that could get him killed. She packed him a lunch, saddled a horse, and kissed him goodbye.

———

Willie traveled for one hour and entered the inn, where people were eating dinner. He quickly spied Julia eating with Megan. He went up to Julia, holding out the boots.

"Mrs. Julia, I brung you dese boots you lef' at the house."

"Thank you very much, Willie. I love these boots so much; I cannot believe I left them. How are things going at the farm with you and Mia? Please sit down and eat something. John came and almost destroyed the farm! He killed the poor Joneses! You must have been terrified, but you helped Samuel and Megan. I am so grateful for your help!" Julia could tell the boy was nervous. She knew he had gone through a lot. "What is happening now at the farm?"

"Mos' of us run off, but Mama and me come back. The farm be fallin' down because nobody be lookin' after it. The magistrate come and as't if any family be goin' to show up and claim it. We don' know of nobody might, miss. Cu'd you come and live there? Mama and I wu'd love it. We wu'd he'p you anyway you want us to. I even know the fields. I works hard, and Mama cooks good."

Julia sat back and thought hard about what he was saying. They were considered traitors now, thanks to John, and stuck here until the war's outcome was clearer.

Julia did not even want to think of how it would impact her and Megan's future if the British won.

"We cannot stay *here* forever. Megan, what do you think about it? We should consider this carefully, especially now that we have Molly with us. When Wiggins comes back, it would be nice to have a place of our own to settle in. I am pregnant and need a proper place for the baby."

"It seems our American adventure must tear from us our familiar ways in England. We cannot replace the life-style we know. But what if a relative *does* appear to claim it as theirs? Let us not risk our last resources on an uncertain proposition. I agree that we cannot stay at the inn forever. What if we offer to pay only a portion of any harvest—as rent?" Megan startled when Willie jumped up and hugged her; both became embarrassed.

"I'll tell Mama. She gon' be so happy! We bin so worrit about new massahs."

"Willie, if we move there, I don't want to be your master. I don't want to own slaves." Julia mirrored British attitudes of the time.

"But missus, we needs you to be our new mistrus, so's nobody be comin' for to take us."

"Willie, I must first learn *if* I can do this. I don't know that we can. I will try and help you and your mama as best I can." Willie was so happy that he finished his meal and ran to his horse to tell his mother.

———

Samuel returned to Daniel Morgan's army with the cover story of taking care of family problems. Samuel was surprised that Julia and Megan had offered to care for his mother. The women were genuinely charitable in doing so. Now he could go back to the war knowing that his parents were out of the horrible indentureship that was breaking them. He still thought of Megan's farewell; she had offered her hands in thanks for helping them as she walked him to the barn where his horse was packed and ready to leave. They stood gripping each other's hands, the current between them growing more potent by the moment while their eyes burned into each other. Overcome, he pulled her to him, and they kissed as if their lives depended upon it. Nothing but manners finally dictated they halt.

Megan said, "Come back to me, unharmed Samuel. I will pray for you every day! I will protect your mother as best I can."

———

The next day Julia secured a carriage and driver from the inn to bring her to see the local magistrate, Mr. Crowley. He was a very handsome man, and wealthy, to judge by his Georgian colonial mansion. A black servant answered the door as Mrs. Crowley stood in the hallway. Julia noticed that they were each due to give birth at about the same time. She found the ride uncomfortable, so she was grateful to disembark and take tea with the Crowleys. As soon as it was socially acceptable to do so, Julia inquired about the farm. She learned she could rent it with the provision that she would have to leave if a relative showed up. She would be expected to see that it was kept in good working condition. She indicated that she would like to buy the farm if her management proved satisfactory. Mr. Crowley offered Julia hot tea in a jug for the return journey since the weather was inclement, and it could be an hour's journey. Mrs. Crowley rose to see to it, leaving Julia and Mr. Crowley alone.

"I am surprised that you allow me to do this since I am declared an enemy of the Crown."

"I am no friend of the Crown myself. You know you are in Patriot country. I enjoy the money and the power of working for the British, but I no longer respect them."

"I take it you have also heard of the situation my sister and I find ourselves in here." When the magistrate nodded, Julia continued. "I tried to be a good wife, but it became impossible for me to stay with my husband. I left him to save my life. I must provide for myself." Julia was ashamed to say this. Shockingly, Crowley approached and sat on the arm of her chair, holding the contract she needed to sign. Julia suddenly became uncomfortable with his nearness.

"You need not explain. We know that you and your sister cannot return to England. Not to worry—I will not turn you in. Is it not difficult taking on a place like that? I know many servants ran off. His face approached hers. Julia twisted in her seat to meet his eyes while leaning away from him in alarm.

"I lived among the Indians for a while, as you probably know. I shouldered my fair share of the labor. No, I am no stranger to hard work. Now is this the agreement I must sign?" Julia leaned as far as possible away from Crowley. She grabbed, then signed the handwritten agreement, wanting to leave in a hurry. Still, Crowley leaned closer into her. Julia was putting up her hands to stop him when he seized them and slowly kissed her palms while intently watching her face.

"What was it like being with that Indian? Did he do terrible things to you? Tell me!" Suddenly, Julia realized that he thought her promiscuous because she had run away with Ki. She closed her eyes, needing to scream and scratch but also requiring the contract to the farm. Now she was looked upon as a whore by this man and probably the whole community. She should have seen this coming. She had hoped for the best, and it wasn't to be, at least not with Mr. Crowley. Julia abruptly stood up and gave him a stern look.

"Thank you for letting me rent the house. I hope we shall not meet again!" With that, Julia headed for the door as fast as she could.

"Mrs. Townset, you must expect to see me soon, as I will be there to collect rent and see how things are doing." Julia was fleeing when Mrs. Crowley returned. Julia realized that Mrs. Crowley was ignorant of her husband's behavior.

"Are you unwell? You look flustered." Mrs. Crowley showed real concern for Julia.

"Yes. I need to go now, and thank you for the tea." With that, Julia quickly left the house. Getting into the carriage, she saw Crowley watching from the window; he was waving goodbye with a big smile.

A Call to Arms

Daniel Morgan knew that his sniper group would play a critical role in the battle of Saratoga. This win would show the rest of the world that this ragtag army could stand up against the British. But the British had other ideas, hoping that this battle would be the end of the war. Morgan's company went into action at Freeman's Farm, and they led the charge there but had to retreat at day's end. Riflemen climbed into trees and spotted for each other, correcting their fellow's aim left or right. They would target the Indian guides first with their long guns. Next, they went after the commanders, knowing them by the crosses on their uniforms. When that commander was shot dead, they would target the next officer in charge. Soon, the British army was in total disarray without anyone to command them. The Brits would yell, "You cowards! Come out and fight like real men, face to face." But the Rebels fighting method was systematically undoing the British army, and they were becoming more and more terrified.

The Patriots followed the Brits, taking sniper shots along the entire march from Canada to Freeman's Farm. Trees were cut down to block the army from moving their cannon and wagons. Morgan's men trapped the British light infantry in a valley with hills on both sides lined with Patriots firing down on them. The British general, Burgoyne, lost five hundred men, so he withdrew his men to Saratoga and dug in. Burgoyne wanted to retreat, but Morgan's men made it impossible because the snipers covered the roads. Burgoyne sent Hessian Colonel Baum with five hundred men for supplies, and all were captured. The Patriots intercepted every message Burgoyne sent out for help. Because Burgoyne had dug in at Saratoga waiting for help that never came, the Patriots in that time were able to call together an army of eighteen thousand to twenty thousand men.

Samuel and Ki had covered the countryside, calling every able-bodied Patriot to arms, and the Patriots came to fight spectacularly, winning the day. Of the seven thousand British soldiers who left Canada, only thirty-five hundred survived when Burgoyne surrendered. Ki took the scalp of every soldier he killed. The British were stunned, and the French who hated England decided to join the fight on the Patriots' side, offering men, money, and ships. This battle, which was supposed to end the Revolution, was a massive defeat to England.

Samuel and Ki celebrated at Morgan's camp after the surrender of Burgoyne. The men drank heavily, and Samuel encouraged Ki to drink. Pretty soon, Samuel and Ki were drunk, and Samuel started speaking rashly.

"I think I might like to know Megan better. She is one hell of a woman. What she did to save her sister, Julia, took a lot of courage!" Samuel knew he had just made a colossal mistake because suddenly the air froze between the two men, and a drunk Ki stared at Samuel.

"How you know Julia? Where is she! Who is Megan? Have you talked with Julia?" Ki's eyes bored into Samuel.

"Ki, Megan came from England and paid the ransom for Julia. They both are at the Rebel inn outside New York, doing well. I was to retrieve the necklace that Megan used for the ransom, so that is how I got involved with the women. After I attained the necklace, Megan and I got Julia and took her back to the inn from Jones's farmhouse. John, her husband, came for her at Jones's farm. They killed the farmer and his wife. I was able to fight them off, but John got away and had Julia and her sister declared the Crown's enemies. So, they sent their man Wiggins, who was there to chaperone Megan, to England to sell off their property in England. I thought Wiggins would need help, so I talked my father into going with him. Ki, I thought we should tell you, but Morgan said no. He made me promise not to say anything to you. You have become very valuable to the campaign, with your shooting skill, so he wants you to keep fighting with us. Julia told me to tell you that she wants to see you."

Ki's anger at the duplicity of Samuel choked his words; Ki thought they had become friends, comrades in arms. Without the latter having noticed, Ki's knife was in hand at Samuel's throat. Morgan, who had overheard the conversation, went into action, driving his fist into Ki's gut. The blade skittered away, making Ki double over. Ki launched himself at Morgan, and the whole company erupted, all striving to quell Ki and protect their leader from the Indian. Blows fell on Ki until a rifle butt to the head knocked him unconscious. Samuel stood over Ki and yelled, "Stop." Morgan was livid.

"I told you to keep this matter from him! Look what your loose talk has done."

"Sorry. I was drunk. It just came out!"

"He will never trust us again. We can't trust *him* now without dangling Julia as bait. What do you suggest we do now, you unlicked cub?"

"We cannot just leave him! I know of an Indian camp that is close. Maybe they will help him." Samuel felt guilty and feared for Ki.

"Take him. We will break up camp and move. Find us later." With that, Morgan turned away with his hand to his bleeding face. The men helped Samuel load up Ki on the horse, and Samuel took off. He had not gotten far when Ki knocked Samuel off the horse with one blow. Samuel had no choice but to grab Ki's leg and pull him off the horse before he got away. The two men fought until another blow to Ki's head made him dizzy and he doubled over, but not before he kicked Samuel in the balls, and Samuel doubled over as well.

Samuel lashed out with the most hurtful words he could summon. "Julia does *not* miss you. I lied to you! She told us she *never* wants to see you again. She blames *you* for everything she has been through!" With that, Samuel held his gun on Ki and jumped on his horse, throwing Ki's gun far into the bushes. Ki went after the gun to shoot, but five Indians were standing around him, having come out of nowhere.

The Onondaga

K i was again sick from the white man's alcohol. The Onondaga village wanted to know all about the warring whites' plans because the Onondagas had also sent some of their warriors to the British but did not trust them. The Onondagas were part of the Indian Nation and friends of the Seneca, so Ki willingly told them everything. It was getting icy, and the snow was deep. He decided to stay for the winter. He helped with the hunting and even went on raiding parties with them. It felt good to be back doing familiar things and living his old customs. He did not want to go back home to his village and admit to failure. His father would tell him that he should have never trusted the white woman. He would like to talk to Julia to see if she in fact no longer cared for him and hear what she planned to do with the baby. He missed her and thought about her all day and even dreamt about her, especially their lovemaking. He felt lonely, angry at her for forsaking him. He did not know what to do about the whole situation, so he did nothing but hunt, fish, and survive. She was from a different world. He hated to think that she had returned to that world and willingly left him behind. He had not completed his father's bargain with the British; instead, he had stolen a British commander's wife. He felt that he had made a mess of things. His father had held high hopes of him learning British warfare and how to defeat them. Well, he had learned war—from the Patriots, and they also hated Indians. They were killing Indians and burning their villages whenever they had the chance to do so.

The Rainsford Farmhouse

Megan and Julia walked through the farmhouse, marveling at the handcrafted furniture. It was modest compared to what she had in England. The rugs were of scraps, hand-braided, coiled, and stitched together. The curved fireplace in the kitchen was tall enough for a person to walk into, with metal hangers for iron pots. A large table stood in front of the fireplace, with a thick hardwood work surface showing scratches from arduous work. The ceiling had massive crude beams and were low compared to Julia's high ceilings in England. Upstairs were comfortable bedrooms with fireplaces connected to the central flues that ran the entire height of the house. There were four bedrooms, with a large one being the master bedroom. Megan said Julia could have that one because she would need more room with the baby coming. Handwoven bedcovers of subtle colors and scraps of material from dresses and shirts—Julia loved the homemade simplicity of it all. The people who made these things had had to carve out time from their busy days to create what was necessary for everyday use. The dressers and beds were all handmade, with little embellishment. Household linens were of homespun domestic fibers like linen, cotton, and hemp to show sympathy with

Patriot resistance to taxation. These people did not have money for expensive, highly decorative things. They had to make the table and then put dinner on it after plowing the fields for their food. Julia admired them for it. Megan also loved it, and together they roamed the house exploring everything.

The barn was large with stalls for ten horses and in the back was room for cows in the winter. There was a large loft with a ladder where hay was kept and chickens roosted. Stools were set out for milking cows. In the back behind the barn was a pig trough with a large fence around it.

There was a coral on the side of the barn for training horses with a door from the barn leading to it.

Three small houses sat fifty feet from the main house that held the slaves. They were one room buildings with a fireplace. This is where Molly said she wanted to live and when Henry came back they would build onto it for Samuel so he could have his own room.

Mia and Willie demonstrated many skills Julia and Megan needed to be self-sufficient, so every day was a new learning experience for Julia and Megan. Molly grew stronger every day until she was able to sew and make candles with her apprentices. At first, Molly tried to keep her station around Julia and Megan, but her true happy nature soon came out. Julia told all of them that she could pay them for their services, and if they wanted to leave, that would be their choice. Julia opposed the idea of slavery, for she had witnessed a runaway slave being beaten and sold and had been sickened by it. But Julia's main worry was John's return. Even in the Patriot country, he

might risk another attack if he commanded enough soldiers. Even more frightening, it could be a sneak attack at
night. She would need the help of the whole community
to fight them off. So, when the need arose for a larger
church, Julia made a handsome contribution.

Julia thought of Ki every time she got water from the
well. She was sorry for the way they had parted and desperately wanted to make amends. Where was he? Was
he still alive? The Patriots had beaten him badly the last
time she had been able to see him. She wanted to tell
him their baby was growing inside of her and they were
doing well. She was getting bigger every day. When she
went to church in the small community close to the farm,
very judgmental looks of disapproval followed her. She
could read their thoughts of *Where is your husband?* and
Why on earth would you run away with an Indian? Gossip
spread quickly about what she had done. "How could she
leave her husband even if he was a British soldier?" "Why
are you an enemy of the Crown?" Julia was lonely, and the
night was the worst. She wore the boots Ki gave her when
she was at home because they made her feel closer to Ki.

Megan and Julia were learning to milk cows, and
Willie was trying to be patient with them. The women
chuckled at their efforts because they could not seem to
get the hang of it.

"Hey, Julia?" When Julia, seated on a small stool,
turned from the cow she was trying to milk, Megan, who
had finally figured it out, squirted milk into her face.
Willie could not help but heehaw also. "Look at how independent we are! Mama and Papa would never believe it."

Megan laughed so hard her stool tipped over, and everyone laughed while Willie helped her up.

"We are ladies who have adapted, are doing well, and even enjoying it! Well, sometimes. There are times I wish I had a warm bath waiting for me. But I can manage, and I like making my own decisions." Megan had gotten up, and Julia put her arms around her sister's and Willie's shoulders. Megan then put her arm around Willie and Julia, proud of their accomplishments as they were leaving the barn.

At that moment two terrifying men loomed at the barn door. They were huge and wore the uniforms of the Hessian army, with their rifles resting on their shoulders. Julia and Megan both screamed at the same time. Willie wondered how he was going to protect them.

Robby Flanagan

The London house and the country estate were both listed for sale in the *Morning Chronicle* and the *London Advertiser*. Henry and Wiggins notified the staff at each home that for now they could remain but the properties would soon sell. The news distressed them because many had lived there for generations, but pensions to be given out relieved their worries. Franklin Townset stormed angrily in, and the servants were quickly dismissed.

"Just what do you think you are doing? I read about the sale in the papers. My brother is due the lion's share of this sale, and I intend to see that he gets it. You cannot legally do this. The law is on my family's side!"

"John violated his contract to buy land for Julia, which John signed, so Rainsford did not regard the marriage as valid. Rainsford's will viewed Julia as unmarried and thus able to inherit everything as an unmarried woman."

"Rainsford agreed that when John returned to England, he would buy the land." Franklin was so enraged he was spitting.

"Do you even know if John lives?"

"Yes. I got a letter. John and Julia are doing well and expecting a baby." Henry and Wiggins tried to keep their knowledge of what had actually happened from their faces, but Franklin read their body language.

"What has happened? What do you know? Have things happened that I don't know about?" Before Franklin could stop himself, he said, "Has Megan found Julia?"

"How did you know that Megan was looking for her sister?" Wiggins was sure they had never discussed with anyone where they were going or why. Franklin realized he had made a colossal mistake.

"Where is Megan? Why did she not come back?"

"Did you have us followed?" It must have been that man Mick Hall.

"I don't know what you are talking about? Why would I have you followed?"

Wiggins boiled with anger; he decided to give as little information as possible. It was in the sisters' best interests for Franklin not to know that Mick Hall had been killed. "Megan is in New York; she wants to sell everything and stay in New York, along with Julia. That is why we were sent to sell everything. John is busy fighting, and they see little of him. Julia has declared their marriage void because of Rainsford's contract and what was never implemented concerning John's part in that contract—buying land in Julia's name. Julia no longer lives with John because of his not honoring the contract."

"John would never agree to any of this! I believe he knows nothing about this. This whole affair is Megan and Julia trying to make off with the entire family fortune, which is John's, and I intend to see that John gets it." Franklin's face was two inches from Wiggins's, and his hands clutched his shirt collar. Wiggins's tic bobbed his head uncontrollably, causing Henry to step in, his pistol pointed at Franklin's head.

"Get out before I shoot off your head." The Irish twang was strong.

"Who in Hades are you?" Franklin soon recovered from his shock. He let go of Wiggins and stepped back. "You will hear from the authorities soon! And my lawyers!" With that, Franklin exited.

An anxious Wiggins nodded rapidly at Henry. "We must sell now and get out of England fast."

"How shall we do that?" Henry put the pistol away.

"Pray that a buyer emerges posthaste. John agreed that he would buy land in Julia's name as a marriage condition, which he violated. Lord Rainsford only permitted the marriage to proceed because of John's lie about Julia expecting a baby. John promised to buy the land when he returned from America, and Rainsford agreed by a handshake that we will pretend never existed. We know nothing about it. If Rainsford had known for sure that Julia was chaste, he might never have approved the union, or he might have sought an annulment. His will indeed named only Megan and Julia, as if the marriage was invalid in his eyes."

The authorities did show up the next day, along with Franklin, but Wiggins had the will and the contract in hand and showed them. Franklin had not realized that the agreement to buy the land *after* John returned from the war had not been written into the contract.

"John had Rainsford's word that he could wait and buy the land when he got back, but you are not going to honor that word." Wiggins played dumb. "I know nothing about an agreement to wait until John came back from the war." Since it was not written into the contract, it would have to be brought up in the courts.

"You have not heard the last of this!" Franklin left with a murderous in his eyes.

———

Two days later a buyer came along, and the sales were completed. Wiggins and Henry had sold the houses with all the furniture and paintings intact. They really could not take anything but jewelry, valuable papers, and paper currency. Anything else would have been time-consuming, if not impossible, to ship due to war in New York and Boston. In the meantime Franklin paid off the authorities and found a lawyer who was willing to lie. Wiggins and Henry were leaving the house when Franklin showed up with the corrupt officers. This time they had guns.

"You will turn over all monies to us now!" Franklin stood with two armed men and a lawyer.

The lawyer stepped forward and declared, "By law, all proceeds of this sale go to the husband of Julia Townset. The money is his by marriage."

"The buyer will deliver the money tomorrow at nine in the morning. He has bought both houses, so if you want the money, come and collect it then." Wiggins's tic was very noticeable. He held his head steady with difficulty. He was also buying them time to get away with the money.

"How do we know you are telling the truth?"

"You have my word." Wiggins conned like a natural. Henry and Wiggins already had their tickets to sail to the colonies. Luck was with them when they found a slaver ship headed to America, with Irish slaves aboard. The commander was even willing to let them have a room with two beds and meals. They had only returned to the London house to meet the buyer and pack a few belongings. Ready to sail at the break of dawn, Henry and Wiggins hoped to flee at night and board the ship before anyone knew they were gone. Around four in the morning, in complete darkness, they left the house headed to the docks. Henry took the reins of a cabriolet they managed to hire. The Irish slaves in chains, as well as cargo and animals, were lined up to go on board. Henry and Wiggins hid behind a storage house.

"We must delay until the last minute in case Franklin has watchers to stop us. If we get on now, he can also board the ship and have us removed. But if we rush on board just as the ship is casting off, they cannot stop it."

"Good plan, but that means we have to run and jump on board at the last minute! Do you think we can do that?"

"As they are pulling up the gangplank, we will quickly jump on it."

"Good Lord, I hope this works!" Henry was beginning to sweat even though it was moist, chilly weather. At that moment, the ship's horn blew, and men moved forward to pull up the gangplank.

"Run!" shouted Wiggins, and they sprang to the ship.

"Stop in the name of the law!" It was Franklin with a gun pointed at them. He had anticipated something like this, so he had waited at the docks. Wiggins and Henry sprinted for their lives, with Henry making it onto the gangplank. Wiggins fell onto it just as a bullet hit him in the arm, but he did not drop the bag of money. Face-first on the plank, he felt Henry grab him and pull him onto the deck while holding the other bag of coins. Luck was in their favor because the sails were entirely aloft, and the boat moved quickly away from the dock into the crowded ship channel. The men at the plank yelled, "What do you think you are doing?"

"We have tickets!" Henry was pulling Wiggins entirely on board and, at the same time, getting the tickets out of his waistcoat. Blood ran down Wiggins's arm, and he looked faint.

"We overslept and nearly missed the boat." Henry tried to explain their lateness.

"*Halt in the name of the Crown! Turn the ship around.*" This time Franklin's hired men joined him, and they fired again at Wiggins. The fast approaching ship captain ducked out of the way from the bullets, but the ship moved sideways from the wind, and the shots went nowhere. There was no way the massive ship could turn around in the ship channel with all the many different ships everywhere.

"What is the meaning of this?" The captain stood up from his deck and felt several gold coins from Wiggins's pocket plop into his hand. Wiggins believed in the power of the bribe.

"We were late getting on board, and we do offer our apologies. But I assure you we have paid for our tickets, and we have purchased rooms on board." Henry handed the captain their tickets, wiping off the blood on them.

"Well, whoever was after you just lost you. It was in your favor that we have a strong wind this morning heading to America. The authorities will not be able to stop us now. I hope this wind will hold to New York and we will be able to land safely. With the war going on, the British are in complete command of the city. You won't be in any trouble with the authorities there, will you?" The captain's eyebrows raised in severe suspicion.

"I assure you there will be no more trouble from us. Do you have a doctor on board? As you can see, I require one."

"No ship's doctor besides me. I can dig that bullet out. With a tot of whiskey, we can heal you back up." The captain was getting his sense of humor back. He showed Wiggins to his chamber, where he and Henry administered cups of whiskey and excised the bullet. Wiggins fainted, his yells quieting to whimpers beforehand.

Wiggins and Henry found that they had to stand guard with the gun in their room at all times. Everyone on board was interested in their enormous bags, the bags with a lot of money in them. They trusted no one, with good reason; the crew looked questionable. Henry took the first round and sat with the gun while Wiggins slept off his crude and grueling procedure. His arm did not want to stop bleeding. Henry was somewhat worried about it. Six days into the trip, the wound grew worse, with Wiggins developing a high fever, and a ring of redness rose around the cut. Henry did not know much about healing, but he started to think he might be left alone on this journey.

"Henry, I don't think I will make it. This is not getting any better. I feel weaker and weaker." Henry had come back with food for Wiggins. He noticed that Wiggins could barely hold the gun up. Someone could have come in, easily overcome him, and stolen the money. "Henry, we have to look at things frankly. I am dying. You will have to take the money back to the girls that I love so much. They have been like daughters to me. Please promise me that you will complete my task. They will make the best use of this money, and they will take care of you and your wife forever. I know this because I love them as my own children. They are the kindest and most beautiful women, and you won't regret doing this. I should have known I couldn't do this, but I tried." Wiggins's breathing was getting short, and he spoke in spurts.

"You will make it! I will see to it. But I promise you that I will take the money back to them and not rob you. I give you my word as a McKinny. You can count on it. I may be poor, but I am a decent man who was taught to keep his word." Looking down on Wiggins, whom he knew was dying, Henry began to worry about what was to happen when Wiggins died. He couldn't stay awake all night with the gun. What would he do when he went to eat? He couldn't carry the bags of interest with him; the crew was already suspicious. Henry knew people were robbed on these ships all the time.

———

Four days later Wiggins died, and the captain held a short funeral on the deck before they slid his body into the sea. That night Henry brought the bags with him to the dining room. He got many questions, such as "What's in the bags?" and "What do you have in there?" On the first night in the dining room, Henry noticed shackled men led in for food. From experience, he knew that they were debtors, to be sold into indentureship. Henry was in luck that they were Irish and not black men. Black men cost a lot more than Irish, and there were no laws regarding the Irish servants. You could beat them and even kill them without repercussions of the law. It would put one back financially if you killed a black slave, but not so an Irish servant, and many were small children. Henry knew many of them had been kidnapped or forcibly taken from Ireland.

He saw a frightened fourteen-year-old. His eyes scanned the room regularly, as if a ghost would appear any minute. Red-haired and blue-eyed, he was big for his age. A beard was beginning to emerge on his cheeks, though not much of one. Henry sat next to him in the dining room on the day Wiggins had died.

"What is your name?" Henry was friendly.

"Robby Flanagan." Robby turned his attention to the fish stew.

"Why are you shackled?" Henry was trying to be pleasant and maybe somewhat fatherly.

"I stole bread for my family. They were starving, and I had to do something to help." There was bitterness in his voice.

"I know how that feels. I was in your place eight years ago. My wife and I were in debtors' prison and sold into indentured servitude and brought to America from Ireland."

"How did you get out?" Robby was curious now.

"A very kind lady bought our servitude. If you are a decent fellow and honest, I could buy yours also." For the first time in months, there was hope in Robby's eyes. He had been living in hell for months, and he had thought his life was over. "You will have to show complete loyalty to my lady, who will buy your service, and me. If you run away or rob me, then my fierce Brit-hating Patriot son will hunt you down and kill you, and I will help him do it. Running away in America is perilous because wild Indians, bears, panthers, or accidents will get you if you run into the woods. If they don't, my son and I will. There are British soldiers everywhere, and they do not like the Irish. They would just as soon shoot you as look at you. So, what do you think? Are you with me or not?" Henry was whispering and looking around as he spoke, trying not to let anyone else hear him.

Robby's eyes had gotten huge when Henry started to tell him what would happen if he ran away or robbed Henry.

"I will accept your good deal, and I will not rob or run away from you." Robby tried to shake Henry's hand, but the shackles allowed little movement. That night Henry purchased Robby Flanagan for seven years. Henry brought Robby into their small room and instructed him on how the gun worked. Robby was a fast learner, and since the place was so tiny, with only two beds and a port window, Henry thought he couldn't miss if someone tried to break in. At first, Henry slept with one eye open to see if he could trust Robby. Then, after about a week, he felt he could.

———

Finally, the voyage ended, and they landed in New York. They learned from drinking men in New York City while sitting in a tavern that the King's Gate had become very corrupt. Henry realized that all you had to do was bribe the guards at the entrance to let you out of New York City, and this was the only way out. Henry was terrified that they would be caught, so he almost peed himself during the transaction while handing over a large solid gold coin. Robby couldn't believe how many British soldiers there were in New York; one could feel the tension of British martial law. The unhappiness of the people and the total lack of food and shelter among the poor were apparent everywhere. They needed horses, and they found a desperate man with two horses and a wagon for sale in the alley of a tavern. They bought corn from a farmer who had just come through the gate for the army. They paid him more than what he would have been paid by the British for the corn, which they piled onto the bags of money to conceal them. When the soldiers inspected the wagon at King's Bridge, they only saw corn and the solid gold coin Henry gave them. They left the city in the dark of night, they hid from the soldiers outside of New York City behind buildings and trees, and with pure luck, they make it home, exhausted. There was much trepidation the entire time, and they were always looking over their shoulders. Robby knew if he was caught, he would be sold again to God knows whom. Henry knew they could be robbed then killed on the spot.

Hessian

Herman Mees and Fredrick Schumer stood before Julia and Megan with the terrified Willie interposing himself. They could see that Willie was trying to be brave and protect the women, so the men quickly put down their guns in peace to let everyone know that there was no danger from them. In broken English and with a hefty German accent, Herman stepped up to the women.

"Wir do no harm, please be not frighted. Wir search werk. Mr. Crowley sen hier. We need werk. You help us?" Julia and Megan were looking very confused.

"You are Hessian soldiers! What on earth are you doing here? You work for the British. Should you not be fighting beside them, rather than here in Patriot country?" Julia thought they could be spies sent on behalf of the British.

"No, we leave army. Washington give near farm land, two pigs und ein cow. Wann Patriots win, wir bekommen citizen." Both men were smiling proudly.

"If you left the British and Hessian army, then you should be fighting with the Patriots right now, not looking for work." Julia knew that the Hessians were a ruthless mercenary group of soldiers sent here by Germany's royalty to increase their country's wealth. They were hired by the British to increase their ranks in America; they were soldiers for hire. So what were they doing here? Herman stepped cautiously up to Julia and showed her the proof the Patriots had given them land. This was land that the Patriots hoped to win with the war, so it was not yet theirs. But it made sense to offer them land to stop them from fighting the Patriots. These men were peasants with no other employment means, so the German authorities used them for their gain. The money made from these arrangements was not given to the soldiers but rather the German royalty.

"Too much fight, fight und no money. Hier gut soil, trees fur haus und fur fier. Zu heim, no money for food, no wood im winter und family freeze. Stay hier wir." Both men nodded their heads in agreement.

"Well, I think you should be fighting with the Patriots right now to make sure that they win." Julia still did not trust them.

"Fredrick leg shoot und mein foot freeze." Herman indicated his bandaged foot. Fredrick wore a huge bandage stained with blood on his leg.

"Wir konnen werk! Wir arms streng. Du wilt see. Wounds better soon. Chop wood und plant und make house wir. Herman kanne—" Fredrick looked confused, trying to recall the correct word, "How du call? Forge smith?" Megan and Julia caught their breath, for a blacksmith could fix many of their problems around the farm. Megan turned to Julia, and so did Willie.

They spoke simultaneously. "We desperately need the help, Julia." Willie was nodding his head as well. They indeed needed help badly. If they knew blacksmithing, it would be wonderful for the community also.

"Sleep in barn wir. Wan no werk du, go werk unser farms, build haus. Gebring wir unser families hier zu leben. Du wilt see. Gut people. Gottly people. Do gut hier, nicht hurt anyone.

"You will bring your families here from Germany?" Megan was speaking up now.

"Yes, gut people sie sind, du wilt see!

"You say Crowley sent you?" The men nodded. "Well, you don't have to sleep in the barn. There are slave houses that you may have. They were abandoned when the slaves ran off. I can't pay you much, but I do need the help. I will check your story with Mr. Crowley to see that you are telling me the truth. On Saturday you may work on building your new houses and your land. Sundays are for the Lord and rest around here." Julia thought of all the things that needed to be done, and despite the worry her new responsibilities brought, she felt a growing sense of accomplishment and control over her fate and the management of the farm.

Ki Comes Back

Some of the Onondaga had gone trading in the white man's community. They were looking for iron pots and—if they were lucky—guns. They were trading with pelts and seed corn, squash, and beans that they excelled at growing. They also were listening for gossip: Who was moving into the area? Would they be friendly or, like so many of the white men, not?

They heard that a new Englishwoman and her sister had taken over an extensive farm; she had left her British husband. The community feared he would find her and bring soldiers, meaning trouble for this Patriot community. The Indians also did not want trouble from the British. They brought this news back to the village, where Ki heard it. Could this have been Julia? Samuel had told him that she did not want to see him again. Was it true? He desperately wanted to see her once more.

Braving the foul weather, Ki went to see if this was Julia. He knew she was pregnant with their child. Would she want to see him, or be rid of him? He had to know. He thought that if she did not want their child, he would take it and return to his tribe and raise the child himself.

Henry had returned with Robby in the middle of the night. The news of Wiggins's death devastated Julia and Megan. He had served them quite selflessly, and guilt overwhelmed both women. He had hated their whole venture but acquiesced out of loyalty to their family. By the grace of God, Henry had returned unharmed with their inheritance. Henry retold his promise to Wiggins on the boat; when a McKinny gave his word, he never broke it. He would get the money to the girls as best as he could. For their part the sisters gratefully accepted Robby Flannagan's help. He could work off his indenture by laboring on the farm, especially at planting and harvesting time, and would receive a small wage if the farm did well. It was decided that Henry would build an extra room onto the little house for Robby.

"I thought our dear Wiggins would be buried alongside us, not in the ocean." Tears marred Megan's face. She longed to beg his forgiveness and console him with gentle pats. They would don black for two months. Franklin's actions were typical of both brothers. He would get word to John, and then John would come looking for them.

"We need loaded guns ready at all times. We must expect him to come." Henry was looking at the Germans sitting around the large table in the kitchen, wondering if they would help. They lived in the small house next to his and seemed to be good men that stayed to themselves. Henry was glad for the help with heavy lifting around the farm.

"We defend your farm. We kee our guns with alway." Herman Mees responded to Henry's gaze.

"When John finds out he did not get his money, he will be primed for bloodshed. He will have the Crown's authority and the British army behind him."

———

Crowley appeared late one evening seeking the rent, making Julia reluctant to invite him in. They stood on the porch as Ki spied them from the forest, so he waited to see what would happen, not knowing if Julia even wanted to see him. It had taken him three days to get there, and he had just come upon the house when he viewed Crowley on the porch. Ki did not know what kind of reception he would get; he wanted to wait and watch the place before going to the door. At that point he viewed Crowley leaning on one arm next to Julia's head as he talked with his face closing in on hers, as if whispering something for her ears only. It looked like the two were very familiar with each other. Who was the man? But there was Julia! Ki wanted to call out to her.

"I will come for the rent every month. If possible, I want to see how well you are keeping up the farm." The lust in his eyes was forceful and intense. "Julia, I want you. It excites me that you are far along in your pregnancy. I know that if you could let an Indian touch you, I won't be so bad." Crowley pinned Julia to the wall with his body. She panicked, hitting at him with her fists. Ki rushed forward, but two large men with guns appeared from one of the smaller houses.

"Frau Townset, you need help?" Herman Mees and Fredrick Schumer had their pointed guns in their hands.

Crowley recoiled in fear of the men, and then fierce indignation filled him.

"I found you work here," Crowley said in accusation, but they stood their ground with stony faces. It dawned on him that they were now loyal to Julia, and he was a threat. Crowley quickly jumped on his horse and rode off. The two Germans nodded their heads at Julia and went back into their small house, but not before Ki had turned around in despair. She had moved on without him; she had others looking out for her. They were possibly guards who would shoot any unwelcome stranger. He did not notice the boots she was wearing, the beloved boots that kept her close to Ki.

Julia stood there on the porch for a moment longer with a feeling of happiness that she could not understand. She had just fought off Crowley and should have been upset, but suddenly she had a sense of great joy. Instinctively Julia looked into the forest around the house. For a moment she had the feeling of Ki close by, but then the mood left, and she sadly walked into the house.

———

Ki went back to the Indian village, feeling even more dejected now that he knew Samuel was right. She probably hated him. Julia might have regretted going to his people and probably lamented the child she was carrying. Would she give the child away in shame? He went straight to the hut of the prostitutes in the village. Most of them were captives from other tribes, and they knew what he wanted; they began to remove his clothing. As one took him in her mouth, another gave him a pipe with special herbs. The herbs made him forget for a little while; he closed his eyes and let their hands wander over his body as they slowly lowered him to the skins.

———

Julia's water broke that night, and she was terrified. She wanted her mother beside her, but she had Molly, Mia, and Megan. Molly and Mia knew about birthing a baby; consequently, they set about the necessary tasks while calming down their mistress. They were gathering linens and setting water to boil as Megan tried her best to settle Julia's fears. Julia's anxiety appeared to be magnified by her situation in America.

"Why did I come to America? I should have stayed in England. Why did I marry John? I should have stood up to my mother and father and refused to marry him. Why did I run off with Ki? He has not come back for me and probably has a new woman." Julia had to stop while a massive contraction overtook her body. She was breathing intensely, rocking back and forth in the bed. "I know he has gone back to his village and forgotten about me. I was a fool, and everyone is laughing at me. John will come back and kill the baby and me." Julia was panting with sweat pouring down her face while another contraction overtook her.

"Julia! Don't talk like this! It is not helping. You don't know what has happened to Ki. Please, concentrate on having a healthy baby and stop worrying!" Megan was beside herself. She, too, wanted her mother right now.

This was not at all what she had imagined for herself and Julia. They were in a foreign country with no relatives or doctors. The two women clung to each other while the contractions got worse, and Julia thought she would die. Suddenly her body started pushing down, and Julia felt the baby tearing through her.

"Push." Both Molly and Mia urged Julia on while sweat covered Julia's entire body. Her hair was matted, and she felt the end of the world was coming to take her.

That is when she screamed with despair and terror, "Ki!"

———

Ki, falling into a deep and satisfying sleep after experiencing sexual released, started dreaming. He and Julia had just finished making love at their house in the village. She was looking at him, tenderly, with her hair about her face from their lovemaking. He was feeling happier than he had ever been in his life when he vividly saw Julia's face change into a mask of terror, and she screamed his name. His eyes tore open, and he listened intently. The women were all asleep, and some were even snoring. He tried to shake his head to remove the drugs' effects, but the scream still echoed in his head. He listened for the dogs, who certainly would have heard it also. All were incredibly quiet; he felt compelled to hurry to Julia; she needed him right at that very moment. He got up and quietly put his clothes back on, gathering his belongings. He took a horse with him; all he knew was that he had heard her calling for him.

Yuma Predicted It

S ally was thinking about Julia and wondering what had happened. She knew Ki had gone after Julia, but no one had heard from either one. It had been strange living in the Indian village, but Sally was getting used to it. Ben adapted better than Sally and had even become a warrior. He loved the Indian way of life. Both of them had a hard time seeing a captive brought in and made to go through the gauntlet. Ben got along with everyone but was challenged by Running Wolf several times to prove his prowess. Running Wolf seemed to be jealous of the physical size and ability that Ben had acquired. Ben had grown a foot since coming to the village and towered over the other Indians. His body had developed into that of mighty warrior that made many jealous and cautious about ever challenging him.

Sally knew what hard work was, so the labor did not bother her. It was nice living with people that did not see her as inferior. She did miss the small house that she and Ben lived in, but when she thought of the house, all she could see was John raping her. Kucma was getting bigger every day. He had chocolate skin and medium-brown curly hair. He was going to be a big boy that would probably tower over the other children. Sally was happy he would have an advantage in the village, where height and weight made a difference. She brought him into the fields with her when she worked. She was coming out of the longhouse when she saw Keme; Sally had learned the language fairly well and rarely spoke English.

"Keme, have you heard anything about Ki?" Sally saw the concern on Keme's face as she spoke in the Seneca language.

"No. I am worried. No one has heard anything, and it has been many moons since Kitchi left us. I want to know about my son; Julia should be having her baby now. I will talk with Yuma and see what he has to say."

It was two nights later that Keme approached Yuma and asked about Kitchi. Yuma was also worried, but he let his worry come out as anger.

"He should never have brought that white woman here. I told him it was trouble. I told him not to go after her and to forget her, but no, he ran off, and now we know nothing!" Keme knew Yuma's ways. When he got mad, he was troubled.

"Maybe we should look for him?" Keme asked very cautiously, knowing her husband would probably say no. "I think maybe Sally would want to come, and Ben will also help if we need him. They can speak the language and ask in places we cannot. I know we will have to be very careful around the white men."

"There is a war that I should never have let my son take part in. I regret it, and I miss him. We will leave in two days; tell Sally and Ben to come with us." Keme sighed in relief. She ran to tell Sally and Ben to get ready, and of course, they would have to take the baby and maybe an extra cradleboard for Julia and their new grand-baby. Keme loved the thought of Julia coming back even though she knew it would anger Yuma. She wanted to see her grandbaby.

———

John had just finished a raid on a Patriot camp that had not gone well. They fought like devils, and the damned Rebel resistance of the area came out of their houses and farms to help the Rebel army! An armed society was a huge problem; they would send out a runner who would alert the farmers, women, ministers, doctors, slaves, youths, and indentured servants of the countryside to the call to arms. Most of the places in the world the British had taken over were unarmed. Every one of these fucking colonists, even the young ones, had a gun and knew how to use it. They would not face you but hide in trees, espe-cially in a forest, then let loose with all their gunpower. John could see the fear beginning to appear on his sol-diers' faces when they went into the forested countryside.

John was already upset by Franklin's letter about Wiggins taking off with all of his money. Several letters had not reached John because of one thing or another. In one letter Franklin explained Rainsford's death and that he had sent Mick Hall to tail Megan, which John already knew. Well, John needed to get control of this situation quickly. He would find Julia and see that she suffered for what she had put him through. Then he would send Julia and Megan to Franklin, on the next boat back to England. No one would expect anything different from him, and John was entirely within his rights, even given the fact that Megan was unmarried. He was walking back to the small church he used for an office when a black man on a horse came to him with a message. It was from a Mr. Crowley, who had just rented a farm to a woman who called herself Julia Townset. She wanted to buy the place but did not have her husband's permission. John nearly exploded when he read the note.

Jason

J ulia had just given birth to a son whom she could not stop fussing over. He looked just like Ki, with very blue and beautiful eyes. He was very demanding when he was hungry, which was all the time. Julia sat in bed and fed him from her breasts while learning how to diaper him properly. Molly was busy making clothes and blankets for him while Mia measured out sackcloth for diapers. Herman was making a rocking chair out of oak. Even though these were uncertain times for Julia, she felt happy and content now that the baby was there. Robby heated water for her bath and lugged pails of it up the stairs. Best of all motherhood was just coming naturally to her.

"What are you going to name him?" Megan was sitting on the bed, trying to learn how to diaper the baby for the first time.

"Jason, after father. I only hope he would approve. I know he is looking down from heaven and shaking his head, with mother at his side."

"Father and mother would be appalled with the way John treated you."

"Do you think they would be appalled, or would they tell me to stay with him and hope that things would change for the best?

"Father would be furious with John. It doesn't matter; we can't go back now. We are here to stay whether we like it or not."

"Megan, I am so sorry that I got you involved with all this. You could be in England right now, happily coming out in society."

"Julia, we will have to make the best of this situation. It will be interesting if the Patriots win. Can you imagine a country without a king? It will be a new era, and we will be a part of it all. I miss all the comforts afforded by servants, but I also like being independent and making my own decisions without asking permission for everything. We will be in control of our destiny, and that is a power we would never have known in England."

"I want to thank all of you for being so patient with me during my labor. I know I was difficult to be with." Julia was looking at all three women. "I don't know what I would have done without all of you. You have been so kind, taking care of the baby and me, making these beautiful things for Jason. I want you to know I am grateful for everything." Suddenly Julia's eyes filled unaccountably. Molly came over, chuckling, as Julia looked on, perplexed and weepy.

"You will cry easily for a while. Then it will stop. It happens after you have a baby. This is what women go through." Mia nodded in agreement. Julia gazed at them both, realizing again how fortunate she was to have these women in her life.

I Know Where You Can Shoot Him

Ben stepped into the Patriot inn to inquire about Julia Townset. He was trying to blend in with the crowd there, but he was getting curious stares, and some were all-out hostile. He began to notice the men whispering among themselves, all the while keeping their eyes on him. They all had their guns close by and ready to use. Ben made up a story about being a former slave of Julia to allay suspicion. He heard she had rented a farmhouse close to the inn. Ben told a story of being captured by the Indians, and now he wanted to unite with his former owner. They reluctantly told him where Julia lived. Ben went back to where Yuma, Keme, Sally, and Kucma were camping in the cold, careful not to alert any Patriots to their location.

———

Willie woke up with a start. Every hair was standing up; he had learned that this was his body telling him trouble was coming and to take cover. Ever since John Townset had gunned down the Joneses, he had learned to sleep with one eye open. He looked over at his mother, sleeping soundly on her bed in their tiny house. The fire had burned low when he heard the horses and other animals in the barn making warning noises. Someone was coming, but it was the middle of the night. Should he wake his mother? He got up and went to the door. He saw lights coming down from the hills behind the house. Mia suddenly sat up.

"What is wrong, Wille?" Then she, too, heard it and sat up quickly. "Willie, get away from the door!" Before they could shut the door, men came riding in hard. Willie recognized John Townset in his uniform, with thirty soldiers.

John shouted from his horse. "Everyone, come out with your hands up!" They all had their guns out, ready to shoot anyone who even tried to disobey them. Herman opened the door to their small house with his gun in hand but quickly dropped it and put up his hands. Fredrick came out behind Herman, also with his hands up. Willie noticed that Townset and the soldiers were all looking at either the main house or the Germans. They had taken their eyes off of Willie, whom they didn't feel was a threat at that moment, so Willie quickly ducked back into the house, glad that John had not recognized him.

"Mama keps lookin at the soldiers and don't say nothin; I going to sneak out the back window and go for help," Willie whispered to Mia, who was trying to shake her head no without looking at her son, but it was too late. Willie was already opening the window and quietly jumping out when Willie heard the main house door open.

"John, what are you doing?" Julia had only a night-gown and robe on when she recognized his voice and stood at the door. Her hell had come about; he was here and would probably kill her and the baby. Willie could tell from her voice that she was terrified and not at all happy to see her husband. Willie heard the baby crying and thought of the fact that Julia was carrying Ki's baby in her arms.

Yuma and Keme told Sally and Ben that they would wait until the morning before approaching the house to wake Julia—and maybe Ki? Their plan changed upon cresting a hill that overlooked the place. They had no warning of the nightmare they were about to enter. Yuma recognized John Townset and remembered what Ki had told him about John beating Julia. Yuma knew that he would not be happy about Ki stealing his wife, for even in the Indian world, this was a crime. But Yuma was a warrior, and he needed to know where his son was, and he prayed that Ki still lived. Ben saw that the place swarmed with soldiers and wanted nothing to do with it.

"We cannot go in there! It is not safe!" Ben locked eyes with Yuma and clutched Sally's arm to make sure that she did not move.

"No! I need to know where my son is!" Yuma sternly returned Ben's gaze. "If you want to stay here, I will go." Yuma started down the hill with Keme following; she would die with him if he were to die. Yuma rode in, holding his spear straight up to the sky in a sign of peace.

Yuma kept his back straight and head up, looking at John the entire time, drawing John's attention from Julia.

Julia could not believe her eyes! First, John had come in the middle of the night with thirty soldiers, then Yuma and Keme.

"Don't shoot! They are friendlies. They presume to be on our side," John said with thick sarcasm while glaring at Yuma. He spat. "What in the hell do you want?"

Yuma was not afraid. "Where my son?" Yuma spoke forcefully, dismounting to face John.

John scoffed in derision. "Well, isn't that rich! Your damned son runs away with *my wife*, and now you ask *me* where he is?" Red suffused John's face; Julia had never seen him more enraged. Megan pressed her hand to her mouth to keep it from trembling while standing behind Julia. Molly and Henry had come out with their hands up, but Robby was not with them, Julia noticed. The soldiers were tying up the Germans. One soldier held a gun to Mia, and more soldiers climbed up the steps, putting their weapons to Julia and Megan. When the soldiers reached the porch, two of them ran into the house to search out anyone hiding there. Other soldiers were going through the small homes to make sure no one was hiding there either. John knew he appeared out of control to his soldiers and that he should work to be more professional, but at this point, he did not care anymore. His wife had made a fool of him, and he was bent on revenge, so he would make an example of Julia and demonstrate the penalty for a wife who disobeyed her husband.

Unobserved, Robby had also climbed out the back window of their small house; he met Willie, and they both ran for the woods. They had not run far when Ben came out from the trees and held up his hand in peace, his other hand to his lips, indicating that they should be quiet.

"We have come with the Seneca chief, who is Ki's father. I saw an army of Patriots camped about five miles from here. One of you go north and alert them. I will go to the inn and warn the Patriots there and ask for help. Robby sped off in the direction Ben pointed.

"Will you stay with my sister and make sure that she does not get near that son of a bitch?" Ben indicated John. Willie nodded. "Whatever you do, don't let him know that she is here. If the soldiers come close, run as far as you can. Sally, keep Kucma quiet!" With that, Ben sprinted in the direction of the inn.

On the front porch, tiny Jason's whimper turned to a bawl. John's attention swiveled back to Julia and the baby. He swaggered up to the bundle and saw a small Ki in her arms, and his restraint immediately fell away. John's arm swung out and knocked the baby from Julia's arms, high in the air off the porch. Yuma sprang forward to catch the baby in midair while Jason screamed in terror.

"My baby!" Julia involuntarily thrust herself forward, but John grabbed her hair and dragged her back to him.

"No you don't, whore," John said in Julia's ear. He turned to Yuma. "Get the fuck out of here, and take your bastard grandchild with you!" There was hesitation from Yuma as he stared at John in complete disdain. Yuma handed the baby to Keme, and she put Jason in the cradleboard attached to her horse. Yuma remounted with dignity and left with Keme following. Yuma and Keme returned for Ben and Sally but were not surprised that they were not there. Yuma assumed they were hiding from the British and would catch up when it was safe because Yuma knew that Sally's baby was John's. Keme could hear Julia wailing for her baby and felt sorry for her, but nothing could be done. The cradleboard fit on the horse's neck, and she could bend down and quiet him with her hands or pick him up if needed. Keme had hoped to bring both Julia and the baby back to the village with them. She worried that they still did not know where Ki was.

Willie and Sally moved to the back of the farmhouse, thinking it would be safer there. They watched in horror as the soldiers took control of everything.

"There is Ki," Sally said quietly to Willie, seeing Ki coming down from the hilltop.

Ki, meanwhile, was watching from the hillside, observing the British; he had just missed his parents. He saw the Germans tied up and everyone with their hands up, but above all Ki noticed Julia with John. After hearing her scream his name in the dream, he came back to Julia and knew she needed him now more than ever.

Willie quietly spoke to Sally. "I will go to him to see if he can help." With that, Willie made his way to Ki.

"Be very careful!" Sally warned.

"Who is Henry?" John demanded of the captives, still holding Julia by the hair. For a moment, all stayed silent until John spat out, "I will start killing people if he doesn't come forth." With that, John grabbed Megan and tore her dress open, "Men? who wants to savor some juicy noble flesh?" His men yelled their assent. Henry came forward, and the men seized him.

"Take him to the barn and beat him until he tells you where the money is; he knows. He was the one who stole from me. Start cutting off his limbs if he won't talk." John released Megan and pushed her to one of the soldiers. "Do what you want to her." The soldier dragged Megan off to the barn. John still had Julia by the hair. "I can do what I want with you now, you bitch. You will tell me where the money is, and I will have fun getting it out of you; now tell me where your bed is!" John was spitting into Julia's ear. Molly was crying hysterically along with Mia.

———

Robby had found the Patriot's camp by smelling the wood fire. He was apprehended long before he got to the campsite, and the scout brought him to Daniel Morgan.

"This here kid says that about thirty British soldiers are holding up a house close by, and they need help. He says one of the British leaders is married to the woman who stays there. Both women have given money to the Patriots before, and they need our help," Daniel spoke with trepidation.

Robby stood there, trying to look brave. Samuel overheard with great apprehension that what he feared most had happened—John had returned.

"We must help them!" Samuel looked straight into Daniel's face. "Have pity! My parents are there, along with Julia and Megan."

"This is not our fight. We cannot get into the middle of people's problems when they don't further the cause." Daniel did not mince words.

"He's a British officer! He will destroy a Patriot stronghold while enriching himself. I beg of you, sir!" Samuel was beside himself.

"Goddamn it, Samuel! I knew getting involved with that British woman would be trouble." But Daniel also knew that Samuel had been one of his best soldiers. Morgan felt he owed him this one favor. "I hope that damned Indian is not there!"

Ki saw a black boy coming to him, holding his hands up in peace. Willie had made a wide circle in the woods to find Ki, who had his long gun ready to shoot just in case he needed it. But the boy looked very troubled.

"You are Julia's Ki? She alu's talks 'bout you. You cun see she in trouble." Willie slowly walked up to Ki, holding his hands out. "The soldiers come quick. Townset mean to kill ev'ryone. He mad at Julia, and he be goin' to hurt her before he kill her and her sistuh."

"Where Townset taking Julia?" Ki's eyes were on the house and the soldiers while trying to see into the windows.

"Pro'ly to her bedrum." It was at that point that Willie had an idea. "I knows where you cun see in her ruhm." Willie carefully started coming in closer to the house, with Ki following. They were going down the hillside approaching the house from the wooded back when through the window Ki spotted John throwing Julia onto a bed. John had slit Julia's bodice with his knife, and he was pushing her down. Curtains narrowed the aperture, but if Ki was vigilant, a decent shot might present itself from where he stood, around two hundred feet from the house. Ki raised his gun; he had waited for this for a long time and tried to get a bead on John, but his target was in motion as Julia kept fighting. At this point Willie slipped a little down from Ki on the hill and offered his shoulder for support of the rifle. It made a perfect resting, and Ki patiently waited for John to hold still, then it happened— he fired.

———

In the house John had locked the bedroom. He wanted to see Julia's face as she begged for mercy, so he lit a lamp.

"John, please don't do this; we are man and wife. I will come back to you if you let me have the baby. I will let you have the money, all of it, as you want and have always wanted."

John became more inflamed. "You are fortunate I did not impale that bastard of yours on my sword. I was tempted! Now take off your dress and spread your legs." John stood for a moment looking down at Julia, relishing the moment.

It happened in a flash; John's head exploded like a watermelon. Julia sat there in shock; she screamed when his body slowly sagged forward onto hers with a stream of blood saturating the bed and wall. Julia scrabbled away from the bed in horror, her hand stifling screams. She heard men yelling, "Who made that shot?" then there were soldiers running up the stairs. For a moment she wanted to keep them out, but they would break down the door. They came in wide-eyed and stood in amazement, trying to comprehend the situation—Julia did not have a gun. They looked to the window that had been blown out from the rifle shot.

"Go find the bastard that did this!" One of the soldiers had taken command, and others that had followed him were now running back down the stairs. Julia staggered to the window with a blanket wrapped around her. Suddenly she knew who had done this, and she could feel him close by. "Ki," she said in a whisper.

———

Ki and Willie, fleeing the searching soldiers, ran straight into Samuel, who was the first to reach the scene.

"What is going on? The British are attacking? My God, where are Megan and Julia?" Samuel was beside himself with worry for Megan and his parents.

"I killed John Townset." Ki was reloading his gun as fast as he could. The two men only had time to exchange looks because the redcoats were coming quickly, so Daniel Morgan ordered his men to take cover and get ready for a fight. Everyone suddenly heard fighting erupt on the other side of the farm. The British soldiers turned and looked in that direction. Patriots from the inn had followed Ben when he had explained that the farmhouse was under attack. This new situation confused the British men going after Ki and Willie, so they turned around and ran to the front of the house. Now the British were encircled by the Patriots in all directions; the Patriots rapidly dispatched the soldiers and advanced on the farm. The redcoats were firing in response but quickly realized they were outnumbered. Samuel desperately scanned the scene for Megan and his parents. He saw his mother take cover behind a barrel, but where was his father, and where was Megan? He crept forward.

In the light from the open barn door, a soldier came out to see who was firing. Choosing his silent knife, Samuel slipped behind the soldier and cut his throat in one motion. He saw his father dangling from a noose in the barn, but Henry's body still moved. The soldiers had dragged him up to the hayloft and draped a rope over the rafters. Samuel almost lost control as he caught sight of Megan's shredded dress up over her head, a redcoat about to enter her. With his pistol, Samuel dropped him; then he focused on the rope. He prayed with everything he had and fired the long rifle. His father fell and hit the floor hard, not moving, while Samuel ran to Megan, who was hysterical.

"Thank God—you came! Samuel, they are everywhere! My God, Samuel, your father, does he live?"

"I don't know!" Samuel felt for a pulse as he knelt by his father. "Alive! I need to go and help fight the bastards. Stay here and hide!" Samuel was reloading his guns as fast as possible as he approached the door, carefully looking out, firing. The two Germans had untied themselves and picked up their weapons and were firing on the British. Mia and Molly were making for Mia's little house to avoid the line of fire while hiding behind whatever they could find. Samuel noticed that men from the inn had shown up to fight. Ben also had joined the battle and fired on the British. One of the Germans was hit in the arm and went down.

Ki entered the house with his rifle pointed in front of him. He found Julia hiding under the bed in shock, and when she saw him, she screamed, "Ki, my God, it was you! I knew you killed him! He was so evil. He wanted to kill our baby! Your parents came, and John threw the baby at them." Julia was telling this in great gulps while tears ran down her face and her hands were dug into Ki's arms. Ki could tell she was out of control, so he grabbed her arms to try and steady her.

"My parents here?"

"Yes, and they took the baby with them and left. Please, we need to find them! Our son is with them, Ki. I have named him Jason." Ki couldn't believe his parents had been here. He was confused. Why had they come in the middle of all this warfare?

"I think they wanted to know where you were. I don't know where Keme and Yuma went. John ran them off with the baby. Ki, we need to find them and get our son back!"

"Stay here. We finish off soldiers." With that, Ki ran back outside. The fighting had finished, and the Patriots from the community were reloading. They gathered in a crowd, along with Daniel Morgan's men. The fight had not lasted long because the British were outnumbered two to one, and they killed every soldier. Mia ran to Herman to inspect his arm and saw that the bullet had gone straight through, so she ran back for whiskey. It was there she saw Willie.

"Thank God you be all right! I was so scart and wor-rit!" She hugged her son.

"Is the fightin' over?" His eyes were huge.

"Yes, I mus' put this on Herman's arm! He be hit." They both ran out to where the men were. Mia began bandaging Herman's arm with a strip from her dress. Robby, who had been firing on the soldiers, told the Patriots what happened when John attacked. A scream came from the barn as Molly stood over Henry, his head in Megan's hands. Henry was immobile when Samuel came over to see if he was still breathing. He was, but shallowly. Molly fetched the semi-filled bucket at the watering trough and splashed the water on Henry. His eyes opened, but still he did not move. A bleeding ring from the rope circled his neck.

"My back! I think it must be broken."

"Dada, can you move?"

"No. It hurts like the devil!" With that, Samuel and another man picked up Henry, who was crying out in pain, and took him to the bed in his small house.

When Ki came out and saw that about sixty Patriots had shown up to fight, Daniel Morgan recognized him, and his face darkened.

"I suppose you are the cause, all of this,"

"I came back for Julia!" The two men stood there, glaring at each other. Ki did not have time to argue and ran back to Julia; he needed to find his baby and parents.

"Julia, stay here!"

But Julia was shaking her head no as she was putting on her riding clothes. "Ki, Jason is a newborn, and I need my baby. Please, we need to find them now!"

"Saddle horse now!" Julia ran to the barn while Ki went for his horse. She saw the damage of the battle, and then Megan; they ran into each other's arms.

"My God, Megan, are you all right?"

"I was almost raped, but Samuel killed him! Julia, this is horrible!"

"Ki and I have to find Jason and his parents. You and Samuel look after the farm. I have to go!"

"Ki is here?"

"Yes. He killed John. I cannot talk; I have to find my baby with Ki."

"Of course. Go find Jason and Ki's parents and bring everyone back." Tears tracked Megan's beautiful face. Willie came into the barn and helped Julia saddle her horse, and Julia hugged him fiercely.

"I showed the window at your bedrum to Ki; let him rest gun on my shoulder." Willie looked as if maybe he had done something wrong.

"You are a brave young man. I love you, Willie. I will never forget what you have done to help Megan and me.

Ki and I need to get Jason back. You help Megan with the farm." Julia was riding out of the barn and saw Daniel and his men confiscating the British soldiers' weapons. She wondered what they would do with all the bodies. She saw Ki on his horse and quickly rode out with him in the direction that Keme and Yuma had gone. They had not gotten out of the farmyard when Ben and Sallie came running out to stop Julia.

"Julia, stop!"

"Sally! Ben! Did you come with Keme and Yuma? Where did they go!"

"Julia, we were terrified when we saw the soldiers, but Yuma was not. He was so worried about Ki, that he went right down there to meet Townset. Keme would not let him go alone. Ben, who hid with me, went for help back at the inn, and the boy, Willie, and I hid. That is when I saw you, Ki, so Willie went to get you. What happened? Did you kill that bastard?"

"Which way? Back to village?" Ki had a dreadful feeling about his parents.

"Yes! I was too scared to come out! I wanted to keep Kucma quiet so that the soldiers would not see us." Kucma started to cry, feeling his mother's anxiety.

"We need to find them so I can get my baby. Go to the house, and tell Mia to find you and Ben a place to stay. My sister Megan is there also. Tell her how we met, and tell her you and Ben are staying with us." Julia and Ki rode out fast.

An old doctor from the community, Moses Donavan, arrived with the men from the inn to look after Herman and Henry. He had been drinking at the inn and joined in the fight. The doctor determined that the bullet had gone through Herman's arm and prescribed whiskey. He then went to Henry, who was in a lot of pain.

"My back is killing me!" Henry sweated and writhed from the overwhelming pain. The doctor felt carefully down the spine and told him it was not broken, but he had likely cracked it. He gave him laudanum and told him to stay in bed for a long time to let it heal. Molly was beside herself, trying to quiet him down. When Samuel realized his father was going to live, he went to look for Megan. That is when he saw Mia showing Ben and Sally where to bed down in the guest room. Samuel tentatively held out his hand in friendship, recognizing Ben and Sally from the kidnapping of Julia. Samuel realized they were Julia's friends, and he figured Ben had helped bring the Patriots from the inn when he saw Ben fighting with them, so he didn't want them to feel mistrustful of him.

"That was smart of you, going to the inn for help." Samuel was trying to be friendly. Ben slowly took Samuel's hand, not trusting him fully.

"Thank you." Ben sighed and introduced Sally. "This Sally, my sister."

At that moment Megan came in from the barn with two massive hams in each arm. She had changed her torn dress, and for a moment, she stood wide-eyed gaping at Sally. She remembered what Julia had told her about John violating the slave girl, and Megan's face went straight to the baby. Sally was a proud woman; she looked hard at Megan, waiting for her to say something demeaning.

"I am so happy to meet you! Julia has talked a lot about you and Ben; now please be our guests. I need to get these hams in the kitchen. Mia and I need to thank these men with a meal. They are starving." With that, Megan sleepwalked into the kitchen. Samuel noted her unusually white face and dilated eyes. She was putting the hams in the brick oven recess of the fireplace when Samuel came up to her.

"Are you all right?"

Megan was in a stupor. She nodded and burst into tears when she found herself in Samuel's arms. "I never thought it would be like this." tears soaked Samuel's shirt.

"Who *does* think their life is going to turn out the way it does? When I was in Ireland, I never imagined I would be here with the Patriots, fighting. But when I think about it, there is no place I'd rather be. I am honored to be with the Patriots. I believe God put me here, and I thank him for it every day. I won't say it is easy. It is hard most of the time, and I don't mind. If we win, I can't wait to see the result; just think! We will have a new world without a king. In this world, I can hold my head up and not feel like I am nothing."

Megan thought about this and how back in England, she'd be judged critically for being with such a scoundrel, but Samuel wasn't a lowlife. He was more honorable than most of the aristocrats she knew in England, and she thought about how he had saved her. Without thinking twice, Megan began kissing Samuel in a manner unbecoming to a maiden, and she didn't care. Samuel was right—it was damn hard here, and scary. But Megan was free to choose whom she wanted. Then, by God, she would pick Samuel! She decided to let him know it with her body. It was at that moment that Mia came in.

"Oh! My! Missy, I will leave."

"No, don't go; we have a lot of hungry mouths to feed. I should be cooking." Megan blushed; so did Samuel as he backed out of the kitchen, looking at Megan with a hunger for more than food.

"Mia, what goes with ham? What do we have to serve these men?" Suddenly Megan called Samuel back in. "I want to give the Patriots more than food. I will give them money, so please tell Daniel for me."

Samuel smiled.

"Did I hear my name?" Daniel Morgan came in looking very serious. "What do you want to do with all the bodies?"

Megan just stood there, wide-eyed and in shock. Samuel quickly stepped in. "Can we dig a pit on the hillside and bury them there?" Megan was still in shock and had no idea how to handle a situation such as this. Her formal education had never prepared her for such a problem; utterly astonished and exhausted, she nodded her head.

"I guess we should start digging right now." Samuel winked at Julia as he left with Daniel.

———

"Can I help? It has been a long time since I was in a kitchen as homey as this." Sally looked around with her child's papoose on her back. Megan couldn't help inspecting the child, and she thought she recognized John's eyes and nose. Then she thought about John being put into the pit that they were digging. Should she allow that? What if the

British army came looking for him and all those soldiers? Sally looked at Megan, waiting for a response.

"We can use all the help we can get around here." Megan turned her face away before Sally could see her dismay. Quietly Megan asked, "What is the baby's name?"

"Kucma." With horrible timing, the Rebel soldiers brought John's body down the stairs at that moment. Blood covered his head where a massive hole gaped. The women stopped working and watched in silence. No one knew what to say.

"I would like to pray. It's been a long time since I prayed with women. No one prays to our Lord in the Indian village." Sally looked around at the women as Mia got down on her knees with her hands folded in front of her, and the other women followed.

"Thank you, Lord, for bringing us safely out of harm's way. Bless these soldiers, all of them, even the British ones."

It was quiet for a moment. Then they all said, "Amen." They got up and started cooking for the men who had answered the call to arms.

Complete Loss

Ki tracked the trail to a campsite at the river, looking for his parents. They were about three miles from the farm when Julia took the lead through the trees to the top of a ridge where there was broken brush and signs of horses in stampede, which alerted Ki to a recent struggle; he told Julia to stop. They both looked down to the river and the coppery odor of spilled blood made Julia's gorge rise, and she leaned sideways to vomit. Yuma lay dead, eyes wide open, an enormous hole in his chest. Keme's body lay over his, her head crushed by a bullet at close range. Flies swarmed. Ki jumped from his horse, throwing himself to his knees, and embraced the bodies as tears ran down his face. Where was the baby? Julia looked around wildly, overturning everything in her way. Then she made herself look into the water, afraid to see her baby there. As the sun came out to help, she saw nothing in the river. Julia dropped to her knees in relief, if only for a moment, then she realized her baby was gone. Slowly, in total defeat, she went to Ki, and they both held each other in desolation.

"Where the baby?"

"I don't know. I have looked everywhere. He is gone."

"He go into the water?"

"I looked; the body is not in the river; unless it went downstream." Sobs welled from deep inside Julia. Ki took her into his arms as they rocked back and forth together, trying to comfort each other.

"Who would have done this?" Julia said through tears.

"Rebels seen them, thought they were a raiding party."

"Jason? Would they have killed him?"

"I not know." Ki slowly got up and looked at Julia. "Are you mad that I came?"

"What! I have been praying that you would come back to me!" Ki realized that Samuel had lied to him as Julia stood up and looked into his eyes. "I still feel the same, and I hope you do too."

Ki nodded his head, then in complete despair seeing his parents so brutally killed before him, he screamed, "Who did this?" Then, in a calmer voice, "I am going to take my parents back to the village to bury them there." Ki noticed that only one horse was standing by the bodies. It was the horse his father had always ridden. "Where is my mother's horse? Who was holding the baby when they left?"

"I only saw John throwing the baby at Yuma. When I tried to go after him, John grabbed me and pulled me back."

"You never saw mother take baby?"

"No, John pulled me behind him." Julia studied Ki's expression. "I will go with you."

"No. I do this alone, tribe not happy, I cannot keep you safe. Seneca need revenge for this. No, I go by myself. You find baby." Julia had never seen Ki look so lost, and she felt he was shutting her out by not looking her in the face.

"Ki! Will you come back? Please tell me you will come back. I have never stopped loving you! I thought about you every day! I hate the way we parted. Please let me come with you?"

"I love you, Julia." Ki was now looking into Julia's face. "You need to find baby. I come back when bury my parents." He carried his parents' bodies to his father's horse. Julia's painful sobs returned as he draped the bodies on the horse. He did not want to suggest that an animal could have carried off the baby because it would only cause more heartache. To leave her some hope for the future, he said only, "Look for baby," though it seemed futile. He had nothing else to say, and they were both overcome with grief.

In a panic, Julia grabbed him and clung to him. "Please come back to me!" Julia herself had never felt so lost. Ki turned out of her embrace and got on his horse, leading his father's.

"Find baby, Julia. I look—" Ki had to stop and take a deep breath before finishing. "I follow river, look for Jason. I face my people; they not be happy."

Julia watched until she couldn't see him anymore. She tried three times before she could mount her horse and return to the farm to face the catastrophe there. She did not feel twenty-one years old; she felt ancient, drained, with all her innocence gone. Coming upon the hill overlooking the farm, Julia could see a pit that held British bodies. It suddenly occurred to her that John's body was there, but it was too much to think about a proper grave or feel any sentiment about John at that time. All Julia could think about was John throwing her baby at Yuma and Ki leaving with his dead parents.

Back in the farmyard, men were eating wherever there was a place to sit; the women served them as best as possible. When Megan saw Julia, she stopped and ran to her horse. The closer Megan got, the more clearly she saw complete desolation on Julia's face.

"Where is Ki? Where is Jason?" Megan was trying to keep panic out of her voice. By this time Samuel had come to her side. He caught the horse, helping Julia down.

"Both are gone!" With that, Julia fell into the arms of Megan.

"How! You two went to get the baby. How did this happen?" Megan was beside herself.

"Yuma and Keme are both dead! We found their bodies by the river. The baby has disappeared! Gone! I looked everywhere but couldn't find him. Ki left to take the bodies back to the tribe. He was completely lost. I have never seen him so forlorn." Julia sat on the porch, stunned. Megan put her hands to her face and began to cry. Samuel put his arm around Megan and became very quiet; he could never reveal that the Patriots had come across Yuma and Keme when running to save Julia and Megan from the British. Daniel Morgan had given the order to kill the Indians, not knowing who they were and assuming they were up to no good. Samuel himself had shot at them, and he had no idea if it was his bullet that had killed Yuma or Keme because so many shots had been fired at once. He remembered one horse running off when the bloodbath started. Could that horse have had the baby on it? Samuel resolved to keep this to himself. The baby was gone! What the hell had they done? What had he done? Maybe the horse would come back here, but no, this was not its home, and the horse's real home was many miles away. Daniel thought of the baby starving on the horse and crying until it died. He would look for the horse himself every chance he got.

Daniel Morgan was motioning to Samuel. "We need to leave and get back on the road."

"Give me leave to stay a while. My father was badly hurt and may not walk again. Morgan, those Indians we killed were Ki's parents. They had their infant grandson with them when we killed them! Ki and Julia could not find the child...I'd like to keep this quiet. Ki is going to be very upset when he finds out what we did."

"Why? A dead Indian is a good thing. They have not helped us in this war. They would have killed us if we hadn't killed them. They will probably send a war party now in revenge. So they had Ki's baby?"

"Yes, apparently his parents came looking for him when John Townset was here, and they left with the babe. Look, Ki helped us a lot."

"We have a job to do, and I aim to do it! I don't need you questioning my authority. Where is Ki now?

"He went back to his tribe to bury his parents." Daniel turned around and called his men to leave.

"Don't be gone long. We need you with us, and remember, I just did you and your girlfriend a big favor." Daniel looked at Megan as she gave the last of the food to the men, along with money. Samuel wanted to cut the talk before Daniel's men let slip that they had killed

Yuma and Keme. He breathed a sigh of relief when they left, taking all the British military weapons and loot from the bodies with them.

———

That night Megan and Julia slept together for comfort. Megan was trying to think of ways to console Julia, but she was not getting very far. Julia just looked at Megan with a helpless expression and tears in her eyes.

"Only one horse was there, and Ki asked me where his mother's horse was. Do you think the other horse ran off with the baby?"

"I don't know, but we will look quietly for him; we cannot tell them that Ki's parents came here because that would terrify the community."

"They already think I am a whore for running away with him and having his baby."

"Then we will deal with that after we have turned over every stone looking for this baby."

Sarah Mackenzie Flynn

Sarah Mackenzie Flynn looked at the baby her husband was handing her after a long childbirth ordeal. She felt overwhelming happiness; this was something she thought would never happen to her—a husband she loved, and now their beautiful baby. The baby would not stop crying; she tried everything while her husband looked at her with a worried expression. She tried giving the baby her breast, but the baby cried even louder.

Suddenly Sarah woke up and realized that the crying was real and coming from outside her door. She tried to get up quickly, but her eighty years and a poor heart hampered her. Without putting on her shoes, she went to the door. There stood a horse decorated with symbols, carrying a sort of large holster on its neck. Inside was the infant of her dream. Sarah quickly moved to the horse, trying to settle it down, speaking soothing words. She got the baby out of the contraption while holding the horse still. The horse appeared relieved to be free of this screaming creature. She led him to the barn where there was hay for the horse as she carried the baby, then shut the barn door, thinking she would deal with the horse later. Sarah recognized the Indian patterns on the cradleboard and blanket. Was this an Indian baby? She carried the baby into the house, realizing that the poor thing was hungry.

First, she would quiet the baby, then come up with some food for it. She had a goat and an old horn from a cow. The horn was hollowed out, and if she washed it, stuffed in a sackcloth to block the hole at the small end, then filled it with goat's milk, maybe the baby could suck the liquid out of it. Sarah sat down in her old rocker and soothed the baby. He was very wet, so she rummaged in the rag bag for thick clouts and diapered him as best she could. Sarah rocked and rocked until the poor wain fell asleep, exhausted. She upended a drawer in her dresser and put the baby in the drawer. She remembered the beautiful cradle her husband had made for their babies, but that was long gone. Sarah felt energized and ran into the barn to milk the goat. She washed the horn with homemade lye soap and drinking water and pushed the absorbent rag into it until it completely covered up the tiny hole at the end of the funnel. She then filled the horn with goat's milk and held it up. Liquid dripped out, but it was not pouring out as she feared it might. No sooner had she finished than the baby woke, starving, so Sarah gave him the horn, and it worked! The baby sucked vigorously, occasionally stopping because it was strange to him.

"I don't know where you came from, but you are a bonny thing. How did you get here?" For the first time in a long time, Sarah smiled. Her little gift ate his fill, his eyes slowly closing. Sarah gently put him on her shoulder and burped him. As she rocked him back to sleep, she could not help but think of the past. Age thirteen, when her parents died in her tiny Scottish village and her penurious uncle's large family indentured her to a ship's captain. He had sold her in New York to a man with many children; the man's wife had picked her out to help. Freddy, the love of her life, had lived next door, and they fell madly in love, but she was not his equal. When his family found out, they told him that they would disown him if he married her. Freddy talked his father into giving him a small portion of his inheritance, and that night he and Sarah left. They were lucky that the man who owned Sarah did not come looking for her. She had put in five years of the seven promised in the indentureship.

Freddy and Sarah had just enough money to buy a small farm far from New York City, where no one would come looking for them. Freddy learned to be a farmer with Sarah's help. The first years were profitable, and they could buy more land. Sarah lost three children to fever and never conceived after that. Now she was alone with five hundred acres of land and couldn't afford the labor to farm it, so she only lived off her garden and sold eggs. She very seldom went into town, only doing so when it was necessary, and that was not often. She did not have any close neighbors; most did not want to be bothered with an old lady.

"Did you come from the ruckus I heard a while back at the river? I heard gunshots, but I did not go lookin' for trouble. I am too old to do that, and there is a war going on. Are people coming for you? Do you have people looking for you?" With arthritic fingers, Sarah tucked thinning gray hair back into her bun. What on earth was she going to do with a small child? She was too old to be doing this. But truth be told, it was a blessing. She had no family, and Freddy's family had disowned him and had never tried to contact them, so who was going to inherit this land? This baby had come from God, an answer to a prayer. Now Sarah knew who was going to inherit the land. No one could find out she had the child, and this would not be hard because she had few visitors. What would she name this little gift?

She smiled and looked into his sweet sleeping face. "Fredrick Flynn." And with that, Sarah fell asleep with him in her arms. She woke up with a screaming, wet baby in her arms two hours later. She hustled to find another cloth for diapering and more milk; all the while, he screamed at the top of his lungs. Over the next few days, Sarah found herself exhausted with the regular chores she had to do to stay alive and now with the baby. He was waking up in the night wanting milk, so her sleep was not peaceful. She told herself she had to do it because God had given her a fourth chance. She sewed late into the night, making diapers and clothes for her little gift from heaven. A plan came into her head: She would go to her neighbors' house as soon as the baby fell asleep for his long nap; she thought she could make it back before he woke up. Sarah would ask the neighbor to have the minister come for lunch. She had an important message to give to him, but she did not want to tell the nosey neighbors. She put the sleeping baby in his drawer and saddled the horse, making it to the neighbor's house in record time for her old age.

"After church, you tell Preacher Turner to come right at twelve and not a minute later. I will have a fine meal ready. Now, remember to tell him not to be late!"

"Sarah, has something happened? Do you need help?" Elisa was looking earnestly into her face.

"No, no. Nothing has happened." Sarah was worried that Elisa could tell she was lying. She decided maybe she should let a little information out. "I am writing a will and need a witness."

"We have been wondering who you were going to leave the land to." Elisa was looking at Sarah imploringly, but Sarah did not bite. She left in a hurry, knowing the baby would be waking up soon. Elisa helped her onto the horse; it took Sarah five minutes to make it onto the old hag. When Sarah got home, the baby was screaming in the drawer, so she had to diaper and fill the horn, then feed the baby. She was breathing hard and fast due to her bad heart.

Sarah began to prepare for Preacher Turner by making her best lamb pie with vegetables, and she even made blackberry wine and apple pie. Sarah kept the baby up as long as she could so he would sleep for a long time, giving them enough time to eat then witness the will. Sarah had made the will out as best as she could, Freddy having shown her many years ago how to read and write. Right before Preacher Turner came, Sarah took an overtired, crying baby to the barn and fed him as much as he would hold, then put him in a wooden box at the back of the barn filled with hay and blankets. She closed the barn door tightly and greeted the preacher, who was on time for a change.

"Sarah, this meal is delightful—and the wine! Did you make this yourself?" The preacher was on his third glass and becoming red in the face. Sarah knew she had to act fast.

"Yes. I love making wine, and I will even give you some for home, but I need you to witness this will I made first, then you can take all the wine you want." Preacher Turner had to get his glasses out; then he had to try to focus on the task at hand. The writing was elementary, but it did make sense.

"Who is Fredrick Flynn? I thought that was your husband?

"It is his nephew in New York City.

"I thought his people—well—had nothing to do with you and Freddy.

"Well, recently, they have been writing to me, and I have decided to give the land to Fredrick, a nephew who was named after my husband. Now, preacher, please just sign your name here. I know you have many things to do and need to be on your way." Sarah put the pen in his hand and pointed out where he needed to sign. As soon as he had approved it and written his name, she got up and poured a substantial amount of wine into a jar with a stopper. Sarah turned around and began moving to the door, hoping to entice him to leave with the wine. Preacher Turner unsteadily stood up and would have liked to have sat a little bit longer to let his head stop spinning, but it appeared that Sarah wanted him to leave. As the preacher was getting on his horse, he heard a funny sound.

"Is that a baby crying?"

"No, no! I have a female cat in the barn with new kittens, and she wants out, so I have to go and let her out, and you need to be on your way. Maybe Elisa would like a visit? I think she makes blackberry wine also. Now you be on your way. Thank you again for doing this." Sarah started to walk with purpose to the barn while looking over her shoulder, praying that the preacher would take the hint that she wanted him gone. He did, and she saw that he was heading to Elisa's house. When she opened the door, she heard a crying baby.

"Well, Freddy, we did it! You now own everything here. Lord, son, your diaper is full and ripe." Suddenly Sarah was exhausted, but she had accomplished everything she had wanted to without anyone finding out she had a baby hidden at her house. She suddenly had a bone-crushing pain in her chest, and for several minutes, she had to hold the baby on a table while she bend over in extreme pain. The pain lasted about ten minutes as the baby screamed in frustration for attention. Sarah had to turn her head quickly to keep from throwing up on the baby, and she was confused for a moment; she had to quickly sit on a barrel to steady herself and try to regain her composure. She knew she should not be raising a child like this, but God had given her an heir out of the goodness of his heart. She would raise this child to help her in her old age, and when the time came, represent him to the community.

"Well, Freddy, I am all you got, so together we just have to make it. You will grow up to be a fine young man I can rely on in my old age."

Seneca Indian Village

The village's scouts saw Ki coming long before he got there; his uncle met him with a deep frown. Running Wolf now wore war paint all the time. His face was red with black stripes, and he had weapons—knives, tomahawk, pistol, and the long gun he had taken from a dead Patriot—on him at all times.

"How did this happen?" Running Wolf was not happy at all.

"I found them dead at a campsite they were trying to set up; I have no idea how they died. They had my son with them, and he is gone."

"Who did this?" asked Raven, Running Wolf's wife.

"I don't know." Ki could not help looking down in shame; he felt responsible for what had happened. More and more of the village was coming out to view the scene; for the first time, Ki felt uncomfortable in his homeland. The looks he was getting were not friendly and welcoming.

"They went looking for you in the land of the white man." Running Wolf was getting madder and madder. "Is this what that white woman did? Did she have something to do with this?"

"No! She had nothing to do with this. Julia would not have harmed them."

"But did she know the people who did this? Where were you, and what were you doing when this happened?" Raven's voice raised in anger as she spoke; many of the tribe's women were gathering around her.

"Julia was in trouble; she needed my help!" Ki was trying to defend himself and was glad he had not let Julia come with him. He saw that his people were going to blame Julia for this.

"What trouble?" Running Wolf was now in Ki's face.

Ki closed his eyes and took a deep breath. "I killed her husband."

"Do you realize what you have done! The British army will want revenge for this. We are in trouble now with the Rebels, and now the British also!"

"I don't think the British will come looking for us."

"Why not?" Raven was now shouting at Ki.

"The Patriots have killed a lot of them; they killed all of the British soldiers who had come with Townset to retrieve Julia. That was when I killed John, and I would do it again if I had to." Ki looked defiantly straight at Running Wolf's face.

"So, you have not been fighting with the British but rather the Patriots?"

"The Patriots took Julia captive, and if I wanted her back, I had to fight alongside them, which I did. I took many scalps."

"You did this knowing that the Patriots hate us for siding with the British? The British were trying to keep the white man from taking all our land. If the Patriots win, they will take all of it!" Raven was screaming. "Julia brought nothing but trouble to us; it was a big mistake to bring her here."

Running Wolf stepped in front of Raven. "Bury your parents in our way. The council will meet to see what will happen to you; you may stay in your parent's longhouse until then."

Raven and Running Wolf walked down to the river, making sure no one followed them.

"We can no longer trust him if he has been with the Patriots." Running Wolf thought that he might be appointed chief now that Yuma was dead, and Raven followed his train of thought.

"You could be chief, but first, Ki needs to leave, and you are right—we can no longer trust him. That woman has poisoned him; Keme should have let him die along with his mother. He is half-white, and now he wants the white man's ways more than ours. If he stays here, there will be trouble from all directions."

Crowley

Crowley could not take the crying of his new baby daughter one minute longer. He loved her, but the crying was nonstop. It drove him out of the house; he told himself it was just for a little while so he could think and drink. He left the house, going straight to the tavern, where he hoped to listen to gossip and maybe learn something thought-provoking. He knew he was playing a dangerous game, playing first like a Loyalist and then a loyal Patriot, whichever side would gain him the most advantage. His Tory wife had brought him a lot of money and power. He loved her, but sex was not high on her list of priorities, and he had found ways to compensate for that. When he entered the tavern, he could see a group of Patriots drinking heavily. Crowley took a table near them to hear their latest tales.

"I didn't know what to do when that blackamoor came charging in here shouting the British were invading that Townset woman's house. I thought it might be a trap! But, by God, he was telling the truth! Zounds! We showed those redcoats what we are made of." The man was red in the face from drink and spitting everywhere when he talked. A friend sitting next to him did not notice because he, too, was drunk and enjoying the tales.

"We were trouncing them when Daniel Morgan showed up. I think we could have taken them even without Morgan." The second man belched loudly. Both men guffawed and almost turned over the table, spilling their beers.

"What do you think they did with all those bodies?"

"They dug a huge hole and buried them. I was ever so glad I did not have to dig that pit. Leave the younger ones to it. But I did tuck into the feast that sister Megan—is that her name?—served."

"I think that was the name—a looker too, and that food was worth the fight. Good thing they buried all those bodies. Could you imagine the stink?" He grimaced with enthusiastic, howling laughter, once again almost overturning the table. Crowley tried to keep from showing his shock.

Daniel Morgan had shown up. *How is that possible?* The Patriots killed the British soldiers and then buried the bodies in a pit! Unbelievable! Crowley wondered how many British soldiers had come and where Julia was during the fight. He couldn't hold his curiosity any longer.

"Gentlemen, I couldn't help but overhear there was a big fight between the Patriots and British at the Townset house. What happened?"

When Crowley saw the men looking at him suspiciously, he smiled and offered to buy them more beer. He slowly sat down while indicating their mugs to the bar wench for filling. "I was happy to hear you got those scoundrels and taught them a lesson they will never forget. I always thought Julia Townset's husband would come looking for her. Is that what happened? What happened to him?" The wench topped off their beer, and the men toasted Crowley with a deep swill.

Then one of them said, "You should have seen the hole in his head. The talk was that Indian got him good." The man turned to his friend. "I heard the Indian shot him from outside the house through the window in the dark!" The man slurred his words and sprayed beery spit. "Those servant women, one black, one white, told us two old Indians showed up before the Patriots got there. Townset threw the baby at them, and they left; guess he didn't like his wife making babies without him. Heard someone killed the Indians when they left, and the bastard is gone."

"What do you mean by 'The baby is gone'?" Where did it go? Did it get killed along with the Indians?" Crowley was snapping his fingers at the bar for more beer so that he could keep them talking.

"No one knows where the sprog is," the man said soberly, and Crowley thought for a minute the men were going to stop talking. "Heard the Indian left 'cause those old Indians were his family, I think." He looked to his friend for help, but the other man had lost concentration. He was having a hard time sitting up. Crowley thought he could fall over any minute.

"Are the sisters at the house now? Are they all right?"

"Yes, they are there, with one of Morgan's men. I heard his parents are servants at the house. Also…" The man snickered, and Crowley thought he would fall out of his chair. "Also…" The man started again, and this time Crowley brought his face close to the man, to try and make him focus. "Also, I saw him kissing that Megan girl." With that, he doubled over with laughter and fell out of his chair.

Crowley cautiously left, all the while making plans. That damnable Morgan raider could be trouble, and he would have to look into the servants. Where had all these people come from? Did Julia employ them within the law?

———

When Crowley got back to his office, he searched the notices for runaway slaves. There was a pair, Sally and Ben, who had run away some time ago, and they were believed to have gone toward Indian territory carrying a baby. Crowley sat back in his chair and thought hard. He would have to get Julia alone, wanting no trouble with the Patriot from Morgan's group, knowing those men were hard and mean. Some had been indentured servants and overall troublemakers from the old country who would shoot you then ask questions later. Crowley decided to go and collect the rent. He would try and act as appropriately as possible, all the while gathering information.

He quickly spied a black man when he entered the farmhouse's front yard; the man was slipping into the barn and watching him. He thought it strange that the black man wore Indian clothes. When he went up to the door and knocked, a pretty black woman with a child on her hip answered.

"Can I help you?"

"I am Mr. Crowley, come to collect the rent; may I enter?" Crowley put on his friendliest face and smiled his most charming smile. When Sally moved to let him in, he asked, "And what would be your name?"

"Sally." She felt uncomfortable with receiving his attention.

"And who is this darling child?" She made no reply, pointing him to the dining table. Megan was teaching a tall man, whom he realized was the Patriot, to read, and he was reading pretty well. Willie and Mia held readers in their hands while Julia read what looked like bills and business papers, stopping to help the students. Interrupted in their chores, they looked unhappy to see him as he uninvitingly sat down in a chair at the table.

"I came to collect the rent. I heard there was a battle here the other night." No one spoke, causing the large man to put his hand on his belt knife.

"Mr. Crowley, when I first came here, I asked if you were a Tory or a Patriot, and you said 'Patriot.' Is that not true?" Julia looked earnestly into his face.

"Yes, I told you that day I am no friend to the British. I heard you gave them a good put down." Crowley tried to be as convincing as possible.

The large man spoke. "We did, indeed."

"And who would you be?" Once again, Crowley smiled pleasantly, but he saw that the large man was not affected by his charm.

"Samuel McKinny"

Julia suddenly spoke up. "I can now buy the farm, my—my husband is no longer living." The room froze with tension, putting Samuel on high alert.

"How did he die?" Crowley quietly asked, keeping his eyes on Samuel's hand.

"Is that important?" Samuel said softly.

"He must be dead without question for me to enact a sale, Mr. McKinny." The two men locked eyes. "How did your husband die, Julia?"

Megan, who was sitting on her hands to keep them from trembling, spoke up. "He died in a battle, fighting the Patriots." She hoped that he would be satisfied with that. Downcast Julia could barely look anyone in the eye.

"Look at how you are upsetting her! Just take the information you've been given and move on with the sale, for God's sake. The woman has also lost a child." Samuel was now leaning forward with anger in his eyes, and his hand was tightly around the knife.

"Sorry, I don't mean to be rude. As I said before, I need truthful information before I can make a sale so that the sale is not disputed in the courts." Crowley stood up and looked at Julia. "I am sorry to hear your husband was killed. I heard that your baby is missing. If I can be of any help finding the child, let me know. I hope I have not caused you any pain, Lady Townset. I will look into getting the documents ready for the sale of the farm. The pain of losing a husband and a child at the same time must be unbearable. I don't know what I would do if my infant daughter disappeared." Crowley slowly got up, letting himself out, taking in as much as possible about the house and its surroundings. Sally was nowhere to be seen, nor was Ben, when he left.

———

Julia tried to return to her day-to-day routine as best she could. But depression marked her every move, causing her to withdraw from everything but the most basic tasks. She felt in charge and happy for the support of the household, which was like a family. Henry was doing better with his back, and the rope marks around his neck were gone; he was even able to do light farm work. Sally and Ben installed themselves with the others nicely; planting and harvesting took a lot of time and effort. Julia had never paid any attention to how the food got to the table, but now it was her constant concern whether there were enough workers to plant and harvest. She found herself up early, getting the day started and catching up on sewing or making candles with the last of the daylight. Previously, she had also never worried about the weather, always enjoying the changes of season. Now she constantly prayed a wet season would not rot the crops or a late frost kill everything in the fields. Ben and Sally were building a small house on the farm for their use. The Germans were finishing up their homes and saving money to bring their families over to the new world. They told many stories of their wives and children, and Julia couldn't wait to meet them. Fredrick's reputation as a blacksmith spread through the community and was bringing him a lot of money.

Julia knew the people judged her relationship with Ki, but they never said anything to her face because of her money. Julia's organization of the building a new church in the small municipality helped occupy her. This also kept some of the gossips at bay, but she was depressed at night, longing for her baby and Ki. She was grateful when, after a long workday, her exhaustion and a long cry would get her to sleep quickly.

Julia felt she had to play the big sister to Megan, who was falling in love with Samuel. One night after going to a barn dance with Samuel, Megan came into the kitchen, whiskey on her breath and not too steady on her feet. Julia met her at the door.

"What are your plans, Megan? Are you and Samuel going to get married? Doesn't he need to get back to the fighting?"

Megan took a deep breath, and her giddy expression fled. "He says sooner or later, he will have to get back, but right now, he is worried about his father. Julia, I love him, and he makes me happy. Happier than I ever thought I would be. I know he is not what mother and father would have wanted me to consider for a husband; America is different. Here people live by their skills and bravery and downright grit. You see what you want, and you carve it out with your own hands and make it work. I love the fact that we are all working together to survive. I love being a part of it, Julia. I know things haven't exactly worked out for you, but I have a strong feeling that the future will get better." Megan bent down to Julia, who was sitting on a chair, and kissed her on the cheek.

"All I ask is that you don't lay with him until you are married." Julia felt it was her responsibility to say this.

"Like you and Ki?" Megan winced at her remark. "I am sorry, Julia. I know you are grieving. I feel that Ki will come back when he has reconciled with his tribe. He was raised there, and he is devastated after the loss of his parents. Who do you think killed them? Maybe you should have gone with him?"

"I have no idea who. I worry that whoever did took Jason with them." Julia couldn't stop the tears coming down her face. She finally put her head down on the table and sobbed.

Megan put her arms around her sister. "I promise I won't cause you any trouble. You have suffered enough with John, and now this situation. I don't blame *you* for running away from John. He was a bastard. I heard the British are looking for him."

"My God, Megan, this could be disastrous!"

"Samuel heard in the tavern that the British want to know what happened and want to know where the soldiers that went with him are. A reward has been proffered." Julia put her hands over her face.

"Oh, Megan, this is horrible. We will hang for treason!"

"No one is talking. Everyone here is a Patriot. They will keep quiet."

"Are you sure, Megan? People are poor here and need the money."

"Samuel feels that no one will talk. If they do, they risk being labeled a traitor. I hate to think about what the Patriots would do to them."

"What if the British win, Megan? What will happen to us? George Washington can't keep this up forever. He is going against the greatest army in the world!"

"Julia, don't think like that! These Patriots are doing things that have never been done before, and they have the resilience to win. I believe this in my heart. We will win, and I thought I would never say this, but now I want to live without a king. I want the people to govern themselves and not be at the mercy of self-serving decisions made by a foreign king."

"Megan, I wish I had your vision for the future. Right now, I only see trouble. We will have to pray all the time that everything will work out."

"Julia, good things are coming your way. I feel it in my heart."

Blackmail (Dragooned)

The household was out of flour, and everyone was busy as usual, so Julia had Robby take her to the gristmill in her carriage. It was there that she happened to meet Crowley, climbing into his carriage with sacks of flour. Crowley latched on to her as if he had been waiting; he considered Robby and directed him away to help load the twenty-pound bags while privately talking to Julia. Julia looked concerned, as though she didn't want to be left alone with him, making Robby quickly load the wagon and creep around the mill to where he could eavesdrop without anyone seeing him.

"At last, Julia, we are alone; your beauty seduces me, and I need you." Horrified, she turned to leave, but Crowley grabbed her arms and pulled her close. "I have you now, and I know what happened at the farm. Have you heard of the reward for information about the whereabouts of your husband and his men?" He drew Julia's face nearer and nearer. She was now fighting to pull away, but he held her fast. Robby felt compelled to stop him, but how? He was an influential person in the community and had the law on his side.

"Julia, I also know you have two runaway slaves at your farm, Ben and Sally. I will personally hand them back to their owner. I will then sell the pickaninnies." Julia's face lost all color, and she felt nauseous. "You do know when I hand you over to the British, you and your sister will hang for treason? You are a whore who ran away with an Indian; the only thing that keeps your head up in the community is your money." Julia could tell that Crowley enjoyed watching tears form in her eyes.

"Don't cry, Julia. You can change these plans if you are willing to come to me every week in private. I will give you the directions or meet you somewhere to show you my secluded cabin. Of course, this meeting must be our little secret. You may have two weeks to think about it. If you don't come to me, I will let the British know where the bodies are buried." Crowley smugly straightened out his jacket and smiled at her. "Oh, I almost forgot. I have written up the homestead sale, which you must sign. Let me hear from you soon." He tipped his hat at her and ran back to climb into his wagon.

Robby returned to the carriage and acted as if he had not been listening. Julia had a hard time expressing her needs to the gristmill operator. Her thoughts simply would not focus on flour; when Robby helped her onto the wagon, his face told her he knew something.

Upon returning, Julia found Megan in the parlor and closed the door so no one could hear. After she told Megan everything, the two held each other in anguish.

"What are you going to do, Julia?"

"I don't know! I have to comply, or else all is lost."

"I will tell Samuel, and he will think of something."

"No! I knew we were headed for disaster, and it has arrived! It is all my fault. I should never have left John;

I brought all of this on us. I got John and all those men killed. If I had stayed with John, you would be back in England at our home. Wiggins would still be alive; oh, Megan, this is all my fault!" Julia sobbed in Megan's arms. "I deserve all that has occurred! This is what happens when a woman turns away from God and family values. This is my punishment for behaving wantonly. Now I need to sacrifice myself for all of us and go to him. I don't want anyone else hurt or killed. I will do what he says to keep us safe. Megan, if you were to hang, I could never be forgiven. God took Jason to punish me, and Ki lost his parents over me! Me!" Julia was pointing at herself as if she deserved to die.

"Stop blaming yourself for everything, Julia! John was a scoundrel who killed his own baby, for God's sake. He could have killed you also. You had to find a way to survive. I will speak with Samuel, and we will figure something out."

"*No! No!* I am to blame for all of this, and I deserve this, so speak to no one about it." The two women didn't hear Samuel leave the hallway, where he had been listening. Robby had run straight to him when they had gotten home from the mill.

Replacing Courage

K i buried his parents and stood at their graves for a long time. He wanted to talk to his father and ask for forgiveness, but he had been denied that. He found the clothes Julia had bought him in the longhouse where his parents had lived. It seemed ages ago that it had happened, and he missed her and wanted her badly. He could imagine his father standing over him with a stern face, saying, "You will have to decide which world you want. Make up your mind and live with it, for you are both Indian and white. These two worlds are not compatible, so you will have to choose."

Could he live without Julia? He did not think so, but giving up this world was hard. Here he felt free, untroubled by the rules and customs of the white man. He saw the white man toiling in the fields all day to stay alive and knew that he would be doing the same if he lived with Julia. Since this was women's work in his world, he asked himself if this was what he wanted. He did not mind the army, even though Daniel Morgan never trusted him because he was an Indian. He knew Morgan admired his ability with a gun and knife. As he was pondering, he felt a presence. Running Wolf stood there, and Ki stood up to meet him eye to eye.

"The council has decided you are to blame for the death of your parents. Because of you, two vital lives have gone from our tribe. You know the Haudenosaunee way—you must replace them. Our people are few, and there are many whites. You have cost us courage in our tribe, and that courage must be replaced with another courage of equal measure. You were adopted into this tribe without question, but we now question your loyalty to it." Running Wolf looked straight into Ki's eyes. Ki knew he would have to find two people to join the tribe, either willingly or as captives. He had no idea how he was going to do this. He packed up and rode out, taking the clothes Julia had given him.

Ki camped several times before he came to the farm. He found Samuel by himself, chopping down a tree in the woods surrounding the house. Sweat was running down his bare back; Samuel failed to notice Ki watching him from a distance. Ki drew close; Samuel felt his nerves jump into high alert, making his hands fly to his rifle.

"Ki! You scared the hell out of me!" Samuel did not know if Ki was still mad at him, and so he kept his hand on the rifle. "Did you find the baby? We have looked everywhere!" Ki had been hoping that Julia had found their son. He felt his heart contract with great disappointment and had to take a deep breath because he knew the baby was gone forever.

"I am sorry, Ki. I thought maybe you had found the child. I knew if anyone could find him, it would be you. I am sorry we parted in anger. I lied to you about Julia not wanting to see you; that was a big mistake. I should have told you the truth." Samuel held out his hand to Ki. Ki knew that his gesture signaled a desire for friendship and forgiveness; gradually, Ki took his hand, and the two men shared a moment of companionship.

"How is Julia?" Ki saw trouble fill Samuel's face.

"Sit down; I have much to say. Julia and Megan do not know that I overheard their troubles. Ki, you know that Megan and I have feelings for each other. And now my parents are living here on the farm. Julia and Megan bought their service. I couldn't be happier for them and me. But Crowley, the magistrate, has threatened to turn us into the British for treason. He knows what happened at the farm and is threatening to tell the British where the bodies are buried. There is a reward for information on the whereabouts of John Townset and the thirty soldiers."

"Who is man?" Ki thought of the man he saw menacing Julia when he first approached the farm.

"He is the official the British appointed to keep track of property and other Crown business. He told Julia that he is a Patriot at heart and would not report her to the British, but now he threatens to do just that."

"Reward?" Ki looked perplexed.

"Coins, wampum, for the person who tells the British what happened to Townset and his soldiers. Julia and Megan could be hung for treason, and you would be wanted for killing Townset. They could try to hang *me*, but first, they would have to catch me. My parents would be homeless again, and Sally, Kucma, Ben, Mia, and Willie could be sold as slaves. Willie was the black boy who showed you where to shoot Townset." Samuel looked deep into Ki's eyes. "I overheard Julia tell Megan—"

"Overheard?" Ki looked to Samuel for an explanation.

"Julia came home from getting flour at the mill very upset. When Julia and Megan were talking in the drawing room, I hid behind a door. Crowley said he wouldn't tell The British if Julia became his"—Samuel had to take a deep breath—"his whore." Ki knew that word. He had heard it used many times by the British and the Patriots. Ki tensed, seeing a nasty picture in his head. Samuel waited for him to speak, but Ki remained tight with a deathly quietness, and suddenly Ki stood up.

"You have any ideas, Ki? Look, we *both* need to protect our women. You want Julia, and I want Megan. Then there are my parents! Tell me what is in that head of yours." Samuel looked worried. For a long time, Ki just looked at Samuel, calculating whether he could depend on him or not. He decided that they were bonded together because of the sisters. At this moment Ki was glad that Samuel was a soldier and not afraid to kill. Samuel had more to lose because of his parents' situation.

"Ki, let us solve this together. You have to tell me what is in your head." Samuel pointed to his head.

"The tribe seeks revenge for my parents. It is my fault they were killed. Tribe's spirit and power must be brought back." Guilt was all over Samuel's face. He hoped Ki did not see it or sense it.

"What do you mean 'seeks revenge'?"

"I take two people to bring in tribe. Revenge for parents." Ki waited for the meaning of his words to fill Samuel's head, and when it did, Samuel's eyes opened wide.

"Who? Who would be willing?"

"Two, where Crowley live?"

Samuel began to smile as he realized what Ki had in mind. "Maybe this problem can be your solution!" Suddenly Samuel thought of a scenario. "You think you can take him? But what would happen if Crowley ever escaped and told the authorities?"

"I tell my tribe sell to Chippewas for fifty wampum beads, the price of two people. That satisfy Seneca. Crowley far west." As Ki talked, Samuel thought hard about the logistics.

"So, if they would be happy with just the appropriate payment, we have to come up with a plan." Samuel concentrated for a while, then he sat up straight. "Crowley told Julia he had a private place to meet. If it is very far from people, it might work for a secret ambush." Samuel was thinking it out; Ki let him talk because he knew more about the situation. "People would notice his absence and try to find him. They might even think your tribe kidnapped him." Samuel was biting his fingernails while he thought. "But what if Julia is not the only woman he tried to bed? Our religion condemns a man who lies with other women when he has a wife, especially if he has a secret place for taking them—and he has such a place. What if we make it look like he ran away from his wife with another woman?"

Ki considered this. His idea only went as far as kidnapping Crowley, but now that he thought about it, he saw that they had to keep suspicion from his tribe as well. Samuel tried to explain the idea as persuasively as possible.

"We could put some women's clothes around this secret cabin he has, as if to suggest he is seeing many women besides his wife. This will anger the community, and they will not be so willing to go looking for him." Samuel was smiling now because he felt he had come up with a good cover-up. "We will get Sally to make a chemise or stockings. Then Sally will spread the rumor around that she saw Crowley going and coming from the cabin's direction. We must leave some of Crowley's things there when we kidnap him." Samuel looked at Ki to see if he approved of his plan.

"Sally do it?" Ki looked off in the distance, thinking.

"Crowley said he would return her and her brother to their owner." Samuel spat out the last of the words. "Then, he would sell her baby."

"Ben and Sally knew this—no one else!" Ki looked hard at Samuel, who held out his hand to seal the deal. The handshake was a tribal brotherhood grasp. Both men now knew what to do. Ki spent a week away from everyone except for Samuel. He badly wanted to go to Julia, but she would not have approved of this plan. Julia would have argued that it was crazy and they all would hang in the end. When Sally and Ben heard of the scheme, Sally agreed to make the garments, but Ben was worried.

"I cannot be a slave," he said. "I will go back and live with the Indians to make sure he can't get me. Tell Ki I will go."

Sally ran to him and cried, "Ben, you don't have to do this. They will make this plan work! Please stay here with me-—I need you." Massive tears rolled down Sally's face.

"Sally, I am afraid of every stranger here! And if Crowley has his way, all of us will be lost! Even Miss Julia and Miss Megan!"

Sally just hung her head. She had to accept her little brother's choice. "When Ki takes Crowley to the tribe, tell him that I am coming."

———

Ki followed Crowley to his private hideaway without him noticing. He saw a pregnant woman come out of the cabin, and Crowley helped her onto a horse. The woman looked unhappy to be there.

When Ki met Samuel at the latter's hiding place, he described the woman to Samuel. "Dark hair and halfway through her maternal way."

"I think I know who she is! I have seen her at church when I go with Megan. She is a widow and has five children. Her husband was a Patriot who was taken prisoner in battle by the Indians. She tries to support herself with sewing and bread making. The problem is she became pregnant after her husband died, and now we know by whom. The community shuns her because they think she willingly let a man get her with child. Poor Amy Walker; I feel sorry for the woman. What if we get her to leave at the same time we take Crowley?" Ki's eyes widened, giving him away to Samuel, but all Ki could think about was her husband, now married to Yo da gent.

Ki could not tell Samuel about Ben Walker and how he had to marry Yo da gent or be killed in his tribe, so he quickly said, "How? Find new home? She have family?

"No, she doesn't have anyone to help her. But what if we were to give her money to leave."

"We have no money. How?"

"Crowley has money in his house. I have seen the jewelry his wife wears. The jewelry would most likely be in a box in the Crowley bedroom. Could you break into the house and steal it without them knowing? It would have to be at night while everyone is sleeping. Could you do that?"

The evening was getting colder as the sun set, and Samuel wanted to use a torchlight on the way to Crowley's house, but Ki said no. He did not want anyone to see them—plus, he needed his eyes to adjust to the darkness. They were in luck to find no dog to alert the Crowleys. When all lights had been out for some time, Ki and Samuel approached the back door. Samuel had brought tiny metal hooks to open the lock on the door and skillfully did so.

When the door was open, Ki slipped in; Samuel marveled at how soundless he was. He floated, shadowlike, going carefully up the stairs in the house, but Ki had to hold his breath when a step creaked under his foot. He waited several minutes, but there was only silence in response. He quietly opened the bedroom door, looked for a box, and saw one lying on a dressing table. He moved to the chest and felt inside a necklace, bracelet, and some rings, which he tucked in the sack around his waist. Just then, the baby woke and started fussing, making Mrs. Crowley rise and pick up the baby. Her unfocused eyes never spied Ki slipping behind the curtains. She nursed the baby for what seemed to Ki a long time. After diapering the baby and putting her back down to sleep, she finally returned to bed, and Ki awaited the soft sounds of sleep. Mr. Crowley slept on undisturbed, and had he opened his eyes, he could have seen Ki's shoes under the curtains. Ki slipped out and took the stairs two at a time, avoiding the noisy step.

The next day Samuel went to Fredrick, confident he would keep their secret. Ki was nervous; he did not know Fredrick Schumer.

"I have to ask you to keep quiet about this. I need you to melt this jewelry down." Fredrick guessed what had happened. "You steal these?"

"For the protection of Julia and Megan." Samuel gauged Fredrick's reaction, but Fredrick had come to know Samuel and liked him. He also knew that Samuel's violent friends would back him up. He believed that Samuel defended the welfare of Julia and Megan. Fredrick was grateful to Julia for his job and the life he had made there. He would not forget his debt to her.

"What shape you want, gelt?" As Samuel looked perplexed, Fredrick added, "Ich konte melt ins coins odor rings."

"Coins will do."

"What you want do mit dem steinen? Ein par sind kostbar—how you say, costly."

"Keep one of them for yourself, and I will take the others. Do this quietly, and let no one see you." Fredrick nodded and realized he would have his house a lot sooner than he had planned. Of course, he would have to spend the diamond far from here.

Revenge

"**W**hat do you mean you are going *away* to hunt?" Megan was looking at Samuel curiously.

"Dad is feeling better. His back doesn't hurt as bad, so we are going hunting for the coming winter. Deer, elk, pig, turkey—and duck, if we get lucky." Megan had never had to worry about these things before.

———

Samuel ambled to Mrs. Walker's house. He remembered fighting along with her husband in the Battle of Saratoga and knew her husband to be a brave man. Samuel figured that the Indians had probably killed him after torturing him. He hated to see her brought low because of Crowley. The poor woman had five youngsters to feed and another coming. Samuel paused at the door, thinking about the dialogue he had rehearsed in his head many times before coming here. He hoped it would work, and with a deep breath, he knocked on the door. Amy Walker answered and looked worried when she saw Samuel. Was another injustice to befall her? At first, the church had tried to help her, but their willingness had quickly faded. Individuals had initially been generous, but that too was now coming to an end. Without Ben's income from the blacksmith shop, they were utterly destitute. Today had been a bad day for her hungry children; they couldn't stop pleading for food that she didn't have. They were growing out of their clothes and shoes. When Crowley offered coinage for sex, what else was she to do? "Whore" was whispered everywhere she went, even at church. Now here was Samuel McKinny standing at her door.

"Please, Mrs. Walker," he said softly, "I mean you no harm. I would like a moment of your time. I come to help you, charitably." She gazed at him for a long time before she stepped back and let him in. When he looked around to see if anyone was watching before he entered, her suspicions were aroused. She did not offer food or drink, for she had none to extend.

"If you leave your mother for a moment, I will give you candy," Samuel offered, holding up the reward to the children. He looked at the thin children and their bare feet and felt sorry for them. They ran out the door to do his bidding. Samuel held out his hands to reassure her. "I mean you no disrespect, but"—Samuel took a deep breath—"I know what Crowley is doing, and I want to help you." Amy Walker looked shocked and backed away. "Mrs. Walker, I am here to help you out of the horrible situation in which you find yourself." Samuel took another deep breath. "I have money that can take you and your children anywhere you want to go. You may not have to work so hard to keep food and shelter for yourselves."

Amy looked incredulous. "What must I do for this help? Why are you doing this?"

"I have money for a small house. Enough will be left-over that if you take in sewing, mayhap you will not have to labor so. Do you have family anywhere that you would like to move near?

"Why are you willing to do this for me? What do you want in return?"

"Mrs. Walker, I knew your husband to be a brave man. This is not how he would want you to live. Crowley takes advantage of you. A godly person, who wants to remain unknown, and I would like to assist you. We want you to take this money to flee this situation you find yourself in by no fault of your own. Is there a place you would like to go? I will take you there, but it will have to be a secret. You can tell no one."

"Why?" Then Amy put her head back and looked at Samuel with a knowing look. "It is Julia!" Amy's eyes grew large, and she put her hand to her mouth, "My God, is he doing the same to her or Megan?"

Samuel turned red and knew he could not lie any-more. "Mrs. Walker—"

"Call me Amy, if you please. Tell me why she wants me gone."

Samuel looked down for a long time, fighting with himself as to how much he should tell her. "Please, I can't tell you. This is no jest; we mean no harm to you in any way. I swear before God. Give me a Bible; I will take an oath upon it. We want to help you, but you must leave, and we will have to go in the middle of the night. I will dis-patch Crowley so that he surely could not revenge himself against you. Amy, please believe me!"

"What are you going to do to Crowley?"

"Don't ask; better you not know."

For a long time, Amy looked at Samuel, remembering what her husband had said about McKinny: "He is a good man, but do not get in his way." These were hard times, with a war going on, and people did not always behave as they would in peacetime. Amy knew Samuel was living at the farm with Julia and Megan Rainsford and that there had been a big fight over there with British losses.

"Does this have anything to do with what happened at the Rainsford farm?"

"All we want to do is get you and your children somewhere safe. This will all be yours." With that, Samuel showed her the coins and a few of the stones from the stolen jewelry. Suddenly tears spilled from her eyes, and soon sobs broke forth. It had been a long time since Amy had felt safe. Now, this rough man offered her safety from the devil who had ruined her. No more starvation or judgmental looks. No more selling her self-respect. She hated Crowley for what he had done to her. She hated herself. If they all stayed here, the children would soon learn their mother had fallen. For a moment, it was like the Lord himself had come to her door, so Amy nodded her head.

"When shall we go? It will have to be Boston. Is that too far?"

"No, Boston will be fine, but remember, you have to keep this a secret. I will need a small personal possession of yours to take care of Crowley—say, a glove? Start packing, stay ready, for I could show up anytime."

Amy just nodded.

Ki had been watching Crowley for days. He repeatedly brought things to improve his hiding place of sexual pleasure. Ben joined Ki and shared that he would return to Ki's tribe because he did not want to be enslaved again. Ki nodded, and they set out to capture Crowley on his way with wood and oil for lamps in the cabin. Crowley was alone on the road when Ben, hidden in the thick woods, ran out, flinging up his hands to stop him. As Crowley reached for his rifle, he was suddenly looking at a demon from hell, face red with black stripes from forehead to chin. Ki had painted himself for war, and in a flash, Ki grabbed the rifle as he leaped into the wagon. Ki hit him with the butt of the gun, and Crowley fell over. Ben and Ki hauled him out of the wagon, then tied and gagged Crowley securely. Ki went on to the cabin and placed the women's clothing around the bed with Amy Walker's glove next to it. Ki went back to Ben, who watched as a furious Crowley, draped over a horse with his head down and his hands tied behind him, awakened.

Ki sent Ben with their captive into the woods to wait for Ki to return. Samuel would need Crowley's wagon to gather up Amy Walker's family for the long trip to Boston. As darkness fell, there was no moon, yet Ki rapidly completed his errand of returning the wagon to Samuel. Fearful of attracting notice, Ben tried not to make a lot of noise, as he had learned to do while living with the Indians.

When Ki returned to Ben, the latter unpacked Crowley and secured his hands with a long rope tied to Ki's horse, making him run behind. Crowley cursed them and threatened them, but it was of no benefit. They would stop and give him food and water and tie him back up at night with the gag. When they reached the tribe, he was exhausted.

———

The tribe put Crowley through the gauntlet, but not before Ki talked to Ben Walker and told him what Crowley had done to his wife, Amy. While Ki was talking to Ben, he noticed Yo da gent, pregnant and holding Peta's hand. Ben let the full range of his anger come forth, and within minutes, Crowley was killed by Ben's hatchet to the side of his head in the gauntlet. The tribe was glad to get Ben back. He had proved his worth as a warrior many times.

Two days later Running Wolf came to Ki. "The council has decided that you may return to us, but Julia will never be welcomed here. She is a colonist Rebel, a sworn enemy. How could you have fought for them? We will have our revenge on them, you will see. Julia brought great trouble to this tribe. If she comes here with your son, even more pain will follow. Because of her and her people, we have lost our most respected leaders. You will have to decide whether you stay or go. You can win back your place here in the tribe, and we will welcome you, but not that pale-faced woman."

"Is this how my mother's clan feels? Have they spoken on this?" Ki was heartbroken by the news.

"The clan gathered, and this is what they decided." Ki felt that Running Wolf wanted him to leave for good so he could be the sachem. Ki went back to the longhouse of his mother and father and threw himself down in their room. He envisioned the house that he and Julia had made, seeing another family living in it. Children were running around the small house, and Ki had a moment during which he wished they were his and Julia's. But that was not to be; destiny had other plans for them. All night he had tried to decide what to do. He never thought he could leave the world he had been brought up to love. These were the families Ki knew and felt comfortable living with. He knew their ways and habits, but he loved Julia. Could he live without Julia? He could not stop thinking about her—she was part of his being. Had she found the baby by some miracle? He wanted to be with her and needed her.

Ben came to see him. "I heard what the tribe decided. Have you decided what to do?"

"They don't want Julia here."

"Can you live with that?"

"Not without great pain. If I leave her, I know I will never love another woman. I will never have a woman like that again."

"Could you try and find another woman and see if you could be happy?" Ben wanted Ki to stay.

"I have no desire to find another woman, and if I did, then I would compare that one to Julia, and I would always be disappointed."

Ben realized he was losing this argument, so he offered some advice while talking in the Seneca language. "Ki, you can pass as a white man. If you go back there, go back as a white man. You will learn how to live in the white man's world with the help of Julia. She is a good woman and will do right by you. What I mean is, she will teach you their ways. It will be difficult because what is important to them is different than what is important to the Seneca, plus they are at war. And you did kill her husband, so watch your back!"

"Are you saying I should leave?"

"I am saying, try to live in their world and see if that is what you want. If not, then come back by yourself. But you will have to live like a white because the British consider the Indian and the black beneath them. They think of us as stupid savages because we don't dress in fancy clothes or talk like them. We don't have their fine things and their money. We don't know how to read their books, so they belittle us for it. But if you show them you can learn their ways, they will hopefully accept you. Then you can learn how to defend the Seneca from the whites. Isn't that what would be best for your tribespeople?" Ki nodded his head and thought about his father telling him to learn the white man's ways so that they would know how to defeat them. He hated to think about it, but maybe Tom was right—the Seneca would have to learn how to live with the white man.

Paleface

With a heavy heart, Ki started on his journey back to Julia. The entire way he debated if this was the right path. He felt betrayed by his people, the people who had raised him. Stepping into the white man's world would be dangerous and confusing. Would they never consider him their equal? He would not bow down to them. He *was* their equal, and he had shown it on the battlefield many times. Yet could he leave the Indian way forever? Ki cut his hair to his shoulders as he sat by the fire alone one night on his journey back to Julia and put on the white-man clothes that Julia had bought him.

He felt the loss of his people and his parents. He knew things would never be the same for him. The wind picked up steadily as he got closer to the farm, and he could hear thunder in the distance. He thought about Julia, and joy came over him, for he wanted her with a need he couldn't deny. He decided that before going to Julia's house, he would visit the place where his parents had died once more.

———

Elsewhere Sarah had been rushing around to get chores done before the rains came. She felt a weariness in her body that told her she was doing too much for an old-timer. The wind had picked up, and she had a hard time closing the barn door because she had no strength left in her body. She felt a sharp pain in her right arm that made her fall to the ground. Suddenly her breathing came quickly, and even with the chill in the air, she started to sweat. The pain was so great that she cried out, but no one heard her as she fell to the ground, and in her last thoughts, she remembered that she had left the baby in the cradle.

"Dear God, please let someone find him." Her eyes closed, and she breathed her last.

———

Ki came to the place where his parents had died, by the river; he sat on his horse for a long time, tears coming down his face. He knew he should seek shelter from the coming rains, which would be powerful because of the heavy winds blowing, but he could not help jumping from his horse to where their bodies had lain. This was the last place his son had been. He remembered Julia praying out to her God for help. Suddenly he knelt and prayed to a God he never knew; he could not explain it, but Ki felt he needed to do this. He needed to say goodbye to his parents and son, the son he would never know or hold in his arms.

———

Jason was sleeping soundly in his cradle when the cabin door banged open with a loud crash, letting the cold draft chill the baby. Jason screamed in complete terror, and when no one came to his rescue, he cried even louder.

———

The wail reached Ki faintly in the blowing wind. He told himself that it was an animal and wondered, *Could it be a bird? A wolf?* In the next gust of wind, the cry of a baby grew distinct. Ki's heart leaped with hope, for could it be his son? But how could that be? Weeks had passed since Jason had disappeared. A newborn could not survive without tending. Yet the cries came louder, and he jumped back on his horse and quickly followed the sound up a small embankment.

Ki rode into the wind, following the sound, across a pasture to a clearing with a house. The door stood open, and he heard the baby now screaming in terror. Ki looked around and saw an aged woman on the ground. The need to know if she was alive fought with his longing to find his son. He ran into the house without concern that anyone else might be inside. Ki ran to the cradle, and there saw Jason, his son. In one motion, he scooped him up and scanned the home to see if he was alone. Thunder crashed down amid a torrent of rain.

Ki walked to the door, looking at the poor woman amid the showers who appeared dead, totally motionless, so his attention returned to his son. He studied the baby's black hair and blue eyes; tears filled his eyes again as laughter burst forth from him. He recognized Julia's nose. Ki put his forehead to the baby's forehead and thanked every God he knew. Eyes wide open, Jason gazed back, fascinated at this new person who had just came into his life.

Ki looked around the cabin to see who else lived there, finding only one bed appropriate in size for a tiny woman. An old musket stood loaded by the door, but there was no other mark of a man living there. For a long time, while the rain poured down, Ki sat in the rocker while he and the baby absorbed each other entirely. Ki found himself cooing to his son and chuckled at this new experience. Soon the baby closed his eyes, and Ki put him back into the cradle. The rain was a drizzle now, so Ki went to the old woman and touched her lifeless flesh. Her hair was gray and white, her skin thin and dry as leaves. He knew this woman had taken care of his son, so he lifted her carefully to the rocker in the house. Her head fell forward when he set her down. He thanked her for finding his son and keeping him alive.

Ki returned to the barn, where his mother's horse stood in the stall, and a Seneca cradleboard hung on a rail. For a moment sorrow for his mother overwhelmed him; he saw her weaving the cradleboard in hopes of riding with her new grandson. He found the goat horn nurser and a pot of goat's milk next to it back in the house. He spied a square of fabric and realized it was a diaper of some sort. Jason woke up as Ki refilled the horn; he hungrily guzzled it down, knowing just what to do. The diaper was a mystery, so Ki bundled the baby in a blanket with the cloth diaper stuffed around his rear end.

"Time to see your mother, who has been longing to see you." As he said this to his son in the Seneca language, the baby burped loudly and then smiled at him. Ki laughed in pure delight and silently thanked the gods again for giving him his son back. Was it Julia's God?

Ki fit the cradle broad to his horse in the Indian fashion with Jason snuggled in it. At first Jason objected to this, but then the horse began to gallop, making Jason intrigued with the ride. Ki led his mother's horse behind him.

———

Samuel crossed himself quickly in the church, making his father smile as he did the same. Both looked at Vicar Turner, who had caught the action and frowned but tried to make allowances for the Catholics in his church. Vicar Turner knew these were unusual times, with the war and everyone having to take sides. The minister also knew that if the Patriots won, they would declare freedom of religion and bring in God knows what. It was hard for the Catholics to worship because the British had outlawed the religion and only wanted the Church of England, the Anglican church, to be the colonies' faith. The McKinnys would have preferred attending church in their own home, but they were trying to please the sisters and the community. Julia, Megan, Samuel, and the entire household came out of the place of worship with the rest of the Patriots' small community. The service had ended, and everyone was glad the storm was over. Mrs. Crowley was there with her infant daughter, looking distraught.

The cabin had been found on Crowley's property when his disappearance had been discovered. Along with Amy and her children, Crowley had disappeared in his own wagon, so it was believed that he had run off with Amy— indeed, they had found Amy's clothes in the cabin. But Mrs. Crowley didn't believe it.

"Why would he run off with that whore with five children who aren't his? He had a good job here that he loved. Besides, we were robbed, and I think this had something to do with it. He loved his daughter and me!" Mrs. Crowley only shut up when she was reminded that Amy got pregnant after Amy's husband had been captured and killed.

Julia was turning to Samuel to ask about bringing the carriage around when she saw him stiffen in total surprise. Julia turned, and Ki was riding up to the church with a crying baby in a cradleboard. She held up her skirts and ran with a quickness she hadn't known she had. When she viewed the baby in the cradleboard, she screamed, "Jason! Oh, thank the Lord. Ki, where did you find him!" Everyone followed in haste to see the Indian in white man's clothes with the lost child.

"Old woman lived close to river where my parents killed where I found him at her house." Ki dismounted to help Julia remove the baby. As soon as Julia had her son in her arms, she put her free arm around Ki and kissed him—shocking the entire congregation.

"Would that be Sarah Flynn?" Vicar Turner was inquiring. Ki just shook his head, not knowing who it was. "Old woman?" Ki nodded. "Where is Sarah now?"

"Old woman died, I got there," Ki stated to gasps and whispers from the worshippers.

Mr. McKay spoke up. "How do we know that you didn't kill her?" Julia turned around to defend Ki, but Samuel spoke up.

"Ki would not do that!"

Mr. Hall then spoke up. "He is a Seneca. They hate us and work with the British. I do not trust any of them." This was supported in unison, and it was clear that the atmosphere was turning hostile.

"Ki was raised as an Indian, but he is half white. He would not kill Sarah." Julia was beginning to panic.

"Ki fought with Daniel Morgan and killed many British soldiers. He has turned Patriot." Samuel was also getting angry.

"How do we know he didn't capture my husband and kill him? I know he had something to do with his disappearance." Mrs. Crowley held onto her baby daughter protectively, hatred coming from her. Several men were picking up their rifles.

"We need to see for ourselves if Sarah was murdered." Mr. Hall spoke up.

"How are you going to do that?" Henry McKinny spoke up while pushing his way to the front.

"Inspect the body for marks of any kind. Let's go now!" The crowd shouted their agreement. The men quickly got on their horses and led Ki out.

"Go back to the house with the baby, and I will see that no harm will come to Ki." Samuel was pushing Julia and Megan to the carriage, where Willie was waiting.

Megan put her arm around Julia and Jason and guided them to the transport.

"Don't worry, Julia; Samuel and Henry will take care of it. They will set them straight. These men just need to see that they can trust Ki." Megan was trying to be positive, but Julia was not buying it.

"Are you sure they will not hurt Ki? They look like they could do something depraved."

"Julia, your baby needs you; I think he is wet, and he looks hungry." Megan lovingly touched Jason, bringing all of Julia's attention back to her child.

When the men got to Sarah Flynn's house, they made Ki wait outside while they went inside, where they found Sarah's body. Ki felt like he would not get a fair chance to defend himself, and this made him very angry. The men took off her clothes and scrutinized the body, looking for any marks. Mr. McKay started looking around the small house and found in a box by the fireplace Sarah's will.

"Who is Fredrick Flynn? Sarah was leaving all this land to him." The rest of the men moved to examine the will, finding the preacher's signature on it.

"Vicar Turner, come here; this is your signature?" The preacher nodded.

"Sarah asked me to come here and witness her new will who she was leaving for a nephew." Turner was pointing at the will when he suddenly remembered the crying. "When I was leaving, I heard crying, like that of a baby;

Sarah just told me it was a mama cat in the barn. But you think it was this child?"

"The Flynns never had any kinsfolks, did they?" Hall spoke.

"I remember asking her about that, and she said that she was in contact with her nephew in New York." Preacher Turner was fingering a whiskey bottle left by the fireplace.

"Preacher Turner, could you write to the Flynn family and inquire about a nephew, Fredrick?" Samuel asked.

"It is possible she named Jason, Fredrick, not knowing his real name and not having any living relative to leave her property to." Henry was scratching his head.

"Is it possible she was hiding the baby, knowing that if she reported it, she would be left without a relative to inherit all of her property?" Preacher Turner pointed to the house as he drank the last drop in the whiskey bottle.

"I think they own the entire hillside but were unable to farm it by themselves." Mr. Hall was also scratching his head.

"They were land rich but money poor and could not afford servants of any kind. Fredrick told me that he had run away with Sarah and his family disowned him for it because Sarah had been a domestic, and the family disapproved of her. I think they had the money for land and this small house, and that was all. They had lost children of their own, and I can't remember why." McKay looked around the house now for things of importance.

"I remember Sarah telling me her children died of fever. I will write to Fredrick's family in New York as soon as we get back, but what are we going to do about Ki?" Preacher Turner asked in a stern voice.

"Well, gentlemen, I think he and Julia should marry since they have a child together," Samuel said emphatically.

"Can we trust the Seneca? They have been killing us all over the countryside," McKay said.

"Was it Ki who killed her husband? I never got the real story," Mr. Hall said.

"Yes, he did, and as I told you, he served with Daniel Morgan and me. He even saved my life when I unloaded my gun and had to reload; he shot several soldiers with his bow and arrows. We had been hiding up in trees and were caught short. If Ki had not been there, I would have died." Samuel looked at each man. "If the British find out that he killed Julia's husband, they will be outraged. Do you know, gentlemen, that Julia and Megan have been declared enemies of the Crown for giving money to the Patriots? They are here to stay and can never go back to England."

"So Ki is the father of Jason?" Mr. Hall looked at Samuel.

"Yes, she ran off with Ki when Townset walloped her and killed the baby that she was carrying at that time."

"Was it Ki's baby?"

"No, it was Townset's, but he had a habit of violently hitting her. The child that is Sally's, the slave girl's, is Townset's also. He would go to Sally's cabin and force himself on her in front of Julia and would put a guard at the door to stop anyone from interfering with him." When Samuel reported this, all the men looked concerned, for these were strict God-fearing men who wanted a godly place to live. "This was at the farmhouse that Julia first lived in when she came with Townset to America. Megan, her sister, told me all of this. The son of a bitch wanted to kill Julia over here in America because it would be easier for him to do it here than in England. He only married her for her money, but he was going to make it look like Ki killed her."

"Did Ki have anything to do with the disappearance of Crowley?" Mr. McKay asked.

At that point Ki came into the building and spoke with deliberate confidence. "I captured him, took him to my village; they killed him." Mr. Hall and McKay reached for their rifles in total disbelief.

Samuel stood up fast to stop a murder. "It is time you know what happened. Crowley got Amy Walker with child because she had no choice, or her children would have starved. Then he told Julia that if she did not come to him, he would inform the British about what had happed at her house. That house where we found Amy's glove and his gear is where Crowley would meet the women. I made it look like he had run off with Amy. Amy Walker is safe in Boston, where I took her."

"How do we know that you are telling the truth?" Mr. McKay said, with Mr. Hall nodding in agreement. They turned to Ki, who was looking at the door with his hand on his gun. Willie and Robby stepped into the house, wanting to add their stories to the mix. Willie was worried about Ki's safety and felt that maybe he could help with his statements. The boys had discussed returning to the farmhouse after church and wanted the truth to come out. Robby felt he needed to speak up at this point.

"I heard Crowley talking to Miss Julia about how she was a whore for running off with an Indian, and then he told her that he was going to tell the British that Ki killed her husband and then tell them where the bodies were buried." Robby was nervous, but he got it all out. "Crowley then said Julia had to meet him at that place—the place where Amy Walker went."

"How do you know this boy?" Mr. Hall said.

"I rode with Miss Julia to the mill that day when Crowley was there, and he told me to help unload a wagon, but I stopped and listened to their talk when they couldn't see me."

"Ki, you killed Julia's husband?" Preacher Turner asked.

Before Ki could talk, Willie spoke up. "He sure as hell did! I tol him where to look into her bedrum window, and there was poor Miss Julia scream'g for him to stop hurt'g her and want'g her baby back. He thro baby at Ki's parents like a sack of flour. I wants to kill him, but there no thing I could do until I sees Ki in woods and show him window and told him to use shoulder as a rest'g place for rifle. Townset's head explod like a pumpkin!" Willie spoke with wonder and respect for Ki while looking at him the whole time with eyes wide open. Everyone was looking at Ki, who sat there with his head high, and the men felt respect for him for the first time.

"How do you think the baby got here? Mr. Hall asked, looking at Ki.

Ki responded, "My parents fired on, not see their attackers; the horse run off after mother shot with cradle-board. The horse come to this house; it close to their bodies." The men fell silent for a moment, feeling the sorrow of one finding one's parents shot to death.

"What are your intentions toward Julia Townset?" Preacher Turner lowered his eyes at Ki in a very judgmental way.

"My wife," Ki stated while looking at each man in the eye. "I protected her, protect her to I die. I stop my Indian ways, be white man."

"You are half-white?" Mr. Hall asked.

"Yes, father French trapper, mother Huron Indian. I raised Seneca."

"I have heard about horrible things that the Seneca do to captives, especially when they are drunk. One story told of the gauntlet the captives are put through—if they reach the end, then they live—but also this one story told of the Indians killing them even though they survived the gauntlet. When they got drunk, they killed a man and cut off his head and put it on a stick and danced around it." McKay was angry.

"It is true, white man taking his land, bring illnesses, killing way of life. I see what white man can do. I no friend to the British when I killed John Townset; I fight on the side of Rebels." Ki looked at each man when he talked, and the air was tense.

"Gentlemen, let us bring this to an end and welcome Ki into our community. Julia and Megan are good people who cannot return to England and have helped us all out in many ways. Julia and her sister have given the Patriots a lot of money. I don't think Julia would have run off with Ki if he hadn't proven himself a trustworthy person. Ki, are you now a Patriot?" Henry spoke up loudly after being quiet and listening to the conversation. He wanted Ki to reaffirm his loyalty. Henry felt like they were essentially building a community of decent and like-minded people.

"I fight with the Patriots, will continue. My people attack Patriots, killing them, not what I do."

"Then we will have a wedding today!" Preacher Turner spoke and nearly knocked the table over as he headed for the door. "Best get Julia and her family to the church so we can get this whole thing over with." He stopped and turned to the men. "We will not talk about Crowley again and leave it as it is. He was an unholy man who preyed on our women; no telling what else would have happened if Ki and Samuel had not"—Vicar Turner lowered his voice—"taken care of the situation."

Wedding

I t was fortunate that Julia had not changed out of her church clothes when the men rode up to the house. Yet she would have unquestionably dressed better had she known it was to be her wedding day. Ki came into the house with the men following him.

"Julia, we go to church to get married now." Ki's expression was somber, giving Julia pause. Julia knew he was out of his element when it came to weddings and marriage in the white man's world, but she would have enjoyed some sense of joy from him. Samuel was happy and had taken Megan's hand after pulling it from her open mouth. The house was utterly silent, with everyone looking at Julia, waiting for her answer. Vicar Turner decided it was time for him to clarify the need for speed.

"Julia, you and Ki have a son together. Ki wants to marry you, and Jason needs a father. So let's get to the church, so come along now."

Julia suddenly realized that they did not want an unwed mother in their community any longer than necessary, so they were taking care of the situation here and now. Julia's answer was to dig in her pocket for two solid gold coins. "Henry, could you take these to Fredrick and ask him to melt them down into wedding rings." Julia looked at Ki, smiling, but his eyes were boring into hers with intensity. The smile left Julia's face as she felt Ki was uncomfortable about the situation. Everyone gathered in the house to hear what was happening and make arrangements for travel to the church. Megan started picking what flowers she could find and trying to make a bouquet.

Samuel laughed at Megan. "Hurry up! We have a wedding!"

"You could have given us some idea that this was to happen today."

"Preacher Turner wants to know that they are wed today so there is no unwed sleeping around." Samuel was helping Megan into the carriage and winked at her before helping in his mother and father. When Julia saw Ki get on his horse, she went for her horse instead of going in the carriage with Megan and Samuel; there was no more room after everyone had piled in. Julia would have liked to have talked to Ki alone but was followed by Preacher Turner, Mr. Hall, and Mr. McKay, so she could not get a moment with him. Ki looked straight ahead without looking once at Julia, which was making her uncomfortable and nervous.

Preacher Turner rang the bell when they got to the church, which brought out several people. Julia took a deep breath, taking Ki's hand, and led him to the altar, where they stood side by side, Samuel next to Ki's and Megan next to Julia. The vows stopped when it was understood that Ki did not have a last name. Preacher Turner was speechless and did not know what to do.

"He will take my name, his name will be Ki Rainsford, and I will be Mrs. Ki Rainsford," Julia stated with exactness; she did not want to be questioned about this or challenged in any way. Ki looked at her with admiration, giving her hope that everything would be all right even though it was unorthodox. When Ki asked if he would take Julia as his wife, he clearly said, "I will" without looking at Julia. This was not at all what Julia had imagined for her wedding. She had wanted joy and happiness all around, and instead, she felt tension and stress from Ki. Finally, the procedure was over; there was so much seriousness from the married couple that the preacher did not even ask Ki to kiss the bride. Megan kissed Julia with a quietness that seemed to ask if anything was wrong, but Samuel grabbed Ki's hand and shook in a heartfelt way, smiling broadly.

To make matters worse, Preacher Turner announced that Jason should be christened next. So, Mia, holding Jason, brought him up to the altar, and everyone moved to the baptismal font. Ki, confused and hesitant, looked to Julia to explain.

"I will explain all of this later when we get back to the house." Ki just looked at her with disapproval. "I promise we will go home in a moment, just please, Ki, have some patience," Julia whispered.

Megan and Samuel were the godparents for Jason. Ki's eyes grew wide when water was put on Jason's head, but he kept quiet. Finally, everything was over, and they could go home when Molly announced, "We better start cooking fast!" Mia was looking at Sally, and they both headed for the carriage. Everyone once again piled in, with Megan holding Jason. Julia and Ki rode on their horses alone for the first time. Megan looked at Samuel worriedly.

"It will be ok; it is just marriage jitters."

Ki galloped ahead, and Julia had to ride fast to catch up. At first she was disappointed in Ki's attitude, but now she got downright mad.

"If you didn't want to marry me, you could have just said so and ran back to your people." Julia was trying to keep the tears from flowing, but it was impossible.

"Those men, they forced me. I do not like forced to do anything." Ki could barely look at Julia; he was so mad.

"Ki, they just wanted to make sure that you would do the right thing by me. Make an honest woman of me."

"What you mean 'honest woman'? You very truthful woman."

"They didn't want an unmarried woman who had a child running around in the community. Vicar Turner's job is to make sure that all the women are married when they give birth. The men were protecting me by making sure you were going to marry me. But if you don't want to—" Julia could not stop the crying.

Her horse had stayed in a grove of trees, so Ki turned around and came to her.

"Julia, I love you. I came to you. I killed husband for you. I protect you. I don't like forced to do anything! Why do men feel they need protect you? Why Vicar Turner want you married?"

"It is a sin to have a child before you are married." Julia took a deep breath; she never wanted to have this discussion with Ki, but now she realized she had to say it. "It is considered a sin that I ran away from John with you and had your baby, Ki." Julia hung her head down, then raised it to him with tears streaming down her face. "They call women like me whores for running away from their husbands to another man, especially when they have babies with that man."

"Why it a sin?" Ki looked stern.

"Ki, I told you when we were together that it is a sin according to our Bible, our religion, for a woman to run away from her husband."

"So, your God want you stay with man who beat you and lie with other women, laugh in your face." Ki's face was getting red from anger and shouting. "What your God want you to do?"

"Pray, and pray!" Tears were dripping from Julia's face.

"Pray! That not help!" Ki barked in real anger.

"It brought you into my life! You came, saved me, and I love you with all my heart for it, Ki." Julia was sobbing. Ki realized that these were the ways of the white man and their religion, and if he was to live in their world, he would have to abide by their rules, even though they made no sense to him. He remembered telling Julia not to walk in front of him at his village and that she always had to get the water. Now it was his turn to accept rules he did not understand. This was already proving to be more challenging than he had thought, but watching her sob made him turn his horse around. Ki pulled her from her horse, and the minute they touched, the old passion hit like a hurricane. At first, Julia was unsure of his love for her, but soon, they kissed with a hunger that needed to be quickly satisfied. Their longing for each other turned to a tsunami of need and desire. They dropped from the horse, quickly finding a grassy area that proved to be the perfect place to reunite far from everyone's attentions, curiosity, demands, and judgements.

We Are Now Bound Together Forever

When Ki and Julia returned home, the first thing they heard was Jason screaming for food. Ki took out the makeshift bottle and showed Julia how to fill it with goat's milk. Everyone was watching to see if it would work, but Ki had other ideas.

"Hold baby to breast, let him suck milk, milk will return." Ki spoke with perfect reason. Julia became embarrassed that he knew about this and that she had never heard of it before.

"How do you know this? Of course! You know this from observing other women in your tribe doing it."

Julia realized Ki would say things that were familiar to him but shameful to say in her society. Ki could see that Julia was embarrassed. "Julia, we not ashamed of our bodies." Julia needed to accept this from Ki and not act ashamed when he pointed out his ways of doing things, things that polite society would not talk about, except in private places.

"You are right, and I will try to let him suck from my breast because I want him to accept me again. I miss doing this for my baby, but it appears that this horn is working, and I am grateful that Sarah found this for him."

"God was taking care of him, Julia, and it is a miracle that we found him and all has worked out." Megan discreetly pulled grass from her sister's hair. "You and Ki go upstairs with the baby and get ready while we get the food going. Look, Jason is falling asleep and needs his old bed; thank God we did not remove it. "Megan felt that Julia and Ki needed time alone, so everyone started moving fast to get things ready for the meal. Samuel looked at Megan with awe and respect at her having taken charge of the situation, having known that Ki felt tense in this new world.

———

Ki couldn't help but stop and stare at the portraits left from the previous owners of the house.

"I couldn't make myself take them down; it was their home first. I felt it was respectful to leave them up," said Julia. Ki nodded in agreement as they went up the staircase to the master bedroom. Julia carefully changed Jason's diaper without waking him, and she breathed a sigh of relief at the fact that she hadn't got rid of any of the baby things as she was putting Jason in the cradle.

"Ki, I prayed that I would find Jason and that you would come back to me. He answered all my prayers."

Ki looked intently into Julia's face. "When coming back, I stop at river where my parents killed, felt sad, tribe told me you not welcome back." When he said this, Julia looked shocked. "I got my knees and prayed, your

God, any God that listen. I hear Jason crying, door where Sarah live open with wind; I hear him. I followed sound, found him. Sarah dead at barn door. She try to close it, died. She is ancient woman."

Julia put her arms around Ki. "God heard your prayers and opened the door!" Julia had tears coming down her face. Ki, the tribe doesn't want me anymore?" Julia was shaking her head in disbelief.

"Running Wolf in charge, he said you not welcome; you the reason Yuma and Keme died." Julia couldn't believe this, but it was true—they had come into the white man's world to where she lived, and now they were dead.

"Why did they come? Who do you think killed them? Ki, I would never bring harm to your parents. I was beginning to love your mother. She was so kind to me and truly tried to help me as best she could. She was teaching me a lot, especially about healing herbs."

"I don't know who killed, but I kill who did this." Julia sucked in her breath.

"When we in Sarah's house, men found will leaving land, house to Fredrick Flynn. Julia, Sarah called Jason, Fredrick Flynn. She left land, house to him. Vicar Turner write to family."

"This is beyond belief—you coming back and finding Jason, us getting married, and now Sarah naming Jason, Fredrick and leaving everything to him. I don't think she had any family that I ever saw or heard of." Julia put her hands on Ki's shoulders. "But Ki, don't kill anyone! You know there have been many Indian attacks on white settlers that the British have encouraged. The people here are terrified of Indians, and now the community has accepted you. You need to show them that Indians are not bad people."

"I afraid British lied to Seneca. They said Patriots not win. Julia, the Patriots win; I saw at Saratoga, we beat them. The Patriots fight like Indians; British not know how to fight back. They fight in straight lines. We killed them like birds. The British told many Indians kill white people, and this they will do."

"Ki, if the tribe is not pleased with you because of me, will they come and attack us?"

"No, not me here with you; safe."

"Did Ben go back to the Seneca? That is what Sally said even though she was not to tell us?" Ki nodded but did not want to tell Julia the whole story of Crowley and where he had taken him.

"So Ben is back with the Seneca! But Ki! What about other tribes that are on the side of the British? Will they attack us also?"

Ki saw the fear in Julia's eyes. "We should prepare."

Julia's eyes got wider. "How? How do you prepare for an Indian attack?" Julia was nearly hysterical.

"We listen to animals at night, that when they attack, dogs let us know, but all women need to learn to shoot, know how to load gun. We practice with guns."

"I have never shot a gun before, but I will learn if I have to. I guess that is what one does in the countryside here. This is so different for me, and I know it is different for you also. We will learn together. I have to change, and we will start to make you new clothes tomorrow." Julia looked into Ki's eyes, realizing that she had become a real American. The two of them would face this new world together, with each other's help; both had to assimilate into the new life that they had created.

"It's late, and I need to see about Jason. I am going up to our room." Ki saw that she was drinking whiskey, which made her mood lighter, and she smiled at him invitingly. Her breathing had gotten heavier, making her breasts move up and down quicker, and her cheeks were red from the drink, making her eyes sparkle; he followed her without hesitation. Jason had been checked on several times during the wedding feast and had slept soundly through it all. He woke up wanting food, so Julia got the horn to fill, but Ki stopped her.

"Put him to breast to get milk, will come back." Julia had Ki untie her dress while she held the baby to her chest. Jason started to suck but got frustrated after no milk appeared. While Julia was doing this, Ki was getting the horn and goat's milk ready, which Jason accepted greedily. Soon Jason's eyes were closing, and Julia changed his diaper. Ki took the baby from Julia and carried his son to his cradle, where he watched him proudly. Jason had their black hair and blue eyes, he had Ki's brood nose, the nose of an Indian, but his chin was Julia's more pointed one. Ki stood over the cradle and watched his son sleep. After a few minutes, he slowly turned around and sucked in his breath. Julia was naked on the bed and holding her arms out to him. He came to her, and they made love slowly and deliberately. Ki loved watching Julia during their love-making, and when she was a little drunk, he discovered she became more aggressive; taking the lead, she climbed on top of him, holding his arms down, teasing him with her mouth. They explored their desires, doing everything they could think of sexually to each other. Afterward, as they were lying together, Julia took his hand.

"These are the white man's symbols for marriage. These rings will tell the whole world that we are married forever." Julia slipped the wedding ring on Ki's hand and put the other ring on her hand. For a moment they held their hands up together, looking at the new rings, which Fredrick had delivered to their house.

"We are now bound together forever."

The next morning Ki woke up to the unfamiliar feeling of a soft bed, hearing the baby making sucking sounds of waking. Julia was sound asleep, and Ki decided to let her sleep, so he quietly slipped out of bed and went to his son after getting back into his clothes. He determined the baby was hungry and headed to the kitchen, where he found bread sitting on the table along with apples and pears. He chewed the apple thoroughly, then spitting it out in his hand, began feeding it to his son. Jason was licking the apple off of Ki's finger when Megan came into the kitchen and became shy with Ki. They did not know each other, he was from a very different culture but was family now and considered the head of the house. Julia and Megan had become very independent and were used to making their own decisions. They often spoke of how they enjoyed their independence from male dominance. Of course, Samuel had been helping out a lot more since his stay at the farm. Megan couldn't help but smile, thinking about how Samuel had kissed her when they were alone last night. It was getting harder for them to stop progressing sexually, but she had promised Julia that she would be good. Megan wondered if things would change now.

"Ki, I have never seen a father feed his children like this; I think it is wonderful." Megan was trying to be sociable.

"Your father fed you?" Ki was always surprised at how different their ways were. A father feeding his son was the most natural thing in the world to him.

"No. We had a nanny for that." When Megan saw that Ki did not understand, she tried to clarify. "A nanny is a servant who takes care of the children. We never saw our parents but a few hours a day right before dinnertime." Ki stared at her, not comprehending. His father had been an enormous influence in his life, along with his uncle, Running Wolf's father. In his earliest memories, he followed them everywhere, and they instructed him on everything.

"How taught?" Ki was curious.

"Our nanny schooled us, and if our parents thought she was doing something wrong, they were quick to point it out to her." For the first time, Megan realized that maybe that wasn't the best way to raise a child. She would have loved a father who fed her, much less chewed the food for her when she couldn't. The intimacy Ki had with his child made Megan jealous that she never had that with her father. A father who showed unconditional love. Ki felt this was uncomfortable for Megan, so he turned the subject to the small houses outside.

"Who lives houses outside?"

"Mia and her son, Willie, live in one, then Henry and Molly and Samuel live in the big one. They added rooms for Samuel and Robby. The Germans built a small shack until they get their houses built on their land. They will then move to the property given them by the Patriots for leaving the British army. The Germans helped us a lot with the farm, and they have become Patriots, but they do not move with the armies to establish their farms. Mia and her son, Willie, lived here before us; when the Joneses lived here, they were their servants." Ki had learned from his time with the British that the black men were slaves. They were bought and sold as the property of the white man. This became clear to him when he saw Sally and Ben at his village and they explained to the tribe that they would rather live with the Indians than be slaves to the white man. The Indians also had slaves that they bought and sold.

"What happened the Jones?" as soon as Ki said this, he noticed Megan become uncomfortable, lowering her eyes.

"John killed them looking for Julia. He charged them with treason and killed them. John made Willie come to us at the tavern with a story about returning because of the boots you gave Julia, which were left here at the farm by her. Julia wanted those boots back, so Samuel and I went together to retrieve them without Julia. We had no idea that John and the soldiers were there, but Samuel became suspicious and had me hide in the bushes with the horses while he checked it out. Willie saw Samuel coming; Willie had been watching for Samuel and warned him of John and the soldiers, so Samuel killed most of them in one fashion or another. He would not tell me how he killed them, but John got on his horse and chased Samuel back toward me. Both men had fired all their weapons when John started running down Samuel with his sword. That is when I came out and threatened to shoot John. I couldn't shoot him; John left, telling me that Julia and I were turncoats of the Crown. I now wish I had shot John. Samuel grabbed the gun out of my hands, but John was gone and out of reach."

"You went back for boots?" Ki was thinking of the boots he had made for Julia.

"Yes, Julia said she really wanted them back, and she even wears them when it gets cold. I have seen her cleaning them; they are the ones you gave her?

"Yes" This was all Ki said, letting it warm his heart to know that Julia had missed him as much as he had missed her. "Why Samuel, his parents live in small house not here?" As soon as Ki asked the question, he saw Megan stiffen. Megan was blushing that she had to explain social structures to Ki. Unless Megan was cautious, she could make Samuel look socially below her status in the British social hierarchy. She did not want Ki to know this, so she took a deep breath, realizing that time had come to step out of the old world and into the new.

"Samuel's parents were indentured servants that Julia and I bought out of servitude. Henry went with Wiggins, our business manager, and chaperone; he accompanied me from England to rescue Julia. He died on the way back from England after selling all our properties there." Ki was beginning to see how busy Samuel had been with Julia and Megan. There was a lot he had kept from Ki, and he was starting to resent it. Samuel had a lot to apologize for.

"Henry got money back?"

"Yes. He promised Wiggins he would, and he did. The McKinnys have been a big help here. I don't know how we would have gotten along without them."

"Robby?"

"When Wiggins died on the way back here, Henry bought him to help guard the money on the ship. He lives here now with us in McKinny's house."

"Henry bought him?"

"Yes. There are a lot of Irish slaves on boats brought over here to work." Megan lowered her head, ashamed for Samuel.

"I know black men slaves, not Irish." Ki could tell that Megan was embarrassed. "Mia, Willie slaves?"

"No, we gave everyone their freedom and pay them what we can. Julia and I do not believe in slavery. These people living on our farm have been a lot of help. This is a large farm, and we need all the help we can get. Ki, in our world, it is"—Megan had to look up and think fast—"not proper for an unmarried woman to live in the same house as an unmarried man if they are not related. Julia and I are not related to the McKinnys, so they have their own house." Ki wanted to ask why their house was more significant in size than the McKinnys, but he could see that Megan was already uncomfortable.

"Sally and Ben? They come from Adams? They slaves?"

"The Adamses don't know they are here, or at least they don't know about Sally, and we would like to keep it that way." Ki was thinking about Crowley and what he had threatened to do—so this was why Ben had gone back.

"Ki, I have to ask you why—why you don't want to be with your tribe or village. Is this strange for you?" Megan felt nervous asking Ki this. Ki thought hard about what he would say. He didn't want to talk about doubts and joys right now, so he decided to explain some of his culture to Megan.

"When man marries woman, not marry her like white man, but live with her, he move in her clan and take her clan as his."

"So, a man is the head of the clan?"

"No, woman, she the clan mother, powerful. She make decision how clan and tribe run."   As soon as the words left Ki's mouth, Megan's eyes all but bugged out of her head. "You mean women have power in your world! Men truly listen to what a woman has to say?" Megan couldn't believe what she was hearing. Without knowing that she was speaking out loud, she said, "No wonder Julia didn't mind living in your world!"

"Yes, men need wisdom women have and honor put upon them." Julia came into the kitchen and stared at Ki, feeding Jason, who was gobbling up the apple from Ki's fingers. She had seen this kind of feeding many times while living with Ki, so it did not surprise her. She loved watching the two bond together, and it gave her a sense of unity and love that she never quite felt in her own family back in England. They were a family at last, and intact. As soon as everyone had eaten breakfast, Julia, Jason, and Ki rode about the farm with Jason in the cradleboard. Ki had never seen a farm this large, and he had to wonder about the fortune of Julia.

"You buy with wealth of your family?"

Julia looked at him with pride in her eyes. "Yes. My family was wealthy, and with the help of Wiggins, who was able to bring the money back here to me, Megan and I have been able to survive well."

"This the money John wanted?"

"Yes. Wiggins was able to get it all because John had not fulfilled the marriage contract that my father made him sign."

"Do you want to go back? You miss it?"

"No. This is my home now; besides, I would be considered a traitor for helping the Patriots." Relief flooded into Ki, who welcomed these words with joy. But it worried him that Megan and Julia were considered traitors. "I am considered an enemy of the Crown." Julia looked at Ki with wide eyes, and he felt the seriousness of the situation. Ki knew the Crown's power, and if Julia was now their enemy, so was he. Ki contemplated this the whole time they rode back to the farmhouse. His tribe had pledged alliance to the British, he had traded sides when Daniel Morgan had made him do it for Julia, but now he was a Patriot by marriage. What would happen if the Patriots did not win?

"You made fools of John and British, Julia?" Ki couldn't help but feel the irony of taking all that John had ever wanted while he smiled at his brave wife.

"I had a lot of help—you, Wiggins, my sister, all the people here at the farm. I have been blessed. Now it is time I show you where I hid the rest of the money." They headed into the back of the barn; in a stall, under thick hay, was a dugout hole with a big box. When Julia opened the box, the sparkle of jewels and solid gold coins jumped into Ki's face. He couldn't help but laugh; it was strange for him—he had never thought about being rich in the white man's world. Did he want that? No. It was not him to act the rich white man. He thought about Julia and realized she was not acting like the rich white women he had viewed in Boston and New York. She was different, and for the first time, he realized that was why he was drawn to her and loved her.

"I love you. You not act as rich white women. You lived with me in small house we build."

"I loved you for protecting me, and I promise you I will try never to act above my means because it is an act. I like to be real, and this is who I am. You and this new country have taught me that, and I thank you. I feel free here for the first time in my life. It is not easy, but I am my own woman. Ki, do you think you can live in the white man's world and be happy? Are you going to want your old life? Will we be enough for you?" Julia was holding her breath, and the tension was so noticeable that Jason looked at his mother and began to cry, feeling her anxiety. Julia held him to her as a shield for what Ki might be telling her. All Ki could see was a strong woman he loved, clutching their child, knowing she felt and knew his dilemma. They had not talked about it because they knew this was going to be problematic. He had not wanted to bring problems to their newfound love. He took a deep breath, gathering them in his arms, feeling the love of his family. But the truth was there, and it was time to express it.

"I don't know. I am white man and Indian. They at war with each other; I feel this inside me. Who am I? I want to live with you, here, but the white man sees Indian, the Indian sees white man." Julia held them both to her.

"I want both, and I don't expect you to give up the way you were raised or what you were taught. The white man and Indian are at war, but this war will end one day. People need to get to know you and see that you are a decent person. It will take time for them to trust you; it will happen. I know it will! I will be there to protect you and help you all I can." Ki couldn't help but smile at this brave woman whom he knew he could trust completely. "When I was in your village, I marveled at how Tom accepted both worlds. He had found his place in both, and I know you will also. Remember that just because you live in the white man's world, it doesn't mean that you have turned your back on the Indian world."

"You saw what Indian does to white man? There is hatred."

"You need to take the good from both sides, and let people see that good. Then they will trust you in time. Have patience, and let things work out. In time, you will find what is right for you. I just want Jason, and I to be there with you."

"I trouble you. The religion, working farm, sleep in soft bed, and eat at table with a spoon." Ki had to smile at Julia teaching him to eat with the white man's manners.

"We will take it slow. Don't try to do everything all at once; feel what is right for you, then act on it. I know that you were taught that certain things were women's work and other things men's work. You and I now need to survive in this new world. It will take making money for some things. I don't know if I can live off the land as you do. I have found that I like farming and working the land because your people taught me this. I know you were taught that this is women's work, but I have a lot of land. That is why I have these people here to help me. I could not do it by myself.

"Julia, I don't want to farm, that woman's work. I want raise horses and sell them." Ki felt his stomach tighten because he knew this was going to be a problem between them. Julia knew in the back of her mind that they would have to deal with this issue also. In her world the men handled the basics of farming. Due to her privilege, she would have never had to think about agriculture, but now it was all up to her. Right now she had enough help, but could she depend on that?"

"If I needed your help, would you do it for me?"

"Yes. I know you do things you not like, carrying water jugs from river to house." Julia knew he was talking about that fateful day when she felt it was too much to ask of her to carry water and be pregnant at the same time.

"I have grown up since then, and I do not feel as entitled as I did back then. I love this farm like I never thought I would, and at the same time, I have realized it is hard work. Forgive me for the way I acted that day; it was all I could think about when we parted, and I thought I would never see you again." Ki took her mouth in a hungry kiss, wanting to make love and tell her how much he had missed her. It was impossible with a baby in between them.

"Did you miss me?"

"Julia, I follow you and join Daniel Morgan and kill British soldiers to see you again. Morgan told me, I killed British soldiers, I see you. Samuel never say what is happening. He tell me he had to go home. Samuel came back, never say anything about you. Daniel told him be quiet. Saratoga, we all drink whiskey all night after fighting. Samuel talk about you and Megan. I know he lie to me. We got in fight, but these his men. I Indian who work with them for hope of seeing you. I not fight them anymore, too many, they gave me to Indian tribe. Samuel tell me you didn't want me. He said I mistake. I not know what to do. I feel I dishonor my father and could not go home, so I live with Indians for long time. One night I hear you call my name in a scream. I feel you call me; I came and found you with John hurting you, and I killed him."

"When I had Jason, I screamed your name because I missed you so much. I felt you had left me and gone back to your village, and I wanted you to come back." Jason had fallen asleep, gently Julia put him down on the hay next to them. "Go lock the barn doors."

Once Julia knew the whole story, she felt the love that many people never got to know in their lives. They both tore into each other, in total submission to every need and desire. They took turns being the aggressive and the subservient one. There was a lot of tenderness and a huge need to bring back the love they had been denied for so long. At one point Ki had to put his hand over Julia's mouth so she wouldn't wake the baby. When they finished, they put their clothes back on and resumed their conversation while Ki looked around the barn lacing up the back of Julia's dress.

"You have many things Indians need. I could trade for furs. Then sell furs to the white man for money."

Julia stiffened when he said this. "Ki, you couldn't sell them guns or weapons of any kind! The Patriots would stop you!"

That is precisely what Ki was thinking of doing, but he also knew that these guns could be used against the white man. The community would never accept him and would drive him away. "Then, it be iron."

"Yes. Pots, plows, and cloth; there are many things they could use." Julia and Ki were beginning to see hope in their future. Jason screamed for attention and food, making both parents look down and smile.

I Might Have

Ki started training horses and breeding them, and
it wasn't long before neighbors with new horses
were coming in need of this. He would take them to the
deep part of the river, and then he would mount them.
The deep water prevented the horses from bucking Ki
off, and eventually, the horse was mastered. He was teaching Robby and Willie to ride without reins or saddle.
Vicar Turner one day came to the house wanting to talk
to Julia and Ki.

"It appears that your son Jason is Fredrick Flynn. I
have checked with the family in New York, and there is
no Fredrick Flynn that they know of, no nephew named
Fredrick Flynn. All of Sarah's land is your son's. You both
are now the largest landholders in the region." Vicar
Turner had the deed of the land, which he handed to Ki.

Julia and the entire household were overwhelmed
with joy after the vicar left. They all gathered a picnic for
viewing the land and Sarah's house. Ki saw Megan and
Samuel taking a particular interest in the place. Everyone
was inspecting the house, barn, and fields.

The animals had long disappeared, except for a few
chickens up in the rafters of the barn. The house showed
signs of mice and rats—it needed a good cleaning. It was

small compared to the main house that Julia and Ki were living in, but it had a promising future.

Ki went down to the river and walked to the place where he had found his parents. The river was like a knife carving out a huge deep gully in the ground. Ki stood staring at the spot and felt the souls of his parents. Would they approve of him now? He did not think so; he wanted to talk to his father and tell him that times were changing, to defend his actions. He felt that they would still think of him as a traitor for leaving his people. Julia joined him there, putting her arms around his erect form. His anger and sadness were very apparent in his stance. Megan spotted them first,

"Ki is still having a hard time with losing his parents." She turned to look at Samuel, who was wide-eyed and had a troubled expression. "Is there something wrong, Samuel?"

Samuel quickly recovered, shaking his head and swiftly walking away, leading Megan back to the house. "Let's go look at the bedrooms." Samuel, trying to be romantic, whispered in Megan's ear, but his stiff and hurried body language did not show romance.

Megan stopped; Samuel could not move her. "Samuel, do you know something that you are not telling me?" Samuel had never been good at lying, especially to Megan. They were beginning to be able to read each other, intuitively knowing when the other avoided an issue that needed to be addressed. Samuel, not knowing how to handle this, decided to use romance as a cover, pulling Megan into the barn where they were alone. He took Megan in his arms, kissing her with a growing desire. A plan had formed in his head, and now was the perfect time to express it.

"Wouldn't it be great if we could have all of this for us? Do you think Julia and Ki would agree to it?" Megan, utterly won over by his desire for her, forgot everything, thinking how delightful living here with Samuel would be. "We could add on, making it even larger, making it ours. I know you are used to a lot better, but we can make it just like you want. Julia wants me to take over the planting and harvesting of everything. That would give us money so you can make this into what you want. But most of all, we would have privacy; it would be ours."

"That would be so wonderful, Samuel, but don't you have to return to Daniel Morgan?" Megan knew that they had been putting off the subject of him going back to fight for a long time, and it needed to be discussed. "Samuel, I want to be your wife, and this place would be perfect for us, but are you going back?"

Samuel took a deep breath, the sexual desire of the moment put out like water thrown on a fire. "Yes, I need to; I could be brought up on charges of desertion. I don't want to go right now because I feel like I am just starting a new life here. But yes, I need to go back. I gave my word that I would support the cause, and I want to, I do, but I never foresaw you coming into my life, I never thought that I could ever have a life like this, and I am afraid that I will lose it all if I leave."

"I don't want you to go either, but if you have to, know this—I will be here waiting and praying for you. Everything will be here waiting for your return. Samuel, I love you with all my heart and soul." Megan had tears in her eyes, causing Samuel to mold her to his body while kissing her.

———

Julia had given the planting and harvesting over to Samuel and his father. The McKinnys knew how to work the land after watching generations do it in Ireland. Henry had always hoped to get a farm on his lord's estate in Ireland instead of being a house servant. Henry would take his two sons to watch the planting and harvesting of the crops whenever possible in hopes that they would do this one day. Samuel wanted to go back to the new land to check the land boundaries and get a good look at the fields to see what needed planting there. Ki saw him coming out of the barn and said he would like to go along; it was about three miles from the main farm.

"I thought you weren't interested in working the land?" Samuel had noticed that Ki had shown no interest in farming.

"I want talk with you; Julia and I decide let you, Megan, have new land when marry." Samuel had to pause his horse for a moment because he was speechless. For a poor boy who had never owned anything except his gun and the clothes on his back, this was a windfall. He and Megan could have a beautiful life there.

"I can't tell you how happy that makes me! Megan and I will make good use of the land. She will be so happy! Hell, for a poor boy, I am so happy!"

"You return to Daniel Morgan?" Ki was looking concerned now.

"I suppose I should, I honestly believe in the cause, and I want us to win. I was telling Megan that I hope I'm not brought up on charges of desertion. But things have gotten crazy around here, some things great and others not. I feel like I have had my hands full. Ki, we can't live under a king! You will hate it, and you have never had to do it, with the Seneca way of life being so different. I know your people took their side, but you cannot trust the British. They lie about everything. Plus, I don't want to leave Megan now." Samuel took a deep breath, concerned over his dilemma.

"We not trust them; they make us servants. They do give us guns!" Ki smiled as he said this.

"The bastards need to go!" Samuel had been so worried over his situation that he had not noticed that they had stopped over the river's embankment where Ki's parents were killed. When Samuel noticed this, his body clenched, guilt was written all over his face, and his eyes moved to Ki, hoping that he hadn't detected it. But Ki had noticed.

"Samuel, you know? Who?" Ki was speaking with deadly seriousness, suspecting that Samuel knew more than he would say. Samuel put himself in Ki's place, for he would want to know who had killed his parents. Julia and Ki were so generous to Megan and him that he felt he owed it to Ki to tell him the truth. For a long time, Samuel just looked at the river, trying to get the right words to come out.

"That night, when we heard that the soldiers were attacking Julia and my family, I was crazy with worry. We started from over there." Samuel was pointing past the river. "We camped by the river, heard about the attack, and ran to the farm to help Julia when we saw your parents over there." Samuel pointed up the river where the murders happened had happened. "There had been Indian attacks around here, and you know how Daniel hated Indians, so he told us to kill them. Ki, if I had known, I would never have hurt your parents, especially if I had known your baby was with them. It was so dark that night. I have so much guilt in me; please know that I had no idea they were your parents!"

For a long time, Ki just glared at the river, then he spoke very quietly and gravely. "You go to Daniel Morgan. Now! You not go back to farm, and you not tell Megan. You not tell parents. You leave now! Take rifle and horse, leave place! You not come back." Ki was looking at Samuel with murder in his eyes.

"Ki, I am sorry; please forgive me!" Samuel was now in disbelief that the situation had gotten entirely out of control. But then again, if he had been in Ki's place, how would he have reacted? Would he have done the same thing? Samuel noticed Ki's hand on his gun; they were eye to eye. Samuel lowered his head, nodded his consent, turned his horse around to the east where he, in time, would find Morgan.

Now that Ki had married Julia, he was in control of the entire fortune. Ki watched him ride away, and then he thought about what he would tell the women. This turn of events would not go over well with Julia, much less with Megan. They would be offended by what he had done? After all, he was the newcomer in the family. Julia had given Samuel a lot of responsibilities that Ki had not wanted, but now he would have to step up. He did not relish the idea of farming, for this had always been women's work, but that would change because there was so much land to farm—the men had to help. What would he say to Samuel's parents? Even though this was bad, he felt he had done justice to his parents, showing them the respect they deserved. After all, he and Julia had lost their baby for agonizing months over this.

———

"What do you mean 'He just left'! He would have told me he was going! We were planning our wedding! Where did he go?" Megan was hysterical, standing by Henry and Molly, who were looking at Ki very suspiciously. When they realized Samuel was gone, they came looking for Ki in the horses' barn.

"He want go back with Daniel Morgan; he afraid?" Ki had to think of the word. "Desertion—he left. Daniel Morgan not a man you play with." Ki was standing next to Julia.

"Ki, do you know more than what you are saying?" Julia was also looking at him with doubt. She noticed his stance was stiff, as if he would not reveal the true nature of the situation. He appeared determined to only say so much in regard to Samuel's departure. When it was apparent that no one was getting any more information, Megan, in tears, went to her room, banging the door shut. Slowly Molly and Henry returned to their modest home, feeling they had been denied the truth.

"Now that we are alone, what happened? Ki, tell me, because I don't want any secrets in our marriage. If we have secrets, then this marriage will not work!" Ki had never seen Julia look so grave and determined. Her face had turned red, with eyes like blue balls of fire. He knew that she needed the truth, and maybe she could explain it to Megan in some way that she would understand.

"Samuel killed my parents!" Ki looked at Julia with loathing.

"What!"

"The night I killed John, Daniel Morgan camped at river, heard attack, crossed river, saw my parents. Daniel told men kill them. They may killed Jason!"

"Do you know for sure that Samuel was the one who did it?"

"Samuel sharpshooter. I saw him kill many times. He knows he did. He not tell us! I told him go back to Daniel Morgan, never come back."

At this, Julia closed her eyes in despair. "Ki, he did not know they were your parents! We have had Indian attacks here, and the Patriots do not trust the Indians because of it. This was a terrible accident!"

"If I near him, I kill him! It good that he left." When Julia looked into Ki's eyes, she saw the truth in what he was saying. If she wanted this marriage to work, then she would have to accept his ways. But how was her sister ever going to recover from the setback? Her sister had shown great loyalty and bravery coming to get her. Now her husband was breaking Megan's heart over an accident. Could she live in the same house with a person she knew had killed her parents? Probably not. Julia tried to stop the tears while she watched Ki walk away.

Julia went upstairs to talk to Megan. She found her crying her eyes out on her bed. Julia walked over to her, not knowing what to say. "Ki told me why he told Samuel to leave."

Megan quickly sat up. "Why?"

"That horrible night when John came, Samuel was camped with Daniel Morgan by the river; this was when they saw Yuma and Keme. They killed them."

"How do you know Samuel was the one who killed them?" Megan's eyes and face were puffy from crying.

"I don't think Samuel ever denied it when Ki asked; besides, they all were deadly shooters."

"They did not know whom they were shooting at! There have been Indian attacks all around here! Samuel told me Daniel Morgan hated Indians."

"I know, but you have to try and look at it from Ki's side. These were his parents."

"What if he doesn't come back! What if he gets killed and I never see him again?"

"Megan, you knew he would have to go back sometime."

Megan nodded her agreement and blew her nose. "But I thought he would at least say goodbye, Julia; he asked me to marry him! Doesn't that mean something? We were making plans!" Julia hugged her sister, patting her back. Suddenly Megan drew away and with wide eyes said, "You love him! You are making excuses for him!"

"Megan, I am not making excuses; all I'm trying to do is see things from Ki's side and Samuel's side also.

Hopefully, this will all blow over, and by the time Samuel comes back, maybe they can be friends again. Megan, they were friends for some time before this."

"I don't know, and I feel something terrible is going to happen." Megan was crying again.

———

Ki saw Molly and Henry working in the small garden behind their house. When they saw Ki, they quickly looked away. Ki thought of his parents and how they would want to know the truth; hell, they had come looking for him and gotten killed for it. Ki also remembered how it had felt when Jason went missing. He went to them, realizing that maybe he would tell them the truth.

"Samuel killed my parents." This was all Ki said.

"I was afraid of that; I knew Samuel came with Daniel Morgan from the same direction as your parents. When I first heard that your parents had been killed, I figured that it might be them. Well, Samuel needed to get back to what he started. He needed to go back and not be charged with desertion. I know that Megan is upset, but Samuel needed to go."

Henry spoke like a true man, and for this, Ki respected him. But Ki could see that Molly was upset and did not feel the same way. Ki walked to his horse and stood patting him for a long time. He had brought unpleasant feelings to the family that he had just entered. The idea that he had made a mistake coming here was heavy in the air. He came from a different world that they knew nothing about. He would separate Julia and Megan, knowing Julia would be loyal to him. Julia found him standing next to his horse, looking like he wanted to leave. Panic hit her, and she ran to him. "You are not going to leave?"

When Ki looked at Julia, all he could see was love in her eyes. "I bring sorry to your family."

"Samuel killed your parents! Everyone will just have to get over it. They will in time, and Samuel did have to get back, and this was as good a time as any. Ki, I can't live without you! We have gone through too much to stop now! We are a family!"

"Your sister?"

"My sister will just have to make do, and I will talk to her. She will come around eventually." Julia needed to prove to Ki that she was telling the truth, so she kissed him hard, using sex, letting her tongue move all over his mouth and lips, enjoying the reaction she got from him.

"Julia, you make me happy!" Ki needed this reminder of their love.

"In my world, people don't marry for love; they marry for money. You love me for who I am. We lived together without my money and were happy. I don't want anything to come between us—ever. Coming here to this new country has taught me that. I can be the woman I want to be, and I want that for you also."

When You See Smoke, Run!

Robby smiled to himself when he saw Elsa Mees at the river doing her family's laundry. He noticed she was wearing the ribbons in her hair that he had saved up for two months to get at the general store. The two were scheduling meetings regularly; their secret encounters had progressed to kissing and holding each other. He silently came up to her as she washed out her father's pants, beating them on a rock. Herman had been teaching him blacksmithing, along with Fredrick. Robby loved it and took to it with enthusiasm when he wasn't farming on Julia's land. The Germans had finished their houses and brought their families here on a ship from Germany. Fredrick had five fair-haired, blue-eyed children, and Herman's six children were of all ages. Their wives were large-boned woman who knew how to do everything to thrive in this wild land, for they had been peasants in their homeland. Beer-making and sausage were their specialties, which they would sell for extra money.

"Oh! You scare me." Robby had his hands around her waist. He bent down to kiss her, and she accepted it with eagerness.

"You knew I would show up; we had a lot of work to do, and it took me a while to get away."

"Mama and pappy know I come." Elsa's English was coming along, and when not working on their farm, she and her siblings attended the one-room school that had just been constructed near the church and general store.

"I know our meetings are noticed. Willie smiles at me when I leave to come here as if he knows just what I am up to."

"I go. I down here long. Pappy come for me; I get back soon."

"One more kiss before you go?" Robby tried to keep his hands from going to her breasts. They kissed long and hard. Finally, they parted. with both panting heavily.

"Two days, I be down here again. Baby's diapers welcome now because they bring me to you." Elsa gathered the laundry into a basket and blew him a kiss as she walked away.

———

Ki sat as still as he could, watching the female wolf returning to her den. He had covered himself with bear oil to mask his smell. He had first seen her coming to the chicken coop, trying to enter it at night. Julia and Ki had made sure that the enclosure was secure from wild animals. Julia loved those birds and considered them her pets. She built cages up high and put a roof over them to protect them from owls and hawks. She had made special enclosures for the laying hens that she had a great fondness for, giving them names. Julia had never known that some hens just wanted to sit all day on eggs and hatch them out. When she brought an egg to her favorite laying hen, it would meet her at the cage's opening and roll the egg back to the nest. Julia loved feeding the chickens and watching the babies grow. She was even beginning to sell eggs and some of the baby chicks.

"Why you bring big eggs to lay hens?" Ki was laughing at Julia, which irritated her.

"I want big chickens, so I pick the largest eggs to give to my layers," Julia stubbornly stated. "Also, I am trying to get the double yoke chickens. You know, the ones that lay only the double yokes."

"You get surprise." Ki was laughing louder.

"What surprise?" Julia wanted to know, but Ki wouldn't say. When the eggs hatched out, Julia soon realized that all she had were roosters. The roosters grew big and aggressive, chasing Julia out of the coop half the time. That is when Julia realized she could kill and pluck a chicken. These were skills that she thought she would never have to learn, but now they made her feel proud to be adding to her family's survival. After that, Julia did not give the laying hens just the large eggs to hatch out.

Ki thought about this as he watched the wolf leave the den after nursing her pups. He knew the puppies were about five weeks old, so this was the time to choose which ones he wanted. Waiting five minutes after she left, he entered her den and chose a big male and a female. They growled at him, making him laugh when he picked up the male. Ki slapped the pup for snarling to let him know who was boss and that this behavior would not be allowed, and he did the same for the female. Making sure they did not kill the chickens was going to take some training on his part. Ki brought the pups into the barn, where he gave them goat's milk. After dinner, he would bring them meat that he had cut up. The mother came two nights to retrieve them, causing Ki to put them in a kitchen box, where they would become familiar with humans. Jason could now waddle to them and pick them up in his chubby little hands, and this kept him amused for hours. The boy was called Koda, and the girl Bala.

The wolves would alert the family to the approach of strangers. The Indian attacks were becoming a much talked about event because farms had been burnt, with the occupants killed, kidnapped, and never seen again. The killings were horrific—baby's heads bashed in, throats cut, and heads scalped.

"Do you think that we will be attacked?" Julia was asking Ki.

"No, they not attack another Indian; we will protect us. I know the Seneca not come here, but another tribe maybe."

This terrified Julia, so she gave Ki money to buy more guns. They had regular practices with the arms and learned how to load them and aim using targets that Ki had set up. Megan was best at hitting the targets.

"Where did you learn to shoot?" Julia was amazed as she saw Megan hitting the target regularly.

"Samuel taught me," Megan said with anger in her words. She was still mad about Samuel leaving without a goodbye. The tension had not lessened in the house.

"Megan, when he comes back, I know things will blow over."

"You don't know that! What if he doesn't come back. What if he is killed?"

"We need to pray for his safe return. Besides, his parents live here, and he will come back." Megan looked at Julia with doubt and went back to the house in a huff. Their relationship was tense, and this worried Julia. She prayed every night for Samuel's safe return. What if Samuel was killed? Would Megan ever forgive her?

———

Robby was slipping the dress off of Elsa's shoulder as he held his breath. She had crept out of the house after everyone was asleep. They were making plans for the future, but right now, all Robby could think of was bedding Elsa. They were just falling on the hay in the barn when the war cries of the Indians surrounded the house. Elsa screamed, making Robby put his hand on her mouth to quiet her. They both were terrified and hid under the hay while hearing horrid screams coming from the house. The children cried and called for help, and Elsa wanted to go to them, but Robby held her back. There were shots and then silence, then fire and smoke.

"They will kill you! Elsa, I am sorry, but it is too late for them." Robby was holding Elsa, trying to think about how they could hide.

"I have to do something!" Elsa was becoming hysterical.

"Elsa, quiet! They will come in here, and we have to hide." Robby grabbed as much hay as he could, trying to cover Elsa and himself. Then they could smell smoke, and at the same time, the Indians entered the barn. Both held their breath; Robby had his hand over Elsa's mouth as their arms circled each other. The Indians ran all over the barn, gathering loot to bring back to their tribe. Suddenly an Indian ran over them, stopping to see what was under the hay and pulling it back.

Robby shouted, "Don't hurt her! Take me!" Robby had never felt such terror; their faces were red, with long black stripes. They looked evil, and Robby knew he had just seen the devil. Elsa screamed for her life; that is when one of the Indians grabbed her by the hair and smiled at Robby as he cut her throat open. Blood spurted like a river from Elsa onto Robby's shirt and pants as her eyes rolled up into her head. He saw the life of Elsa leave her body. Robby was speechless and felt vomit come up through his throat. One of the Indians held his arms behind his back, but he barely noticed because all he could do was look at Elsa. The Indians laughed while he threw up, then loud sobs came from him, making them laugh even more wildly.

"Go to hell, all of you fucking heathens!"

Robby received the butt of a rifle on his head; he lost consciousness. He was hauled off over the shoulder of Running Wolf.

"The dogs are howling in the directions of the Mees house." Julia had gotten out of bed because of the noise. She hoped the dogs would not wake Jason from his sleep. It was a clear night, and from the horizon came flames.

"Ki, there are flames and smoke! Is it an attack?" Ki jumped out of bed and came to the window.

"I will go and see it." Ki quickly went down the stairs and found Henry standing in front of his house.

"Robby is gone! I think he went to see Elsa Mees. Oh my God, their place is on fire!" said Henry.

"Get everyone up, get guns. Everyone be ready to fight! I go over there, see what happening!" Ki was running to the barn and mounted his horse without saddle or bridle. Henry started yelling for everyone to get up and get the guns. Mia and Willie came out; Sally came out holding Kucma's hand; all had their guns loaded as they had been taught. Henry got as much ammunition as they had and got all the women into the main house. Megan was holding her gun as she sat in front of her window. All stood in a window with the children in the middle of the kitchen, hopefully out of the way of stray bullets, watching for danger to come. Ki commanded the wolves to stay at the house as he rode away.

"Where's Robby?" Willie cried from his window, holding his rifle.

"He is at Elsa's house!" Henry yelled at him.

"That's where the attack is." Willie was trying to keep from shaking.

"Ki went to see what is happening; let's pray that it is just fire and not an attack." Julia tried her best to calm everyone down, but she was terrified, letting Jason feel this, so he screamed in terror.

They sat there all night and into the morning. Mia put her gun down to make breakfast, which she brought to each person at their window. Weariness had set in, along with uncertainty, making everyone irritable. The children had fallen asleep on the floor. Everyone was on high alert, not wanting to look away.

Finally, Megan yelled down to Julia, "Don't you think he would be back by now?"

"He might be helping with the fire."

Megan could not see the strain on Julia's face. "Well, we will just have to pray that he comes back unharmed," Megan said sarcastically, remembering what Julia had told her about Samuel.

"Now is not the time, Megan!" Julia was about to lose her temper.

"Now you know how I feel!"

"Do you have to be such a bitch right now?" Julia was fighting tears of hurt and fear for Ki. Henry could feel this was getting out of control, so he stepped in between the two sisters.

"For the love of God, be quiet! We could be under attack at any time." Julia and Megan were suddenly quiet, both thinking that Henry sounded a lot like their father when he was upset.

———

Robby woke up, and the first thing he saw was Running Wolf combing out the scalp of Elsa. He knew this was her hair because it still had the ribbons he had bought for her. Running Wolf was smiling at him as he did it, knowing Robby had purchased these for Elsa. He set the hair near the fire to dry out so he could proudly put it on his belt. Robby tasted blood and knew it was Elsa's; as gruesome as it was, Robby knew this was the last of Elsa he would ever see. Robby was wondering why he was still alive. He sat up and noticed three other Indians with them. He suddenly needed to vomit yet again, but nothing was in his stomach; only dry heaves came up. The Indians laughed at him. Robby knew the Indians took captives to induct into the tribe; he would not submit. But then again, if he didn't, he knew what the punishment was—burning for days, tied to a stake. Robby could not get the picture out of his head of Running Wolf, smiling at him, as he cut the throat of Elsa. Robby had been through a lot in his short life; being sold as an indentured servant from Ireland had given him the rage to kill. Now he had it fearsomely he wanted to kill them all. Robby worked the ties on his hands to loosen them, and to his surprise, they were coming loose, but what would he do if he got free? There were four of them, and he knew he could not take them all without any weapons.

Ki had been tracking them all night. He knew it was his tribe that had committed the massacres on the Mees family. When he got to the Mees house, it was on fire, and inside were the Mees family's bodies. Mr. and Mrs., along with six children ranging from seventeen to six months. The mother had her throat cut, and the father had been stabbed many times. All were missing their scalps. The fireplace was dripping with the blood of the young children whose heads had been bashed against it. The barn was also on fire, and most of the animals taken. Ki knew they would take away a captive, and he figured it would be Robby. The Seneca needed new warriors—and he had been right, he knew as he observed Running Wolf from a tree. Ki saw Running Wolf smiling at Robby and thought about the fact that this Indian had always had an aberrant nature. He had liked to torture small animals before killing them, even though the elders would admonish him for doing this. Ki had brought with him his rifle and a pistol, along with ammunition; he tied his horse to a tree about half a mile away because he did not want the horse to give his hiding place away.

Ki knew they would come to this spot because of the river; they needed water. Running Wolf and another Indian left to find wood for the fire, and this was when Ki figured he could attack. Running Wolf was running with the Delaware Indians, and when one was busy with the food at the fire, Ki ran up to him and cut his throat. Robby saw this and quickly worked his hands free of the rope to help Ki. The other Indian turned and came at Ki with his tomahawk, but Robby grabbed him by the leg as he was running, tripping him. Ki was on him and cut his throat; when the third Indian came in and fought with Ki, they squared off, and the two went down in a fighting mass with Ki on the bottom. Ki turned his gun upward, shooting the Indian.

Running Wolf heard the noise and came back, climbing up a tree, quietly hanging over Ki. Ki was busy telling Robby to run when Running Wolf jumped on Ki from the tree and tried to bury his tomahawk into Ki's arm. Both Robby and Ki were so active that they had not heard Running Wolf. Running Wolf grabbed Ki and brought his knife to Ki's throat, making Robby freeze; he did not know what to do because he did not have a weapon. Both thought this was the end until they saw an arrow slice through Running Wolf's throat. Astonished, they turned to see Ben standing there, in full Indian dress, for he had grown even more into a sizable man, making a formidable picture dressed in his Indian clothes with the weapons on his belt. Ben stepped into the campsite, quickly going to Ki and dressing his wound with a cloth from one of the Indian's blankets, trying to stop the bleeding.

"Ben! What you doing here?" Ki sank to the ground, exhausted and losing blood. Ben redid the cloth, tying it tighter to stop the blood. Ki looked Ben in the face and said thank you in the Seneca's tongue. Ben was silent as he worked with Ki's arm; he stood back.

"I am going back; I decided to return to my sister. I was on my way back to her when I heard of the raid Running Wolf was on. I knew they would come here." Ben was looking at Ki, who was trying to stand up but was light-headed from blood loss. "Running Wolf brought in a Rebel captive who wanted me to free him, and the Rebel told me that if I joined the Rebel militia, I would be a free man at the end of the war. I tried to free him, but Running Wolf found out and burned him alive. Running Wolf and I haven't been getting along." Ben said this with contempt in his voice. "Did you bring a horse, because I think you will need it."

"Yes, tied up." Ki was pointing to the east, and Ben took off for the horse. Robby looked with concern at Ki, who was having a hard time standing up.

"We need to get you home quickly. Molly and Mia will know what to do with that arm." Robby helped Ki stand when Ben came back with the horse, and both helped Ki onto it.

———

Julia helped with the burial of the bodies at the Mees house. Sobs could be heard everywhere, along with cussing from the men at the carnage in the burnt house and barn. All Julia could think about was how hopeful Herman Mees had been that day in the barn. Everyone was scared and angry at the Indians but mostly at the British for encouraging them to attack the settlers. The British told them only to attack those who were Patriots, but the Indians did not know who was a Patriot versus a Loyalist, so they attacked everyone. The Loyalists soon became Patriots when they realized the British would not defend them and, in fact, put their very lives in danger when supplying the Indians with arms.

"Where is Ki?" Vicar Turner asked Julia in a harsh voice as she helped with Elsa's burial. "And where is Robby?

"Robby was here with Elsa when the attack came. They took him, and Ki went after them."

"Ki is not a part of this?"

"No. He would not do this!" Julia was mad at the Vicar for the asking. "He is trying to save Robby!"

"How do you know that?" the vicar asked Julia, who was getting angrier, but at that moment, Robby came into the clearing. He looked like he had been through hell; he was covered with dried blood. Both Julia and the vicar ran to him.

"My God, Robby, you are safe!" Julia put both of her arms around him.

"Ki saved me; he killed them, with Ben's help. Ben is back, and you need to go to Ki because he took a toma-hawk to the arm and he needs your help." Julia ran to her horse and jumped on it, taking off at a dead run.

"Robby, what happened here?" The vicar was talking to him, but Robby knelt by the newly dug grave.

"Is this her grave?" Robby couldn't keep the tears from falling. "They came in fast and attacked the house and killed everyone. Elsa and I were in the barn; we tried to hide, but they found us. I stood there as they cut her throat." Robby broke down and sobbed. Vicar Turner put his arms around him. "I don't think I would be alive if it weren't for Ki. He and Ben killed all of them. One was Seneca, and three were Delaware."

"Don't blame yourself! There was nothing you could have done. Thank God you survived."

———

Julia came running into the house to find Mia sewing up the cut on Ki's arm. It was bleeding down his arm, and he did not look good. Julia ran to him and hugged him without disturbing Mia. Julia had never seen a cut this size being sewn up with needle and thread. Her eyes grew large; she wanted to put her hand to her mouth because she knew it had to hurt a lot. When she hugged Ki, he felt hot with fever.

"You are burning up! But thank God you are alive!" Julia kissed Ki on the cheek.

"Ben came back; making sweat lodge, help with fever." Mia was pouring whiskey on the cut and wrapping it up tight to stop the bleeding. Julia looked at Mia, who was shaking her head.

"This is a deep cut. I hope these stitches will hold up; fever concerns me." Julia could see from the redness that the cut was becoming infected.

"Will Ki be all right? He will be well, won't he?" Julia was becoming hysterical, so Ki took her hand to reassure her.

"I be well, you see; I need fever out."

"Come to bed and rest." Julia helped Ki get to their bed. He was sleepy, needing rest. She took off his clothes and bathed him as best she could, making him weakly laugh.

"I need jump in river; wash away blood faster, take fever away.

"No. Let me do this for you. I remember when your mother dunked me in the river! I thought she was crazy, but it did work. I am using cold water from the well; it should help with the fever. God, I am so glad you are alive." Julia kissed him all over his face, noticing that he was exhausted; she sat there with him until he slept. She thought about what her mother did when she was ill—make chicken soup. Julia got up and went down to the coop and stared at the rooster who had tried to attack her that morning when gathering eggs. She grabbed the hatch with murder in her eyes. The rooster just stood there, looking at her with disdain, as if challenging her to a fight. Usually, this would have scared Julia because he had big spurs on his legs that could do some damage. Julia stood there with the hatch and dared him to come, and he did in one enormous spurt. She squared her legs, holding the blade like a club, and swung, taking off his head with one motion. Then she held the chicken up so the blood left the body.

"My God, Julia, what are you doing?" Megan had never seen her sister so determined.

"I am going to make chicken soup for Ki. Don't you remember—that is what mom did for us when we were sick?" Julia held the chicken with pride, amazed at what she had just done, then she headed to the house to ask Sally how to do the rest. For the first time, Julia plucked a chicken, learned how to cut one up, and made chicken soup, while Megan watched, laughing at her attempts to cook.

———

Ben and Sally made a sweat lodge out of saplings covered with blankets. He made sure that the rocks he used did not have air pockets that would explode in the fire. He knew some of the traditional words of the ceremony used in the sweat lodge.

It began to work because the fever lessened every day, with the additional help of rum-soaked clothes on the cut.

"This seems to be working; it worked when Ki brought me to the village after I lost my little girl, and I was very ill," Julia said to Ben.

"Ki has not told you the reason I came back? I will join the Rebel militia to be a free man when this war is over. I will be taking Sally and Kucma with me. They will also be free at the end of this war. They will be camp followers while I fight." Julia was taken aback by the words. She and Sally had always been friends, and Julia depended on her for many things. But if Julia had the label of a slave on her back, she would want it removed. "There is more; I would like for you to give us money so we can buy a small piece of land in Vermont, where they have declared slavery illegal." Julia knew Ben had saved Ki's life, and they had been through hell because of what John had done to Sally. This was the least Julia could do for them.

"It will never excuse what John did to Sally and what both of you have had to do to be free, so I will give you a diamond that can be easily hidden from thieves while you are in the militia camp. I will miss Sally! I have grown to love Kucma, even though it has been hard for me."

Julia found Sally in the kitchen and ran to her, putting her arms around Sally's waist. "I will miss you so much, but I understand why you want to go."

Sally had tears in her eyes. "I am so glad you understand why we need to leave. I don't think the Adamses are looking for us anymore, but I know there are papers still out there with our names on them.

"I understand perfectly, and I hope you someday find the happiness you deserve. You and I have been through a lot, but I have found peace, so you need to find yours." Julia hugged Sally.

A week later Ben, Sally, and Kucma would leave the farm. Julia couldn't help but think this was the last reminder of John she would ever have to see. The farm had almost doubled in size now that they had acquired the new land, and Julia would miss their help and the memories of everything they had been through and seen.

"What is this?" Julia brought the steaming soup into their bedroom on a tray.

"This is what I was taught to do when you are sick. It is chicken soup; it may help. Try it. I made it just for you." Ki looked at it suspiciously, but he did not want to hurt Julia's feelings, so he tried it. It was tasteless, but he acted like it was delicious, making himself eat the whole thing because Julia was standing over him, hands on hips like his mother used to do when he was a child. Ki looked at her anxious face and knew she loved him. She was breathtaking to him at that moment. He set the bowl down and took her hand in his, and pulled her to the bed. Julia felt his head.

"I think your fever is going down. Well, it sure looks like you are feeling better." Ki was kissing Julia's neck as he removed her chemise.

All We Have Is Each Other

J ulia was in the beautiful gown that her mother had chosen for her to wear in London. She knew she was beautiful and was enjoying the moment. John was trying to get her attention, but she teased him by dancing with everyone but him. She enjoyed the sour expression on his face as she danced the night away. Julia had forgotten how much she enjoyed dancing with the fresh summer winds coming in from the ballroom's open doors. The food was delicious, and the punch was how she loved it. Her parents enjoyed watching her; this was how they hoped to win a proper suitor for her. Suddenly loud cries came from the doorways as Indians dressed in full war battle mode began running in. They started killing everyone and setting fire to the ballroom. Julia looked to her parents and saw an Indian start to scalp her father. He looked at her and yelled, "*Run.*" Julia saw another Indian grab her mother as he held a knife to her throat. Julia ran outside, where she saw that she was the only one there. She turned to look back and saw her parents on the large porch with the Indians holding them, knives to their throats. John was there with them, and he had a very large Indian holding him as blood came from his head and throat. Julia couldn't believe it, but her father waved goodbye to her as blood spouted from his throat, then he fell off the terrace.

"Noooo!" Julia sat up in the bed with sweat all over her body. Her scream woke the baby. Ki woke up with a start and put his arms around Julia, realizing she had just had a nightmare.

"Dream; I am here." Ki got up for Jason, who was crying loudly after hearing his mother scream. He brought the baby to the bed, where Julia took him and rocked him gently to get him back to sleep while nursing him because her milk had come back in. Ki wrapped his arms around both of them as they leaned back into the pillows.

"Tell me ?"

"It doesn't make any sense. I was back in London dancing; John was there. Indians came in and attacked us. My father told me to run as he was being killed, so I ran outside, and that is when I saw everyone on the porch with the Indians killing them, but my father waved goodbye to me."

"You dream your old life, and new life come into it; you miss old life?"

"A part of me does. I was enjoying myself until the Indians came."

"You feel safe?"

"I don't know." Julia went deeper into Ki's arms.

"You happy, Julia?"

Julia thought about it. "I am happy for the woman I have become. I am so glad to be married to the man

I love. But there are things that I miss. I don't want to go around wearing fancy clothes and jewelry all day. But I was having fun dancing and being young again. What about you? You have had to change into this life we now live? Do you have bad dreams also?" Ki had to choose his words carefully.

"Many things I miss. Indians don't make money. Here everything is money. I miss freedom of only hunting, giving shelter, that enough, now it is not. I have bad dreams; I cannot protect you and Jason." Julia sat up and looked closely into Ki's face.

"Are you happy here?"

"I change like you. I enjoy comfort of house, feel becoming—" Ki had to think of the right words. "Soft."

"Ki, are you happy?"

"You, yes. New for us. White man hates Indian in me; it is hard. Why you keep asking?"

"This life is so different from what you are accustomed to, and I seriously don't know if I can do this without you. You have been my rock almost from the time I got to this new world. I keep thinking that you are going to want to go back, and it worries me."

"Julia, you strong woman. You needed change, and you do it. When we apart, you survived. Tom right; Indian will need change after war. I hope I help my people when they need me."

A sense of protectiveness filled Julia, and she felt the challenge of going forward into this new life. Life had given her a curve, but she would be dammed if she would let it bring her and the family she loved down. She thought of the Bible, of 1 Corinthians 13:11: "When

I was a child, I talked like a child, I thought like a child, I reasoned like a child. When I became a man, I put the ways of childhood behind me."

The old life was gone, and this was a new one that brought new challenges every single day. Dancing in ballrooms and wearing ball dresses were over and gone, but Julia felt a strength she never knew she had in her. It was the modern world challenging her: "Can you do this? What kind of woman are you?"

The Patriot

Samuel McKinny found himself in the Corps of Light Infantry, which on June 12, 1779, formed as an elite seasonal combat organization under the command of Anthony Wayne. They were to attack Stony Point, about ten miles south of West Point and thirty-five miles north of New York City. The British had set up their stronghold with cannons, five irons, four mortars, and four small howitzers. Also, there was The British Seventy-First Regiment, the Royal Artillery, and the Royal Navy gunboat on the Hudson River. Last of all came the Loyal American Regiment, made of Loyalists from America; these men were deemed inferior soldiers by the British, simply because they were American and uncivilized. The armed sloop, the Vulture, was anchored outside the river to oversee the British's safety. In all, there were 8,000 British and only 1,350 Patriots to bring them down.

Washington observed all of this through a telescope from Buckberg Mountain, and he formed a plan. Samuel was told to go to the local tavern to see what he could find out about the stronghold. The Patriots often used this plan because the British were known to get drunk and reveal things. He acted as a local farmer and went to the inn, hoping to learn about the garrison's strength and, most importantly, the sentries' placement. He needed information on how the southern stronghold was fortified because this was where the Patriots planned to attack. Samuel had collected money from the Patriots soldiers to buy rounds of beer at the tavern. That was where he found a British soldier who looked as if he had been up all day and night drinking by himself. The soldier was young and seemed to be somewhat wet behind the ears—just what Samuel needed.

"Let me buy you a tanker; you look like you could use it." Samuel put his hand on the man's shoulder.

"And why would you do that?" The soldier looked surprised. Samuel pulled up a chair next to the young soldier and put on his most genuine smile.

"I hate them Sons of Liberty; they destroyed my farm. They came in and took all the livestock and what little food I had in the fields. My wife and children are starving now. I have to start all over again!" Samuel looked mad as he fixed about the tavern hoping others would hear him and not suspect him a fraud.

"I hear them Sons of Liberty are bastards. Thanks—I could use a tanker." The soldier appeared to relax. Samuel could tell he was exhausted.

"Been up all night?" Samuel held his breath.

"Been up since four this morning and worked until four in the afternoon." The soldier rubbed his face and eyes with his hand. This was precisely what Samuel needed to know.

"Hell, I get up at four every morning and work until sunset on the farm. Those cows needed milking, but now they are gone, thanks to those bastard Patriots. Are those your regular hours?" Samuel looked sympathetic while signaling for another round of beer.

"Yes, and it is about to kill me." Samuel laughed at this.

"Don't farm; it will kill you for sure." Samuel needed to know more about the south side of Stony Point. "The wind sure has been coming from the south strong at night. It makes it nice to sleep, not so hot." This was the only thing Samuel could think of to get the soldier talking about the south end of the stronghold, and he knew it was lame.

"London, where I am from, is cool at this time of the year; I am a city boy."

Samuel rolled his eyes and tried to think of a different way to get him back to talking about the stronghold's south end. "I saw them Patriots attack the center of the stronghold; they actually thought they could take you British." Samuel acted like he was getting drunk and moved in closer to the soldier. Samuel knew this had been a false attack to fool the British into thinking that they would come in from the stronghold center.

"They are so stupid, we have fortified it heavily." The man was slurring his words, so now Samuel decided it was time to call for whiskey. He waved the maid over.

"Bring your finest whiskey!"

She just nodded her head and left to retrieve it. When the whiskey came, Samuel took his glass and downed half of it to show his manliness, hoping the soldier would do the same. It worked; the soldier, with shaking hands, tried to down the whiskey as he rocked in his seat with glassy eyes that were having a hard time focusing. Samuel leaned in closer and looked worried.

"What if they come from a different direction? Will you be able to stop them? Those bastards are sneaky."

It took a minute for the words to register in the soldier's head, and he had a hard time forming a sentence. His mouth moved without words coming out, but then he finally said, "Colonel says they too stupid to do that. It also hard for them to come from the south. There's two to four feet of water on that side." Samuel took note of that and would have to warn Wayne about it.

Samuel decided to push for more, so he shook his head. "I don't know; they are such a pain in the arse that they could just come from a different way."

Once again, it took the soldier a while to answer. "No. The colonel knows they come from the center."

For a second, Samuel thought he would throw up on the table, but he still needed the guard shift times. "Well, now that I think of it, maybe your guard shift isn't so bad after all. The other shift must be at night, and that is a hard time to stay awake?" Samuel was thinking, *Come on, give me what I need to know!*

"The other shift is from four in the afternoon to three in the morning, then we"—the soldier rocked forward as if he was going to pass out, his eyes fell shut for a moment, so Samuel gently shook his arm to make him continue, and finally he spoke—"we have shift change in the main room." The soldier started to laugh and almost choked, whiskey dripping from his chin. Samuel looked around the room to see if anyone noticed, but everyone was interested in their drinks and conversations. The soldier laughed harder, and his face turned red.

"What is so funny?" Samuel was still looking around the room to see if anyone was watching. The soldier was all but giggling.

"When we do shift change, no one is on post." Samuel turned his attention back to the soldier with alarming interest.

"Isn't that dangerous?" Samuel couldn't believe his luck. The soldier could no longer talk he was so intoxicated; he just nodded his head and laughed again at the situation's foolishness. Samuel thought he had gotten enough out of the soldier, and it was time to leave before being noticed.

"Well, good luck with them bastards; you will show them." The soldier laughed, and whiskey spurted out of his mouth again. "I must be getting back to the wife and brood." Samuel got up quickly, looking over the room for anyone spying on him, but there were only drunken soldiers emptying their tankers. He took a circular route back to the Patriot camp, ensuring he was not followed, and reported everything to Washington.

———

Samuel woke up with excruciating pain at his ankle. He reached for it to stop the agony and saw that he was in a barn with several other soldiers. One soldier on a table had a piece of wood in his mouth while the doctor sawed off his leg at the knee. Three other men held the man down, and tears were pouring from his eyes while the doctor tried to stop the bleeding. Whiskey was being drunk by all, including the doctor. Samuel looked at the scene with disgust. He examined his ankle and saw that the flesh was gone around a large hole, and when he removed the bandages, the blood began to flow. A woman ran up to him, telling him to let the applications alone and that he was next for doctor's table. Samuel looked at the man on the table, and the hair on his neck stood up. The man was no longer writhing in pain but was perfectly still, his arms outstretched beside him as the doctor was listening to his chest. The doctor shook his head no, and the three men removed the dead man from the table. Samuel made up his mind; he would not let them take his foot.

"Samuel, your foot is not going to heal, and you need to let us take it off." The doctor was tired and did not want to have an argumentative discussion. He had done too many of these and was sick of it.

"No. You will not do that to me. Did we win?" Suddenly the doctor perked up, and there was a small sign of happiness on his tried face.

"Yes, you Patriots did proudly. You scaled up the side of the embankment and broke into the garrison and took that son of a bitch in twenty-five minutes. It was hard going through the water, but you guys did it perfectly. Knowing when the guard shift time was happening was brilliant because that was when the attack came. Washington is proud. Don't you remember it?"

Samuel tried to remember, but all he could see in his mind was the British soldier coming at him. He remembered bayoneting him with his gun before the Brit could fire off his weapon. Samuel realized that the Brit must have fallen with his gun hitting the ground, causing it to go off, striking Samuel in the ankle. Samuel tried to turn away but tripped because of his foot, falling directly on the metal ring of a barrel of whiskey with his head, knocking him out cold. He felt his head, where a sizeable purple bump was throbbing. Samuel fell back onto the makeshift bed, mentally thanking whoever had brought him back to safety.

"Thank God we won!" Samuel could feel happy for a moment before the pain made him suck in his breath. "I want to go home and have the doctor there look at my ankle."

The doctor was shaking his head, and his eyes were almost closed. Then in an exhausted voice, he said, "If you make it home. This will not heal. We need to take it off now, and if you survive, you will need to serve out the rest of your service." Samuel looked at the doctor in surprise. "Washington needs you to come work in the garrison or recruit soldiers. You will only get half pay because you no longer can be on the field fighting."

"If I survive? Well, I will! I want to go home and let the doc there see what he can do."

"Are you sure that the doc you are talking about isn't helping Washington now? He probably won't be there when you get home. Washington requires every able doctor he can get." The doc looked hard at Samuel. "Do you have parents at home and someone waiting for you?" Samuel nodded yes. The doc had seen this before; the young man wanted to go back to his mother and have her take care of him. He wanted familiar surroundings, and maybe he could just survive that way. The girlfriend wouldn't hurt either; she could give him some hope of staying alive if he made it home.

The next day a soldier with a disabled hand helped Samuel on a cart with other injured soldiers who did not have immediate family care. The drivers were all soldiers who had survived injures that had left them unable to fight on the battlefield. They were heading out when the man sitting next to Samuel started writing. His leg had been cut off several inches above the ankle. The man was sweating even though it was not hot but rather chilly for the time of year. The bandages around the stump leaked blood on the wagon, and there was a foul smell coming off the leg. He was having a hard time with the bumpy cart, but this did not hinder him from staying on task. Even though Samuel was in pain, he wanted to help the man, but realizing he was not good with his letters, he did not volunteer to help. The reading lessons he had with Megan had been developing with much speed and success when Ki had asked him to leave.

There were cries of pain from the wounded men when going over a bump, then curses, some directed at the drivers and others at no one in peculiar. The drivers appeared to be used to the language and paid no attention to it. They all were headed in somewhat the same direction, to be delivered at different places.

When night came, the drivers unloaded the soldiers, placed them around a fire, and commenced making dinner for everyone. They were handed a stinking jar to pee into, and if one had to defecate, the drivers would put him over a log until he was finished.

The man had stopped writing due to his breathing becoming short and deliberate. He was having a hard time keeping his eyes open when he grabbed Samuel's arm.

"I am not going to make it home. I assume that we are going in the direction of your home?"

Samuel looked sadly down at him. "Yes, I live about a day from here; try to hang on." Samuel thought to offer words of comfort to him.

The poor man had nothing left to give. "Then please give this to my parents; they have to live close to you. Their names are Timothy Jones and Anna Jones; I am their only son. I have been a poor son in not writing for a long time. I should have made an effort to write more, but it seems I never got the chance." The man had to stop and gather his strength to talk. "My name is Lucas Jones; tell them that I love them very much and ask them to try to forgive me for not writing more."

Samuel was holding his breath as realization washed over him like an icy waterfall. He had to lick his lips serval times before he could get the courage to speak. At this moment, all he could see was the *J* carved into the barn door that he had looked at a hundred times. Samuel knew the *J* stood for "Jones," but he had never known what the *L* stood for. He had seen a heart craved into a tree outside the barn with *L* and *C* inside. Now he knew it stood for Lucas.

"I think I know the place; is there a large *J* craved into the barn door?" Samuel held his breath, waiting for the man to speak, but all Lucas could do was smile, remembering a memory as his breathing became very shallow. He tried to talk, but it was difficult, so Samuel had to put his head close to his mouth to hear him.

"I craved that *J* myself. Tell my parents I love them, and I will see them someday in heaven; I will be waiting for them."

Samuel's felt tears come into his eyes as he whispered in Lucas's ear while he held his hand, "They are already there, and they are waiting for you; go to them now, and be happy." Samuel held Lucas's hand until he took his last breath.

"I see them!" Lucas had a smile on his face when it went slack. Samuel called the drivers over to see the dead man, telling them that they both would be dropped off at the old Jones house that was now the home of Ki and Julia Rainsford.

———————

The next day Samuel took a turn for the worse. The pain was overtaking his body and mind. The wagon's motion was not helping; as they crossed the river, they had to submerge his leg in dirty water as the drivers got the horses through it. It was there that his leg took on a different throbbing that made his heart and head pound with desire to get out of the damn wagon.

Koda and Bala heard the wagon first, and both put their heads back with a long howl to warn their masters. Everyone stopped to see who was coming. Megan looked out the window and, with a whispered prayer, hoped it was Samuel coming home. But why wasn't he on his horse? Everyone came out to see; the men and boys had their guns handy, just in case. Megan was the first to get to the wagon, and upon seeing Samuel, she let out a cry of joy. The joy soon fell away when she saw Samuel's condition and the pain consuming him. Megan couldn't believe the damage to his foot in the dirty bloody bandages. Samuel grabbed Megan's hand, and they just looked at each other.

"God, I have missed you, Megan!"

"We have to get a doctor! Julia, we have to get a doctor now!" Megan's hands were on Samuel as Henry and the drivers tried to get him out of the wagon. Samuel could not bear the pain any longer, and he cursed with a vengeance as they moved him into the tiny room of the cabin.

"Who is this?" Julia was asking the driver as they put a body wrapped in heavy cloth on the ground.

"Lucas Jones said he lived here. He didn't make it, as you can see. He died a day out on the road coming here. Samuel appeared to know him." As the driver was getting back on the wagon to deliver more poor souls home, recognition came to Julia. She put her hands to her face as Ki looked to her for answers.

"My God! This poor man is the only son of the Joneses, who lived here before John killed them! Oh, the poor man; he probably didn't know his parents had been killed!"

"We bury him hill with parents." Ki bent down and hoisted the body over his shoulder, going to the barn, where he laid him out on a large pile of hay. "We have problems." Ki was looking into Julia's eyes, and she knew what he meant.

"There is no doctor! They have all gone to help Washington! Did you see his leg? Ki, it looks like it needs to come off!" Julia was becoming emotional.

All Ki did was nod his head in agreement. "There is old man who is eighties; I don't know if he come here."

"Where does he live?" Ki covered Lucas in hay to alleviate the dead's smell, which was getting stronger by the moment.

"He live about five leagues from church, going west. I can't remember name." Julia was looking worriedly over her shoulder at Henry's house as Megan came running out. Tears were running down her face.

"He needs a doctor now! He is going to die!" Megan was visibly hysterical.

Ki got on his horse in one motion. "I bring him back here. I stop at Vicar Turner's house for directions." Before anyone could say another thing, Ki was out of the barn and headed down the road. Megan ran back to the house to be with Samuel.

"Don't let them take my foot, Megan; I want to die before that happens. I won't be good anymore to anyone." Sweat was pouring off of Samuel's fevered forehead.

"Samuel, you need to stay alive for us. I have missed you so much! I love you!"

Willie and Robby dug a grave on the hill overlooking the farm. They buried Lucas Jones next to his parents in a crude coffin. Julia was there picking all the flowers she could find and laying them on the grave. Vicar Turner came to say the proper prayers over the small funeral, and suddenly Julia felt overwhelmed with emotions. Willie and Robby had gone back to the house, leaving

Julia there by herself; Ki was gone to find the doctor. Koda and Bala were her ever companions.

"Most women get small fluffy dogs from their husbands, but I get two wolves." Julia had to smile because she loved the domesticated wolves, who made her feel safe. She never worried when she went away from the house about being attacked by anything. This made her reflect upon her new life and how it was so different from what she had expected. She looked upon the graves and spoke to the people that were now in heaven.

"I promise to take care of your beautiful farm; this place has given me a life I never dreamt I would ever have. I was taught to worship wealth, that it was all that mattered. This beautiful place has taught me to love the simple life, that it is not wealth that makes you happy but genuine love and family. This incredible country is now my home, and I love it even though it can be damn hard to live here. But it has shown me the real woman I could be and am growing to be."

Julia had moved to the hillside next to the graves, where she could look down on her farm. The sun was setting, turning the sky pink-gold with clouds, and the trees whispered in the wind. She sat quietly with the wolves on either side of her, peacefully staring into the wind with eyes half-closed. This was a wild country that challenged you every day to survive in it, and Julia was beginning to believe that maybe she could. Ki and the Indians had taught her not to chase the material world, and it was such a relief not to have to reach for the status quo continuously. She was doing things she never thought she would ever have to do—shoot a gun, live with the Indians, run a farm, and be self-efficient. Julia had become more asser-tive and smarter than she ever dreamt possible. At that moment she thanked God for bringing her here and prayed that he would protect her beautiful family.

Moses Donovan, the Drunken Doctor

"**A**re you that Indian that married that high-born British woman?" The older man had lost most of his teeth. The absence of a woman's touch in the cabin was noticeable. His clothes were dirty, along with most of the dishes. There was an odor coming from the small fireplace that Ki did not want to view. Vicar Turner had told him his name was Moses Donavan when Ki had stopped to ask about the man.

"You probably will have to bribe him with whiskey to come. He can be a mean old drunk," the vicar had told Ki. So to help out the dire situation, Vicar Turner gave Ki a bottle of whiskey, which Ki knew was a sacrifice for the vicar also. Ki held up the jar to the old, watery eyes. Ki thought he recognized the doctor from when he had treated Henry that day in the barn, but it had been a while since he saw or thought about him.

"We need doctor. A soldier got foot shot. Come now, and there could be more of this."

Donovan was shaking his head no. "I'm too old and drunk, and I can't do that anymore."

The only thing left for Ki was to get out his knife and threaten Donovan, who sighed deeply and moved to the dilapidated barn with a bag of tools in his hand. Donavon followed Ki, asking for the bottle serval times, but Ki firmly told him no. Serval times Ki thought he would fall off his horse, which was the oldest thing Ki had ever seen. When they got back to the farm, Megan came running out.

"He's going mad with the pain and fever. We are having a hard time keeping him in the bed." When Megan looked at the doctor, her hopes vanished.

"Is this the doctor?" Megan stepped out of the way as Ki showed Donavan Samuel's foot. Everyone stood in shock as they looked upon the dirty old man. From when Donovan had treated him, Henry recognized him and realized the old man had aged quite a lot. At first Donovan just stood looking at the foot, but then he seemed to wake up and become the doctor he once was. His look became intense as he poured some of the precious whiskey on his hands before examining the wound. Red lines had started to creep up from the injury.

"This needs to come off now, or he will die."

"Noooo! Let me die!" screamed Samuel. He was thrashing around the bed, crazy with pain. Molly and Megan tried to calm him, but he pushed them away as he screamed at the doctor.

Donovan sadly looked at Samuel. "Son, you are still young. It will be hard, but you can do it. Now get me my tools. I need the saw, knives, and more whiskey. We will also need boiling water and men to hold him down. Also, a stick for the mouth so the screams won't be so loud." The situation had sobered up Donovan, and a take-charge attitude was firmly in place as he carefully inspected the foot.

"Noooo!" Samuel had become hysterical and was fighting off all who tried to touch him. Ki did the only thing he knew to do in this situation: he walked up to Samuel, manhandled him so that he could get on top of him, doubled his fist, and then walloped Samuel hard on the chin, knocking him out cold. Then Ki took a deep breath and went to get the doctor's bag of tools. It took Henry, Ki, Willie, and Robby to hold Samuel down during the operation.

Samuel had a raging fever for days; half the time he did not know where he was. Cold water was regularly applied across his body to bring the temperature down. When he was in his right mind, he hated everyone who had had a hand in amputating his foot. Samuel used vulgar language with all who tried to comfort him, even Vicar Turner, who came to see how he was doing. Ki had to retrieve Moses once again when it looked like Samuel was going to die, so the old man spent several nights with Henry and Molly. Molly washed the old man's clothes and even sewed him some new things.

"He is going to need your support when he can get out of bed." Moses was looking at Henry, Molly, and Megan.

"He is so mad at all of us! When will that change?" Megan was especially feeling the rejection of Samuel.

"He will stay that way until he sees hope in his future."

"How do we do that?" Megan was trying to keep tears from falling.

"I saw a device for men who have lost a foot. It is a large leather cup, and the stump fits into a soft cushion in the middle, with straps that tie around the knee. The bottom of the cup has a large round wooden ball mounted on it so he can walk. His saddle will have to be reworked to fit it, but since it is his right foot, he should still be able to get on a horse."

"Do you think you can draw a picture of what you are talking about?" Henry asked.

"Yes, and you can take it to a tack worker and see what he can do." Moses was turning out to be a lifesaver. Megan went to tell Samuel, whose fever had finally left, but he was weak and frustrated from having been in bed so long. He was tired of everyone waiting on him, and he needed his freedom.

"Samuel, it is going to be all right. Moses told us about a device that can fit where your foot was so that you can walk on it. Your saddle will have to be redone to accommodate it. But the best thing is you will be able to walk and ride again." Megan spoke with hope, thinking that they could return to normalcy in their relationship, but that was not to be.

"You think everything will be normal again? Well, let me tell you, it will not! We can never be normal again! This changes everything!" Samuel was all but screaming at Megan, who took two steps away from him. Henry and Molly came rushing in when they heard the yelling.

"Son, don't you talk to her that way! She is here trying to help you because she cares about you." Henry was mad and had had enough of Samuel's foul mood.

"I don't want anyone to help me! I wanted to die! And now look at me; I am a cripple and worthless. A good-for-nothing buffoon!" Samuel was so mad that he was spitting as the cruel words left his mouth. "I hate all of you! And as soon as I can, I will return to the army!"

"Surely not, son; you have lost your foot." Henry was shaking his head.

"Oh, yes, father, they are not finished with me yet. Hopefully, this time I can get killed and put out of my misery. I realize that I will not get full pay because I am a cripple now, but I still can do all the dirty work that needs to be done, like taking the wounded home, doing garrison work, or maybe recruiting new soldiers. If you want to help me, then all of you leave me the hell alone. Every time I look at your faces, I see betrayal. Especially you, Megan; I told you I wanted to die, and now look at what all of you have done." Samuel tore the sheet back so everyone could see the swollen red stump. Megan was turning to leave with tears in her eyes, "Wait, I have a message for you to give that damn Indian who knocked me out so that drunk old man could take off my foot. Tell him we are even now; he took my foot for taking his parents." Megan could not believe her ears. "That's not true! You were dying, and he got the doctor who saved your life. If he wanted you dead, why would he get the doctor several times to save your life?"

"You don't understand! So he can laugh! Are you that stupid?" Samuel was screaming now at Megan. She had never seen him so mad, and it was frightening. Megan ran back to her bedroom, where she cried for hours. If anyone felt betrayed, it was she. Megan thought their relationship was strong and that he would want to live for her sake. Well, she now saw the situation as it was—gone forever.

Samuel began to get out of bed a little every day. He hopped around the room while cussing at not being able to stand up properly. At first he needed furniture to lean on; then, Henry made him a crutch that he could use to keep his balance. Slowly Samuel got to where he could move better. Julia and Henry took the design that Moses had drawn to a tacker who worked with leather. Samuel rejected it at first, but then he tried it and found he could keep his balance. The tacker had made it so that Samuel's legs were even on the ground; still, he needed the crutch to walk. After many rituals of learning how to walk with the device, Samuel began to walk without the crutch. The tacker reworked his stirrup to accommodate the foot device so he could lift himself on a horse and his foot would stay in the stirrup.

Megan watched him from her bedroom window, feeling let down by his behavior. They had not talked in weeks, and it looked like Samuel was getting ready to go back to his post. Samuel had not spoken to anyone except his parents; he had not even thanked Julia for paying for the foot device. Megan told Ki what Samuel had said about being even, and Ki had just shrugged it off.

When everyone was asleep, Samuel would leave the house and sit in the shallows where no one could see him. He would look into Megan's bedroom window, hoping to see her. What would he say? He was still angry and confused. It was better if he left and went back to his post to think about it, where he felt he could clear his head, free from this place. He needed to get away from the place where so much pain had driven him almost mad, and he required his self-esteem back but did not know how to do that.

Samuel packed his clothes, and Molly made food for the road, and early one morning, he left. Most of the household came out to see him go, and when getting on his horse, Samuel could not figure out how to get the device into the stirrup and began to cuss. Megan, who had just come out of the house, wanted to run and help, but Ki held out his arm to stop her. Samuel readjusted the device and eventually got it to work, and without looking back, he rode off to war.

The Southern War

Samuel headed back to West Point, the headquarters of General Washington. It was there he got a huge surprise. He was getting off his horse when a hand fell upon his shoulder.

"Well, look who's coming back." Daniel Morgan was smiling.

Samuel was shocked and overjoyed to see his friend. "Daniel, I thought you had resigned!"

"I did in seventy-nine; was passed over for a promotion that I should have gotten, but a year later, I got promoted to brigadier general."

"So, you are back. What are you up to?"

"They want me in the Southern Department; I am heading down to Charlotte, North Carolina, and will be working under Nathanael Green, commander of the Southern Department of the Rebel Continental Forces." Samuel was shocked. The British had taken control of Charleston, the capital of South Carolina. The Southern colonies had suffered one Patriot disaster after another. "Want to come with me?"

"Daniel, I would love to, but my foot is gone. I will slow you down; I lost the damn thing at the Battle of Stoney

Point. There is going to be some fierce fighting there in the South. The British won't give up Charleston easily."

"You can still shoot a gun! You were one of my best shots. You will have to learn to fight on your horse and not fall off." Daniel was laughing.

"If you will have me, I would love to fight under you again." Samuel had not been this happy for a long time. He felt his self-worth coming back.

"We will be taking the Maryland Line with us." Samuel's eyes grew large because this was the highly trained regiment of the Rebel forces. So this was going to be one hell of a fight. Samuel couldn't stop smiling now as the old Rebel juices started to rage up inside of him. Samuel leaned into Daniel.

"Let's go give them hell!"

Battle of Hannah's Cowpens"

"We will make a stand at the Broad River on two low hills in the open woodland." Daniel had gathered his men and was shouting as loud as he could. He stood on a wagon overlooking the soldiers.

"Tarleton will be right on our ass!" one soldier yelled at Morgan. Tarleton was the British forces' hero; only twenty-six, he had won many battles against the Rebel forces and relished defeating them for good. He had shown the British that he knew how to command an army and win at a young age.

"Our strategy will be to keep him running after us. Tarleton will come at us with an army that has been chasing us for days, and we will keep that army running to catch us until we wear them out. It is at that point that we will stop and then surround them. We will look like we are retreating, but we will not. We will keep backing up and making them run after us; they will be losing formations until they are utterly exhausted. That is when we will encircle them, just as they are thinking we are retreating and losing. We will be in three lines, and the first will be the sharpshooters, who will take out as many commanders as possible. Picken's irregular militia will manage the second line, taking out more commanders. Remember, look for their uniforms to see who the commanders are. Picken, you will look like you are retreating, but you will in fact fall behind the third line. The third line will be the Maryland and Delaware regulars who we all know are very seasoned warriors of this war."

God was with them because Tarleton had thought Morgan was going for Ninety Six's fort, which was held by American Loyalists, but Morgan wasn't there. When Tarleton found this out, he and his command had to go through rough terrain to get to Morgan, without food or sleep. They arrive on the battlefield exhausted, so Morgan's constant retreating plan, making Tarleton's army have to charge over and over until they were completely out of physical energy, worked right up to the moment that the Rebel army was able to surround the exhausted British army.

Samuel was shooting from his horse when he saw the second line retreating. He had just shot a British commander and turned his horse when a shot hit his horse. The horse rose, unseating Samuel and displacing the foot device in the process. Samuel could pull himself out from under the dead horse, but he could not flee from the British in time to prevent his capture. He tried to run, but it was no use without his foot device, which had been left under the horse. He was tied up and put into a wagon with other captives.

"Where are they taking us?" One of the young Rebels, who had not been able to retreat fast enough when he had stopped to help a dying friend, looked at Samuel. His name was Kane McLaughlin; he was around nineteen years old, with long blond hair and sky-blue eyes. He was tall, and one could see that he had worked hard in his short years because of the well-developed muscles throughout his body. He had been an indentured servant to an English farmer who was a Loyalist living around Yorktown, Virginia. When the fight came to Yorktown, the English farmer went to fight with the British, and Kane ran away to the Patriots. The mistress of the house where he lived had sent dogs out after him when he ran, so he had had to wade through creeks and rivers to cover up his scent.

"I think we are going to Charlotte to see what Cornwallis will have to say about all this. They just lost and will be very angry, livid." Samuel fiercely wanted to rub his foot, which was swollen and hurting.

"Do you think they will shoot us?"

"Don't know, but keep your head about you."

"Cornwallis is the head man, isn't he?"

"Sure is; he is the leader of the entire British army."

When they arrived in Charlotte, they saw a disheveled Tarleton talking to a red-faced, shocked Cornwallis. Cornwallis was leaning on his sword as he heard Tarleton's words, and suddenly his sword snapped from the force. Samuel tried to keep from laughing out loud; he thought he would die happy if he had to die, knowing that this new country was winning.

"Kane, if we do die, then know that we are defeating the greatest army in the world and that you helped do it. The people who will come after us will never have to apologize for who they are ever again. Every man will stand on his worth. You helped to do this!" Kane smiled at Samuel, but his life was just beginning, and he wanted to see the fruits of his labor; plus, he had a girlfriend waiting for him at home.

"You got a girl at home waiting for you?" Samuel had seen that faraway look in Kane's eyes.

"Yes, she's something to look at; her name is Mary. I miss her terribly. She has red hair and blue eyes—she is Irish like me—and a temper, but she can be so sweet when she wants to be. She can cook like you wouldn't believe. She is indentured like me and was only nine years old when she was put up for sale in America. Her parents were killed by the British, and the bastards sold her. My father was killed when he tried to stop a British soldier from raping my mother. I was only ten, but I tried to stop them." Kane had to look down to stop his emotions from showing on his face. "That is when my mother tried to protect me, and they hit her in the head with their guns. She never recovered. She died a week later. I was gathered up with other orphaned children and sold."

"My parents were indentured also, and I had to work my way over here on a ship. I found them and lived with them for a while until the war began. I gave my parents' owners free labor just to be able to live with them. The English farmer was a mean bastard who worked us hard. But now they are in a decent place. A nice lady bought them for me, and we live at her house."

Samuel was thinking of Megan and the mess he had made of his life back home. Would she ever forgive him? Would she find someone else? Someone equal in her social world? Someone who had money? He could see her telling Julia that in the back of her mind, she knew it had always been a mistake getting involved with Irish trash. Could he blame her for the way he treated her? He thought of his leaving that morning and not even turning around to say goodbye. Damn, what a fucking fool he was! If he ever got the chance to be with Megan again, he would beg for her forgiveness and never treat her or his parents like dirt ever again.

They received a small amount of food and ate it in the rain while Samuel rubbed his aching stub. They were bound up again and put on a wagon after they relieved themselves in the woods with guards watching. Kane tried to help Samuel walk, letting him use his shoulder to steady himself. Samuel heard Cornwallis talking to the driver of the wagon.

"Take them to Wilmington, and put them on a ship bound for the *Jersey*." Samuel closed his eyes, but not before Kane saw his expression.

"What is the *Jersey*?"

Samuel just looked sadly at Kane. "A prison ship in New York; it is a death sentence. Start praying for your very soul!"

"Where is Samuel McKinny?" Morgan had been drinking with his men in joyful bliss after the battle. Morgan couldn't believe his scheme had worked, and he was taking count of his men. One soldier looked sadly at Morgan and shook his head.

"Was he killed?" The soldier shook his head again.

"Horse shot out from under him, and he couldn't run with his foot gone, so they captured him."

The joy of the moment drained from Morgan's face. "Which way did they go with him? Did anyone see where they took him?"

"They looked like they were headed north, probably to load them up on a ship." All happiness left Morgan—if they were taking Samuel up the coast to New York to the *Jersey*, that would be a death sentence for sure. The *Jersey* was a hell-on-earth prison ship in the New York Harbor. It was there that they starved men and broke them until finally they gave up and died, letting the rats eat their bodies. Morgan decided he should write to his family because, after all, he knew where they lived, and maybe they could send money to pay for food and provisions while he was on the ship.

———

Samuel was grateful for Kane's help, which made it so Samuel could walk; Samuel had even found a stick to aid him, but it was knocked out of Samuel's hand when he was led up the *Jersey* plank. Kane threw up upon entering the ship's hull, where the prisoner's defeated faces greeted them. Rats ran around the feces of men who couldn't get up, and this combined with the smell of death every-where. Cries of help from men with boils and fever from multiple diseases were a never-ending song of the ship.

"I bet the one without a foot won't last a month." Jack looked at his partner in crime.

"Well, that kid is helping him, and the kid is pretty young, so he could hold out for a while."

"I bet you five that he doesn't last a month." Jack needed the money; he had lost terribly in a card game last night. Jack and George had gotten the unlucky job of working on the *Jersey* when they had shown cowardness in a battle. They both had run the opposite way when the bullets had started firing. This was their punishment.

"We could play with the kid," Jack looked at George and felt himself grow hard. They had not been with a woman in a long time, and Kane was looking pretty good to them. Jack and George never seemed to have money for the many whores who worked in New York City, or the time off. Their job was to feed the prisoners, so to amuse themselves, they would put the food in the hull's front and watch the prisoners run to get it. They would bet on who could make it first to the grub. As the men got weaker, the first one to the foodstuff would change day-to-day. Jack and George created situations where men would fight for food, and they enjoyed gambling on who would win. They laughed at how the starving men fought over food that was full of bugs and rancid. They would laugh even more when the race winner threw up the food because the meat was raw and crawling with worms.

Kane was making it to the food first and getting enough for both of them. One day as Kane ran to the food, he was blocked by George, who held him off with his bayonet. That day they didn't eat, and the next four days were the same. Kane and Samuel were getting weaker and weaker. That is when George called Kane over to talk.

"You hungry?" George was eating an apple in front of Kane. It was all Kane could do not to grab it.

"If you and your partner want food, then all you have to do is come with me and Jack into that room." Kane looked into the room and saw the beds where the soldiers slept. Kane knew what was being offered, and his pride at that point was more significant than his need for food. He shook his head and went back to his dirty blanket where he and Samuel lay.

"Don't do it!" Samuel also knew what was being suggested to the kid.

"I told him no." Kane looked at Samuel, who was growing weaker by the day. That night as Kane tried to sleep, he saw Samuel sit up quietly, trying not to wake Kane. He thought Samuel needed to readjust his sleeping position, but then he heard chewing sounds. Kane found Samuel eating lice off of himself, and he knew then he would tell George yes.

Everyone heard the rider come in, and they gathered around Julia to read the letter handed to her and Henry. Could Samuel be wounded or dead? Had he been taken prisoner? Julia began reading aloud to the small crowd.

To the Parents of Samuel McKinny,

I want to tell you that your son fought with honor at the Battle of Cowpens. Samuel showed unmistakable bravery on the battlefield. But he was captured, and I fear taken to the Jersey in New York Harbor. This situation has given me much grief, and I hope that you can send money for food and comfort. I am not sure that he was taken there, but it would be reasonable to think that he is being held there. I hope this letter finds you in good health so you can help your son in any way possible.

Yours Truly, Daniel Morgan

Julia bowed her head after reading this. Megan let out a half scream that was covered up by her handkerchief. Molly started to sob and ran back into their little house, with Megan following her. No one knew what to say or do, so they returned to their work—except for Henry, who talked to Ki.

"Do you think he's dead?" Ki just shook his head. "We can go and see and offer money." Henry was amazed that Ki would even consider helping Samuel, knowing that they were not on good terms.

"How would we get into New York without a pass?"

"Let me think, make plan." Ki turned and went back to working the new horses he had just received. He was beginning to breed and train all kinds of horses for different functions. He even worked with the Clydesdales, teaching them to pull a plow. Ki wanted to trade with the Seneca, showing them how to use the horses and the plow, a new invention for the Indians, but now was not a good time, with the war going on. In this new environment with the white men he now lived with, he could not help the Seneca. But there would be a time coming when he could help his people, and he vowed to do it.

———

Megan had started seeing a new magistrate from the area who professed to be a Patriot but looked and acted like a Loyalist. He wore a lot of white powder with very red cheeks, making his face appear deathly pale. His mannerisms were very English—carrying snuff, snorting it periodically in a most delicate manner from a tiny gold box. It was uncomfortable when he came to the house because he appeared uneasy with Ki; it was apparent that he looked down on him. His name was Alexander Howard, well educated in England, old money. He had an Irish indentured servant for a driver who managed two beautiful horses pulling a magnificent black and gold-trimmed carriage. Julia tried to accept that Alexander was precisely who her parents would have wanted for Megan. Julia did the proper thing by sitting with them in the parlor for a short time when Alexander visited Megan. She could tell that Megan wasn't in love with him and would stare in dismay when he would get out the snuff and snort it in the most proper English matter. Julia recognized that this wasn't a suitable English home setting but a functional American farm, and she heard Alexander's judgmental opinions concerning the way they lived. He now lived in the house of the Crowleys, because Mrs. Crowley had moved back in with her parents in New York City and sold the property to Alexander, who got her husband's old job.

Julia was proud of her hard work on the farm, and they were making money with the crops, and with Ki selling his horses, they were coming out with a sizeable income. She enjoyed making bread and found that when she wanted to take her frustrations out on something, pummeling dough was the perfect thing to do, causing great bread in the process. Julia also had her beloved chickens and eggs to gather and the exhausting planting, buying seed, and harvesting.

"Do you want to ride in the country for a while?" Alexander looked at Megan like a wolf smelling a rabbit, and Julia realized he was sexually attracted to Megan. When Alexander put his hands on Megan, it felt like soft chilled dough that had no mark of any real physical work. Once when they were alone, he had grabbed her with a quick kiss that felt like a wet fish hard-pressed to her lips. It was all she could do to keep from wiping her mouth. All she saw was Samuel and the love they had and longed for; they had been making plans, but that was gone forever. Megan had decided to try and move on with her life and entertained the idea of a new suitor, but it was not going very well.

"I think Megan would love that." Megan gave Julia a quick sneer, almost making Julia laugh, and Julia heard Megan say, "Bitch" under her breath.

But then Julia thought of Samuel and the love they once had, and it sobered her. "Now that I think of it, I do need Megan to help me with some embroidery." Megan looked relieved. Alexander was disappointed.

"Maybe tomorrow?" Alexander was all but licking his lips.

Bring 'Em Back Alive

The tension at the Rainsford Farm was heavy. Molly and Henry were terrified that they would never see their only son again. The war was heating up, causing everyone to be on edge. Julia found Ki becoming more subdued and contemplative, so she went to confront him in the barn as he inspected the foot of a horse he had been working with.

"What are you planning on now? I know you. When you get silent, that means you are planning something." Ki just smiled; this was one of the pleasures of marriage, or was it a hindrance? They were beginning to read each other.

"I dress in Indian clothes, I demand, have right as Seneca Indian, take Samuel, kill him because he kill my parents."

"How would you even get into New York without a pass? Do you think they would recognize you?" Julia's nerves were getting the better of her, making her eyes large amid a red face. Ki knew he had to speak calmly to her, or else she would start crying and pleading for him not to go.

"I show up and demand Samuel. I know is Indian killer, a killer of my parents. Since we, Seneca, taken side of the British, they owe me this."

"Have the Seneca done this before?" Julia was getting more anxious.

"Yes. The British gives prisoners who killed Seneca to us. It will work. I tell the truth; they know I not lie. I tell Henry about plans."

"I am glad you have decided to forgive Samuel. I was very proud of you for getting the doctor when he needed his foot taken off. I know he didn't appreciate what you did for him, but that was very brave of you." Ki had wondered if he would have reacted the same way Samuel did if someone had tried to take his foot off. The answer to that question brought a strong feeling of reality to him— he thought he might have. The feeling of losing his family over something like this was thought-provoking for Ki. Maybe it was time to bring Samuel back into the family; he had suffered enough.

Molly and Henry were relieved to hear the plan. Ki would have to go alone, but at least something was being done to get their son back, even if he wasn't on the ship. Molly made two suits of clothes for Ki to take to Samuel in anticipation of his homecoming.

"Samuel will need these if he is on the ship; I know he will be covered in lice and will need to burn his old clothes. Here is food for the trip, and these soda cakes are Samuel's favorite."

Ki took the food and clothes from Molly. He also had his Seneca clothes, a wool jacket with white buttons, which was simply made, and necklace of beads, with a large round silver clasp that was three inches thick and multi-colored. The band was tight against his neck, covering up his tattoos. Before he came to the King's Bridge entrance into New York City, guarded by the British, he stopped and changed into his Seneca clothes. He felt it was too dangerous to wear these clothes while on the road with Patriots all around the countryside who greatly feared the Seneca. He planned to braid his hair with feathers in one braid and wrap the other one with a thick leather strap. He carried his tomahawk, pistol, and knife on his belt and his ever-present long rifle. He brought a small razor-sharp blade concealed in a small pocket on his hip. He could gut a deer with one cut with the small hooked knife. He had ammunition in a pouch on his belt with a horn of gunpowder. He decided not to paint his face.

———

The paleface British guard stood staring at Ki, speech-less, with his partner doing the same. They had just come from England as fresh recruits, never having seen an Indian before. This one was so different from what everyone described as the usual Indian. He was tall and had blue eyes and could even speak English, standing a head taller than everyone, looking mean as hell and fully armed. The Indian did not have a pass and was on foot, wanting to see the person in charge. The new guard ran back to the post house, where they were all living.

"Sergeant Sheahan, there is this rather large mean-looking Indian out there wanting to speak with you."

"I told you not to bother me; what does he want?"

"He says that there is a prisoner on the *Jersey* who killed his parents, and he wants to take the prisoner back to his village and kill him."

"What!" The Sergeant was just getting up from a nap when this occurred. He straightened his uniform, leaving the bunkhouse quickly. There stood this enormous Indian at the guard post of the entrance to New York City, to his dismay.

"You want a prisoner from the *Jersey* who killed your parents? You are Seneca?"

Ki just nodded. Now Sergeant Sheahan knew that the Iroquois were on the British side, and the English were doing everything to encourage their continued participation. These Indians were treated with respect, even though behind their backs, the English would make fun of them.

"Yes, Samuel McKinny killed Chief Yuma and wife Keme, my parents. I take him to my village to kill." Ki had waited patiently. Many people were staring at him, giving him ample space even though there was a crowd at the post.

"So, this is personal for you and your village?" Sheahan knew that the *Jersey* was overcrowded, so he did not see a problem with releasing a prisoner to this Indian to be killed by him.

"We punish him for what he did to us."

"I will give you a pass with instructions saying that you are to receive a Samuel McKinny as your prisoner to execute as you see fit. You will have to take a boat out to the *Jersey*. There are boats in the harbor that you can rent to take you there." Ki took the pass and only nodded his head in thanks and left.

———

Kane McLaughlin was sitting on his filthy, worn-out blanket with his head down on his raised knees. He wouldn't talk or look at anyone, and it was becoming very worrisome to Samuel.

"I told you not to do it, Kane, and now look at you." Kane had heard this serval times from Samuel, and his anger came to the boiling point.

"What the hell was I supposed to do; damn you! We were starving! They wouldn't give us food!" Samuel saw tears in the boy's eyes, and it just about killed him.

"Don't worry about me! This is my life, and if I want to starve, then so be it. I don't expect you to help me. It is every man for himself here."

"Right! It is every man for himself, but I don't want to starve either. At least we are given somewhat better food. I know it is still terrible and not fit for humans. Hell, the pigs would not want it." Kane was wiping tears from his cheeks. "I don't want to die!"

Samuel couldn't fault him. He hated to see the young man disgrace himself and knew it would scar him. Kane wanted to live, and that was a powerful enticement to do whatever necessary. But to let these men take one's body was an extreme shame. Samuel had resolved that he would die here, but he couldn't blame Kane for wanting to live. The horrid food had let them live another miserable day. Samuel put his arms around the boy.

"You are a good boy, and if you want to cheat death, then you do it!"

———

Ki had a mission in mind beyond saving Samuel. He had heard that the British had some beautiful horses stabled in New York. He looked around New York until he found the British officers' stables on Long Island. People stared at him as he wandered about the place, and he had to dodge the British soldiers, so he kept to the alleys, trying to stay out of the main streets. When he came around the alley corner, Ki saw the most beautiful horse he had ever seen in this life.

General Cornwallis was on a huge black stallion, and Ki wanted him, for he was seventeen hands high, broad across the chest, beautiful, young, and powerful. Next to the black stud was a female that stood sixteen hands and just as gorgeous, being ridden by an officer. He wanted both animals for breeding, but to do this was going to take some planning, courage, and speed. He knew Samuel couldn't walk, so Ki would have to carry him running back to the stables from the *Jersey*. The *Jersey* was in Wallabout Harbor on Long Island, so he planned to get Samuel off the ship and then come back and steal the horses. This was a crazy idea, but if it worked, he would save Samuel and get two breeding horses that would make him one of the best breeders in New York. After the general had left, Ki went into the stables to look around.

"Can I help you, sir?" The stable boy was trying to appear brave but had a hard time of it, judging by his trembling hands, as he looked up at Ki. Ki just smiled at him, wanting to put him at ease. He could tell the lad was impoverished by the clothes he wore and his shoes, which had holes, and he thought the British probably didn't pay him but gave him food instead of money.

"You care for horses?" Ki was slowly walking up to him with a friendly smile, thinking he would need to catch him if he started to run. "I won't hurt; I want look at beautiful animals. You do great job. Not everyone do good job as you." Ki held his hands out in a sign of surrender, and the boy was starting to puff out his chest but was cautious. "You need be proud; not everyone care of horses as you. I am friendly Indian, works with British. The British pay you much money?" The boy looked down sadly and shook his head no. "Where you live?" Ki knew the boy lived in the barn, as he pointed to a small room in the back. "I do better for you?" With his eyes growing large, Ki took out four pure gold coins. "These yours when I get back with man. We take horses. You no tell?"

The boy just stood there, not knowing what to do, but when Ki took out another gold coin, he said, "Yes, sir, I will tell no one and will keep a lookout for you." The boy had never seen so much money in his life.

"Indians have horses, not beautiful ones."

"I feed them good oats every day and ride them and brush them."

"When I take them, I feed oats and brush like you. I do just like you. I give horses good home as you. I leave, come back, these coins yours, you stay quiet, not tell anyone." Ki was holding his finger to his lips. "What your name?"

"Darcy McGregor"

"You have parents?"

"No. The general bought me in Ireland to look after his horses."

"How old?"

"Thirteen"

"You do one thing more?" This time Darcy looked suspicious. "I give you lot of money; I need you help me. I need you let all horses loose when I leave."

"You mean, let them all loose out of the stables to run down the street so no one can catch them?" Darcy's eyes were huge.

"Yes!" Ki was holding the money in his hand so Darcy could get a good look at it. Darcy stared at the gold for a long time, then slowly nodded his head yes.

"Don't know when come back—soon, look for me."

———

Ki went to the harbor, where he found a woman who brought food and other articles out to the *Jersey* on her boat. She was reluctant to let him on her dinghy when she saw him, but the money changed her mind. Ki told her to wait for him, that more money would be hers; when they got to the ship, Ki held out the pass and boarded the *Jersey*. George was standing in front of his superior with the admission form that the sergeant had filled out for Ki.

"This Indian has come aboard with a pass saying he has the right to take Samuel McKinny because he killed many Indians, including his parents."

"Let me see this pass." Lieutenant Johns was worried about this situation—it was unusual—but the pass looked original and proper. Finally, he walked over to Samuel.

"This Indian says you killed his parents? Did you?" Samuel was shocked to see Ki in his Indian clothes and fully armed, and for a minute, all he could do was stare at him. Ki was also stunned at seeing the condition of Samuel.

"Yes, I did. I killed both of them." The officer nodded his head after looking at the pass again.

"Looks good, so let him have Samuel McKinny. I hear that they torture the hell out of them for days before they die." Ki went to pick him up, and that is when Samuel let himself fall against Ki.

He whispered, "Get the one next to me; we need him. *Please.*" Samuel was looking at Kane. Ki looked at Samuel, then at Kane, and saw the youth fading quickly. Ki let out a long breath.

"I want that one; he killed many Indians." Ki was trying to sound convincing.

"I don't know; the pass doesn't say anything about Kane." George didn't want their newest sexual victim to leave.

"I saw him kill many Indians!" Ki was now sounding and looking mad as he put his hand on the pistol at his belt.

"Lieutenant, the Indian wants Kane also." George was shouting to the lieutenant, who didn't seem to mind as he was walking off. He had more prisoners than he could handle or feed.

"Let the Indian have both; I don't care." This upset George, who had to think fast.

"I have to talk to this one first before you can take him." Samuel became upset and looked at Ki helplessly. At that moment, Ki realized they were going to hurt Kane somehow.

"Stop!" Ki went up to Kane, acting as if he wanted a better look at him, holding out his hand like he was inspecting Kane's hand. Ki slipped the small hooked knife into his hand as George dragged Kane off to the beds. As soon as he got Kane to the mattresses, he started laughing. "I need another go at you for a farewell gift before you leave."

"You have to save him!" Samuel looked at Ki as Ki smiled at him, and then Samuel knew Ki had given him a weapon; Samuel closed his eyes and prayed.

Kane tasted revenge so great that he waited for George to get hard, even acting complacent and bending over for him like he wanted this to be over soon. That is when Kane whipped around, cutting his manhood off, and before the shocked George could scream, Kane cut his throat. Kane pulled up his pants, pulled a blanket from another bed, mopped up the blood, and got George in bed with the covers over his head. The bloody blanket went under the bed. Kane came out with blood on his shirt, and Samuel began to have an anxiety attack.

Samuel started hitting Ki, screaming, "Please don't let this heathen take us. He will torture us to death." The guards began laughing, enjoying the show.

"Shut mouth; I make you bleed like him." Ki was pointing at Kane. Ki threw Samuel over his shoulder and quickly climbed down the rope ladder to the woman waiting in the boat. Kane followed, confused, but he knew this scary Indian had just saved him. When they got to the little dinghy, Ki told the woman to move fast. Her eyes sprang open when she saw the blood on Kane.

"I don't want no problems." She was rowing as quickly as she could, but Ki grabbed the paddles out of her hand and began to move with much stronger strokes. This made her mad, but she was not going to argue with the big Indian. Samuel had tears in his eyes as he looked at Ki, while Kane was utterly bewildered.

"What is going on?" Kane looked from face to face for an answer. Samuel's eyes went to the woman and motioned to Kane to be quiet. Samuel did not trust the woman and what she would do if questioned by the authorities. Kane noticed that Samuel appeared relieved and not at all threatened; Samuel seemed to be pleased, even smiling. When they got to Long Island, Ki paid the woman more money than she had seen in a long time.

"We hurry before they find who you kill." Ki took off with Samuel, and Kane ran to keep up with the two of them.

"Who are you?"

Before Ki could answer, Samuel laughingly said, "Our savior, Kane; this is my friend Ki. He may look like he is going to kill us, but he is not; we will be safe if we can get out of here!" Samuel was having a hard time talking while Ki ran with him over his shoulder. Kane decided to keep quiet and just follow. But he needed to thank Ki for saving him also.

"Thank you, Ki, for saving me." Ki didn't look at him but nodded his head in agreement. Ki seemed hell-bent on getting somewhere quick, looking around for any trouble, suddenly stopping, and motioning for Kane to wait as he looked around a corner cautiously.

"What's the plan for getting out of here?" Samuel was trying to stay serene while riding on Ki's back and shoulder.

"We get to stables without the soldiers seeing."

"Are we hiding in the stables?"

"No. We steal horses."

"Good God, Ki, we can't get away with that! They will come after us." Now Samuel looked worried, and Kane began to develop more anxiety. Ki didn't answer but ran down backstreets, always on the lookout for soldiers. They ran into a stable in one alley, with a boy holding two horses with saddles on them. Ki quickly placed Samuel onto the big magnificent horse and motioned Kane to get on the mare.

"Whose horses are these? These belong to a rich man! My God, they are the general's horses, aren't they?" Ki ignored Samuel and talked to Darcy.

"Let other horses loose; get them out! Here is money!" Ki was handing the boy gold coins, but the boy was shaking his head no.

"They will kill me!" The boy was trembling with tears in his eyes. For a moment, Ki did not know what to do. He had to think fast and make a decision quickly, or they would all be dead.

"Kane, help get all horses out stable!" As he was told, Kane opened all the gates to the stalls and headed the horses out the door. As soon as the horses saw the open exit, they ran down the alley.

"They will beat me to death!" Darcy was screaming now; Ki jumped on the big horse behind Samuel.

"Kane, get boy, go!" Kane reached down and hauled Darcy onto the horse behind him. They thundered out of the stables while shouts of warning came. One soldier got in the way as Ki nearly ran him over.

"Stay down!" Just as Ki said that, a bullet came over Kane's shoulder. Fortunately, they knew to stay low over the horse's neck. They heard shots, but the winding, busy streets helped, and the soldiers couldn't get a straight shot. The streets were crowded, with people screaming to get out of their way, making the soldiers reluctant to shoot. By the time the soldiers had gathered, the loose horses, Ki, Samuel, Kane, and Darcy were long gone. The four were heading into unknown land on Long Island to hide.

Ki had laid out an escape path when he had decided to steal the horses. He prayed to the gods that his plan would work, and to his surprise, he even prayed to Julia's God. This was the second time he had prayed to this God, and it had worked. Of course, they weren't home yet.
They headed deep into the countryside of Long Island, always on the lookout for trouble. All Kane and Darcy knew to do was follow and hope that it would all work. Finally, they stopped by a creek, right before sunset; Ki jumped off the beautiful horse and reached for Samuel.

"Samuel, Kane, need to wash; get lice off, use dirt to scrub."

"Yes, that will work, scrubbing with dirt. Kane, come over here and help me into the cold-as-hell creek." Kane was still just doing what he was told to, along with Darcy, but his eyes widened when he saw Ki pull out extra clothing.

"Thank God, my mother made two suits of clothing. Kane, try these." Kane looked at the new clothes, knowing that his old ones were full of lice, and he just nodded his head. The nights were getting colder, making the bath freezing, but it felt wonderful to get the mites off.

"We not make a fire; I have soda bread. When get farther away, we hunt and have fire. It good that you put blankets on horses."

"Where are we going?" Darcy was still wondering if he had made a rational decision to go with them. "Are you going to give me my money? You said you would if I let you steal the horses."

"You go?" Ki challenged the boy, who heard a coyote calling for his friends, and the boy's eyes got big. Ki laughed and motioned for the boy to come closer. Darcy slowly came over to Ki, looking somewhat scared.

"I not give you money. I give you home. You not go hungry, need anything. You work with these horses."

"What if I don't want that? What if I want my money now?" Darcy was trying to stand tall like a man. So Ki took out the money and handed it to Darcy, who heard more coyotes howling closer. Ki knew the boy was scared, and he laughed.

"Take money. You go by yourself; we not share our horses with you or food." Samuel was listening and took pity on the boy.

"You will have a decent home there, Darcy. I know because I live there—or used to, before I ran away from it. The food is plenty and the women lovely. You will have work to do just like we all do. I am Irish also, and my Irish parents live there. They were indentured servants until this wonderful lady bought them and gave us all a beautiful home. That woman is Ki's wife, and she and her sister are the most generous people on earth."

"Is she a white woman?" Kane, who had been listening, said in disbelief. "But you are an Indian?"

Samuel spoke up in Ki's defense. "An Indian who saved her life from a bad man who mistreated her."

"I thought the Indians were on the side of the British?"

"I fight with Patriots." Ki looked serious. Kane realized he should shut up and be grateful for being rescued by this blue-eyed Indian.

"What if this lady doesn't want me? She doesn't know me?" Darcy spoke up.

"Julia and Megan will help you, and it is what they do." Samuel answered him.

"How far away from this farm are we?"

"Far, and if I am correct, we will have to cross the East River to get back." Samuel was looking at Ki for verification. Ki was bringing out the smashed bread he had in his sack. Ki handed the pieces to each person and tried not to stare as Samuel and Kane ate it ravenously. Ki hated to see the condition Samuel was in when he had seen them bathing in the creek. They were walking skeletons with dark circles on their faces, arms, legs, and hands. Some of the spots on Samuel were seeping yellow liquid. They needed decent shelter soon, and Ki needed to hunt food

448

for them, but it was too dangerous for a fire this close to the British. They spent a cold night hiding. Before sunrise they were on their way again; Ki was thankful for Kane's help with Samuel. They headed for the East River.

"Are we going to have to look for a ferry?" Samuel was looking at Ki and wondering how on earth they were going to get the horses across.

"We can find smugglers." Ki knew there were a lot of smuggling in this area because many whiskey barrels and draughts were brought in the area and taken to New York City. It would have been so much easier if he hadn't stolen the horses. They would also be in the open on the water where they could be spotted by the British.

When they made it to the coast of Little Bay Dog Run, they watched for a boat. They spied one; it was a smuggler. Ki had everyone hide in the forest while he went to talk to the smuggler. Ki changed out of his Seneca clothes and tied his hair back in a ponytail down his back. The man pulled his gun on Ki as soon as he saw him.

"I need go Throgs Neck with load. Can help me? I have money." The man looked dangerous and mistrustful.

"How much do you have?" Ki wasn't going to fall for that one.

"Enough." Ki looked at the man with his hand on his gun.

"How much is enough?" he asked.

"Enough for all us and horses across river."

"What's your business over there?"

"Get home." Ki was getting impatient with the man.

"Are you running from the British?" At this point Ki decided to be honest with the man because he did not look or act like a Loyalist. This man looked like he had lived his life in the open, making his way as best as he could, smuggling whatever he had.

"Yes." Ki held his breath.

"How many are you?" Ki motioned for everyone to come out of the woods. The man let out a curse.

"We are going to need a bigger boat. Unless I can make two trips."

"No. Leave all at once. Where is bigger boat?" The man pointed across the East River. "Can get it today?"

"No. The tide is bad right now. I can get it tomorrow. But I will need to see how much money you have." Slowly Ki brought out two gold coins and saw the man's eyes light up.

"I will get the other boat first thing in the morning, and the next day we can leave."

"Not today?" Ki mainly wanted to get off this Island.

"No. We can make camp tonight, and tomorrow I will leave first thing."

"Safe to have a fire?" Ki wanted to hunt for food.

"No. The British could see it, but I have food in the boat. I have some bread and salted fish and whiskey."

"I pay you for food. What is your name?" Ki had three sixpences, which he gave to the man.

"Caleb."

They had moved to a flat place in the woods and began to make camp. It wasn't freezing, but it was cold; the food was much-needed. Caleb looked at Samuel and Kane, noticing their skeletal bodies and the way they were eating.

"Prisoners, are we?" Samuel nodded his head first, then Kane. "How did you escape?" Caleb looked at Ki as he figured the answer. Ki did not want to tell him the story, so everyone stayed silent. When Caleb saw he wasn't going to get a response, he went to another subject.

"Those are some mighty fine looking horses you got; where did they come from?" Again no response; Kane and Darcy looked from face to face, wondering how long they were going to stay silent. Samuel and Ki just kept eating as if nothing unusual was happening.

"I saw the British general once from a long distance, and I swear he had a horse that looked just like this one." The tension was hanging in the air like heavy morning fog, but Kane and Darcy did as Samuel and Ki did and kept their heads down and continued to eat. Suddenly Caleb laughed out loud, showing three missing teeth, and slapped his skinny leg.

"You stole these horses, didn't you?" No reply. Darcy and Kane were having a hard time keeping a smile off their faces; snickers broke loose from both of them. "That certainly took some big balls!" This time Kane and Darcy started to laugh. Samuel looked to them to shut up, but the friction had broken, and everyone felt some sense of relief.

That night Ki kept awake to make sure that Caleb did as he said he would. When everyone was asleep, Samuel sat up next to Ki and spoke very softly.

"Ki, it means the world to me that you saved Kane and me." Ki just sat there. "You didn't have to do it, especially the way I left. I was an asshole; I guess I thought I could go to war without getting shot. What a stupid dumbass I was." Ki looked at Samuel with a big smile.

"Now?" Ki knew he should be serious-minded, but he couldn't help it. After all, they had formed a bond of some sort over the time they had spent together, and they also loved two sisters. Who would have ever thought that a Seneca Indian and an Irish immigrant would have ever developed a friendship and ended up in a family together?

"I deserved that, but four months on, the *Jersey* took it all out of me. When we get home, I will kiss the ground. If I ever complain again, please, you have my permission to kick me in the ass. How is everyone? I miss all of them!" Ki knew whom Samuel missed the most, so he intentionally talked about everyone except Megan. Samuel listened intently, but Ki could see that he wanted to hear Megan's name. That was when he got silent and pretended to inspect his gun and the powder, acting like he didn't have any more to say.

"Goddamn you!" Samuel said this as quietly as he could without waking everyone up. "How is Megan? Does she hate me even now? I don't blame her, with the way I left without even saying goodbye." Ki just shook his head and continued to look at his gun.

Finally, Ki said, "She has suitor; he rich, wears powder on his face." Ki was motioning all over his face. He could feel Samuel slumping down as he scratched his bug invested hair. But Ki also knew that Megan still loved Samuel. Ki saw the way Megan would move away from Alexander when he tried to sit next to her and the way she would get bored when Alexander arrogantly talked about himself. But it would do Samuel good to have to win her back. Megan deserved that much from Samuel for the way he had left.

"Does she love him?" Samuel asked earnestly, and Ki had to look away to keep the smile off of his face.

"Don't know." Ki thought that he should tell Samuel that Megan still loved him, but it was up to both of them to find what they had lost.

"I will tell her I am sorry and ask her to forgive me. Do you think that will do?" Samuel was beginning to get very worried. Ki shook his head, still wanting to laugh, but put a serious look on his face when he turned back to Samuel.

"Don't know; Alexander wealthy, has black gold carriage and beautiful horses. He lives Crowley's large house, Crowley's wife sold it." Ki had to get up so Samuel wouldn't see him smiling. "I pee." As Ki walked into the woods, he could hear Samuel cussing.

———

The next day Caleb went for the bigger boat and was able to come back by nightfall. They spent another night in the cold, so it was a good thing that Caleb had come back with more food. They loaded up everyone on the boat and were crossing when soldiers came upon the bank.

"Hold up and turn around, or we will shoot." Ki and the others turned the horses around on the flatboat so they could use them as cover.

"They won't shoot them. The soldiers know general's horses." Ki had his gun aimed at the ten soldiers. Samuel motioned for Caleb to hand over his rifle. Caleb figured that Samuel probably knew how to use it better than he did, having younger eyes. Samuel stood up, leaning on the mare, and aimed over her back. The current was taking them at a fast rate away. That was when Darcy couldn't help but peek around the mare to see if he recognized any of the soldiers. A shot rang out, and the face of Darcy blew off, knocking him into the water. Everyone on the boat just watched in shock as the boy's body floated away in the red stream. Anger filled Ki and Samuel so that in unison, they both sighted in their targets.

"You take the one on the horse to your left, and I will try and take the one in the middle on the horse." Kane and Caleb watched as the shots proved deadly, taking out the leaders; the other soldiers decided to run.

"You two sharpshooters? Sorry about the boy; was he a relative?"

"No!" Ki said in anger and reloaded, looking around for more enemies, feeling like he wanted to shoot another British soldier in revenge. Why had he taken the boy? He should have left him, then he probably would still be alive. Ki never cussed in the white man's language, but the temptation was too great.

"It's not your fault; he should not have looked." Samuel was trying to console Ki, who was desperately trying to control his anger. Samuel heard something that shocked him.

"Fuck white men!" Everyone on the boat got quiet and tried to stay out of Ki's way, and it was that way all the way home. They headed out into Patriot country, where Ki could hunt and have a fire.

Irish Lacy

"**K**i has been gone for three weeks now." Megan couldn't keep the tension inside her anymore. She and Julia were deciding on how to harvest the crops, which would be a monumental task. All hands needed to bring in the bounty, and they were short of hands. Everyone was exhausted at the end of the day from harvesting. Mia stayed back to cook and wash dirty clothes. The barn was becoming full of corn, apples, pears, cabbage, potatoes, squash, and sweet potatoes.

"I pray every minute that I can keep on." Julia was sitting at the table, feeding Jason on her lap. Julia was worried sick; if something had happened, how would they ever know? How could they continue as if nothing had happened? Julia had told Ki that she didn't know if she could do this without him; she needed his strength and encouragement. Alexander had sent over some of his servants to help out with the harvesting, which was much appreciated. The next morning, when Julia was walking to the barn, she saw a dead rat that the cat had decapitated. The cat had been a gift from Alexander to Megan in hopes of her accepting a marriage proposal. Vomit came up without any warning, making her bend over at the waist. "Oh Lord, I am pregnant again! Please, Lord, bring them home whole and healthy."

How many months had it been since her monthly periods? Julia knew she had had five after Ki came home with Jason, but since then? Her head was swimming when she heard Koda and Bala howling, which meant riders were coming in. Alexander had taken Megan out on a much-needed ride in the country in his beautiful carriage. They were laughing as Alexander pulled up next to the barn. But the wolves kept howling and looking east, telling everyone that more was coming. Julia held her breath, and Megan couldn't hear a thing Alexander was saying to her at that moment because she too held her breath in anticipation of Samuel coming home. Molly and Henry came out, along with Mia, carrying Jason, Willie, and Robby.

"I see them! They are on horses!" Willie was jumping up and down.

At that point Ki came riding in on the most beautiful horse Julia had ever seen. The other horse held a young man no one knew, but Samuel was behind him.

"Samuel!" Molly screamed and ran for her son. Megan couldn't help the tears coming down her cheeks, so she quickly brushed them away. Julia ran with Molly to the riders. Ki stopped and picked up Julia and kissed her hard on the mouth. Julia couldn't stop touching him all over. As soon as they were all in the barn, Henry helped his son off the horse.

"Son, we thought we would never see you again." Tears were running down Henry's cheeks unchecked. Molly couldn't stop kissing Samuel as soon as his foot was on the ground. Megan came in to watch the reunion and noticed that Samuel would look over at her every fifteen seconds or so. There was no anger or judgment in his face as before, and he gazed at her with what looked to be yearning. Megan was horrified at his condition, for he looked as if he had aged. As soon as Samuel could break away from his parents, he turned to Kane.

"This is Kane McLaughlin; I couldn't have made it without him. He has proved to be a loyal friend, and Ki saved both of us from that godforsaken hell ship." Samuel started to introduce Kane to everyone so Kane could learn their names. When he got to Megan, Samuel had to stop for a moment and just gaze at her. "This beautiful woman standing here is Megan Rainsford." Tears spilled from Megan's eyes; she couldn't believe how pitiful he looked. His hair was long and shaggy, and the beard was coming out in clumps with dark spots on his skin and face. She desperately wanted to hold him to her, but pride got the better of her; Megan turned around and ran to the house. Alexander ran after her, calling her name.

Finally, Henry spoke. "Samuel and Kane, come into the house and eat. I know Julia and Ki want to be alone."

"Dada." Jason was holding out his little arms to his father, and everyone laughed.

"He is calling for you, Ki, he is saying, 'dada.'" Julia brought their son to Ki, who hugged and kissed him.

"Where did you get these beautiful horses?" Julia was looking at the huge stallion. Suddenly everything went quiet; all looked to Ki for an answer. Ki ignored the question and continued to walk with his son toward the house. Julia looked perplexed and looked to Samuel, who was holding on to his father, but he just shrugged and limped away with Kane and his family.

———

"Why are you crying?" Alexander was trying to hold Megan while she was pushing him away.

"You need to go; I don't want you." Megan was trying to get control over herself while having to deal with Alexander at the same time. But Alexander was getting angry.

"What do you mean you don't want me? I have been very tolerant of you, Megan."

"What does that mean?" Megan was shocked to hear him say that.

"Why do you reach beneath you for these rustics? You are better than they are; I know you were taught to believe this. You were raised to be a woman of high standards. Look at what your sister did? Marrying an Indian!"

Megan looked into his face with loathing. "You know nothing! That man is noble and brave, and yes, he might have much pride; he is my brother-in-law. As for my sister, she more than likely wouldn't be alive if it weren't for Ki."

"Why then did you lead me on? Why did you make me feel that you were in the market for a husband?" Alexander was getting angrier and angrier, making his face turn red, with spit was coming from his mouth. They were in the sitting room, and their voices were getting louder and louder.

"I am sorry you thought that I was looking for a husband, but I am not. You need to go now." Megan was trying to be reasonable as she pointed to the door.

"No. I have put too much time and effort into you." Alexander wrapped his large hands around her arms, pulling Megan to his mouth.

The next thing Alexander sensed was a knife suddenly at his throat and a quiet voice saying, "You leave." Ki looked to Megan more dangerous than she had ever seen him. Alexander picked himself up off the couch in fear for his life and quickly moved to the door.

"Thank you, Ki." Megan was embarrassed that Ki and Julia had had to witness the shameful behavior, and that Ki had had to come to her rescue, so she ran upstairs to her room. She felt foolish for having encouraged Alexander even though she did not even like him. Megan was overwhelmed by the feeling of seeing Samuel again; all the love she had repressed came screaming out of her heart. But pride stood in the way of going to Samuel. He had hurt her badly.

Molly was making a big fuss over Samuel coming home, making a huge meal with thought of sharing the food in the big house. Julia had gone up to their bedroom, where Ki was putting Jason down in his bed.

"I am so happy you are alive!" Julia hugged Ki, who wasn't his usual self; now he appeared standoffish and troubled. "What is wrong?" Ki didn't like having to explain himself; it wasn't the Indian way, and he felt that the next question would be "Where did the horses come from?" He knew Julia would think it careless of him to have stolen the horses, risking everyone's lives, and stealing was not a thing she would do. Stealing from the white man was very much what the Indians did, even though it was an unwritten rule that they never stole from each other. He relished the fact that he had pulled off the scheme and did not want to hear that it was a bad thing. But when she looked at him with those loving eyes of trust and devotion while running her hand down his body, he knew he had to talk.

"I made boy at New York City help steal horses. Darcy worked for British. British bought him take care of horses; I asked him help steal them. I pay him, and he wanted take it, but he thought British kill him for helping me."

"Darcy was probably right." Julia was looking curious.

"He come with us, we left all horses out of stable so British couldn't go for us. We made to the river when British found us. We on a boat with the horses. I told everyone stay behind the horses need cover. Darcy look, and they shot him, his body gone in river, dead."

"How old was he?"

"Eleven or twelve." Ki was looking at Jason in the cradle.

"Do you think I am mad at you? I am not; I was worried sick when it took so long for you to come back. As for the horses, I think it was a crazy plan, and I can't believe you did that. Were you going to bring the boy here? Did he have a family?"

"No. General bought him in Ireland to keep horses."

"My God—are these the general's horses?"

"Yes." Ki smiled. Julia had to absorb it.

"That was extremely dangerous, do you think they will come for the horses?

"No, British now only in New York City the Patriots have run them out of all colonies and they only in that place."

"So the Patriots are winning then with the help of the French. Tom Mulligan was right we will win. Did it look good in New York City? What was it like there?" Julia couldn't believe that she said we are winning and it dawned on her that she truly was an American now.

"Washington fires on them everyday with cannons." Her eyes were huge for a few minutes before she could function, "How did it go on the *Jersey*?"

"They let me take Samuel. Samuel told me Kane helped him. I told guard I wanted Kane; he killed many Indians as Samuel did. The guard took him to a room and was on him like a woman. Kane killed guard with knife I gave him. We then stole horses and left." Julia closed her eyes, thinking how dangerous the situation was and how it could have been a total disaster. She pulled Ki to her, letting her hands enjoy the feel of him again. It was a good thing that Jason was napping as they moved to the bed.

"How did you get them off the boat before they discovered the body of the soldier he killed?"

"Hid body in blankets on bed, we leave fast, before they knew he dead."

"I can't believe you did that! Ki you cannot steal anymore, or the Patriots will not trust you."

"I only steal from people don't like"

"Ki, we have laws against stealing and you are going to have to abide by them. Do you think you can abide by these laws?" Ki gathered clean clothes.

"I go to river to wash." Julia realized he was getting mad at her. So she decided to show him her loyalty.

"No, you lay down on the bed and I will bring water and heat it, then fill the bathtub up for you." Ki enjoyed watching Julia getting water from the well, then heating it and carrying buckets up the stairs for his bath using the big wooden tub in their bedroom. When he was in the tub she washed him thoroughly until he pulled her in with him. Isn't this what a woman did to show her love, it was in the Indian world.

———

Everyone gathered at Julia's table for the celebration of their return one day later. Molly had had a new foot brace and stirrup for Samuel's horse made, even though she did not know if Samuel would ever make it back alive. She did this with the thinking that if she stayed positive, then everything would turn out ok. She had lovingly shaved both men and cut their hair, then demanded that they bathe in saltwater while vigorously scrubbing the first layer of skin off to make sure the mites were gone. With some quick practice, Samuel was able to walk again.

Everyone bowed their heads as Julia said a prayer of thanks for delivering everyone back home safely. The only one not at the table was Megan, who had said she did not feel well. Pride would not let Megan come down because she knew she couldn't be around Samuel without making a fool of herself, so she sat in her room feeling sorry for herself.

"I saw Alexander leave quickly." Samuel was looking around the table for an answer, but no one wanted to say anything. When Samuel did not get a response, he asked, "Why?"

"He not want blood on his shirt." Ki said; Samuel's eyes got big while Kane laughed out loud.

"You had to make him leave! Why?" Samuel just wanted to hear the words that Megan had told Alexander to leave for good. But Ki was getting weary of the tension in the room caused by Samuel and Megan. He was simply happy that Julia was not mad at him for stealing the horses, and he wanted things to get back to normal.

"Samuel is coward." Ki was losing tolerance, and Samuel knew it was time for him to act. Samuel put down his napkin and excused himself as he went to the bottom of the staircase, then calling up the staircase to Megan's room. "Megan, come down here, please?" Samuel was using his most convincing voice.

There was silence for several minutes, then a very tiny voice said, "Why?" It was apparent that Megan had been crying.

"I have something I want to tell you, so you need to come down now."

Everyone held their breath as light, hesitating steps came down the stairs then Megan slowly entered the dining room, looking all around her.

"Please go outside with me. I would like to talk to you." Samuel gently led Megan out the door. When they got out, Samuel took her in his arms. "There hasn't been a moment that I did not think about you. I thought I would never get to see you again. Megan, I love you!

Please forgive me for the way I treated you; I promise that I will never repeat that."

"You were so mean!" Megan said through tears.

"I know! I have learned my lesson never to do that again. Please, Megan, forgive me? I have thought about you for so long, and I want you so much." Samuel kissed Megan while pushing her up against the wall and imprinting his body against hers. She could feel his need for her, and all resistance stopped. As soon as Samuel felt this, he grabbed Megan, and they made for his little room in Henry's house. The clothes flew off as Samuel lowered her to his bed. He couldn't enter her fast realizing she was a virgin. He had to show some acknowledgment of her needs, so he slowed things down and was gentle entering her. This made her more than ready and wet, and it did not take long before he was entirely in, and they moved in harmony. They climaxed at the same time.

"Marry me?" Samuel felt he had been given a second chance at life with the woman he loved.

"I guess I have no choice now that you have had your way with me." Megan was smiling because it felt so good to be back in his arms. Then she became sober. "I want a big wedding. I would like the whole community to come."

Samuel and Megan had not noticed that Henry, Molly, and Kane had returned to the house. It had become apparent that Samuel and Megan were not coming back to the table, so when everyone had finished eating, they all returned to the small house. Kane stayed in the little cabin that Sally and Ben had been using but was curious about Samuel and Megan. They entered, not knowing what to expect, so when they saw Samuel's door closed,

Molly and Henry decided to be nosy. They stood at the door listening with Kane trying not to laugh. Kane felt he had not been entertained this well for a long time.

It was at that moment that Molly heard Megan through the door say, "I want a beautiful wedding dress, but I don't know how to make one."

"I will make you a beautiful dress with lace!" Molly had pushed the door open with a naked Samuel and Megan on the bed.

Samuel quickly covered them up with the blanket, looking around wildly, but Megan did not miss a beat, "Can you make that beautiful Irish lace that I saw in London? Everyone I know had it at their weddings." Samuel was astounded that neither Megan nor his mother showed any shock at their being found naked in bed. Henry was standing sheepishly at the door, shrugging his shoulders at Samuel, while Kane let his laughter roar.

"Yes, and I can teach you, but we will have to hurry because if I know my son, he already got you pregnant. We don't want people counting on their fingers." Samuel laid back down and laughed.

"We will need our own house."

The household was bustling, getting ready for the wedding and bringing in the harvest. Molly was teaching Julia and Megan how to make Irish lace, and all the men needed suits. Finally, the day had come to gather for the wedding and feast, with the entire community having been invited through announcements at church. A whole pig was on the pit, with corn and potatoes roasting in the fire. Wildflowers decorated the tables that had set up in the church's newly added meeting room, as well as the doorways. Barrels of whiskey and beer were ready for use.

Ki was trying to fix the ruffles on his shirt; he and Samuel had the same suits, a hunter green coat with a straight collar and waistcoat of the same color with breeches that reached their knees and black boots that went to the top of their knees. The shirts had ruffles at the collar and bottom of the sleeves, which came out of the coat. Samuel noticed Ki struggling with unfamiliar clothes and decided to help.

"This is much trouble for wedding." He was trying to be good-natured for Samuel, but his patience with details was becoming slimmer and slimmer.

"Yes, but tonight it will be wonderful. Women are very passionate in bed after a wedding. Wasn't Julia?" Ki was thinking about how they hadn't even made it home before they made love. Samuel laughed. "If I remember correctly, Megan was picking grass out of Julia's hair when the two of you came home from your wedding."

"You two not together since night you told Megan you loved her?"

"Mother made it clear that I was to respect her and I had to wait until after the wedding. This is why we men put up with all this." Samuel was pointing around the church with the flowers and then pointed to their clothes. "Indians don't put up with all this, do they?"

"No." Ki wanted to laugh at Samuel for being sexually frustrated and having to wait until the ceremony was over.

"Ki, please, only one class of whiskey. I don't want any fighting."

Ki breathed in and tried not to argue; he did not want to be angry with Samuel today, but he was thinking of the few times he had drunk the stuff—it had not turned out good. Ki was standing next to Samuel at the altar as best man. He watched Julia come down the aisle in a pink empire dress embroidered with yellow flowers. The gown gathered at the back with two large buttons in a V formation, and there was also a V in the front of her dress, showing ample amounts of her breasts. Puffed sleeves with lace coming down her arms and white gloves finished off the gown. Her dark hair set off the pale color of the dress. Ki realized he had never really seen Julia this dressed up and beautiful; he couldn't stop looking at her. Megan came next after Julia, on Henry's arm, wearing the same dress as Julia, but with a lace veil covering her face. Julia had had two gold coins melted down for wedding rings.

A wedding cake decorated with flowers sat on a table next to all sorts of things used as musical instruments for Irish peasant dancing. Ki just sat and watched, holding Jason while Molly and Julia organized the food and drink. Julia, very much the hostess, talked to everyone, making sure they were enjoying themselves. Megan and Samuel started dancing, even though it was hard for him with the foot device.

Ki knew that he didn't need another whiskey, but he wanted it while watching the celebration expanding around him by the minute. The men were getting rowdier, and the ones who hadn't wanted to dance at first were now dancing and laughing. Everyone enjoyed themselves, so it was easy for Ki to fill his large mug with whiskey for the second time. He began to feel light-headed and somewhat dizzy as he watched the new owner of the gristmill talking to Julia. Mr. Berkley was a young widower who had lost his wife in childbirth. He was not fighting with the Patriots because of his newly bought business, but he gave them generous donations when he could. Berkley was very handsome and could easily engage in conversations, being an educated man. He was quick-witted and laughed easily, causing a lot of women to blush when talking to him. His clothes were of the latest fashion and fit him perfectly. Julia appeared entirely taken with him by the way she was laughing and agreeing with whatever he said. Ki thought they were having an educated conversation about subjects that he would not know anything about. As his thinking became more clouded, jealousy began to grow, and then anger. He felt she was disrespecting him and realized that she could have done a lot better with an educated man of her own culture. He was not drunk enough to want to cause a scene; after all, he had promised Samuel that he wouldn't. But it was getting harder and harder for him to watch them as Julia bent down to give the man a piece of cake, showing her ample breasts.

If Ki hadn't been drinking, he would have seen that Julia was having a very innocent conversation about growing wheat in this area. The only thing Ki knew to do was leave because he couldn't watch them anymore. He gave Jason to Mia in a hurried fashion, and she noticed that he was getting drunk and angry. Ki sat by himself and drank the rest of the whiskey on the church's steps, becoming quite drunk. This is where Julia found him.

"Here you are; I have been looking for you." Julia was flushed by the whiskey also, having drunk a lot more than usual. Ki took this as Julia having been so impressed by Berkley that she had fallen totally in love with him.

"You want him?" The words just spilled out of his mouth as he watched Julia's expression of total confusion appear on her face.

"Whom are you talking about?" Julia stepped back from Ki as he came toward her with an anger that she had never seen before.

"Berkley, women want him. He rich, educated, handsome. I saw you talking." Ki's words were slurring.

"We were talking about growing wheat next season. I don't want Berkley! Ki, what are you doing?"

Ki grabbed Julia by the shoulders and began to shake her hard. Julia didn't know what to do, so she slapped Ki across the face. A dark expression of anger filled Ki, who felt that she had given him the ultimate sign of disrespect. He drew back and backhanded her hard across her face, causing her lip to break and bleed. Julia's eyes filled with tears, and a look of total mistrust and hurt filled her face. Ki had seen this face before when she had looked at John. In a moment of clarity, Ki saw what he had done; he tried to grab Julia to hold against him, apologizing. It didn't work because Julia was terrified and ran. Ki was too drunk to follow, feeling he had disgraced himself and needed to escape. He knew he had lost control and wasn't in any condition to understand how to repair it. Ki got on his stallion, which he had named Black, and rode away into the dark, heading for the people he missed, Indians who knew just how he was feeling at that moment. Ki rode all night, getting sleepy, when he didn't notice the low hanging branch. Black made it under the tree's arm, but it caught Ki across the forehead, flipping him off the horse's back; he landed hard on the ground. It knocked the breath out of him, and he passed out.

A Pox on Your House

Something was licking his face when Ki opened his eyes. Black was trying to wake him up; he slowly sat up, causing vomit to rain everywhere. Then the realization of what he had done came rushing over him, and he lay back down. Why had he drunk that second glass? Why did he think that he could drink like the Englishmen? It made him mad that he couldn't. When Ki remembered Julia's face as she ran away, he put his hands to his eyes to keep tears from falling. What had he done? Samuel had warned him not to do it, but he had felt he could handle it. Did he just destroy his marriage, his family? It was at that moment that Black alerted him to people. He sat up as quickly as he could with one hand on his gun and the other on his knife.

"Kitchi." It was a hunting party from his tribe. "Is that your horse? We were trying to catch it?" They were speaking in Seneca.

"Yes," Ki answered in Seneca.

"Can we have him? What are you doing here?" Ten young warriors out hunting were now surrounding Ki. Ki had been pondering the idea of using Black as a stud for their horses. It was the least he could do for his tribe.

"He is my horse."

"What are you doing on the ground? What are those clothes you have on?" They had observed him sitting there and probably smelled the vomit. Ki decided to ignore the question and pretend nothing unusual had happened.

"I was at a party with a white man." Slowly getting up so he wouldn't vomit again, he knew that he should get back to Julia and his son, but truth be told, he was too ashamed. He had no idea how he could correct what he had done without losing his pride. Ki got on his horse and started for the village.

It took them two days to get there because they stopped to hunt. Ki learned from the warriors that the village had suffered from smallpox, along with the Patriots launching an army against them, destroying fields of food and housing, and killing warriors. His people had suffered much while he was gone.

"Is smallpox gone from the village?" Ki did not want to get the horrible disease.

"Yes." Lone wolf was the leader of the warriors. "Our village has suffered."

"I want to use Black as a stud for your horses. We will need to pen the mares up with Black." Ki thought that they would have to construct a large pen for this project. He was already thinking about how much wood they would need to accomplish making the corral.

When they got to the village, he saw Ben Walker and Yo da gent, with a young child on her back. The clan mother greeted him and invited him back into the longhouse. Much had changed; most of the individual houses had burned, including the one he and Julia had built. The fields of corn, beans, squash, and fruit trees were all burnt. It was depressing for Ki to see this; he felt his heritage was dying.

"Where is Tom Mulligan?" Ki asked Lone Wolf.

"He went to find you."

"Why?" A feeling of apprehension came on Ki.

"He wanted to talk to you about the future."

"What about the future?" Ki was now suspicious after seeing what had happened to his people.

"I do not know for sure, but he thinks the Patriots will win, and we have to prepare for that." Ki thought about what Tom had said about the Patriots winning the war. What would happen to the Iroquois Nation? Would the Patriots want to kill them all for taking the side of the British? He knew they wanted their land.

A feeling of guilt came over Ki as he could see Julia telling Tom that she had no idea where he had gone after getting drunk. Tom would have a pretty good idea where Ki had gone; his people who would not judge. Well, he had a job to do, so he got busy making a large pen for the mares and chopping down trees for the corral he had seen in many white man's farms. The corral worked perfectly when the mares went into heat, and Black did his job.

"Are you going back?" Ki's aunt, Little Bird, was now the clan mother and hoping he would not return to the white man.

"Yes." Ki was eating around the fire cross-legged and trying not to look at a young squaw who had grown into a beautiful unmarried woman. She had been following him around, letting him know she was interested. "I have a wife and son whom I need to get back to." He said this loud enough for the squaw to hear, but she never stopped her intense stare. That night she came to his blanket and slipped in while he was asleep. He had been having a dream about Julia and how she liked being the aggressor, holding his arms down while getting on top. Julia had taught him how the white man kissed with their tongues while making love, so when he moved his tongue along her mouth, he heard, "What are you doing?" This brought his eyes wide open; he was staring into the squaw's face. He jumped up, giving her the sign for no, got dressed quickly, and decided it was time to leave. He needed to find Tom Mulligan's place to see what he had to say, and then he would be on his way home; he was long overdue. What was he doing?

———

"You wanted to see me?" Ki greeted his old friend and looked to the new Mrs. Mulligan. Tom's place was a day's ride from the village, going east. He had been granted this land by the Indians and had married a captive brought in on a raid.

"Mary, this is Ki." Mary was a beautiful redhead. The house was hand-built of stone and wood. It wasn't large, but it wasn't small either. Tom began making a fire in the stone fireplace, and Ki helped him bring in wood from the woodpile, even though this was work done by the Indian women. Mary started to make breakfast for them.

"She was a captive brought in." Tom and Ki were sitting on the floor next to the fire. "She was completely terrified." Tom was looking at his new bride in their new house, and Ki could tell he loved her from the way he kept looking at her. Ki just nodded his head in agreement while getting a pang of guilt, thinking about Julia and his son. "We were married by a priest." It surprised Ki that the tribe had let that happen, but the Seneca loved Tom; they considered him one of their own and would have granted him this wish.

"What did you want of me?" Ki looked seriously at Tom.

"We need to prepare for the future of the Seneca. I told you that I know the Patriots will win. When that happens, the new government will have to deal with the Iroquois. I want to help them with agreements that will be made and see that they are treated fairly. You can read in English, and I want you to help me with this. Also, I want us, you and I, to start a trading business between the Iroquois and the white man." The men talked in Seneca.

"I have already thought about trading with my people, but the Patriots are worried that we will trade furs for guns. They will stop anyone who tries to do this."

"Right; all we could trade is furs for iron products and blankets. But that should change once the Patriots win. The tribes require food after the destruction of many villages by the Patriots."

"I can't see the Patriots ever letting us sell the Seneca guns." Ki was shaking his head at Tom.

"We could sell brandy, as the British do to the tribes."

"No!" Ki saw himself hitting Julia. "That would be their destruction. The white man's drink has been bad for us."

"There will be a lot of traders doing this." Tom also knew the devastating effects of the white man's drink on the Indians. Tom knew that they could not handle the alcohol; he had seen the Indians appoint younger Indians to stay sober when they drank, men who would not let things get out of control. The sober ones had to go so far as to bury their weapons in a secret place so the drunk ones couldn't find them when the bloodlust came on. Tom himself had been appointed to stay sober once, and it had been a horrifying situation. "I know what you are saying; the men are now letting their women drink."

"That is not good!" Ki was surprised to hear this. When he was living with the Seneca, the women were not allowed to drink. This was not good at all; it sounded like things were getting out of control.

"I am afraid for them; I have come to respect and love the Seneca and the whole Iroquois Nation. The Patriots want democracy badly, but you people have had it for many years. Ki, let's support them as best as we can, with our knowledge of the English ways and language."

"I will do as you ask; I do not want to see my people wiped off the face of this earth." The two men grabbed each other's hands in agreement.

"I am surprised that you are here, actually. When I went to see you at your house, there was a black sign on the door."

"Black sign?" Ki was confused.

"It means smallpox. Does your family have smallpox?" Tom was looking at Ki curiously. Tom saw the complete surprise on Ki's face, then the total shock.

"They did not have it when I left; I need to go!"

"Maybe you should wait; if you go now, you will get it."

"No. I will leave now." Ki was heading out the door without having eaten the food Mary was preparing. He nodded goodbye to her as he ran for the door. All Ki could see was Julia and his son dying without him. He got on Black and headed home with thoughts of how he had left them. Was this his punishment for what he had done? Mary looked at Tom in confusion.

"Ki did not know his family has smallpox. I couldn't get him to stay. I hope he doesn't get it."

Ki rode Black hard, thinking this was his punishment for what he had done, and he deserved this. He had betrayed Julia and his son, so now he was being punished. He remembered praying at the river where his parents were killed and how he had found Jason, and he began to pray again to the white man's God. He told God that if he saved his family, he would never touch the devil water again because it wanted to destroy everything he loved. While riding back, Ki was between cussing and praying the entire way.

———

A few weeks before, Mia was milking one of the cows, not noticing the open sores on the udders. The cat came up to her wanting milk, so Mia sprayed milk on the floor and petted the cat in a friendly gesture. What Mia did not know was that she had gotten some of the pus from the cow's sore on her hand, and now the cat had it on him. The cat then came into the house and began begging for food when everyone was at the table. The cat wrapped around everyone's feet, begging for a drop of food and infecting the whole household with the cow's pus. Mia noticed that she had inflamed sores on her hand while cooking days after, but she continued preparing the food, and so the infection went from person to person. Soon everyone noticed tiredness and sore throats. Then a fever broke out on Jason, and the sores began to cover him. Shortly, everyone had a fever and sores.

This is what greeted Ki went he came crashing through the door in desperation to see his family. The first person he saw at the table was Samuel, looking miserable with fever and pocks all over his body.

"Smallpox?" Ki asked Samuel, who was too sick to get up and could barely raise his head.

"Don't know, but if you don't have it, then you should go back to wherever the hell you have been. You picked a good time to leave, and just where the hell have you been?" Samuel was angry with Ki for getting drunk, hitting Julia, then leaving without saying a word.

"Where's Julia and Jason?"

"Where do you think they are—sick as hell and in your bedroom with a fever. Where the hell have you been?" Ki did not answer Samuel; he took the stairs two at a time, and then he found Julia with sores on her body, holding Jason, who was crying and also had sores; both were hot with fever.

"I am sorry, Julia, I promise never drink again." Julia turned away from him, holding the baby, and this nearly killed Ki. He knew he should not touch them, but he could not stop himself from taking both of them in his arms. He held them tightly to him, knowing that this could be a death sentence. "I promise never hit you." Julia was so sick that she could not struggle. "I go get doctor and bring him back here."

"He won't come if he thinks this is smallpox, and you should leave so you don't get sick." Julia was trying to push him away, but he had them in a death grip.

"I make him come! I did before, and I do it again." Ki kissed both of them and got up to leave. Julia was too sick to argue with him. When Ki went back down to the kitchen, he saw Samuel still sitting there. "Where is Megan?"

"In our room sick with pocks and fever." At that moment Willie came in with wood for the fire. He also had pocks but did not appear to have fever.

"You not sick?" Ki directed the question to Willie, but Samuel answered for him.

"Julia and Megan are worse than any of us because they are expecting." This stopped Ki in his tracks; Julia had not told him they were to have another child, making him feel even more guilty.

"I bring doctor back." Ki went out the door in a hurry. He needed to rest Black, but these were dire times, and he had to push the horse to his limits.

———

Moses Donavan was in worse condition than the last time Ki had gone to get him. He was already drinking at ten in the morning.

"I need to come with me; we have the pox." The doctor moved as in slow motion. Ki helped him up from his chair on the porch. "Where are tools?" The older man couldn't talk for a moment, and then he slowly started to move.

"Smallpox, you said?" The doc spoke slowly.

"Yes, afraid?" Ki was praying to God that he would come.

But to his surprise, Moses smiled and said, "No, had cowpox years ago and can't get smallpox now." Ki helped him on his old nag after saddling him up, getting his tools, and closing up his dirty house, and off they went. "You got any whiskey on you?"

"At house, you have after you see everyone." Ki was trying to speed the old man along, which was almost impossible. When they got to the house at nightfall, Ki was relieved to see Kane cooking stew on the fireplace. It was hanging from a big hook, and he could smell cornbread. Kane had pocks also, but he did not have the fever, so he was able to get around a lot better than the rest of the family. As soon as the doc started looking at the patients, he once again sobered up and took the job seriously. He inspected the pus coming from the pox on each person, going to Henry's house then to Mia's house. When he finished looking at everyone, he asked to see the cows. Ki took him to the barn, where the doc looked at the udders. Moses called Ki over to inspect one of the udders and pointed to a swollen sore on the cow, and then he took Ki over to two more cows, where he pointed out more swollen sores on more udders.

"See these; this is where you got the cowpox." Then Moses started to laugh. "This is good! It is not fatal, and no one will ever get smallpox." Ki was bending over, looking at where the doc was pointing.

THE INDIAN AND ME

"No one die?" Ki almost wanted to fall to his knees in relief. The white man's God had given him a miracle again.

"Women? They are with child."

"They are not that far along, so they should be ok. Now, where is that whiskey, and did I smell stew and cornbread?" Ki gladly took him back to the kitchen, where they informed everyone that it was cowpox, and they would not die and could never get smallpox. This brought much relief to everyone. Ki fed the old doc, gave him whiskey, made a bed for him in the kitchen by the fireplace. Samuel was taking some up for Megan, then would take stew to his parents and Robby, who were all in bed. When Ki brought stew up to Julia and the baby, he noticed Samuel in Megan's room, spoon-feeding her while discussing plans for remodeling Sarah's old house.

"Julia, you have to eat for the baby." Ki was patting Julia's stomach. Ki was more than willing to spoon-feed Julia, anything to keep her happy and not thinking about where he had been.

"Who told you?"

"Samuel, he tell why you and Megan are so sick. Eat, you give me one more strong son." Jason was happy to be with both parents again and the center of attention. He was eagerly opening his mouth for the food that Ki was offering him.

"I think his fever is gone. I heard what the doc said about the cowpox and that we could never get smallpox. Ki, you need to get this also so you will never have that horrible disease." Ki took a deep breath and agreed with her, but who wanted to be sick with even this infection? "Why did you leave?" Ki tensed. He was hoping that he wouldn't have to face this and explain himself. Ki did not want to confess his shame; he did not want to admit he had made a fool of himself.

"Julia, know I never do again. You have my promise. I never want to be John." Julia wanting an explanation of more depth and was looking intently at him, making Ki yearn to change the subject, so he blurted out, "I go to church with you." Ki could tell from her reaction that he had accomplished this.

"You will! What has happened to make you want to do this?"

"I prayed to your God three times, and your God gave me what I asked. Jason not smallpox. Julia, I try to be Christian, but—new to me. I need to learn read better. Tom Mulligan and I help Seneca people with treaties. I need read for them and know they are good for my people." Julia was delighted with all of this; she knew she should have been mad, but she did not feel the need for it. Is this what marriage was all about, forgiveness?

"So you went back to the village?"

"Yes, bad; house we build burn." Julia hated to hear this. "Much burn; no food for people."

"Well, we will have lessons as soon as I feel better, and when you get sick, because you will, you can stay in bed and study. The lessons won't be like before but much harder and I will expect you to take them seriously. I won't be the nice teacher anymore." This made Ki smirk, and Julia felt a little sense of revenge for what he had put her through.

Breeding Humans

K ane asked if he could bring his girlfriend to live on their farm, and Julia was more than grateful for the extra help that might come with her. Kane made plans to steal her away in the middle of the night since they both were still in their indentureship.

"You will need this." Ki was leading a horse with a saddle to Kane in the barn. Samuel and Henry also handed him a gun, some money, and a makeshift map.

"I have never been treated this well, not since my parents were killed. You have no idea how grateful I am for all of this."

"You kept my son alive; it is our turn to help you." Henry was handing Kane food for the road that Molly had made.

It took him a week and a half to get to the farm where he and Mary McDouglas had lived. He waited until night, when the household was asleep, before approaching the cabins of the servants. Kane knew Mary worked in the kitchen and would need to clean up after dinner, causing her to come back to her house late. Kane waited behind the barn for his chance to grab Mary. A big black man went into her cabin, and ten minutes later, Kane saw Mary heading there also. Confusion set in as he watched Mary shut the door for the night. Anger filled Kane; she had not waited for him. But she had not known where he was or when he was coming back; she hadn't even known if he was alive or dead.

It looked like many things had changed since he had left. Maybe Mary no longer loved him or even thought about him. Kane felt stupid for having come all this way, and for what? He was sure that Mary loved him because they had made plans for the future after making love the night he left. She told him that there would never be anyone again for her, even if he did not return. He had been gone for almost one year, and a lot could change in that time. Finally, Kane decided that he needed to talk to her before he left. He felt like kicking down the door with his gun blazing, but that would draw too much attention, so he quietly walked to the door and knocked. He was grateful that there weren't any windows in the front of the cabin, thinking they might not let him in if they knew who it was. Kane had his gun out and cocked when the large black man answered the door. The man had only his breeches on, which fueled Kane's anger even more; he came in and banged the door shut with his foot.

"*Kane.*" Mary ran to him with her nightgown half on and half off. What stopped her from tackling him was the gun that looked like it would go off any minute. The black man put up his hands in surrender,

"I don't want any trouble; if this is your woman, you take her. I was forced to do this." Mary stood in front of the black man to defend him. This made Kane even angrier, Mary could tell, so she also held out her hands in surrender to Kane.

"Kane, Joe is right! We were ordered to do this! Master Hawkins directed us to make babies for more slaves." Kane just stood there with his mouth open. Could life get even uglier?

"I have a wife and kids that I love, but Master Hawkins wants slaves half-white and half-black. I don't want this." Kane knew they were telling the truth, and he wanted to kill Hawkins with a vengeance. When Kane had left to go with the Patriots, he knew Hawkins was getting crazier and crazier, but to do this?

"Kane, I love only you, but I didn't know if you were coming back. Master Hawkins was so mad that you left, and two more indentured men left after you. Master Hawkins wanted more slaves to replace—"

"*Stop! Stop* calling him Master Hawkins. I want to kill him." Kane was so mad he was spitting. Joe started shaking his head at Kane's outburst.

"That not be wise; he has lots of crazy friends who kill us all. Leave now! Mary takes him to creek and follow it to river, so when he puts dogs on you, water cover your tracks." This woke up Kane.

"Mary, get your things, and let's leave. I have a horse, so we can maybe get down the road before he knows we are gone." Mary started to gather two dresses, shoes, and a comb, all of which went into a pillowcase.

"I will tell Hawkins that when I woke up, you were gone. I hope that will work." Joe was looking scared. Mary thought that Hawkins would probably torture Joe to find out where they had gone. Joe knew what Mary was thinking, "I swear I will not tell him anything."

"Thank you, Joe!" Mary was starting to get emotional, but she had no time for that because Kane had pushed her out the door. The dogs barked, making Kane and Mary run fast to the horse he had left in the pasture. When they got on the horse, they listened for voices but heard only Joe telling the dogs to be quiet. They went to the creek and then the river, like Joe had told them to do. They did not stop for a day and a half until both got hungry and tired, along with the horse. They were afraid of having a fire, so they wrapped themselves in the horse blanket for warmth.

"Do you still love me even though I had to be with Joe?" Kane thought about this, and the ugly picture of him being raped on the *Jersey* materialized in his vision.

"Yes." Kane had to stop and find the words to tell Mary what happened on the ship. "I had to do some ugly things to survive also while on the *Jersey*, but we braved it. We will make a pact to never be like those horrible people. I never want to be that depraved; all I want is to live free with you and by my own hands.

"What is the *Jersey*?" Mary was kissing his lips and face.

"Someday, I will tell you, but right now, all I want to do is make love to you."

A week and a half later, they were back at the Rainsfords' farm in their little cabin. There was a small wedding and, of course, Irish dancing, but Ki did not drink.

Christmas and Potluck

A meeting hall connected to the church stood prepared for Christmas Eve services and a potluck afterward. Ki stood in amazement as he watched the Germans cut a tree and bring it into the building, decorating it with candles. All he could think of was the building burning down. Julia came to stand next to him.

"They call it a Christmas tree."

"It burn the place?" Ki looked around at the Christmas hall decorated with holly while Christmas songs were sung from memory. There were hams, potatoes, sweet potatoes, turkey, cranberries, and pumpkin and blueberry pie. The children were running around happily with their presents from the church of apples, pears, and whatever fruit the church could get that time of the year. After dinner the children got restless, so Ki directed them to the massive fireplace at the end of the hall, where he took corn kernels from his pouch and put them into a pan with oil. He held the pan with a lid over the fire and kept it moving. Popping sounds came from the lid of the pan as the children watched in wonder. Pretty soon the cover lifted, with white balls coming out. The children screamed in joy as Ki poured out the popcorn on the table and he ate a handful to show that it was good. Soon everyone was helping themselves to it.

Megan and Samuel chewed, and after a few bites, Megan said, "I wonder what this would taste like with butter and salt?"

REFERENCES

———

Note: Some of the characters in this book are based on historical people captured by the Indians; in such cases names have been changed.

The Account of Mary Rowlandson and Other Indian Captivity Narratives

Shawnee Captive: The Story of Mary Draper Ingles

Wikipedia: "British, Hessian, and Loyalist Prisoners"

How the Iroquois Great Law of Peace Shaped US Democracy

Babes in Bondage: Indentured Irish Children in Philadelphia in the Nineteenth Century

Indentured Servitude by Carla Tardi

What Is Cowpox? What Are the Symptoms of the Disease?

Native American Women in Colonial America

"Battle of Cowpens," History.com

Great Law of Peace

Black Loyalist Military Units

List of American Revolutionary War Battles

Seneca People

Indian Clans or Gens

The History Place American Revolution

The Saratoga Rifleman by Donald Norman Moran

History of the Colonization of America and the Original Thirteen Colonies

Life in Seventeenth Century Colonial New England

Colonial American Ministers

British Army during the American War of Independence

Myth-Busting Inheritance Law in the Regency Era, by C. Allyn Pierson

History of New York

The Six Nations Confederacy During the American Revolution

Seneca Nation of Indians

CPSIA information can be obtained
at www.ICGtesting.com
Printed in the USA
BVHW081952070521
606760BV00004B/1228